Threads of the Heart

Threads of the Heart

by

Jeannie Levig

2015

THREADS OF THE HEART

ISBN 13: 978-1-62639-410-0

This Trade Paperback Original Is Published By
Bold Strokes Books, Inc.
P.O. Box 249
Valley Falls, NY 12185

First Edition: July 2015

Credits
Editors: Victoria Oldham and Cindy Cresap
Production Design: Susan Ramundo
Cover Design By Gabrielle Pendergrast

Acknowledgments

As it says on the cover, no one travels this life alone, and when a lifelong dream is realized, there are many people to thank. So here goes.

My deepest love and gratitude to Jamie Sullivan Patterson for her unwavering belief in me in all ways, for standing by me through all the permutations of everything we've been to one another and what we share, and for being the best first/ideal reader any writer could hope for.

Immeasurable love and appreciation to Lisa Elzy Watson for loving me unconditionally and teaching me the only way life makes sense. You have changed me in so many ways and given me the gift of knowing who I am. Don't think you're done, though.

An enormous thank you to Craig Levig for showing me that first little ad from the local paper for a writers' workshop so many years ago and encouraging me to attend and for your loving support as I began my journey in writing.

Heartfelt acknowledgement and gratitude to my children—Erik, Kelly, and Mindy Levig and Chris Dison—for your constant love and support and all that our family shares. I love you all so much.

Thank you to my circle, my spiritual family, for always loving me no matter what, for celebrating with me my successes, and for holding me steady when I stumble.

An enormous thank you to Sheila Calderwood who so very long ago when I was making my very first attempt at writing a novel plunking away on a typewriter—yes, it was electric, but still—helped me buy my first word processor. Thank you, Sheila, for believing in me as a writer.

Thank you to Debbie Bailey, my very first writing partner, for all those many hours at my dining room table as we each worked on our projects, all the plotting, all the trips down to Orange County RWA meetings, all those shared cups of coffee, all the laughter…all the memories.

And, of course, my deepest gratitude to everyone at Bold Strokes Books: to Radclyffe and Sandy Lowe for inviting me into the Bold Strokes family; to Sandy for being so generous and available with the answer to any question and help with any difficulty; to Victoria Oldham who made my first editing experience easy and fun with her patience, clarity, and humor; to Cindy Cresap for her immaculate copy editing and for all she's done in moving my book through the production process; to Gabrielle Pendergrast for my fabulous cover; and to all the behind the scenes people who finish out the entire project. It is an honor to be counted among such a talented group of authors and to be a part of a team so dedicated to excellence in writing and publishing. Thank you all.

And finally, thank you to the readers who share this story with me. I hope you enjoy these characters as much as I do.

Dedication

To Kathryn Errecart
Sept. 4, 1925–Oct. 22, 2013

You lived a life of meaning that touched and profoundly influenced the lives of so many students. Your legacy lives on in all of our accomplishments.

I love you, Mom.

CHAPTER ONE

1995

Maggie Rae-McInnis came through the kitchen doorway just in time to catch the full view of slender buttocks clad in a pair of red Jockeys for Her.

Dusty Gardner stood bent over, examining the contents of the refrigerator. As their longest-standing tenant and semi-exhibitionist, she had managed to make her cute little heinie a relatively familiar part of the decor, one that Maggie normally didn't mind stealing a glimpse of from time to time. This morning, however, Maggie wanted it hidden until the guest she was expecting had come and gone.

"Dusty, luv."

"Aye, me lady?" Dusty answered with the lilt she sometimes used to mimic Maggie's Irish accent.

"Would you please go upstairs and cover yourself? We're havin' company."

Baxter, Maggie's three-year-old Rottweiler, nudged her hand with the ball he carried in his mouth, and she absently scratched his ear.

Dusty turned, a Tupperware container in one hand and a jar of mustard in the other. Her *I Like Dyke* T-shirt barely concealed her Jockeys, and her favorite baseball cap sat backward on her head, taming the morning wildness of her collar-length blond hair. "I'm covered." Her ocean blue eyes shone with mischief. "All that's showing are my legs."

"Your legs aren't what I noticed when I entered the room." Maggie hoped her tone came off stern, in spite of her amusement.

"Hey, I can't help it if you're obsessed with the more alluring parts of the female anatomy." Dusty padded on bare feet to the island in the center of the kitchen and added what she held to a small collection of containers already on the counter.

"Who's obsessed with the female anatomy?" Addison sauntered in through the dining room entrance, the morning paper tucked under her arm. The corners of her lips—those full lips Maggie could never get enough of—curved upward in a hint of a smirk. Her dark brown hair, still damp from her shower, curled softly at her nape in that way that always made Maggie want to play with it.

"She is." Dusty waved a jar of mayonnaise in Maggie's direction.

"No one is." Maggie blushed. Even after twelve years, she still sometimes felt like a tittering schoolgirl when Addison caught her by surprise. "I simply asked Dusty to go put somethin' on."

"What?" Addison pressed one hand to her heart and fanned herself with the other. "And cover up all the raw sex appeal that the bar babes go wild over? C'mon, Dusty, give us *the stance*. Show Maggie how you entice those sweet things."

Playfully, Dusty leaned an elbow against the white tile and lowered her eyelids to partially veil a smoldering gaze. With her free hand, she picked up the jar of Grey Poupon and held it in front of her. "This is a Corona, of course."

Maggie frowned. "Of course."

Addison hissed and shuddered. "How could any healthy libido resist that?"

"Well, dawtie," Maggie said, using the Irish endearment she saved for Addison alone. "If you're so stimulated by it all, maybe the two of you should see if you can get somethin' goin'." She shot her a glance and raised an eyebrow.

Addison took a moment and studied Dusty, seeming to weigh her options. "Naw," she said, dropping the newspaper onto the counter. "I prefer my women softer." She crossed the lightwood floor and slipped her arms around Maggie's waist. She nuzzled her neck.

Maggie smiled and let her body mold into the curves of Addison's. "Ah, who do you think you're foolin'? The biggest thing keepin' the two of you apart is not bein' able to decide who'd lead."

"I would," both women said in unison.

Maggie chuckled. "I rest my case." She wiggled from Addison's grasp and ran her fingers through her hair, smoothing what Addison had mussed. "Don't think I was kiddin' about puttin' some clothes on, luv. She'll be here any time."

"Who'll be here?" Dusty took two slices of bread from the loaf and laid them side by side.

"Eve Jacobs. She's the niece of my friend Carolyn. She'll be lookin' at Della's room." Maggie opened the dishwasher and began emptying it.

Dusty snorted but remained focused on her sandwich. "Why would anyone want to look at Della's room?"

"To rent it. Eve's goin' through a spot of trouble and needs a place to stay for a bit."

"Della's renting out her room?"

Maggie sighed. "No, *I'm* rentin' out the room. I own the house, remember? Addison and I? Della moved out last week."

"Della moved?" Dusty looked up. "Nobody told me. She didn't even say good-bye."

Maggie set the last glass in the cupboard and closed the cabinet door. "Darlin', if you're goin' to be galavantin' around with your girlfriends all week, you're goin' to be missin' a few things here at home."

"She could have left me a note or something." Dusty plopped a spoonful of cold macaroni and cheese on top of ham slices, then reached for the peaches. "She's always leaving me those damned little sticky notes about the toothpaste and stuff in the bathroom. She could have at least left me one that said good-bye."

Maggie smiled. Dusty talked a tough game, but in reality she was as hard as a freshly baked muffin. "I'm sure she'll be back to visit. She's not movin' to Kansas or anythin'."

"Where *did* she go?" Dusty asked, still pouting.

"She moved in with Nat." Addison sat down in the breakfast nook.

"Nat?"

Maggie nodded. "You know, Natalie? Nat?" she said, turning from the silverware drawer to study Dusty's face for any sign of recognition. "The woman Della's been datin' for the past three months?" She couldn't fathom how Dusty managed to even maneuver through traffic some days, she lived her life in such a state of oblivion. Sometimes, though, Maggie also suspected Dusty's lack of awareness was simply an act.

"Oh, yeah. *Nat.*" Dusty scoffed. "That's not a name. It's a bug."

Maggie pursed her lips and returned her attention to her task. "And you wonder why Della didn't say good-bye to you."

"Good morning, everyone." Tess Rossini, the other tenant who shared their home, strolled into the kitchen with characteristic grace, the softness of her voice a contrast to whatever turmoil Dusty was causing at any given moment. Her deep olive complexion glowed against the pale blue of a button-up shirt, knotted at her waist, and her white cotton shorts. She wore her sleek, sable hair in a French braid that tucked under at the base of her neck.

"Hey, Tess." Addison looked up from the paper. "Sleep good?"

"Mm-hmm." Tess made her way to the coffee maker and retrieved a cup from the mug tree beside it.

Dusty offered her a sly smile but said nothing, then slapped the top piece of bread onto the layer of peaches she had added to her creation.

"*That's* disgusting." Addison glanced at the dripping sandwich before returning to the day's headlines.

"Hey, it's a fully balanced meal all in one bite."

Tess smiled and filled her cup with the spiced butter rum blend Maggie had brewed. Her eyes shimmered with the illusive peace that, over the past year, had little by little begun to replace the pain and fear that once haunted them.

Maggie had suspected for some time that this gradual change had something to do with Dusty but had chosen to mind her own affairs. She leaned against the edge of the counter and watched the three women dearest to her go about their activities.

Tess added creamer to her coffee while Dusty returned everything she had dragged out to its proper place in the refrigerator—something it had taken Maggie two years to get her to do. Addison sat peeling an orange from the fruit bowl on the table while she continued to peruse the newspaper.

The scene seemed ordinary enough, but it was one that warmed Maggie's heart.

The room for rent had come and gone to various individuals in diverse stages of transition over the years, but the four of them had remained constant for quite some time. Dusty had been with Maggie and Addison for five years, using their home as a haven in her otherwise wild and unsettled life. Tess had lived there for three, ever since the loss of her partner in a car accident. They were a good mix. They were family.

"So, Dusty, tell me about your latest conquest." Addison's voice brought Maggie back to the present. "I'm sure I have some catching up to do. I haven't talked to you in two days."

Dusty laughed. "Oh, you're way behind." She plopped her sandwich onto a plate and strode to the table. "Wait'll you hear about the looker I picked up the other night. She was almost more woman than I knew what to do with."

"I seriously doubt that."

"I said *almost*." Dusty grinned. "She loved my Harley, too. Was on the back in a heartbeat."

"Hold on." Maggie held up a hand. "Before you get all wrapped up in your escapades, you get upstairs and get dressed like I asked you to." She wagged a finger at Dusty to punctuate her order.

Dusty winked. "Anything for you, Maggie Mae. I'll tell you about it when I get back," she said to Addison before she trotted out of the room.

Maggie listened to the heavy footsteps as Dusty took the stairs to the second floor two at a time. "That girl." She shook her head, but her fondness for Dusty softened her. "She's thirty-two, and do you think she'll ever settle down?" She filled two mugs with coffee and crossed the kitchen to set one in front of Addison.

"Oh, someday I'm sure she'll find what she's looking for."

"And what do you suppose that is?"

"Someone just like you to melt her heart." Addison leaned back in her chair and grasped Maggie's hips.

She gazed up at her, and Maggie saw the gold flecks in her green eyes reflect the morning sunlight. "You think so, do you?"

"Yeah, I do."

Maggie leaned down and brushed a soft kiss across Addison's lips. "You do a pretty good job of meltin' a heart yourself, dawtie."

The moment shattered with the thunder of Dusty's return trek down the stairs, and Maggie straightened. She turned to find Tess, still at the counter, watching them with an expression Maggie knew was a reminiscence of her own days gone by.

Tess hadn't yet recovered from the loss of her partner and the life they had shared. To make matters even more difficult, her lover's disapproving parents had swooped in after the funeral and claimed everything in their daughter's name, including the house in which she and Tess had lived. Tess had been left with very little evidence of her past life and love.

Although Maggie could sympathize, she didn't pretend to comprehend the true depth of the wound Tess had been left with. All Maggie could do was be there as her friend.

"Tess, would you like to join me on the patio for coffee? Spare yourself the details of Dusty's wanderin's?"

"That sounds nice. I have to return a phone call from last night, though. It'll only take a minute. Quick, save yourself," she added as Dusty bounded back into the room. "I'll be out shortly."

The only difference in Dusty's attire was the addition of a pair of miniscule cut-off jeans. Oh well, Maggie thought with resignation. All she had said was cover yourself.

As she opened the sliding glass door and stepped out into the sunshine, Baxter close at her heels, she heard the eagerness in Addison's voice.

"Let's hear about your little date."

She pulled the door closed behind her, the barricade of glass muffling Dusty's answer. She wondered briefly about Addison's recent increased interest in their younger housemate's promiscuity and casual—at best—relationships. A twinge of something rippled through the back of her mind. Uneasiness? Suspicion?

Addison had been in her mid-twenties when they had gotten together and had very little experience with other women. Coming to Maggie directly from her only other relationship, she had never had the opportunity to play the field. In addition, Maggie was thirteen years older than Addison and had always feared that as time passed Addison might find her less attractive and want someone younger. She thought of herself in her twenties, of her first love, Julia, and how much Maggie had hurt her. Julia had been older and ready to settle down, but Maggie had been a bit wild and wanted adventure. Unlike Maggie at that age, though, Addison had seemed sure of what she wanted at the time she and Maggie had made their commitment. *And now that my age is showing? Don't be ridiculous. You're forty-nine, not a hundred and forty-nine. Addison loves you. She's been with you for over a decade and has never once given you reason to doubt her.*

She forced the matter from her musings and pulled a chair out from the rattan patio set. She settled into the cushioned seat at the table. "Well, Baxter, lad. If Eve Jacobs decides to take the room, we're goin' to have less than a bit of time to ourselves today. We'd best get to enjoyin' it."

The dog stared up at her and cocked his large black head as if to contemplate her words.

She chuckled and stroked the underside of his chin. The peace she always found in her backyard enveloped her. She closed her eyes and raised her coffee mug to her lips.

She remembered her astonishment twenty-five years earlier, the day she had first ventured up into the Hollywood Hills with her inheritance from her grandfather and her Realtor and discovered this lushly hidden neighborhood surrounded by the urban chaos of Los Angeles County. At the time, the beauty of the house itself had seemed simply a perk of its gorgeous locale. Without hesitation, she had made it her home—and later *their* home, hers and Addison's. In the beginning, it hadn't been her intention to take in renters. That had simply evolved—a friend going through a breakup needing a place to stay, a friend of a friend in town for a temporary job, and before she knew it, she had a houseful. She learned quickly that she loved the energy of so much life around her.

She listened to the melody of the birds in the pine trees that covered the mountainside sloping high above the three-story house and the soft splash of water flowing from the lava rock fountain into the fishpond. A cool breeze feathered across her cheeks. The last remnants of her earlier tension eased with its caress, and she relaxed.

It was no surprise to Maggie that so many of her tenants over the years had found solace and refuge in this place during their times of trouble or change. The house seemed to have a vibration that drew those with wounds to heal or transformations to make, and Maggie did her best to be a presence that nurtured and supported those who came through her home as they found their peace. She believed in the interconnectedness of life, that what you give to another, you give to yourself. She felt it everywhere, every time she offered a smile, every time she cooked a meal, every time she shared a moment. Caring for others brought *her* peace.

She opened her eyes and took in the hot pinks and purples of the bougainvillea that lined the back wall. She smiled. Perhaps Eve Jacobs's peace could be found here as well.

CHAPTER TWO

Eve Jacobs gave one final tug on her emergency brake, securing her metallic gold Volvo into its parking space on the steep slope of Skycrest Drive. She couldn't imagine leaving her car on such an incline every night, worried about whether it would hold or if she'd remembered to turn the wheels toward the curb—and what about the commute to the office? From here, it would be almost twice as long as from the home she'd shared with Jeremy and the boys for the past eight years.

Who did she think she was kidding, though, really? It was neither the hill nor the drive to work that made her want to turn and run from the room for rent her aunt had mentioned. In truth, it was her own fear of what the future might hold. The butterflies in her stomach felt more like bats. Her hands began to tremble.

What was she doing here? Why couldn't she just be happy with a wonderful husband and two beautiful sons—with the life she knew and at least a part of her loved so much? Why couldn't she simply go back to ignoring those other feelings, pushing them down deep within her as she had done for so many years? That thought, however, terrified her even more than the house across the street.

No, she had to find out, once and for all. She needed to know who she really was and what she really wanted. She steeled her resolve and studied the home of Maggie Rae-McInnis for whatever hints of the woman's character it might reveal.

Set back into the hillside, the large, slate-colored house stretched tall above the landscaped gradient that acted as its front yard, and a lush blanket of purple flowers spilled over the edge of the sidewalk at street level. Several azalea trees grew on either side of one of the lower multi-paned windows.

Eve drank in the beauty. If the interior of the house and its inhabitants were even half as inviting, maybe she could find asylum here long enough to sort out her life. With renewed courage, she pushed open her car door and stepped out into the late-morning sunshine.

The warm air fanned the bare skin of her legs and arms, and the sweet smell of pine caressed her senses as she crossed the road and started up the L-shaped concrete staircase to the double front doors. A hunter green Ford Explorer sat on one side of the driveway, and a maroon Sunbird occupied the parking space at the curb.

Eve combined the final step onto the stoop with an adjustment of her purse strap over her shoulder. Okay, now be calm, she reminded herself. Don't talk too fast. Don't use big words. Don't let your eyes dart around the room like a kid in a toy store. She didn't want to appear nervous. She straightened to her full five feet five inches and pressed the button for the bell. She listened to the aria of the chimes from inside—"I Can't Get No Satisfaction."

Hurried footsteps sounded on the other side of the door, and with a jerk, it swung open.

Eve jumped but held her ground. She stared into the fiery features of a blonde in a baseball cap and extremely short cut-offs. The word *dyke* leapt from her chest and clouded Eve's vision.

She dropped her gaze to the woman's legs, muscular but not overly developed, her bare feet, slender but masculine in their stance. This couldn't be Maggie. Aunt Carolyn had described Maggie as gentle-spirited and warm. This woman was...Eve didn't know what this woman was. She let her stare travel back up the loosely-clad contours of the blonde's torso. She felt a flurry in her stomach—not butterflies, not even bats. Pterodactyls, maybe?

"Like what you see?" The surprisingly feminine voice jarred Eve from her daze. A mocking grin spread across the woman's lips, and she leaned against the doorjamb. "I could show you more."

Eve's mouth went dry. "I, uh..." She swallowed. "I'm here regarding the procurement of your room?" It came out more as a question than a statement.

The woman studied her. "Procurement? What's that, a new kind of paint?"

"What?" *Damn*. She was doing it. Whenever she was nervous or unsure of herself, her vocabulary developed a mind of its own. Her therapist called it *maintaining a one-up position*. "Oh, no, I mean rent. I'm here about the room you have for rent."

"Oh, yeah." The blonde's bold stare moved from Eve's face to her neck, then down to the cleavage peeking out from the vee of her sundress. "I guess you don't look much like a painter."

Eve suddenly felt conspicuous in the light cotton fabric that draped her body. Her long, flowing hair and her immaculately manicured nails, both of which usually boosted her confidence, now seemed frivolous, even foofy. She felt like a groomed French poodle under the scrutiny of a wild mountain wolf.

"I'm Dusty Gardner. And you're…Dang it, what did Maggie say your name was?"

Oh, thank God. This isn't Maggie. "Eve Jacobs. I'm, uh, here about the room." Embarrassment heated her cheeks. She sounded like a moron.

Dusty's grin broadened. "So you said." She held firm in the doorway, obviously enjoying Eve's discomfort.

Eve's anger rose at the woman's arrogance, and she shifted her weight. Perhaps a one-up position would be beneficial in this case. "Now that we've introduced ourselves, do you think it might be possible for you to apprise Ms. Rae-McInnis of my advent?"

Dusty shrugged then straightened. "Sure. If you want to just *advent* your way in here, I'll get her." She stepped back a pace and, with a wave of her hand, motioned for Eve to enter.

Relieved not to be face-to-face with the annoyingly intriguing woman, Eve moved into the foyer, but her respite was short-lived. As she passed Dusty in the narrow doorway, her arm brushed the front of Dusty's T-shirt. A chill ran through her. She found herself wanting more of a touch but at the same time desiring nothing more than to get as far away from those feelings as possible. She couldn't conceive of living here, not if this kind of emotional conflict accompanied it.

"Wait here," Dusty said, her voice entirely too close to Eve's ear.

Eve nodded and watched the woman's long strides carry her out of sight. Grateful for the solitude, she struggled to collect her thoughts. *Get a grip.*

She thought about the woman's T-shirt, the word dyke. Her stomach clenched. *God, I can barely think of myself as a lesbian, never mind dyke or butch or femme, or God knows how many other words I don't even know.* She was so out of her element. Okay, she couldn't live here. That was definite. So, now what?

Now, it was just a matter of conducting a polite conversation with Aunt Carolyn's friend, going through the pretense of looking at the room, then saying she'd get back to her with an answer shortly. Later, a quick phone call and the ordeal would be over—but then what? Where would she go? Back with Jeremy to live what might be a lie? She closed her eyes and fought back tears.

She had to gain some clarity. She recalled her recent conversation with Aunt Carolyn. "Take it one step at a time. You're only thirty years old, sweetie. You don't have to figure out everything right this minute. Go talk to Maggie. Make a commitment of only a month if you want, but give yourself at least that." Aunt Carolyn was wise. Eve knew that.

Her nerves began to settle. She mentally began to repeat the mantra she'd learned to depend on years earlier—*breathe in...take in the scenery...breathe out...take in the scenery.* It was Aunt Carolyn's favorite motto, along with *life's full of choices*. Although, Eve didn't care for the latter nearly as much.

*Breathe in...take in the scenery...*She glanced around the circular foyer. To the left, she noticed two doorways leading to different rooms, and to the right, a closet and a hallway. *Breathe out...take in the scenery.*

Directly ahead sat a mahogany commode cabinet, the sort that, Eve knew from Jeremy's infatuation with antiques, had graced the bedrooms of many a farmhouse in the late nineteenth and early twentieth centuries. At that time, a fluted ceramic washbowl and pitcher would have occupied the marble top, but now the polished stone provided the perfect platform for a bronze depiction of Botticelli's *Birth of Venus*. Behind the sculpture, a flight of steps had a miniature bronze on every stair edge, many of which were small nudes, graceful and nubile in their innocent poses.

Eve released a deep sigh and began to relax. The atmosphere of the interior of the house, at least what little of it she could see, held the same enticing serenity that had captivated her from the outside—such an emotional contrast to what had greeted her at the door. In fact, if it hadn't been for that Dusty person, she'd have been sure about a decision for the first time in years.

"Good mornin' to you, Eve. It's so nice to finally meet you."

Eve turned her attention toward the voice and met a pale blue gaze, friendly and warm, nothing like Dusty's.

A small-framed woman with dark auburn hair extended her hand. "I'm Maggie." She carried herself with an air of nobility in spite of her casual attire and small stature. Dressed in khaki walking shorts and a forest green blouse, she appeared at ease with her task of interviewing a prospective tenant.

Eve smiled and reached to accept the handshake, but at the sight of the large black dog coming up behind Maggie, she froze.

The animal's head came to Maggie's waist, and the breadth of its chest was almost that of Maggie's. Granted, she was fairly diminutive, but it still presented an impressive picture.

"Oh, this is Baxter. Don't you be worryin' about him. He's harmless." Maggie laughed and rubbed his head. "You'll get used to him."

Baxter looked up at her adoringly.

"What kind of dog is he?" Eve asked, mostly for the sake of conversation. The animal still made her nervous.

"A Rottweiler." Maggie turned and, with Baxter at her heels, took a step into the room behind her. "Why don't you come make yourself at home, and we can get to know one another a bit."

Eve followed, but came to an abrupt halt just inside the doorway. The view stole her breath. The entire far wall of the living room consisted of floor-to-ceiling windows, with a sliding glass door that opened onto cement decking. Clear water flowed down a lava rock fountain into a sparkling pond, and lavish greenery sprinkled with splashes of colored blossoms filled a small space beyond a lush lawn. High on the wooded hillside reaching above the ivy-covered back fence, two deer stood munching on a shrub. It could've been a mural.

Eve stared in awe.

"Beautiful, isn't it?" Maggie's tone possessed pride.

"It's absolutely gorgeous," Eve whispered.

"Why don't you sit down and enjoy it for a spell? I was just about to brew some tea. Would you care for some?"

Eve tore her gaze from the splendor before her and took in the long sofa that dominated the center of the decidedly feminine room and pale rose carpet that brought out a hint of pink in the alabaster walls. "That would be lovely, thank you."

Maggie smiled.

Eve watched as Maggie made her way through an open dining area and into the kitchen beyond. From what Eve could see through the doorway, it was bright and cheery. She settled into her cushioned seat and shifted her interest to the far wall where a flagstone fireplace sat dormant in the early fall climate, but she could imagine quiet flames on a winter evening casting their shadows out to mingle with those of the numerous candles placed about the room. Above the fireplace hung a beautiful marble wall sculpture depicting a woman caught in the moves of a dance, the lines of her body and flowing gown forming a gracefully subtle, musical treble clef.

The peace that embraced Eve overwhelmed her. Aunt Carolyn had been right—this would be the ideal environment in which to examine her feelings, evaluate her life, and make her decisions. She set her purse down and easily envisioned herself living in these exquisite surroundings.

Maggie returned carrying a small tray of cookies and placed it on the beveled glass and wood coffee table. "The tea will be ready shortly," she said, easing into one of the occasional swivel chairs at either end of the couch. "I thought we could start with these."

"Thank you, they look delicious."

"Your aunt's told me a bit about your struggles. I'm sorry to hear you're havin' such a tough time with it all."

Eve tensed at the immediate focus on her dilemma. She considered Maggie.

Maggie's soft features and smooth complexion gave her the appearance of a nurturer, a motherly type, but her expression reflected a more direct manner. A knowing smile deepened the laugh lines around her eyes. "Be warned, I can be a bit blunt at times. If I've made you uncomfortable, I apologize."

With a sigh, Eve chuckled. "No, it's all right. As Aunt Carolyn said, that's what I'm here for, to face my questions. And she assured me that if I *am* willing to face them, you're someone who can help."

"Well, I'll be happy to offer what I can, but you're the only one who really knows your own sexuality."

Eve stiffened. She couldn't believe she was actually going to sit here in broad daylight and discuss her quandary of whether she was straight or gay with a complete stranger. The only other living person she'd ever told had been Jeremy—and Aunt Carolyn, of course—but even that had only been recently.

"Many of us have been through it to one degree or another, but still, it's always an individual thing."

"I just have so many questions spinning around in my head."

Humor accompanied by a tender glint flickered in Maggie's eyes. "This would be the place for you, then. You'll have a whole houseful of lesbians to ask."

Lesbian? There it was. Eve felt the blood rush from her face.

Maggie examined her. "Not ready for the word yet, are you?"

Eve looked away for only an instant then returned her gaze to Maggie.

With a cluck of her tongue, Maggie raised an eyebrow. "Don't let Dusty know that."

The name alone brought back the fluttering in Eve's stomach, but the concern in Maggie's expression strengthened it to a churning.

"Don't let me know what?"

Eve froze. She already knew that voice.

Maggie swiveled in her chair to face the entrance from the foyer. Arms on the rests, her legs crossed, she was the epitome of nonchalance. "If we'd wanted you to know, I wouldn't be sittin' here warnin' Eve off you, now would I?"

Slightly fortified by Maggie's air, Eve shot a glance at Dusty.

"Oooh." Dusty slapped her hand to her heart. "You're a cold woman, Maggie Mae."

"And don't you be forgettin' it, either." Playfulness danced in Maggie's eyes.

A low whistle revved, then shrieked, from the kitchen.

"Be a love," Maggie said to Dusty, "and bring the kettle and cups for us, will you?"

"Oh, sure. I can fetch and carry for you, but I can't be let in on any secrets." Dusty's mutterings faded in the opposite direction.

Eve assumed the hall she'd seen off the foyer circled around to the back of the kitchen. She had to admit, she was grateful for Dusty's departure. Relief washed through her and it must have shown.

"Try not to pay the girl any mind. You'll get used to her," Maggie said.

Like the Rottweiler? Eve looked down at Baxter, who watched her closely from the floor beside Maggie's chair. She doubted it, but she only smiled.

With a clatter, Dusty appeared in the dining room, carrying a second tray. Elbows extended and chin jutting, she crossed with exaggerated strides to where they sat. "Tea for me ladies," she said in a taut voice as she stepped between them and set the service on the table.

Maggie laughed. "You've missed your callin', girl."

"Yeah. I should have been an actress."

"Actually, I was referrin' to the style with which you serve."

Eve giggled and reached for a cookie. She brought it to her mouth.

Dusty frowned. "So," she said directly to Eve, "you gonna take the room?"

Oh, God. Eve halted mid-bite. *She's talking to me again.*

Maggie poured hot water into the two cups Dusty had brought, evidently unaware of Eve's anxiety.

"I, uh…" She cleared her throat. "I haven't had the opportunity to enumerate the pros and cons yet."

"Uh-huh."

Maggie eyed Eve briefly. "We haven't as yet discussed the room," she said to Dusty.

"Oh. Okay. Isn't the rest of the house great?" Dusty lifted the hem of her T-shirt and shoved her hands into the back pockets of her cutoffs. She shifted her weight to one bare leg.

"The view is astounding. Who could have imagined that all this resplendence could be found in the center of a metropolis like LA?" Eve swallowed.

Maggie stared at her with a gentle expression.

"As for the interior, I find the collection of art particularly poignant." She gestured to the two bronze statues—Mercury and Diana—that decorated either end of the marble surface of the large mahogany buffet in the dining area.

Dusty's gaze followed the motion. "You mean the guy in the loincloth with the wings on his feet?"

"Yes, Mercury, the Roman messenger of the gods."

"Oh."

"Dusty," Maggie said. "Aren't you goin' in to work at noon today?"

"Work? Oh." Dusty glanced at the clock on the bookshelf. "Jeez, yeah. I gotta get going." With no further interest in Eve, she raced out the door and up the stairs.

Maggie dipped a tea bag into a cup of steaming water. She considered Eve for a long moment. "Would you care to tell me what on earth that was about?" She eased the mug across the table.

Eve's cheeks heated. She felt like a fool. It was one thing to play her word games with someone like Dusty, but she'd never fool anyone like Maggie into thinking she was confident and sure of herself. She sighed, allowing her head to fall against the back of the couch. "I'm so sorry. I don't know why I do that. I mean, I know why I do it, I just don't know why…" She lifted her hands in a gesture of helplessness.

"Have some tea, darlin'. It'll help." Maggie raised her own drink to her lips and settled back in her chair.

After several swallows of the blackberry brew, Eve looked up to meet Maggie's patient gaze. It held understanding, acceptance. Even though she'd only just met Maggie, Eve somehow knew she could trust her. "I wanted so badly to fit in here. I'm so confused and feel as though I don't fit even in my own life anymore. I just needed a place where I could figure out who I am."

"This could be that very place," Maggie said, her tone soft. "It's been good for some."

"That's what Aunt Carolyn said, and I had hopes. But then *Dusty* had to answer the door." She realized she spoke the name with a bite. "I was fairly sure of myself, then there she was with that grin and her snippy remarks."

Maggie arched her brow. "I surely am aware of Dusty's shortcomin's, but she's hardly the devil incarnate, now is she? What's really the problem?"

Eve considered the question. "I don't know. It's just when I met her and when she came back in just now, I felt so…so…I don't know what I felt. I've never felt it before."

"Ah, so that's it." Maggie smiled, comprehension shaping her features. "Dusty has that effect on people. Whatever you've never felt before, she'll be the one most likely to bring it out in you."

Afraid of the repercussions the truth of that statement might have, Eve dismissed the thought. "Oh, that's ridiculous."

"Is it, now? Well, another possibility is that you're findin' yourself attracted to her, and she's not exactly the type you're comfortable bein' attracted to."

"Oh, no. *That's* even more ridiculous. That feeling I do know. I've been attracted to people—to women—before, and believe me, they weren't like Dusty." She laughed and took another drink. "Besides, it's the recognition of those feelings that's brought me to this point already. I know I'm attracted to women. That's what I have to think through."

"Think, is it? In my experience it's been feelin's that bring me more understandin', especially in matters of the heart."

"Not meaning any disrespect, but *I* approach things from the head. I find it much more productive."

"It sounds as though you know yourself pretty well," Maggie said with a smile. "I'm sure since your problem with Dusty is neither of the things I suggested, you'll figure it out soon enough."

Above their heads, a door banged shut. Footsteps thudded on the stairs. Eve couldn't imagine how all those little statues she'd seen from the foyer stayed in place.

Dusty stopped in the doorway wearing blue jeans and a black motorcycle jacket. She carried a helmet under one arm. "Gotta go, Maggie Mae."

"Will you be home for supper?"

"Dunno. If there's anything left, save it for me. Otherwise, don't worry about it." She finished pulling up the zipper and winked at Eve. "Maybe I'll see you around." The next sound was the slam of the front door.

Eve shot a pensive glance toward the point of Dusty's departure, then turned to see Maggie watching her. Before either of them had a chance to speak, another set of footsteps sounded on the stairs, these much slower, quieter.

A few seconds later, a tall, slender woman sauntered into the room. A pair of white jeans covered her long legs, and a Green Bay Packers football jersey was tucked in at the waist. "Was that Dusty that just left?"

Maggie chuckled. "Could it have been anyone else?"

The woman smiled and crossed to the chair. She took Maggie's hand.

"Eve, this is my partner, Addison." Maggie gazed up into Addison's face then kissed the back of her fingers near the ring that matched her own.

Eve hadn't been around many female couples, and watching their affectionate interaction gave her a sense of yearning, as if the hope for something long suppressed could actually be kindled.

"Addison," Maggie continued, "this is Eve Jacobs. She's lookin' at the vacant room."

"It's nice to meet you. Have you seen it yet?"

"No, we were just talking and getting to know each other a little. And I've been enjoying the beauty of your home. It's lovely."

"Thanks to Maggie." Addison combed her fingers through Maggie's hair. "She's the one with all the style."

Eve smiled.

"I have to run down to the office for a while, babe," Addison said to Maggie. "I should be home for dinner, though."

"I thought you'd planned to work at home today."

"I did, but Michael called earlier, and he has a new client who wants to focus some advertising on the community. He asked if I could meet with them and give some suggestions."

"All right, then," Maggie said. "I'll see you when you get home."

Addison bent and kissed her before she turned back to Eve. "It was nice meeting you. Even if you don't take the room, I hope we see you again."

Her words felt genuine, filled with warmth. "Thank you," Eve said. "But I've already made my decision. I'll take it." She knew that the room, sight-unseen, would be just as beautiful and peaceful as everything else about this sanctuary—everything, that is, except Dusty Gardner. And perhaps Maggie was right. Maybe she could get used to Dusty.

CHAPTER THREE

Addison sat at the stoplight at Lankershim and Ventura Boulevard where her lush hillside neighborhood butted up against the southeast boundary of the San Fernando Valley. The ivory leather upholstery of her Explorer felt pliant in the warmth of the midday sunshine, molding comfortably beneath the contours of her body. When the signal turned green, she crossed the intersection and pulled into the gas station on the opposite corner.

Bright and airy, the day should have been the kind that lifted her spirits and cleared away darker moods, but the same unsettled feeling that'd been plaguing her for several weeks held her in its tenacious grip. Her gaze traveled to the woman across the way, not exactly the whole woman, but more specifically the tanned, smooth legs that met the frayed edges of snug Levi shorts.

Addison pulled the release lever for the fuel tank and slipped out from the driver's seat. She rounded the back of the vehicle and swiped her credit card through the automatic payment slot, trying to keep her eyes focused on what she was doing.

"Nice wheels. I love that shade of green," the woman called from the other side of the pumps. Her broad smile shone in contrast to her sun-darkened flesh, and a tie-dyed bandana that matched her tank top held back her strawberry-blond hair.

"Thanks." Addison searched for something to say about the dented and primer-splotched MG the woman stood beside. It looked like it might have been yellow in a previous life. "Beautiful day, isn't it?"

It seemed to be enough of an invitation for the other woman. "Gorgeous." She crossed the island and walked toward Addison. "My ex had an Explorer, but it was much older, and, even then, she never could've afforded the Eddie Bauer edition."

Ah, *she*—the all-important pronoun. Addison sometimes pondered just how many unasked questions could be answered with such a small word. She inserted the nozzle into the tank and locked it into position. "Ever wonder who Eddie Bauer is?" She grinned. "I mean, I know he's always associated with the luxury version of everything—cars, furniture, clothes. But who the hell is he?"

The redhead laughed. "Somebody very spoiled." She appeared to consider Addison, then forged ahead. "Do you live around here, or did you just pull off the freeway?"

"I live right up the hill." Addison motioned across the street. "You?"

"No, I have an apartment in North Hollywood. I started waiting tables at Miceli's last week." She pointed down the road in the direction of the Italian restaurant. "I just picked up my schedule."

"Oh, really? I've eaten there a number of times. It's a pretty good place."

"How long have you lived here?"

"Twelve years."

The woman nodded as if summing up the information she'd been receiving. "My name's Brenda, by the way."

"Addison Rae-McInnis." Addison extended her hand.

Brenda shook it with a tentative grip. Her attention seemed otherwise occupied, and obvious surprise showed in her raised eyebrows. "Rae-McInnis? Is that hyphenated?" She glanced down at the rainbow sticker on the bumper of the Explorer.

"Yeah, my partner, Maggie's, last name was McInnis, mine was Rae. We just put them together and both took the same name."

"Oh," Brenda said, with a puzzled expression. "Are you still with her?"

"Well, yes." Addison paused, a little confused. "Why?"

Brenda studied her and smiled. "It's just that you don't come off as being unavailable." A glint of intrigue flashed in her blue eyes. "Are you?"

The gas pump clicked off. Addison stood staring at Brenda. *What does she mean I don't come off as being unavailable? I just told her I'm with someone. Of course I'm unavailable.* She laughed more out of politeness than amusement. "I've been with Maggie for twelve years. I think that makes me pretty unavailable."

"Not necessarily. I've known a lot of people in long-term relationships who are very *available* for certain things." Brenda's gaze traveled down Addison's figure and back up to her face. It almost seemed she was more interested now than before. "There's nothing saying we can't just have some fun."

An almost unrecognizable pang wriggled through the pit of her stomach, no, lower. It was a feeling she hadn't experienced in years. It felt dangerous, yet exciting. The mere possibility of an afternoon of casual sex with this woman conjured flashes of images in Addison's mind, stirred responses in her body. Then she envisioned Maggie.

What was she thinking? She loved Maggie. Their life together meant everything to her. "I, uh…" She forced her focus back to Brenda. "I'm sorry, I don't think so."

"You don't think so?" Brenda tilted her head. Laughter played in her eyes.

"I mean, no. No, thanks. I'm in a committed relationship."

Brenda's smile broadened. "If you don't mind my saying so, I kind of see that commitment slipping. And when it does…" She turned but kept her gaze fixed on Addison. "Come by Miceli's."

Addison stared after her. She couldn't let her think that. "No, really. I'm not interested. And I won't be later." Why did it matter to her what this woman thought?

Brenda stopped with her hand on the open driver's side door. She watched Addison for a long moment. "Well, if that *is* the case, you might want to work the word *we* into your conversations." She slipped in behind the wheel and started the engine. "It'll avoid misunderstandings," she called over her shoulder with a grin, then stepped on the gas.

As Addison watched the MG turn onto the busy street and disappear beneath the freeway overpass, her emotions began to calm, but her mind still raced. *What was that about? Nobody's hit on me in ages.* Maybe that's the reason it had caught her so off guard. She had always just assumed it was due to the fact that she was getting older and didn't look the way she used to. But Dusty had said something a while back, that day Addison and Maggie had argued about fish food…or filters—something to do with the koi pond, something stupid. There'd been that woman in the supply store Addison couldn't stop sneaking looks at, and she'd ended up feeling unsettled and, somehow, unattractive. And when she was getting down on herself, what had Dusty said? She recalled the conversation.

"Are you kidding?" Dusty's tone had been incredulous. "Women notice you all the time. You're the one who doesn't see anything—or anyone."

"Oh, yeah, I'm sure. That's why I get so many propositions, isn't it?" Addison laughed at the idea.

"You don't get offers because you don't give out those kind of signals."

Addison chuckled. "What're you talking about?" For a while now, Dusty had been coming home with some interesting bits of wisdom, usually from her friend Rebecca, but this one sounded more out there. Addison didn't see herself giving out any signal at all.

"The *signals*. You know, those little vibes that go out into the room and tap women on the shoulder saying, 'Hey, look my way. I got something special to show you.'" She lifted an eyebrow in a suggestive arch and leaned back in her chair. "Everything *you* put out says, 'I'm in love with Maggie Mae, and I show *her* all my special stuff.'"

"What's wrong with that? I am in love with Maggie."

"Of course you are, and nothing's wrong with it. But if a woman's looking for a good time or even something more, she's not gonna waste her moves on someone who's not in the market for the same thing. I'm just saying. It's all in the signals. You get back what you put out."

A horn honked, jarring Addison out of the past. "Hey, lady," a man yelled from the car that'd pulled up behind her. "If you're making a career out of this, you wanna fill me up?"

With a start, she jerked the nozzle from her tank. "Sorry," she called. "I'll be done in a second." She quickly replaced the gas cap and climbed into the driver's seat.

Once again at the intersection, she glanced toward the freeway entrance and thought of Brenda. Had she gotten on the 170? Without hesitation, Addison decided to take Ventura Boulevard all the way to the office. The last thing she wanted was to somehow catch up to the MG. But why?

She remembered Brenda's advice. *You might want to work the word* we *into your conversations*. Addison had always talked about herself and Maggie as a couple. She even thought in those terms. Yet today, apparently, she hadn't.

The signal changed, and she pressed the accelerator. The Explorer eased into motion, and Addison instinctively took control. Her mind was on its own journey, though.

She considered her years with Maggie. They'd had some difficult times, but nothing like many of their friends had experienced. Their biggest hardships had occurred during the addition of the master suite and art studio on the third level of the house and a period of Baxter's puppyhood during which he'd decided to chew up and bury anything and everything he could find that belonged to Addison, including her leather-bound art kit. They'd survived both, though. They'd never disagreed on the important relationship issues that many couples struggled with, least of all, monogamy and trust. That was Dusty's arena.

Her thoughts returned to Dusty and her stories of freedom, the excitement of exploring a new lover every time, but Addison didn't want that. She wanted Maggie. She wanted familiarity, the true intimacy that comes from waking up together each morning and going to bed together each night.

Something dark, something disturbing, snaked through her, coiling in her gut. She tightened her grip on the steering wheel. She'd had this feeling before but had always pushed it aside, buried it to keep it dormant. Maybe it was time to look at it.

She glanced down the road then pulled out to pass a camper.

She recalled listening to Dusty, hearing tales of the lady du jour, the thrill of not knowing where something or someone might lead. She'd felt that disturbance in contrast to Dusty's excitement. What exactly was it? Sadness? Regret? She let it begin to wriggle its way to the surface, allowed it to swell within her. It grew stronger, intensified, and finally crested. She realized it was envy. Or maybe even worse—maybe envy and loss combined. Her chest constricted.

Addison had never had the kind of experiences that constituted Dusty's life. At eighteen, she'd started a six-year relationship with

Donna, her college girlfriend and her only ex. Then she'd quickly fallen uncontrollably in love with Maggie. She'd never had the wildness, the freedom, the fun of single life.

She accelerated to make it through a yellow light.

How could she be thinking this way? She didn't want those things, or at least she never had. She wanted a home, a life filled with love and commitment, someone with whom to grow old. She wanted Maggie, the woman who knew her so well that she knew every one of Addison's faults and shortcomings, who loved her so deeply that she accepted them all. At least, that's the way she'd always felt before. Recently, however, those things seemed almost stifling, suffocating. She was beginning to realize a part of her felt trapped.

Addison shook her head. *I've got to get control of myself, of whatever this is. It's ridiculous. Some woman—one woman—hits on me in a gas station, and I'm imagining myself as Dusty, or at least heading in that direction.* It was merely a compliment and should only be taken as one. It simply meant she was still attractive.

What about what Dusty had said, though? *You get back what you put out*. Addison shifted uncomfortably. That'd been a while ago, and it was just chitchat over coffee. What did Dusty know, anyway? She'd never had a serious relationship in her life.

Addison rolled her shoulders and relegated the entire matter back to the deep recesses of her consciousness. She slowed to a stop at Van Nuys Boulevard and waited for the signal to change. It was time to start concentrating on real life, not some inane encounter with a redheaded waitress. She glanced around the congested street heading into Sherman Oaks and began to relax into the familiarity of daily routine. Yes, routine. That's what she wanted. That's what she loved. Of course.

She passed the row of seedy, one-story shops and businesses that greeted her each morning on her way to work—a tattoo parlor, a used clothing store, a record shop with a video rental branch across the street. The marquee of what once had been a neighborhood theater stood tall and garish, but now, instead of spelling out the titles of movies, it read, *The Gap*. What once had been the box office held an array of modern fashions.

All these sights soothed her, reminded her that her life was intact. As reality returned, Addison began to see the humor in the experience of the last half-hour. She must be losing her mind—or it could be early menopause, maybe? Whatever it'd been, she felt silly. The best she could do was leave it behind her and be grateful no one had been around to witness her idiocy.

Finally, Addison steered the Explorer into the underground parking garage of the eleven-story structure that housed the Milton and Ryan Advertising Agency where she'd worked for the past nine years. She maneuvered into her assigned slot. She recognized how much of her life was set, how strongly she could depend upon certain aspects—a parking spot, a paycheck, the love of her beautiful Maggie. She smiled and headed for the elevator.

The building was fairly new and from the outside looked like nothing more than a glass box, but the suite of offices that the agency leased on the top floor marked them as the up-and-coming advertising firm that they were. The elevator doors opened into a plush reception area with rich burgundy carpet and finely textured walls that offered abstract patterns of swirls and twists. Three clusters of comfortable chairs dotted the large room, and a floor-to-ceiling fish aquarium acted as a divider between the reception desk and the small maze of offices and conference rooms behind it.

It always felt a bit odd to Addison when she came in on weekends in casual attire. During normal work hours, jeans, even if they were white, and a football jersey would be grounds for a reprimand, but Michael had said the client today was pretty laid-back, concerned more with what the agency could do for her than what they looked like on a Saturday afternoon.

She rounded the end of the enormous aquarium and raised her hand to tap her usual salutation to the large, colorful fish that swam languidly back and forth in their quiet world. Today, though, she hesitated and pressed her fingertips to the glass. She envied them the serenity of their existence—nothing to prove, nothing to figure out, nothing to lose. Voices drifted to her from down the hall, comfortable laughter, then a pause. Michael and his client must have finished lunch and returned to the office early.

Evidently the client owned a restaurant up in the Bay Area, one that had become quite successful over the course of the past several years. She was now opening a second somewhere in Studio City, and she'd hired Milton and Ryan to put together an extensive advertising campaign on the recommendation of one of their satisfied clients.

Although her establishments didn't cater exclusively to the gay and lesbian community, she had specifically asked for a portion of the strategy to be focused there.

Addison stepped into the doorway of Michael Helton's office.

"Ah, there she is," he said, smiling at her from behind his desk. His cherubic features and the slight cowlick that was never fully controlled at the crown of his blond head always reminded her of the first of several broken-hearted little boys in her distant past. "Addison Rae-McInnis, Victoria Fontaine. Victoria, Addison." He motioned to a young woman who looked to be in her mid-twenties seated in a white upholstered swivel chair in front of him.

She rose and extended her hand. "It's nice to meet you, Addison. Michael speaks highly of you."

She stood about an inch shorter than Addison, and her dark blond, mid-length hair accentuated her gold-rimmed brown eyes. A silk fuchsia blouse and pair of navy Guess jeans amply emphasized her body's natural attributes—seductively subtle cleavage and shapely hips and legs. Diamond-cut gold earrings glinted against the soft wave of her hair.

Addison laughed. "He has to. I do his evaluations." She shot a quick glance in his direction. "It's a pleasure to meet you, too." She shook Victoria's hand.

Victoria's grip was firm, confident. A smile tugged at the corners of her mouth. "I'm glad to see that kind of playfulness between you two. It's been my experience in my own business that when people play well together they also work well together." Her words and manner belied her obviously youthful years.

Addison wondered if Victoria was actually older than she looked, in order to be opening a second restaurant of her own. "We certainly do both around here," she said with a grin, remembering Michael's jig on the table at last year's Christmas party. "And I have no doubt that we'll be able to give you everything you're looking for." She lowered herself into the other swivel chair and settled in for discussion.

Victoria reclaimed her own seat and smiled. "Everything I'm looking for? I have to say, that's the best news I've heard in a very long time."

Addison thought she detected a hint of innuendo in Victoria's tone then immediately dismissed it. She wasn't going there again. This was her job. This woman wanted a professional service. She wasn't the redhead in the gas station. Hell, she wasn't Maggie. She was a client. "Let's get started and see what we can do. From what Michael's told me, I'm assuming you and he already have a general outline on the main portion of your campaign?"

"Definitely. He's drawn up some great ideas."

"Will you be using the same ads in both the mainstream and the gay markets?"

"Yes, I think what Michael has put together will cover both areas. Mostly what I want in the gay and lesbian community is visibility. I just want to get the word out that everyone is welcome at Fontaine's. We need more places where we can have romantic dinners, celebrate anniversaries—just be ourselves."

Addison nodded. "And my part in this is to give some ideas on where to advertise, right?"

"Right," Michael said. "Newspapers, publications, radio stations. I know about *The Pink Pages*, of course, but we're looking for some of the less obvious places to advertise that'll really get Fontaine's embedded in the community's mind."

"That shouldn't be too hard. I could probably pull together a pretty thorough list by the end of the week." Addison glanced at Victoria and caught her gaze moving back up from Addison's body. "Would that be soon enough?"

"Certainly," she said without missing a beat. "We're just now beginning the renovations on the building. We're still several months away from opening."

"Great. I'll get going on it so you're sure to have it when you need it. It really won't take me much time at all."

"That'd be fantastic," Michael said, his tone holding an obvious edge of finality. "I really appreciate you coming in today, Addison. I wanted you and Victoria to meet before I leave for the conference in New York. In fact, I need to get out of here and start packing. I'm flying out tomorrow."

"Oh, yeah. I forgot about that. You try not to have too much fun while you're out there. It's supposed to be work, you know?"

Michael straightened and saluted. "Absolutely not. No fun whatsoever."

Addison chuckled and rose. She turned to Victoria. "If you need anything while Michael's out of town, feel free to give me a call. I'd be happy to fill in for him."

"Thank you. I really appreciate that." Victoria retrieved a purse from beside her chair. "I'd better get going, too, and let you two get on with your day. Addison, it was truly a pleasure meeting you. I look forward to seeing you again."

"Same here."

They shook hands once more, and Addison said her good-byes to both of them. She entered her own office a few doors down the hallway and crossed to the row of windows that provided an impressive view of the skyscrapers of Encino, but she barely took notice of them.

Instead, she remained focused on Victoria Fontaine and the allure that seemed to smolder just beneath her surface, on the redhead who'd been much more direct but whose interest seemed to be the same, on Dusty's words, and on her own confusion. Maybe she just needed sex. She and Maggie hadn't made love in a while, not since… When was it? Other things—work, friends, social obligations—all seemed to get in the way too damned often. That's all this was. She needed to connect with Maggie, feel her close. They could have a quiet evening tonight.

She'd stop and pick up Chinese food on her way home—Maggie's favorite. They could retreat to their room, have a picnic in bed, maybe watch a movie. After all, isn't that why they'd added the third floor, so they'd have a sanctuary in a house full of renters? Then she'd make love to Maggie like she hadn't in a long time, slowly, passionately, with all the desire she felt for her.

A light knock sounded behind her.

She turned to face Victoria Fontaine.

"Hello again." Victoria's voice was softer than it'd been earlier. "I'm sorry to bother you."

"It's no bother. What can I do for you?"

"I was just wondering," she said, crossing to where Addison stood. "I really don't know anyone here all that well, but I'd like to get out and see some of the hotspots. You know, maybe a couple of the more popular lesbian bars. The nightlife? I'm starting to go nuts in the evenings." She laughed. Her demeanor was easy, relaxed.

"Oh, sure, I can give you the names of some places."

Victoria fixed a warm gaze on Addison. "I was hoping more for an escort. Someone to show me around."

Addison fell into the depths of Victoria's eyes. They enticed. They suggested. Hope seemed to linger in their cast. She could imagine staring into them on a dance floor as she held her close.

Victoria? On the dance floor? She forced her mind away from such thoughts. Didn't she mean Maggie? Why wasn't it Maggie she saw herself embracing to the music? What was happening?

Taking Victoria out on the town was a job much better suited for someone like Dusty, but for some reason, she couldn't imagine introducing this woman to Dusty. If all she wanted was some company, what was the harm in that? "Oh. Well, yeah, that shouldn't be a problem. I could show you around." She recalled Brenda's advice. "Or, *we*. We could show you around."

Amusement shaped Victoria's expression, and she glanced down at the picture of Maggie and Addison on the desk. "Is this your partner?"

"Mm-hm. Maggie."

Victoria trailed a finger across the top of the silver frame and studied the photo. "It's a great picture of you. You look very sexy."

Addison had always loved the photograph, but more for Maggie's likeness than her own—the warmth in her expression, the joy in her eyes, her vibrant smile that seemed to reach out and touch anyone who cared to notice. Victoria, however, didn't. All she appeared to see was Addison. "Thanks," she said, omitting the rest of her thoughts. It was enough that Victoria knew about Maggie.

"Michael said you and Maggie have been together for a long time."

Addison frowned slightly, wondering why her personal life had come up in the conversation at all. "Twelve years. What about you? Anyone special?"

"I know a lot of special people, but no *one* in particular." Victoria leaned a hip against the edge of the desk. "I don't know, maybe it's because I work too much. There never seem to be enough hours in the day."

"No kidding. Even when you have a relationship, sometimes it gets pushed aside by other priorities."

"How have you done it? Twelve years is so long."

Addison thought for a moment. It hadn't seemed that difficult. "Love and commitment, I guess." She felt a little foolish with such a trite answer, but she couldn't think of another one.

Victoria gave no response. She eased forward slightly and watched Addison as if waiting for more. The angle provided a perfect view of the swell of a breast just beneath the silk fabric of her blouse. It seemed too casual to be deliberate, and yet Victoria watched her with intensity.

Addison realized the boldness of her own stare. She felt the heat rise in her body.

"That's it?" Victoria's words broke her trance.

"What?"

"Love and commitment? That's the answer?"

"Uh…" *Oh, yeah, Maggie. Twelve years.* "It's the only one I have. And maybe some luck." Addison struggled to regain her focus.

"What about trust?"

Addison shoved her hands into the front pockets of her jeans. A twinge of uneasiness tightened her stomach. She could guess where this was going. "Of course, trust too."

"Have you ever violated that trust?" Victoria's delivery sounded pensive, as though she were searching for something, but her eyes displayed knowledge beyond her apparent years.

This woman is dangerous. Addison sensed it throughout her entire body, throughout her entire being. She made Brenda look like a fairy princess. Was this whole day some kind of test? Was she supposed to prove her love for Maggie all of a sudden? Prove it to whom? The powers that be? Herself? *You get back what you put out.* But she hadn't known Victoria long enough to put out anything yet. "No, I've never violated that trust." She answered the question more to escape her own confusion than to continue the conversation.

"I admire that." Victoria smiled. "Someday I hope I can find a relationship like yours. I think it's very rare."

Addison blinked. It was hardly the response she'd expected from a woman who seemed to have a totally different direction in mind.

Victoria picked up a paper clip and twirled it between her fingers. She flashed a sincere smile, with no trace of the devious look that Addison had *thought* she'd seen.

"Well, I really do have to get going. I'm catching a flight up to the Bay Area later this afternoon. I have to touch base with my manager up there, but I'll be back Monday. Maybe you, Maggie, and I can get together next week?"

"Oh, okay. That sounds good." Relief mingled with disappointment. Had Addison imagined everything—the suggestive tone, the leading questions? Did this attractive, younger woman *not* find her interesting? This was how it should be, though—Victoria, the client, being entertained by Addison, the account executive, and her lovely partner, Maggie.

"Thanks again for everything," Victoria said as she strode toward the door. "I'll give you a call at the beginning of the week."

"And I'll check with Maggie on her schedule so we can set something up."

Victoria smiled and disappeared around the corner.

Addison released an exasperated sigh. What the hell was happening to her? Was she going insane? It must've been all those ridiculous thoughts she'd allowed herself to entertain on the way over here. Maybe all of this *was* a test. Maybe it was a sign. Of what, though? That she needed a therapist? That she needed to be spending more time with Maggie?

Whatever it was, she knew it was her own stuff and only hers. She had to leave Victoria Fontaine out of it, along with any other poor, unsuspecting female who happened to cross her path.

CHAPTER FOUR

Tess Rossini stared at the open message box on her computer screen.

The cursor blinked back at her, silently screaming its demand for her response.

The e-mail system that the university had set up to enable more direct communication between the students and professors provided some wonderful benefits from an academic stance. It allowed for clarification of assignments and more in-depth questions on lecture points and permitted those pupils with a deeper interest in a subject to inquire about additional resources, but it also had a tendency to boost the courage of some and give them that little bit of anonymity they needed in order to approach her on a more personal level.

She received this type of correspondence each year. They usually began similarly. *Dear Dr. Rossini*—or, sometimes, *Dear Tess—I can't believe I'm writing this to you*, or *How can I begin to tell you how I feel?* From the more romantic, she even had a few love sonnets written in her name. She took these letters seriously. She had no desire to hurt anyone's feelings or shatter someone's confidence, but they always left her feeling a little unsettled, all too aware of the void that remained in her life. She would never consider having a relationship with a student, and their interest in her served as a painful reminder that her fear of suffering another loss prevented her from taking the risk with anyone.

What, though, was she supposed to say to these young women, and sometimes men? Although her orientation was fairly well known around campus, she still occasionally heard from the male population.

She realized that she could always just say it was against the rules for faculty and students to date, but that seemed like such a cold response. Besides, there were plenty of instructors who didn't play by that particular rule, so that stance wouldn't necessarily hold without argument.

It had been much simpler for her when she had been with Alicia. Her answer had been pat. *I'm very flattered by your interest, but I am in a committed relationship with someone I love very much. I would never want to mislead anyone. You are a bright...*She would then go on with words of encouragement and reassurance that pertained on an individual basis. Since Alicia's death, however, responding to such notes was more difficult. She no longer knew what to say without going into more personal detail than she preferred.

As she continued to stare at the blank screen, she considered the ease with which she had been able to deal with JoAnn Bennett, a psychology professor at the college, when she had invited Tess to dinner. That seemed different, though. JoAnn was close to Tess's age, an equal professionally, someone with enough history of her own to understand a loss like Tess had experienced. Tess had felt comfortable sharing more with her. When JoAnn had asked her out, it had been simple enough to explain that she still had healing to do from her past with Alicia, and even now when JoAnn periodically checked in with her or invited her to an informal event, Tess was able to decline with merely an apologetic look.

"Can't you just lie?" Dusty had asked one night while reading over Tess's shoulder. "Just tell them you're with somebody. Tell them you're with me."

The thought had made Tess smile, but the answer to the question was no, she couldn't just lie. Or rather she wouldn't.

She considered herself honest and open, and her students, particularly ones who developed crushes on her and were courageous enough to voice their feelings, deserved at least that much. She always found some way to handle such situations. She trusted that this time would be no different.

The Waterford clock on the corner of the large, L-shaped desk began to chime.

Tess glanced at the face—five o'clock.

The house had been quiet for the afternoon, with only herself and Maggie at home. She had managed to finish outlining the class syllabus for a course on contemporary British novels that she was teaching for the first time in the spring as well as get caught up on most of her e-mail. All that remained was this one message.

She leaned back in her swivel chair and gazed out the doorway of her bedroom.

Located at the very end of the second floor, the room that had been hers for the past three years overlooked the full length of the wide hall. So many times, Tess had followed its path past the alabaster walls hung with numerous photographs—many depicting various members of the McInnis and Rae families intermixed with pictures of past tenants at social gatherings. This house, and its sometimes odd string of inhabitants, had given Tess a miracle when she had needed one most.

The car accident that had taken Alicia's life had swept Tess's away as well. The telephone call she had received as a result of the emergency card in Alicia's wallet had started the spiral that would later result in her losing everything. She had rushed to the hospital to find her partner in the intensive care unit already on a ventilator and connected to every kind of monitor imaginable. The doctors encouraged Tess to contact the parents who hadn't spoken to Alicia in the eight years she and Tess had been together. Upon their arrival, they mandated that only *real family* be allowed into the ICU to see their daughter.

Tess never laid eyes on her partner again, though Alicia never woke to know that.

Four days later, Alicia's body was shipped back to Iowa for funeral services that Tess was told didn't concern her.

Within a month, she received a court order evicting her from their house which was still in only Alicia's name—a legality they had always meant to remedy, but hadn't gotten around to. The edict demanded that she take only her clothing and personal items.

Engulfed in grief, she hadn't had the strength to fight, and now, in retrospect, she realized it had been a blessing. Without Alicia there calling her name down the hallway or leaving wet towels balled up in the corner of the bathroom, the house felt like a tomb. Left on her own, Tess doubted she ever would have been able to leave it, and yet, it was no longer a place for life.

This was, however. Tess glanced around her. Even when she had first moved in, when the walls were bare and the furnishings comprised only her computer and a bed and dresser that Maggie had supplied, it had been her haven, her retreat for solitude, comfort, and healing. She had spent the first couple of months either buried in her work or isolated in her room, emerging only for an occasional meal or sometimes light conversations with Maggie when no one else was home. The nights were filled with tears, longing for the past, and the loneliness of the present.

Little by little, however, Maggie lured her out under any and all pretenses—help moving the large, potted fichus downstairs, assistance assembling the new patio furniture, company while cleaning the fish pond in the backyard. Each task would lead to tea and conversation, gradually to tears, and eventually to laughter.

The decorating had been Maggie's idea as well. Tess recalled the day vividly.

"I'm goin' down to the mall. They're havin' flannel sheets on sale before the cool weather comes along." Maggie stood in the doorway of Tess's room, wearing the same determined expression she always wore when she had made up her mind to pull Tess into the world for a while. "I could use some help pickin' them out. Care to join me?"

Tess turned and considered the firm set of Maggie's jaw, her steady gaze that said she wouldn't leave without Tess in tow. She smiled. "I just can't imagine how you managed before I moved in."

"You don't have any idea what it takes to keep a house like this runnin'." Maggie's eyes flashed with amusement.

Tess studied this precious gift she had no doubt had been sent to her by the Goddess. The laugh lines around her eyes attested to how thoroughly she enjoyed her life, and the sincerity in her manner promised genuine caring. Even after living there for only a few months, Tess knew exactly how much it took for Maggie to run the household the way she did and the effect this one woman had on the worlds of those around her.

Tenderness and gratitude welled within her. "Yes, I do," she said softly. "And I would love to get out for a while and go to the mall with you."

A broad smile brightened Maggie's face. "Good. We'll need to pick up a set for Dusty as well. She says hers are gettin'…" She hesitated for a moment, her brow furrowing. "Nubbly, if I remember correctly."

Tess laughed and rose to find her shoes.

"I'll be waitin' for you downstairs." Maggie turned to leave, then called over her shoulder. "Who knows, maybe you'll find somethin' in the housewares department for your room as well. If you've decided to stay with us, you should get some color around you."

That was the day it had started—Tess's gradual delivery back into the world of the living, the very first steps of rebuilding a life without Alicia.

Now, three years later, rich hunter green carpet and matching curtains with maroon accents warmed the once stark white walls. The far end of the large rectangular room held a Victorian-style double bed with an antique, silvery finish and glass-topped nightstands. The hand-painted ivy and berry-wine-colored blossoms that twined around the curved tops of the head- and footboards—compliments of Maggie's artistic talents—seemed to flow directly from the floral pattern of the cotton comforter that covered the mattress. A tall, open-backed shelving unit separated her sleeping area from the section she used as an office, and the walls offered several tasteful nudes of women and a painting Tess had found at an artisans' fair of the mythological muses picnicking in a meadow. These days her private living space gave her peace and contentment rather than the emptiness of the past.

A quiet knock drew Tess from her reminiscence. She turned to find Maggie standing in the exact position she had imagined her in moments earlier. Still enveloped in the memories of how much this woman had done for her, she extended a warm smile. "Have I told you lately how much you mean to me?"

Maggie leaned against the doorjamb, Baxter at her side. "My, my, what've you been doin' up here?" Tenderness tempered her tone.

"Oh, just counting my blessings, I suppose."

Chuckling, Maggie straightened. "Well, if you're done with your real work, why don't you come downstairs and help me count some other things? I've got lasagna noodles, tomatoes, all sorts of things that need countin'."

Tess laughed. "Is that your way of telling me there's no way you can make dinner without me?"

"Exactly."

"I'd be glad to help." Tess glanced at her computer screen. She could finish that last e-mail tomorrow. She rounded the end of her desk and headed down the hall with Maggie and Baxter.

As they neared the stairs, Tess looped her arm through Maggie's and slowed to a stop. "I was serious about what I asked. I want you to know what a special friend you are to me, how much I've grown to love you. I don't think I tell you often enough."

Maggie patted Tess's hand. "You tell me every day, darlin', every time I see your smile."

In the kitchen, Maggie retrieved two packages of Italian sausage from the refrigerator while Tess gathered a pot for the noodles, a large skillet for the meat, and a baking dish. The two of them had made this meal together many times and had it down to an art form.

"I saw you in and out of Della's old room this afternoon. Is it all ready for the new tenant?" Tess asked. She placed the pot in the sink and turned on the faucet.

"It wasn't the room that was the problem. Della left it spotless. It was that bathroom of Dusty's." Maggie rolled her eyes. "The girl's a slob when there's no one to keep watch over her."

The long bathroom that stretched between Dusty's room and the third rental on the second floor at times developed its own persona, actually evolving into what seemed like a separate entity walking around the house. Its main purpose appeared to be causing conflict rather than the simple function of eliminating waste and washing away the day's dirt. Everything about it had been argued over repeatedly—its cleanliness, its decor, whether the window should remain open or closed, whether or not the shower could or should be used for drying nylons, T-shirts, hats…on and on.

Tess felt guilty at times for not being involved in any of the disputes or their resolutions. She felt relatively certain she could successfully share the bathroom in question with Dusty, but the room connected to it was too small to act as both a bedroom and an office combined. She needed the extra space of the one she now occupied.

"No, you don't." Maggie interrupted her musings as if reading her mind. "Don't you be thinkin' this is your problem to solve. You pay extra for the bigger livin' area and a bathroom to yourself. Besides, I decided long ago that anyone movin' into that other room upstairs, whether she knows it or not, has signed up for some interestin' lessons with Ms. Dusty Renee Gardner in this lifetime. And vice-versa." Maggie emptied both packages of meat into the frying pan and turned on the burner beneath it.

Baxter surveyed the kitchen activities with obvious dogly enthusiasm. He sniffed the air as the sausage began to cook.

"It just seems so silly to let it cause so much trouble."

"I don't know why you always think that *you'd* have any easier time than anyone else usin' the same bathroom with her?" Maggie's voice trailed upward at the end as if she were asking a question.

Tess ignored it. She knew why, but for some reason, had never been able to share it with Maggie. Perhaps she was embarrassed. "Maybe you're right. I'd probably be just as upset as everyone else who's had the experience." She smiled and found the noodles in the pantry. "What did you say the new tenant's name was? Eve?"

"Mm-hm, Eve Jacobs. And to tell you the truth, whatever friction might result from that bloody bathroom is the least of my concerns about her and Dusty."

"What do you mean?" Tess set the pasta on the island counter and opened the refrigerator.

Suddenly, Baxter was her best friend. As she leaned forward and retrieved the cheese from the deli compartment, he pushed up under her arm and landed a wet kiss on her cheek.

"That's very sweet, Bax, but you still don't get anything." Laughing, she stroked his head.

"It's not usually my practice," Maggie said, "to go meddlin' into anythin' that would naturally go on between anyone livin' here, but Eve's a bit different from what we're accustomed to." She stirred the meat and added some seasoning. "She's very confused about herself. She's leavin' her husband to try to figure out if she's a lesbian or not."

"She doesn't know?"

"No. From what I gathered talkin' to her this mornin', she's more of a thinker than a feeler. But she must've felt somethin' somewhere to be questionin' her sexuality."

Tess tore into a package of mozzarella then opened a drawer to find the grater. "What's that have to do with Dusty?" she asked, rummaging through the contents.

Maggie laughed. “You should’ve seen the show that girl put on. It was like watchin’ the dance of the peacock. She was more than a bit interested in Eve.”

Tess tensed slightly. “Really?” She had never met any of the women Dusty dated, but she sometimes wondered about them. What were they like? What was Dusty’s *type*, as they say?

“Mm. But I think she scares the poor girl to death.”

Tess giggled. “I suppose if you weren’t sure of your sexuality Dusty would be pretty scary.”

Maggie nodded and removed the skillet from the heat. “I think I’m goin’ to have a chat with her. She has enough girlfriends. She doesn’t need one here at home.”

The front door opened and the small wind chimes that hung from the top of the door sang wildly with the force.

“I’m home.” Dusty’s voice rang out. “Anybody here?”

The dog dashed from the room.

“In the kitchen,” Maggie called. She glanced at Tess. “Speakin’ of our proud little peacock.”

“Hey, bud, how ya doing?” Dusty’s booted footsteps, accompanied by the clicking of Baxter’s toenails on the teak floor, grew louder as the pair moved down the hall then appeared from around the corner. Her black leather jacket hung open to reveal a fluorescent green T-shirt beneath, and the denim of her blue jeans hugged the contours of her firm thighs.

“Mmmm. Something smells good.” She ran her fingers through her hair, disheveled by the helmet she now carried, and smoothed it back to its more customary state. She scanned the kitchen and grinned. “Lasagna? Boy, am I glad I came home.”

Tess smiled and pulled her gaze from Dusty. She began grating the cheese.

“I’m glad you came home, too, darlin’,” Maggie said. “There’s somethin’ I want to talk to you about.”

“Oh, yeah?”

“Be a love and put the pasta in the water for me, will you? But wash up first.”

Baxter settled in the corner, apparently giving up his quest for any treats.

Dusty set her helmet on the counter and rinsed her hands at the sink. "That's what you want to talk about?" She grabbed the noodles and ripped open the package. She dumped them into the bubbling liquid.

"No, it's about Eve."

"Who?"

Maggie frowned. "Eve Jacobs, the woman you met here this mornin'?"

Dusty stood poking at the portion of the noodles still sticking up above the water level. "Oh, yeah. Is she gonna take the room?"

Maggie stepped up beside her. She swatted the back of her hand with a fork then stirred the contents of the pot until everything disappeared below the surface. "Yes, she's movin' most of her things over tomorrow."

Dusty shifted and leaned against the tile edge of the built-in stove. She smiled at Tess while Maggie's attention was on the boiling pasta.

"I want you to stay away from her." One of the things for which Maggie could always be counted on was directness.

Dusty's jaw went slack. She turned to face Maggie. "What do you mean?"

"You know exactly what I mean." Maggie wagged the fork in front of Dusty's nose. "Play your flirtin' games somewhere else. This girl's fragile right now. She doesn't need to be toyed with."

"Toyed with?" Astonishment resonated in Dusty's voice. "Me?"

Tess shook her head and smiled to herself. She knew it was now Maggie with whom Dusty was playing. Whether or not Dusty had ever had any real interest in Eve Jacobs would never be known. When it was all said and done, she would, of course, do whatever Maggie said, but in the meantime, she would have some fun. Tess watched with the same intrigue she always felt when witnessing one of these performances.

Dusty was an enigma, a conundrum that defied a solution. She seemed to expend a great deal of energy convincing the rest of the household of her shallowness and lack of any genuine emotion, yet Tess had seen the warm, caring side of her that belied the very notion. She allowed everyone else to believe, at times, that entire days were spent in bed with a hangover when Tess knew she was curled up in her room with a book she had borrowed the night before.

"Can I help it if women can't resist my magnetism?" Dusty quipped in response to whatever Maggie's last warning had been.

Oh, well. Tess supposed everyone had secrets and chose carefully the people they trusted to keep them. Dusty kept Tess's. It seemed only fair for Tess to keep Dusty's.

"What's wrong with her, anyway?" Dusty asked. She shrugged her jacket off and tossed it across the end of the island where Tess worked.

Maggie shot Dusty a stern look. "Nothin's *wrong* with her. She's just a bit confused and needs some time to sort things out."

"Confused about what?" Dusty rested her elbows on the tiled surface next to Tess.

Tess inhaled the citrus aroma of the shampoo Dusty used. She coaxed her focus back to the mozzarella.

"That's none of your concern. You just do what I ask." As though finished with the conversation, Maggie walked to the pantry and began collecting cans of tomato sauce.

"Aw, c'mon. How come I can't know?" Dusty cast a sideways glance at Tess. "I'll bet Tess knows."

Amused by Dusty's ploy, Tess stifled a smile. The last place she wanted to be was between these two women on this topic.

"How come she gets to know and I don't?" Dusty asked.

"Because she's a sincere, caring person who might be able to offer Eve some insight," Maggie said with exaggerated enunciation.

Dusty straightened and planted her hands on her hips. "I care," she said. "I have things to offer, too, you know."

"Of course you do, darlin', and if we ever need someone to take Eve for a motorcycle ride or get her so bloody drunk she can't see straight, you'll be the first person we call." Maggie's words were sarcastic, but her gaze held a glint of fondness.

Dusty considered her for a long moment before she turned to Tess with apparent deliberation. She sidled close and slipped her arm around Tess's waist. "Will you tell me what's wrong with her?" she whispered. Her warm breath caressed Tess's ear.

Tess hid her small intake of air with a laugh and turned to look into Dusty's pleading, dark blue eyes. "Not if you strung me up on the hanging tree and let the birds peck at my flesh."

"Whoa." Dusty's eyes widened. "That literature stuff can really warp your mind, can't it? I was just thinking of plying you with chocolate."

Tess chuckled. She slid the last bit of cheese between Dusty's lips. "That won't work, either. If you know what's good for you, you'll do as Maggie says." She looked up to find Maggie watching with a loving smile. Tess eased back. She gave Dusty a playful shove and pushed her away.

"Okay, fine. You two just keep your little secrets. See if I care. And next time *I* have one, I won't tell you, either." She slouched against the counter again and munched on her cheese.

Tess and Maggie laughed.

"Now that that's settled…" Maggie said.

Dusty glared at Tess.

"There's the bathroom." Maggie stirred the noodles again.

"Oh, God, not the bathroom." Dusty buried her face in her hands. "I'll try to keep it cleaner, or I'll open the window, or I'll turn the shampoo upside down, or right side up, or I'll balance it on my nose. Whatever anybody wants."

The front door creaked, and Baxter took off at a vigilant trot.

"All I was goin' to say," Maggie continued, "is to be sure to give Eve her privacy in there."

Dusty looked up. "I'm not a peeper, you know."

Maggie chuckled. "I don't think you are, luv. I'm simply askin' you to be aware that there might be someone else in there. You've had it to yourself for a bit now, with Della gone."

"Not really," Dusty grumbled and rolled her eyes. "I didn't even know I had my own bathroom till this morning. Which brings up another point—"

"Hey, everybody." Addison stood in the kitchen doorway, holding a bag that read *Panda Palace* on the side. "I brought Chinese food. Anyone interested?" She grinned at Maggie.

Maggie stared back with a stunned expression. Then irritation settled into her features. "Tess and I've been makin' lasagna for the past half hour."

Addison's smile faded. Her gaze traveled to the stovetop, to the counter, and finally to the baking dish awaiting the layers of ingredients. She turned back to Maggie, an odd mixture of remorse and hope mingling in her eyes. "Well, it's not done yet." She faltered slightly. "Could we save it for tomorrow?"

Tess glanced at Maggie. At this point, it would take just as much work to prepare the dish for storage as for eating.

Maggie still stood watching Addison with obvious bewilderment. "Do you think we could save the Chinese for tomorrow?"

"Really, Addison," Dusty said. "They've been working hard on dinner. Besides, I love their lasagna."

Annoyance replaced any other emotion showing in Addison's face, and she walked to the breakfast nook. "Whatever." She dropped the bag onto the table.

Dusty looked back and forth between Maggie and Addison. "Hey, you know, if you'd called, it might have helped."

"Shut up, Dusty." Addison tossed her keys down beside the food.

Dusty raised her hands as if in surrender. "Sorry. Just making a point." She grabbed her jacket and helmet and headed out the door.

Maggie frowned. She removed the pasta from the burner. "That was a bit uncalled for, don't you think?" she asked Addison.

"It's none of her business."

"She made the exact point I was thinkin'. Is it my business?"

Addison stiffened and turned to face Maggie. "I just wanted to surprise you." She glanced at Tess. "But you're right. I should've called. Maybe you could've penciled it in." She pivoted and stalked from the room.

Tess pursed her lips. "What was that about?"

Maggie shook her head. She eyed the empty doorway, concern creasing her brow. "I don't know what the problem is lately. She's beginnin' to act so different. She's been distant, moody…never like this, though." She shifted her gaze to Tess. "But I can't get her to talk."

"What does she say when you ask her about it?"

Maggie sighed. "She's busy at work. She hasn't been sleepin' well. She loves me, and I shouldn't worry."

Tess bit her lower lip. "I'll finish things down here. Why don't you go up and try to talk to her? Take the Chinese food and see if you can work out whatever's wrong."

"What?" Maggie asked in evident disbelief. "And reward her for this little display?"

"Maggie, she isn't Baxter. You don't reward her when she sits on command and discipline her when she doesn't." Tess took Maggie's hand. "She's your partner, your lover. And I think she needs you."

Maggie softened and looked into Tess's eyes, uncertainty and maybe even a little fear clouding her normally confident air. Her gaze drifted as if following a thought. "Maybe you're right," she said gently. "You don't mind bein' left with all this mess?"

"Not a bit. You go. Take care of your sweetie."

"Thank you, darlin'." Maggie patted Tess's arm and retrieved the takeout food. She took a deep breath and started toward the hall. "Oh," she said, coming to a halt. "And you'll feed Dusty?"

Tess laughed. "Of course, I'll feed Dusty."

"And Baxter?"

Tess glanced at the dog. "And Baxter." She winked at him. "I'll feed them both lasagna."

CHAPTER FIVE

Maggie drifted from a deep, dreamless sleep to an awareness of rustling ivy on the hillside behind the house and the gurgling of the fountain in the backyard below. A cool morning breeze wisped through the open window and played across her cheek. Eyes still closed, she absorbed the caress of Addison's bare skin pressed against her own.

Spooned behind her, Addison held her in a gentle embrace.

Maggie released a peaceful sigh and snuggled deeper between the satin sheets. She took Addison's hand and brought it to her lips. She kissed the fingers still redolent with traces of the previous night's lovemaking—if that is what it had been. Whatever it had been, it had stolen Maggie's breath.

She had come upstairs after the disagreement in the kitchen to find Addison sitting on the far side of their king-sized brass bed, staring into space. The last rays of late afternoon sunlight poured through the large window at the opposite end of the room, intensifying the brilliant colors of the Georgia O'Keefe paintings that graced the subtly textured walls. The decor presented a stark contrast to Addison's somber portrait.

Maggie eased the door closed behind her.

Addison remained silent, motionless, obviously carried far away by her thoughts. She looked incredibly sad, the corners of her mouth drooped with a frown.

Regret swelled in Maggie's heart. Hurting Addison always affected her deeply. From their very first argument when they were dating so many years ago, she hadn't been able to stand the thought that something she had done had brought this beautiful woman pain. It was one of the ways Maggie had known this relationship was different, that Addison was the one with whom she wanted to spend the rest of her life. All earlier irritation faded. Addison had only been trying to be thoughtful. Maggie knew that. "Would you still like to have Chinese?" she asked apologetically.

Addison didn't respond. She appeared not to have heard the question. Then, slowly, she turned her head, her gaze still distant. As her eyes began to focus, confusion showed in their depths. "Maggie," she said, her voice barely above a whisper. She seemed surprised, not that someone was there, but at the fact that it was Maggie.

"Were you expectin' someone else, luv?" Maggie smiled.

"No." Addison's tone strengthened. She looked away. "Of course not. But I wasn't expecting you, either."

Maggie studied her. She felt the wall go up between them, the same barrier that had been separating them for the past couple of months whenever Maggie tried to get Addison to talk about what was bothering her. Maggie set the bag of takeout food on the Indian rug beside the bed and lowered herself onto the mattress. "Don't I always come to you after we've quarreled?"

"Always?"

Maggie reconsidered. There had been times when her temper had bested her. "All right then, usually?" She moved further onto the ivory satin comforter. She brushed several strands of hair from Addison's forehead. "I'm sorry I was cross. I'm sorry I hurt your feelin's."

Addison pursed her lips and leaned into Maggie's touch. "I'm sorry I didn't call."

Tension continued to pulse between them. Apologies said, they both seemed to know that dinner wasn't the issue.

"Dawtie, tell me what's wrong," Maggie whispered. She stroked Addison's cheek. "You've been so far away these days."

Addison squeezed her eyes shut and inhaled deeply. "I don't know," she said, her words slightly choked. "I don't know anything."

Maggie felt one stone in the wall crumble. At least Addison was no longer denying there was a problem. She took her face between her palms. "Talk to me, luv. We can figure it out together." She eased closer.

Addison's eyelids fluttered open, her lashes moist with the beginnings of tears. She looked like a lost child in a supermarket, afraid and alone. She grasped Maggie's hands. "I need you."

"I'm right here, dawtie. Tell me what you need."

Addison answered with a kiss. She grazed her lips across Maggie's gently. Then something shifted. She twined her fingers into the thickness of Maggie's hair and pulled her against her, her grip firm, her mouth insistent.

Startled, Maggie gasped. She tried to draw back.

Addison held her tightly, passionate, demanding. It had been a long time since they had kissed this way.

Maggie's body began to respond. She surrendered to Addison's hold, merged with her desire. Slipping her arms around Addison's neck, she molded to her and returned the fervent kiss.

Addison moaned and lowered her to the bed. She pressed her full weight down on Maggie. Her breathing quickened. She tore her mouth from Maggie's and gazed down at her. No trace of that frightened child remained, no sign of confusion. Though she still wasn't talking, at least Maggie knew what she needed, and it was something she could give.

Addison stirred behind her, bringing Maggie back to the serenity of the morning.

Memories of lust and passion lingered in her body and mind. She remembered Addison's eager hands, her searching mouth, her probing fingers, her thrusting hips. Maggie had yielded to them all, her own excitement heightening to match the intensity of Addison's hunger. They had continued late into the night, the waves of their arousal cresting over and over again until, finally satiated, they drifted into tranquil sleep.

It had been like years ago, when their attraction to one another had seemed like the only thing that existed, when each other's bodies had been uncharted, unexplored. It had almost seemed as though Addison had been somebody new, somebody different—or perhaps as if she had seen Maggie as such.

An unsettling ripple wormed its way through Maggie's mind. She opened her eyes. She turned over in Addison's arms and gazed into her unguarded features. She touched the soft lips that had been so bruising the night before.

The corners of Addison's mouth lifted in sleep.

Maggie tensed. What was she dreaming this morning? What had she been thinking while they made love? Was she fantasizing about someone else? Maggie recalled Addison's growing interest in Dusty's sexual exploits. She wondered if it held any meaning. She had wondered about it before.

Was Addison beginning to wander? Was she restless in their relationship? Were the things that brought Maggie comfort and security causing her partner boredom and suffocation?

These were all questions Maggie had brought up in the beginning, issues about which she'd had reservations. The thirteen-year age difference between them had been cause for concern. The difference in their backgrounds raised some doubts. Maggie also wondered, though, if her suspicions and fears sprang from her own breakup with Julia so many years ago, and any residual guilt she felt. These were all the same points that had caused her concern, at the age of twenty-two, about committing to a relationship with someone older. She'd always known the importance of experimenting, of playing the field, and she hadn't wanted to take that away from Addison. But Addison had convinced her, and it had been a wonderful twelve years. So why was she doubting now?'

"Such a worried face for so early in the morning. Something wrong?"

Addison's quiet voice startled Maggie back to the moment. She looked into Addison's still-sleepy features and considered the affection in her gaze, the familiarity in her expression. The stranger from last night was gone—or had she ever been there? Maggie smiled. "What could possibly be wrong?"

"Mmm." Addison tightened her embrace and snuggled closer. "Not a thing. You're incredible."

Maggie laughed. "I'm incredible? No, *we're* incredible." She trailed her fingertip down Addison's neck and along her collarbone. "Last night reminded me of the way we used to be."

Addison blinked. "What? You mean we've done that before?"

"Mm-hm." Maggie chuckled. "When we were young and wild. It's been a long time."

Addison settled back onto the pillow. Her manner grew serious. "It's been too long, Maggie. I miss it."

"You've thought about it?" Maggie searched Addison's face. If the problem was as simple as this, why had she not merely said so? "Before last night?"

Addison hesitated. Her gaze left Maggie's. "I met a woman."

Maggie's stomach clenched. Her throat closed. She had feared this for years, and yet, she was still unprepared.

"You know, Michael's client? The one I met with yesterday?"

Yesterday? All this had happened yesterday? She nodded.

"She asked me about our relationship." Something flickered across Addison's face—thoughts not followed, words unspoken—then vanished.

Maggie waited.

"She asked how we'd made it last for so long. She said she didn't have anybody special because she works so much. It just got me thinking. I do have somebody special. Somebody very special." Addison returned her focus to Maggie. "And I take it for granted."

"Take it for granted?" Maggie was stunned. She mentally had Addison, the woman she loved more than anyone else in the world, being unfaithful, wandering off, and Addison was simply worried about taking their relationship for granted? Maggie felt foolish, but more than that, she felt guilty.

"It just seems like we put everything else first," Addison said. "Work, the house, our tenants, your hospice patients. Even our friends. You and me kind of get lost in it all. I don't want to lose you, Maggie."

Maggie raised up on her elbow and searched Addison's expression. She saw uncertainty, remorse. Love streamed through her. "You're never goin' to lose me. You're me dawtie," she said softly. She caressed the hollow of Addison's throat as her mind once again returned to the time of their beginning. She giggled. "Do you remember the first time I called you that?"

Addison laughed. "Yeah, we were in bed. I still think you called me Dottie."

"Oh, I did not."

"I was so mad, I left and didn't talk to you for two days."

"Yes, but not before you'd gotten what you wanted, if I recall correctly."

"Hey, I worked hard for you." Addison grinned. "I wasn't about to throw it away at a crucial moment over some ex-lover's name."

Maggie gave her a playful slap then stared down at her. "So, that's been the problem, has it? We need more time for us?"

Addison sobered. She brushed her thumb across Maggie's temple. "I think so. I love you, Maggie, and I want to hold on to what we have."

"As do I, luv. As do I." Maggie kissed her long and deep, pressing their naked bodies against one another. She felt the embers from the previous night rekindle. "When would you like to start?" She smiled against Addison's lips.

"Let's see. How's a week from Thursday at one o'clock?"

Maggie nibbled Addison's ear and draped her leg over her thighs. "Right now works a bit better."

"Mmmm, I see what you mean," Addison whispered. She slipped her arms around Maggie's waist. "Oh, there's one more thing. You know that woman I told you about? She wants to go out."

A joke, right? Maggie chuckled and ran the tip of her tongue down the side of Addison's slender neck. "With you? Or me?"

Addison released a slow moan. "Actually, both."

Maggie halted. "Both?"

Addison laughed. "She's new in town. She's just here for the remodeling and opening of her restaurant, and she doesn't know anyone."

Maggie gazed into Addison's eyes, aware of every point where their bodies touched. She forced her attention to the words.

"She asked if we could take her out to some of the bars sometime this week." Addison began to stroke the small of Maggie's back, her hands slow and deliberate. "Maybe introduce her to some friends."

"Our friends…" Maggie closed her eyes, succumbing to Addison's caress. "…don't hang out in the bars. Except Dusty. Perhaps she…"

Addison made a noise of dismissal. "She could probably meet some people on her own. She just doesn't want to go alone." She shifted her position and pressed herself into Maggie.

Maggie gasped, her arousal mounting. She clenched her legs around Addison. "If I agree, can we stop talkin' about this woman?"

Addison flicked Maggie's nipple with the tip of her tongue. "Then what?"

Maggie squirmed against her. She opened her eyes to find Addison grinning at her. "You're an evil thing. But you know that, don't you?"

"I'm *your* evil thing. I know *that*."

Maggie laughed, then rolled over and pulled Addison onto her. "Then forget your other woman and show me."

CHAPTER SIX

At two o'clock on Sunday afternoon, Eve found herself pulling her Volvo up to the same curb on Skycrest Drive she'd parked at the previous day. This time, though, she brought all of her personal belongings needed for daily life, as well as a few cherished items to ease the aching in her heart. Glancing down, she picked up the gold-framed picture of her two boys from atop the box nestled into the passenger's seat.

Daniel's hazel eyes, pensive and serious, seemed to question her, probing for answers in their customary fashion, while the image of his younger brother, Enos, flashed the carefree grin that always made her smile. This time was no exception, but as though in punishment, the voices in her head started their condemnation. *How can you leave your children? How can you be so selfish? You're blessed with a beautiful family that anyone else would be grateful for. Why can't you just be happy?*

Eve steeled herself against the attack. She'd heard it all before. She'd *said* it all before. There were no answers, no excuses. All she knew was that she'd lived as long as she could without understanding for certain what was missing from her life. She thought she'd figured it out, but thinking was no longer enough.

Replacing the photograph, she checked her rearview mirror.

Her aunt's black pickup eased to a stop behind her, its bed filled with Eve's beloved rocker that she'd inherited from her grandmother, an inexpensive shelving unit she'd picked up at the swap meet, and boxes of clothing, books, CDs, and toiletries. Aunt Carolyn had insisted that Eve needed help moving, but more importantly, she needed the love that went along with it.

Her husband, Jeremy, had offered as well—he was trying so hard to understand—but Aunt Carolyn had cautioned that the day might be too emotionally charged for both of them. “You’re taking a big step,” she’d told Eve. “I think having Jeremy there will only make it more difficult.” And of course she’d been right. Even waking up in the same house this morning had been too much for them.

On the surface, everything had looked normal. She’d made a nice breakfast for all of them, cleaned up afterward, and read the funnies with the boys while Jeremy showered and dressed. The tension, however, had been palpable. She’d found it impossible to look Jeremy in the eye. And the boys—well, they knew she was going to stay with a friend for a while and would spend time with them regularly, but there was the usual sadness, similar to when she left on a business trip.

She and Jeremy had decided it would be best if the boys weren’t there when Eve packed, so Jeremy had taken them to the zoo for the day. As hard as it’d been to say good-bye to her family, Eve had been grateful to watch the car pull out of the driveway, and would be even more grateful to have the entire move behind her.

With renewed resolution, she opened the door and stepped out into the warm afternoon.

“I’ve always loved this neighborhood,” Aunt Carolyn said, climbing down from the cab with mastered efficiency. Her salt-and-pepper hair tapered back from her heart-shaped face, and the white strands gleamed in the sunlight. “Why don’t we go up and say hello before we start unloading?”

They ascended the steps and rang the bell.

As they waited for an answer, Eve remembered Dusty Gardner’s greeting from the day before. She’d been caught off guard then, but today she was ready.

The door opened.

Eve straightened to her full height and lifted her chin.

“Hello, darlin’,” Maggie said with a broad smile. “Carolyn, what a wonderful surprise.”

A prick of disappointment deflated Eve’s poise. No matter. She’d save it for later. Surely she’d need it eventually.

Maggie stepped outside and enveloped Aunt Carolyn in an affectionate embrace. The brown and mahogany hues woven into the floral pattern of her shorts outfit enhanced the highlights of her hair, and her complexion seemed to glow. "I had no idea you were goin' to come with Eve today. Please come in, both of you."

They followed Maggie into the foyer.

"It's kind of a rough day for her." Aunt Carolyn slipped her arm around Eve's waist. "I thought maybe she could use some support."

"I sure can." Eve gave a weak laugh, struggling to keep the irrational voices from filling her mind again.

"Well, you're here, now." Maggie patted Eve's hand. "Try to relax and take things a bit at a time."

The comforting energy of the two women washed through Eve like a soothing wave. For an instant, her confusion ebbed and her fears receded. If only she could freeze time in this moment.

"Oh, and before I forget." Maggie turned and snatched a key from the corner of the antique cabinet and laid it in Eve's palm. "This is for you. Don't you ever feel as though you need to ring the bell again. This is your home now."

Home. The word echoed in Eve's ears. She stared down at the metal object. It represented such ambivalence. In its polished finish shone the promise of discovery—knowing once and for all who she really was. Its jagged edge, however, symbolized what might very well turn out to be a severed past, the loss of her family, the loss of her boys. She clamped her fist closed and retreated from the dilemma.

"Don't let her fool you. Everyone in LA has one." Addison descended the steps with an easy gait, a wide grin conveying her humor. Her slim body moved fluidly beneath a pair of gray drawstring jogging pants and a red cropped T-shirt.

"You hush," Maggie scolded her in response. "We've lots of friends." She gave what appeared to be an almost embarrassed shrug.

"Yeah, and they all have to have access to our house at any hour of the day or night." Addison stopped at the bottom of the stairs. She slid her arms around Maggie and kissed her on the cheek.

Maggie rolled her eyes, but a tender glint tinged their cast.

"Hi, Carolyn, it's good to see you." Addison said.

Aunt Carolyn laughed. "And it's always a pleasure to see you, too."

Eve heard a door at the top of the stairs open and close again.

"Hey, we having a party?" Dusty's voice ruffled Eve's composure.

Where was that confidence she'd mustered a few minutes ago, that resistance to letting this woman affect her? She looked up to see Dusty's tautly-muscled legs as she made her way downstairs. Eve took in the frayed cutoffs and yellow tank top that revealed well-shaped shoulders. When Dusty's face came into view, Eve straightened and looked directly into those vibrant eyes.

But Dusty didn't even seem to notice her. She averted her gaze and focused on Aunt Carolyn. "Wow, long time no see."

"Yes, it's been a while," Maggie said. "Before you called about Eve, I don't think I've talked with you since the Renaissance Fair last spring. Things just get so busy."

"Has it been that long?" Aunt Carolyn sounded surprised. "Maybe after I help Eve get settled, you and I can visit for a while."

Addison looked from Aunt Carolyn to Maggie. "I have a better idea. Why don't Dusty and I unload Eve's things, she can put them away, and you two can do some catching up?"

Maggie leaned into Addison. "That's very sweet, dawtie. Thank you."

"Oh. No, that's okay." Eve motioned toward the car, her hand trembling. "I can get my stuff up to my room. There isn't that much."

"You wouldn't say that if you'd ever carried much up the stairs in this place," Addison said with a grin.

Eve hesitated. She wouldn't mind some help. The sooner she could finish with this whole moving process, the sooner her doubts and uncertainties might be calmed, but she didn't want to take advantage, either. "I'm sure Dusty has—"

"Dusty doesn't mind, do you, Dusty?" Addison slapped her on the shoulder.

Dusty eyed her and shoved her fingertips into the front pockets of her cutoffs. "I dunno," she said in a sulky tone. "Are you still mad at me for last night?"

"Of course not."

"She was never angry with you, luv. You were simply too close to the hand grenade, as me da used to say." Maggie gestured Aunt Carolyn toward the living room.

"Besides"—Addison pinched Dusty's cheek—"you're too cute to be mad at."

Eve watched with amusement.

"Ooow."

"Oh, quit being a baby. What happened to the big bad biker dyke?" She turned and headed toward the front door. "C'mon."

Without hesitation, Dusty followed. "I think you ought to at least apologize. You hurt my feelings. I think you should have to sing the Super Sorry Song."

Addison laughed. "No way. I was in the no-song zone," she said, stepping out onto the stoop.

"Nuh-uh." Dusty shook her head vehemently. "The no-song zone's around the couch in the TV room."

"That's during the first and third weeks of the thirty-day months. Yesterday, the no-song zone was the kitchen."

Dusty paused and frowned. "Dang it." She pulled the door closed behind them.

Eve smiled at Maggie. "The Super Sorry Song?"

Maggie laughed. "It's the penance for all manner of infractions. I'm certain you'll be hearin' it. We sing it around here quite a bit at times."

Moments later, Eve rounded the corner of the stairwell on the second floor and proceeded down the quiet hall toward her new living space. At the far end, a door to another room stood ajar. Maggie had told her that it was rented by a woman named Tess, but Eve had yet to meet her.

It felt so odd to be walking around the place alone, to know she'd be sharing it with total strangers. She'd lived in a house for eight years with the man she knew intimately and the boys she'd given birth to. That was what a home was, a place you occupied with people who were significant, most important, in your life.

Yet, the women who lived here, although not blood related, seemed as close and intimate as any family. Maybe there was a chance she, too, could fit in here.

She entered the room she'd rented and dropped her purse onto the white antique dresser. The previous day when she'd first seen it, her attention had been drawn to the leaf-patterned stenciling, the color of frost, that decorated the tops of the Prussian blue walls, its wispy lines dancing along just below the ceiling. The same design painted in shades of blue adorned the ivory headboard of the bed whose carved trim matched that of the chest of drawers. Powder blue carpet covered the floor, its tone mingling with the other hues to soften the overall effect.

Eve sighed. Like every other room in this house, this one emanated peace, beauty, healing. Just standing there calmed her nerves somewhat. Once she got her own things added into the equation, she felt sure that this would be the perfect place to sort out her life. She gazed out the lace-covered window to the lush hillside. The tension she'd been dragging around most of the day began to ease.

"Okay, so tell us where you want everything, Madam Supervisor," Addison said, her voice bold and cheerful.

Eve turned with a start.

Addison and Dusty stood just inside the room, each holding a section of bookshelves. "Do you want these right here?" Addison pointed to the empty space along the wall beside the bathroom door. "Or would you like the furniture arranged differently?"

The sincerity in her questions was genuine, and Eve could tell that all she'd have to do is ask, and Addison would move anything anywhere she wanted. She was touched by the thought.

Dusty waited, examining the artificial wood finish on the piece she held, looking utterly bored.

"Oh, right there is fine." Eve motioned at the first space Addison had indicated. "Everything else is great where it is."

Addison nodded. She set her section down and stepped back. "Why don't you put those together, and I'll go get the third piece."

"I—" Dusty began, but Addison was past her and gone before she could get anything else out. She looked at Eve and shrugged.

It was the first eye contact they'd made since Eve's arrival.

Eve froze. She faced Dusty with as much confidence as she could manage, but it wasn't nearly as much as she would have liked.

Without a word, Dusty bent and centered the piece of shelving Addison had left along the wall. She didn't appear nearly as interested in Eve as she'd been the day before.

A part of Eve was grateful, but another part wondered if she'd done something wrong. Maybe her silly word game had offended Dusty. "Is there anything I can do to help?" she asked, trying to ease the tension she felt.

"Nope, not a thing." Focused on her task, Dusty lined up the dowels on the bottom of one section with the holes of the other then snapped the pieces together. She strode out the door.

Eve looked at the ceiling. She'd blown it. Because of her ridiculous behavior, Dusty now hated her, and she had no one to blame but herself. She'd been a total ass yesterday, trying to appear so much better than Dusty. Now she had to live with someone who already didn't like her, and she hadn't even fully moved in yet.

Dusty had frightened her, though, in an intriguing sort of way—all that attention, the suggestive comments, the kind of interest she sometimes received from men. But this had come from a woman. Eve knew she was attracted to women, but it'd always been unspoken, unexpressed, and she'd never been in the position of having another woman attracted to her, at least, not to her knowledge.

She frowned. Maybe it was for the best. She hadn't been able to think with Dusty taking so much notice of her, and that's what this whole experience was for—to think things through, figure things out. It would be easier without distractions.

Footsteps on the stairs announced Addison's and Dusty's next trip to the second floor. They appeared in the doorway, and within seconds, Addison had the top section of shelving in place. Dusty set two clothing boxes in front of the dresser.

As they continued to bring Eve's possessions to her, she began the job of putting them away. Underwear in the top drawer, nightgowns beside them, shorts below—just like home, everything had its place. Addison hung the dresses and blouses in the closet that Eve would have to arrange later, and Dusty stacked the two crates of books beside the shelves before leaving the room once again, without a word.

Finally, Addison brought in the rocking chair and set it in the one free corner. "That's about it," she said, her hands on her hips. "Is there anything I can help you with up here?"

"No, you've done more than enough already. Thank you so much."

"Okay, but you just yell if you need anything. We'll be around all afternoon."

Eve smiled. "Thank you, Addison. I can't tell you how much I appreciate everything all of you are doing for me. You're really very special people."

"You're welcome," Addison said, her tone softer than usual. "I hope you're going to be happy here."

Alone in her new room, Eve surveyed her surroundings. She stared in amazement. The things she'd brought, the items most important to her, seemed like they belonged there. The seat and back cushions of the rocker were an almost exact match for the color of the walls, the gold frames of her photographs accentuated the brass handles on the dresser beautifully, and the dried flower arrangement that her sons had given her for her last birthday held the same shades featured in the stenciling on the headboard.

Then her gaze fell on the picture of Daniel and Enos. Her heart lurched. How could things seem so right and at the same time so wrong? If this was where she was supposed to be, there was no room for her boys. If her life was with them, there could very well be no place for *her*. If she was a...lesbian...she couldn't be their mother. Could she? Not wanting to consider either possibility, she shook off the thought. It was too soon to decide anything, too soon to be analyzing anything. She wasn't even unpacked.

She sat cross-legged on the floor in front of the shelves and opened a crate. She arranged the small portion of her library she'd brought with her alphabetically by title, filling the bottom section with her self-help category and the next level with her Bestsellers-I-Never-Got-To collection. She leafed through each book as she pondered what would be most beneficial to read first—fiction to relax or psychology to help her mind start looking inward. She reached for another. Her fingers grazed a paper bag. Anxiety gripped her.

She'd forgotten about those, the purchases she'd made the one time she'd scraped together enough courage to go to A Different Light, the gay and lesbian bookstore in West Hollywood. She'd worn sunglasses and a hat and had avoided eye contact with everyone she passed. The one woman who'd smiled at her and said hello had sent her in terrified retreat to the cash register. She'd picked out five books. That should be plenty, she'd reasoned.

But she'd never looked at them once she'd gotten them home. She'd always been too worried that Jeremy would catch her, that the boys would walk in. She didn't even remember what she'd bought. She opened the bag and peeked inside.

Her stomach tightened. Her shoulders tensed. She felt as paranoid as the time she'd sneaked a cigarette in the garage when she was ten. *What if someone sees? What if they tell?*

Tell who? Scanning the room, she realized how silly she was being. She reached into the sack and retrieved the books.

From Wedded Wife to Lesbian Life. She remembered finding this one and being amazed that there was an entire book on the subject. Apparently, she wasn't the only one to whom this had happened. Maybe she should read that one first. She set it aside.

Lesbian Couples. She glanced through the pages. She wasn't in a couple yet—not with a woman—nor was she even sure she ever would be. She placed that one beside the other.

Lesbian Sex—the words leapt off the hot pink cover. Eve's mouth dropped open. She found it difficult to believe that she'd ever conjured the nerve even to take this book off the shelf, what's more carry it to the register and pay for it. Slowly, she opened it. She perused the contents: "This Is Your Life—Where We Start," "You Don't Have to Know Latin to Know Your Body," "Barriers to Sexuality." It seemed basic enough. She continued. "Physiology." "What We Do In Bed." "Fantasies." Her gaze halted. She tensed. She'd had fantasies and had often wondered if they were normal. Arousal fluttered in her abdomen. She tried to go on, but she couldn't coax her eyes to function.

"Knock, knock." Dusty's voice resonated within the walls of the room.

Eve jumped. A scream fled her throat. The book flipped from her grasp and landed on the floor beside her.

"Wow, I'm sorry. I didn't mean to scare you. I just wanted to bring you these." Dusty held something out to her. "We must have dropped them out of one of the boxes."

But all Eve could see was that bright pink book cover against the powder blue carpet, like a neon sign flashing *lesbian sex, Lesbian Sex, LESBIAN SEX*. Her heart pounded.

"You okay? You're really pale."

"Yes." Eve cleared her throat. "I'm fine." She forced her gaze to the object Dusty held. A pair of her red silk panties dangled from Dusty's fingers. *Oh, God, can this moment get any more humiliating?* "Thank you." Her voice squeaked. She snatched the undergarment from Dusty. Maybe she would leave now and never even notice the book.

"Lesbian Sex?" Dusty read aloud. "Who needs a book on that?" She laughed and reached for the paperback.

Eve grabbed it and sprang to her feet. The sudden movement caused what little blood remained in her face to flood to her toes. Her vision darkened, and she swayed. She felt arms around her, holding her, supporting her. She teetered into a body—*God, not Dusty's.*

"Easy. I got you." Dusty's lips spoke close to Eve's ear. "Come over to the bed."

Eve let Dusty guide her, steady her, for no other reason than she had little choice. Her feet stumbled. Her head swirled.

Dusty eased her down onto the mattress and gently laid her back.

Eve's vision began to clear.

Dusty leaned over her. "You all right?"

Eve stared up into those fiery eyes, those self-assured features. "I must have lost my equilibrium." *Oh, God, I'm doing it again.*

"You're what?"

"I mean, my balance." Eve brushed a hand over her face. "I think I stood up too fast."

"Oh, yeah? I thought maybe this got you too excited." Dusty giggled and fanned Eve with the book.

Eve's temper flared. Her cheeks flamed. She jerked the paperback from Dusty's hand. "Thank you for your help." She clenched her jaw. "I'm fine now."

Dusty stood and retreated a pace. "Okay, sorry." She raised her hands and edged toward the door. "Jeez, everybody's so touchy these days." She walked out, still grumbling under her breath about grouchy people.

Eve buried her face in the pillow and groaned. If she'd ever been as embarrassed as she was right at that moment, she couldn't recall it. How could she be so stupid, so immature? Sex was sex, wasn't it? Why had she allowed this ridiculous book and Dusty Gardner to transform her into a moron?

She sat up and glanced at the cover. Maybe it was because she'd refused to consider sex with a woman for so long, keeping the thought far from her consciousness except on those occasions when a fantasy would sneak its way into her daydreams. Maybe she'd made it too much of a taboo for herself, so now that she wanted to think about it, examine it, she had to overcome all of that.

That was it. She just had to jump in and do it—read about it, think about it, give herself permission to be curious about it.

What about Dusty, though? How did she play into all this? Surely Eve wasn't attracted to her. She'd never been attracted to a woman like her—never even *known* a woman like her. The women Eve had been drawn to in the past were soft, gentle. She paused.

The sensation of Dusty's arms around her skittered across her flesh. The sound of her reassuring words caressed Eve's ear. Dusty had been gentle, but that was only a moment. In general, there was nothing gentle about her, and there was no point in thinking about her. Whatever Eve felt when Dusty was around would pass as soon as she'd developed a better understanding of herself.

With that, she picked up the book again and stared at the cover. She began saying the title over and over again in her mind. The more she said it, the more familiar she knew it would become and the more comfortable she'd be with both the words and the concept. She was here for a purpose. If she was going to figure out who she was and what she wanted, she might as well start now.

Chapter Seven

The Wednesday afternoon staff meeting at the Milton and Ryan ad agency ran long. By the time Addison got back to her office, the late-day sun reflected off the silver picture frame on her desk, its radiance not quite rivaling Maggie's smile. The past few days had been wonderful. Since their time together over the weekend, talking, laughing, making love, they seemed to have rediscovered the feelings that'd brought them together and kept them together for so long.

Addison's restlessness, her discontent, seemed to be settling. She'd been more focused at work, more attentive at home. She knew where she belonged. She knew she loved Maggie. She knew how to show it, and she intended to do so.

She glanced at her watch. She'd thought the meeting would break up in time to get some flowers ordered. Maybe it wasn't too late to get them delivered before Maggie left for her evening plans with Carolyn.

Addison grabbed the phone and flipped through her rolodex. "L" for Lavender Rose—she used to know the number by heart. She frowned and punched the buttons on the receiver. She listened to the rings on the other end of the line.

"Good afternoon. Lavender Rose," a soft, familiar voice said. "This is Monica. How may I help you?"

"Hi, Monica, this is Addison Rae-McInnis—"

"Well, hello. We haven't heard from you in a while."

"Yeah, I know," Addison said with a chuckle tinged with a combination of guilt and embarrassment. "I've been neglectful. But I'm turning over a new leaf."

Monica laughed. “Then I’ll assume your order is going to Maggie?”

“My one and only.”

“Same address?”

“Oh, yeah, Maggie would never give up that house.”

“And one half-dozen Sonya roses.” Monica drew out her words the way she did when she was writing.

Addison shifted her weight. Was it good or bad that her florist knew her order before she said it? “What can I say? They’re her favorite, and she’s definitely a creature of habit,” she said, feeling the need to explain.

“What would you like the card to say?”

“Hmm, let’s see.” Addison picked up the picture of Maggie and herself and studied it. She thought of the past few days, then the last twelve years. She smiled. “Because you make my life so beautiful. I love you. Just sign it ‘A.’”

“All rightie,” Monica said with the abruptness of someone who’d heard every sentiment anyone could possibly think of many times before. “I’ll try to get this to her today, but it’s kind of late.”

“Yeah, I know. I meant to get the order in earlier, but the day got away from me.”

“I know how that goes. Hey, are you and Maggie having your Halloween party again this year?”

“Of course. If there’re two things you can count on in this world they’re our Halloween party and our Christmas party.”

“Great. I’m seeing someone new. I want everybody to meet her.”

“Bring her along.”

“I plan to win that costume contest this year, too. I’m on a search for the perfect outfit. Any idea what Dusty has in that twisted little mind of hers?”

“Not a clue.” Addison chuckled, remembering the previous year when Dusty had trotted downstairs in nothing but a strip of duct tape over her mouth and a nightshirt that read *Strong enough for a man—but made for a woman* on the front. Everyone had to wait until the unmasking at midnight to find out that she’d come as a Secret, a play on the deodorant by the same name with the same tagline. They all agreed, though, that it’d been the quietest evening anyone had ever spent with Dusty.

"I guess we'll just have to wait and see," Monica said. "For now, let me get going on this order for your lady and see if I can get it delivered today."

"Thanks. And we'll be sending out info on the party next week. You have a nice evening."

"Thanks. You, too."

Addison hung up the phone, still smiling at the thought of Dusty with her mouth taped shut. It'd been an historical event, especially when Tess, dressed as a beautiful Greek nymph, had discovered the fun of tickling Dusty's neck with her shaft of wheat. Dusty had been as vulnerable and helpless as anyone had ever seen her.

The soft chime of the intercom on the desk brought Addison back to the moment, and she pressed the button to answer it. "Yes, Peggy?" she said, a leftover chuckle sneaking into her voice.

"There's a call for you on line one," the receptionist announced with the utmost efficiency. "Victoria Fontaine."

The name registered with a flash of Victoria's image in Addison's mind. She frowned. She'd only half-finished the list of potential advertisement options she'd promised Michael's client. "Okay, thanks." She disconnected from the in-house line and picked up the receiver. She pressed the flashing button on the phone. "Hello, Victoria. How was your trip up north?"

"It was great. They're doing just fine without me." Victoria's response was light. "A little too fine, I think," she added with a laugh.

"That's the problem with us indispensable types—the rest of the world doesn't always recognize who we are." She opened a drawer and rummaged through the contents in search of the file she'd started for Victoria. "What can I do for you this afternoon?"

"I was hoping we could get together and go out like we talked about last Saturday. I know I was supposed to call earlier in the week, but things have just been so hectic."

Addison paused. "Oh." Relieved, she closed the drawer. "Sure. I just thought since I didn't hear from you Monday you'd changed your mind."

"No, not at all. In fact, I could really use some fun. I can't even remember the last time I went out that wasn't work related. When would be good for you and…Maggie, was it?"

"Uh, yes, Maggie. Any night this week would be fine. Except tonight. Maggie has other plans."

A pause hovered on the other end of the line. "Oh," Victoria said finally, a twinge of disappointment in her voice. "Tonight's the only night I can make it until next Wednesday. The rest of the week is booked. Then I head back up to the Bay Area for a few days."

"How about when you get back?" Addison flipped through the pages of her desk calendar.

"I guess that'll have to do. I was hoping to get out tonight and relax a little, though. I could really use it." Victoria sighed. "Hey, do *you* have plans? You said Maggie was busy."

"Me? No. I don't suppose I do."

"Would Maggie object if you showed me some of the nightlife tonight? I mean, if you want to, of course."

"Uh, well, sure." Addison remembered her conversation with Maggie about Victoria. It wasn't as though Maggie didn't know she was just a client. "That'd probably be fine."

"Great!" Victoria's pitch rose with obvious excitement.

Addison smiled. She couldn't recall the last time anyone had shown such eagerness to spend an evening with her. "What time are you free? I have some work to finish up here."

"Me, too. Let's see, maybe around seven? We can get some dinner, then you can show me around?"

"Sounds good. Can I pick you up?"

"Oh, that would be perfect. I'm staying at the San Vicente Inn in West Hollywood. Do you know where that is?"

"I've seen it. Isn't it right off Santa Monica Boulevard?"

"That's the place. I'm in room S, up at the front. Just ring the bell and I'll be ready." Victoria let out a giggle. "Oh, this is so wonderful. I can't tell you how much I need this."

Addison laughed. "Yeah, I can tell. I'll see you later, then."

"Okay. Bye for now."

Addison heard another giggle before the line went dead. She chuckled and shook her head. If only it were this simple to make everyone in life so happy. She disconnected from the call and dialed her home number.

"Hello, you've reached the Rae-McInnis household." Maggie's voice answered on the fourth ring. "If you've a message for Addison,

Maggie, Tess, or Eve, feel free to leave it at the tone. If you're lookin' for Dusty, join the club. You can leave a message, but there's no tellin' when she'll be gettin' it. Oh, and please, if you could let us know if you find her first, we'd be oh so appreciative."

"Hey, Maggie, it's me. Are you there?" Addison said after the beep. "Tess? Dusty? Eve? Anybody?"

No one answered.

"Okay, well, I was just calling to let you know I'm going to be taking a client out to dinner tonight, and I've still got quite a bit of work to finish here, so I think I'll just stay at the office until it's time to go." She glanced down at her tan slacks and white oxford shirt. *If it's good enough for the office, it's good enough for the bars*. "I won't be too late. I love you. Bye." She hung up. She wondered if she should've mentioned the client was Victoria, and if she should have, why she hadn't.

She pushed the thought aside and settled at her drafting table to start on some ideas for one of her accounts. As she worked, several people stuck their heads in her doorway and said good night, and little by little, the office fell silent. The time passed quickly, and when she next checked her watch, it was six fifteen. She took the canyon route through the hills and found herself pulling up to the curb in front of the San Vicente Inn a few minutes before seven.

Addison rang the bell next to the S on a panel of buttons beside a locked gate. The grounds around the entrance were well kept, and a number of summer blossoms still bloomed in the flowerbeds.

Within seconds, a voice crackled from the speaker. "Hello? Addison, is that you?" Victoria asked. Her tone didn't seem nearly as excited as it had earlier.

"Yeah, it's me. You ready for a fun-filled night on the town?"

"Just a minute."

Almost immediately, Addison heard a door open from behind the gate and a series of footsteps. The wrought iron panel swung open.

Victoria stood there wearing a terry cloth robe and a towel wrapped around her head. "I'm so sorry. I'm running late. Come in."

Addison paused, glancing at Victoria's attire. "I can wait in the car." She gestured toward the street.

"Don't be silly. I promise I'm harmless. Come in and relax." Without waiting for a reply, Victoria retreated to the left and up several steps to the room at the very front of the building.

Addison followed and closed the door behind them. She really should wait outside. She knew that. Victoria was a client, not a buddy. And she was in a robe. Addison started to wonder about what it concealed, but caught herself. *Knock it off. You're not going there again.*

The entrance led into a sitting area furnished with a short, taupe couch, a wicker chair with a cream-colored cushion, and a glass-topped coffee table. An archway to the right emptied into a second room that housed a queen-sized bed with a dark wood headboard. Several bottles of perfume, a jewelry case, and a haphazard array of magazines were strewn along the top of a matching dresser against the far wall. In the corner sat a television set. The hardwood floor shone with a high gloss.

"Wow, this is pretty nice," Addison said. "It's much homier than most hotels."

"That's one thing I like about it. I figured since I'd be living here for a while, I might as well stay someplace that feels comfortable." Victoria scooped an open briefcase from the couch and set it on the floor. "Please sit down. I'm really sorry. I'm usually more punctual."

"Don't worry about it. We're not on any kind of schedule, are we?" Addison settled onto the sofa and leaned back against the cushion. She could use a breather from the long day. "Take your time."

Victoria smiled. "Would you like a drink while you wait?" She waved her hand toward a small refrigerator in the corner by the window. "I have a few sodas and some wine."

"No, thanks. I'm fine."

"Okay. Give me about fifteen minutes, and I'll be ready." She pulled the towel from her head and her wet hair tumbled down past her shoulders. She opened a set of louvered doors on the opposite wall and disappeared into a narrow bathroom.

The door remained slightly ajar.

Addison glanced out the high, arched window at the front of the suite at a fenced-in courtyard. Tall bushes lined the edges to hide the grounds and the room from the outside world.

"Did you get all your work done?" Victoria called.

"Yeah, most of it." She turned back toward Victoria's voice. Through the crack of the bathroom door, she saw a side view of Victoria's naked body. It swayed with her movements as she brushed her hair. Fingers of sensation stroked desire within Addison. Embarrassed, she looked away. *Client. Client. Client.*

"That's what held me up tonight," Victoria continued. "I was trying to tie up some loose ends, and I kept getting interrupted."

"How are your renovations going?" Addison leaned forward and picked up a Chinese takeout menu from the table. She heard the sound of something hitting the counter in the bathroom and glanced up.

Victoria seemed to be looking at herself in a mirror. She raised her arms and ran her fingers through her hair as if spreading something through it.

At this angle, Addison could see her profile from her head all the way down to her feet.

Her breast lifted high with her reach, the nipple soft and relaxed. One leg bent forward in front of the other just enough to keep the lower part of her body a mystery.

Addison couldn't look away, no matter that her brain was screaming for her to do so. A throb of arousal began to pulse between her thighs.

"Everything's coming along just fine." Victoria's attention was still on her reflection. Her voice startled Addison out of her lust-haze.

She forced her eyes back to the card she held. She cleared her throat. "That's good," was all she could manage. It seemed even now, with her gaze averted, Victoria's nude form ruled her focus. Even her peripheral vision betrayed her desire. She stood and crossed to the refrigerator. "Can I change my mind about that drink?"

"Of course. Help yourself." Victoria's voice sounded clearer.

With a slight jerk, Addison turned to find her peering out from behind the louvered door, her body hidden. Addison felt a blush rise in her cheeks. "Thanks."

Victoria smiled, the glow of her moist skin highlighting her eyes. "I have to dry my hair now, so I won't be able to hear you."

"Oh. No problem." Relief flooded Addison like a cool bath. She hoped her uneasiness, her guilt, weren't evident.

Victoria vanished back into the bathroom.

Addison sighed and rolled her eyes. *What the hell's the matter with me? It's not like I've never seen a naked woman before.* She heard a blow dryer whir to life. She yanked open the fridge.

There was a partial bottle of white zinfandel and several diet colas, a collection of takeout containers, and an assortment of flavored, low-fat yogurts.

Addison considered the wine then realized she'd have to actually knock on the now-closed bathroom door and ask Victoria for a glass, since she didn't see any around. She snatched up a soda and shut the refrigerator. She popped the top and stepped to the window. She stared outside.

Her thoughts tumbled in her head. How could she have been so rude as to sit and watch someone in the privacy of their own bathroom? Was this more of what she'd experienced the day she'd met Victoria—the day she'd run into that redhead? She'd been thinking so clearly since she and Maggie had talked. She'd been so certain that whatever she'd been feeling was just a need for more closeness with Maggie.

She took a drink of her cola and found it hard to swallow.

This was ridiculous. She *had* been a little confused the other day. She wasn't used to women hitting on her out of the blue. That was over now, though. Victoria *wasn't* hitting on her. Victoria hadn't even known the bathroom door was open. She was a client of the agency's, nothing more, nothing less. There was no doubt in Addison's mind that she loved Maggie, that Maggie excited her. Besides, she'd only *looked* at Victoria. Victoria was a beautiful woman. You'd have to be a houseplant not to look.

The blow dryer switched off, and the door to the bathroom opened.

Addison heard Victoria move across the hardwood floor, but kept her gaze on the courtyard outside.

"Just one more minute," Victoria said.

"Okay." Addison took another swallow of soda. She caught the faint reflection of Victoria's once-again robed body on the other side of the bed in the adjoining room.

She tossed a garment onto the comforter.

Addison froze. She tried to study the bushes outside closely enough to determine their kind, but even then she saw Victoria reach for the tie at her waist. She saw her slender fingers work the knot.

Addison went rigid. She couldn't do this again. It was just wrong. She considered excusing herself and going outside, but she feared making Victoria as uncomfortable as she was. She closed her eyes and raised the soda can to her lips. She took a long, slow drink. She listened to the rustling of clothing behind her. After a few seconds, she swallowed. Was it safe? She opened her eyes just in time to catch a glimpse of a full frontal view of Victoria's shapely body right before the light fabric of a summer dress slipped over it. A part of her watched as Victoria turned to the chest of drawers and put on some earrings, and then sprayed perfume onto her neck and shoulders, but the image she'd just seen kept the other part of her well occupied.

"Okay, I think I'm set," Victoria said as she came into the room.

With a sigh, though whether of relief or disappointment she couldn't have said, Addison turned around.

Victoria slipped her bare feet into a pair of tan sandals that highlighted the amber tones in her haltered sundress, colors that flattered her complexion. Pride rainbow beads dangled on varying lengths of thin gold chain from her ears.

Addison considered her. The sweet fragrance of the cologne caressed her senses as Victoria closed the distance between them. The fit of her dress, her bare legs, her tantalizing scent all kept the thrum of arousal in Addison's body from dying out completely, but at least everyone had clothes on. "You look great. I think I should've taken the time to run home and change."

A smile lifted the corners of Victoria's full lips and touched her eyes. She adjusted the collar of Addison's shirt. "I think you look just great, too."

Addison laughed. "Shall we go, then?"

"Absolutely. I'm starving, but can we eat someplace quick? What I really want is to get onto a dance floor."

By a quarter to nine, they were heading into Dusty's favorite hangout, Vibes. Addison had been there a few times in the past and had decided it might be a good place to take Victoria because of its diversity of patrons. If what she wanted was to meet other women, she'd find every type there.

Vibes held varied appeal partly due to its layout. The split-level arrangement allowed for a lower room, accoutered with an antique, dark wood bar, a gathering of tables, and a number of conversation areas. At the far end, four wide steps with polished brass handrails led to the upper level where more tables and a couple of satellite bars encircled a large dance floor, with a DJ's booth at the opposite end. Unlike many bars, this one provided for quieter conversation away from the music as well as seating and dancing for those in high-party mode.

The place wasn't too crowded, it being a weeknight, and Addison started to guide Victoria to a vacant table toward the center of the room.

Victoria broke into a grin and grabbed Addison's hand. "Come dance with me," she said. Without waiting for a response, she pulled Addison toward the dance floor.

Addison chuckled and followed. There was very little sign tonight of the serious, restrained businesswoman that Addison had met the previous Saturday.

At dinner, Victoria had shared a lot about herself. The professional image had been replaced with a playful and, at times, painfully genuine profile of an open and somewhat vulnerable young woman.

Addison had learned that Victoria originally came from a small town in Utah, her mother had died when Victoria was young, and her father supported her and her two brothers by running a small grocery store. She'd been Mormon when she was a child but had turned her back on any religion long ago. Her first lesbian experience took place when she was fifteen and had been an affair with her biology teacher. She'd run away later that same year when the town gossips caught up with them, and her father, in his shame and humiliation, had beaten her into unconsciousness.

Addison's stomach turned at the thought. She'd never been able to understand the reasoning of violence, especially that between parent and child. She almost felt guilty when she heard stories like Victoria's. Her own coming out experience with her parents had been easy, quite uneventful. She'd taken them out for dinner and told them she was gay shortly before she introduced them to her first serious girlfriend. All they'd said was that they'd suspected for several years and they were happy she trusted them enough to be open about it. A week later, they'd accepted Donna, and years later had taken Maggie into the family with open arms. No real tale to tell, but she had shared it with Victoria all the same.

They came to a stop on the dance floor, and Addison found herself staring into Victoria's eyes. They were no longer distant as they'd been during the conversation at dinner. They were vibrant and alive, her broad smile, infectious. "Come on." She started moving to the fast beat of the music.

Addison laughed and joined in. At first, she felt awkward. It'd been so long since she'd been dancing. Her movements seemed stiff and jerky. She felt self-conscious, but before too long, her attention was riveted to Victoria's movements, not her own.

In spite of the hard, pounding beat of the song that played, Victoria's body flowed from side to side with the grace of a silk scarf caught in a breeze. Her hips slid one way while her torso and arms swayed the other. She raised her hands high over her head, her fingers fluttering through the air. Her breasts lifted with the motion, the nipples Addison knew were bare forming soft points beneath the thin fabric of her dress.

Addison felt her own body respond with stirrings and tingles. She averted her eyes and tried to listen to the music, but Victoria twirled and danced in front of her once again. Finally, the music stopped, and Addison smiled, breathing a little harder than she would've hoped. She started to turn and leave the dance floor, but she felt Victoria's long, slender fingers lace through her own and pull her back around just as another song began to play.

"Again," Victoria yelled over the scream of an electric guitar. She held tight to Addison while she slipped her other hand around the back of Addison's neck and thrust her hips to the beat.

Their energy mingled even though their bodies weren't quite touching. Heat rose between them.

Addison fought the urge to grasp Victoria's rocking hips and pull her to her. She wanted to feel their bodies pressed together.

As if reading Addison's mind, Victoria smiled more broadly and lifted the hand that held Addison's. Then slowly, inch by inch with each beat of the drum, she closed the space between them until, finally, her breasts pressed into Addison's and her pelvis lightly rubbed Addison's thigh.

Addison tensed, but kept dancing. She lowered her eyelids slightly and inhaled the sweet, alluring scent of Victoria's perfume.

Their arms still raised, Victoria shifted and began moving to the side, her body sliding across Addison's. Their slight difference in height allowed her to duck beneath Addison's arm without missing a beat, and as she did, she dipped down in a longer stroke of their bodies.

Addison couldn't hold back a soft moan and was grateful for the volume of the music. She hoped Victoria hadn't heard, or noticed her shudder. She felt Victoria step around to her backside.

In an easy motion, Victoria released her hand and gripped her hips. She pulled Addison to her, pressing her pelvis to her buttocks, her breasts against Addison's back. The heat of her thighs penetrated the weak barrier of their clothing. Victoria's grip was strong, and she moved Addison, controlled her, to suit her motions.

Addison remembered Victoria's naked form in the bathroom, the sight of her dress sliding down to cover her flesh, and she gave herself over to *all* thoughts of Victoria.

When the song finally ended, Addison was on fire.

They made their way back down the steps to where the conversation tables were arranged and found one toward the back wall. While Victoria rested, Addison went to the bar and bought two cosmopolitans—Victoria's choice.

"That was fun," Victoria said with a laugh as Addison set the drinks on the table and sat across from her. "I love to dance."

"I can tell." Addison smiled, hesitant to say much else until her body and mind calmed down. The trip to the bar had helped, but her thoughts still revolved predominantly around the sight of Victoria's seductive swaying, the feel of her breasts and thighs, and the imaginings of her moves in even more provocative places than a dance floor.

"Did you enjoy it?" Victoria asked, running the tip of a finger around the rim of her glass.

Addison couldn't tell if the question was truly innocent or if Victoria was deliberately teasing her. "Yeah, it was fun. I haven't been dancing in a long time."

"You and Maggie don't go dancing?"

Addison tensed with sudden discomfort from talking about Maggie while her body raged with desire for another woman. She took a swallow of her drink to drown some of the guilt. "Um, we used to. We haven't been in a while."

Victoria broke into the playful grin she'd flashed when they'd first arrived. "When we're finished with our drinks, we'll go out there and loosen you up some more."

"Well, hey there, buddy. What brings you out into the party world?"

Addison winced at the sound of Dusty's voice. Could she get any more uncomfortable? Only if she were naked—and it were Maggie's voice instead of Dusty's. Had she seen them dancing? Addison turned and watched Dusty saunter up to the table, holding a bottle of beer. "Hey, Dusty. What's going on?"

"Not much with me." Dusty shifted a quizzical gaze from Addison to Victoria then back to Addison. "But what's up with you? Out partying with a gorgeous woman? And on a school night no less."

Addison felt her already-heated face grow hotter still. She watched helplessly as Victoria's gaze took in those alluring eyes and the charismatic grin that most women found so irresistible, before it moved down the length of Dusty's lean build and back up. She felt a jealous anger begin to simmer in her belly. She knew she had no right to feel that way. Victoria and Dusty were both single—both free—and she wasn't. In truth, the best thing that could happen tonight would be for Victoria and Dusty to go back to Victoria's room together and for Addison to go home, right now. She drew in a calming breath. "Dusty, this is Victoria Fontaine. She's a client. Victoria, this is Dusty Gardner, one of our housemates."

"Good to meet you," Dusty said, offering her hand.

Victoria shook it. "I'm sure," she said with a smile and a glint in her eyes that seemed more of a challenge than a flirtation.

Dusty pulled out a chair, flipped it around and straddled it backward. "Where's Maggie?"

Addison eased back in her seat. "She had dinner plans with Carolyn, so I offered to show Victoria around. She's from the Bay Area."

Dusty grinned and turned back to Victoria. "The Bay Area, huh? What do you do there?"

"I own a restaurant, and I'm opening another one here. Addison's agency is handling my advertising."

"That's great." Dusty nodded. "If I can show you around while you're here, or maybe keep you company, don't hesitate to get my number from Addison. I'd be glad to show you a good time." She took a swig of her beer.

"Oh, thank you. That's sweet. But Addison has been doing a wonderful job showing me the spots." Victoria smiled and scooted her chair away from the table. "If you'll both excuse me, I'm going to run to the restroom."

Addison was stunned. She'd never seen any woman just turn away from Dusty so blatantly. Even if someone wasn't particularly interested, she'd usually be flattered by Dusty's attention.

Dusty turned to watch Victoria walk away. She gave a low whistle. "Buddy, watch out for *that*."

Addison stared at Dusty. "What just happened?"

As the bathroom door swung closed behind Victoria's swaying hips, Dusty turned back to face Addison. "Recognition just happened here."

"What do you mean? You know Victoria?"

Dusty laughed. "Yeah, buddy, I *know* Victoria. And she knows I know her. She's after you for no reason other than you are *un-available*. She's playing with you. And she doesn't play fair. Watch out."

Addison felt a surge of that anger again, but this time it wasn't jealousy, but indignation. "Oh, so she couldn't just like spending time with me because I'm interesting or easy to talk to?"

"Of course she could. But she doesn't. She wants one thing and one thing only—to prove she can have something that she shouldn't be able to have. And once she gets it, she'll be done. And then where will you be with Maggie?"

Addison seethed. "I'm not going to have this conversation with you. You don't know anything about Victoria. She's a client and nothing more. I'm *not* going to do anything with *anyone* other than Maggie. And you don't know a damned thing about *anything*!"

Clearly unaffected by Addison's attack, Dusty took another slow swallow of beer. "I know *this* a lot better than you do. Trust me. I recognize Victoria because I've *been* Victoria." She studied Addison. "Where does Maggie think you are tonight?"

"Not that it's any of your business, but Maggie knows I'm showing Victoria around town. She's fine with it. Nothing's going on."

"Did everyone say what they needed to say while I was gone?" Victoria asked as she approached the table. "Or should I kill some more time ordering another round of drinks?"

"Yep, we're done," Dusty said with a smile.

"All is well, I trust?" Victoria met Dusty's direct gaze.

"Absolutely."

Addison continued to watch the interaction with a mingling of fascination and irritation. She just wanted Dusty to leave. No, she wanted her never to have shown up in the first place, never to have seen her and Victoria together. She downed the remainder of her cosmopolitan with a grimace. She wanted a drink of Dusty's beer.

"You want to dance?" Dusty's question jolted Addison's attention back to the table.

"Oh, no, thank you. Addison is doing a great job of that as well. And speaking of which, Addison, are you ready to hit the dance floor again?"

"Sure," Addison said, still amazed by this new turn of events. In what universe did women choose her over Dusty?

"You'll excuse us, won't you?" Victoria asked Dusty.

"Of course. You kids behave." Dusty lifted her beer bottle to them as they turned to leave.

They stepped onto the dance floor in the middle of a fast song. It felt good to let loose. The tension of the last twenty minutes drained out of Addison's shoulders, the anger at Dusty's intrusion settling down into some dark place. Once again, Addison felt herself drawn in by Victoria's movements, by her smile, by her beauty, by her unwavering attention. It was the latter she found the most seductive.

When the next song began, it was a slow version of the old song "Yours," one sung by a woman, Belinda something. Or was it Bernita? Addison loved this version. It was from some movie soundtrack. She couldn't remember which one. It seemed the movie itself wasn't very good, but the song…Victoria stepped into her arms, and all other thoughts ceased.

"When the lights go down and the music plays, I see only you as your body sways," the woman sang. "You are the breeze that fans my desire. Your eyes hold the spark that lights me on fire."

Victoria tightened her arms around Addison's neck and pressed their bodies firmly together. Her intent was undeniably, utterly, clear.

The intensity of Victoria's gaze made Addison slightly weak. She closed her eyes for an instant and was sheathed in scent. She inhaled deeply of Victoria's perfume, her hair, her sweat. As they turned on the dance floor, their bodies rubbed. Addison grew dizzy. She opened her eyes to steady herself.

"I see only you in the midst of the dancers. My body asks how, and your body answers. When you move to the beat, I start to shaking. When you sway to the music, I'm yours for the taking."

Victoria's heated eyes held Addison like a web holding a spider's prey. Addison felt the danger but couldn't save herself, wasn't even sure she wanted to.

Was Dusty right about this woman, right about what was going on? At the thought of her friend, Addison managed to break her gaze from Victoria's. She looked around the bar, down among the tables.

Dusty was gone.

Chapter Eight

Dusty maneuvered her Harley through the light, Wednesday evening traffic with the mindlessness of familiarity. She'd ridden the route between Vibes and the house so many times she could do it asleep, after drinking way too much, with her mind still riveted on whatever woman she'd just been with.

Tonight, it was Victoria Fontaine that occupied her, but not in the way it would have six months earlier. Dusty was changing, and she knew it. Sometimes the change felt right. Sometimes she fought it, but it was happening, all the same. Not very long ago, she would've been obsessed with Victoria Fontaine's beauty, her inherent seductiveness. She would've taken Victoria's blatant dismissal of her as a challenge and would've set her intention to bed her at all cost—and she would've succeeded.

Tonight, however, all she could think of was Addison and Maggie, what they had, what they'd spent twelve years creating and building. She couldn't escape the memory of that all-too-familiar glint in Victoria's eyes—the glint that Dusty had flashed so many times—that said, *this one is mine*. Dusty thought back to all the women, the so very, very many women, who might have had or did have partners, husbands, children at home, lives that either were, or could possibly have been, shattered because of Dusty's relentless pursuits and conquests for no other reason than to bolster and display her skills and prowess. Now it seemed it was coming back around to hit her close to home—that *Law* her friend Rebecca was always talking about. Granted, it wasn't her own relationship teetering in the balance. How could it be? She'd never had one. It was her home and her chosen family that could be at risk, though. What would life be like if Maggie and Addison broke up? What would it feel like around the house without Addison there, with Maggie's heart broken? Dusty couldn't even imagine, and yet, she had done the same thing many times, without a thought of anyone being on the other end, without a single care for anyone's heart.

She'd wanted to be mad at Victoria Fontaine as she'd watched them walk back to the dance floor. She'd wanted to hate her. How could she, though? Victoria was her, and she was Victoria. It might as well have been Dusty seducing Addison.

But what about Addison? What was *she* thinking? How could she risk what she had with Maggie? Dusty had always admired Addison for her commitment and loyalty. *What a joke.* Dusty clenched her teeth. Where had that commitment and loyalty been tonight? Then again, where had Dusty's loyalty been? Maybe she should've stayed. She was Addison's friend, after all. Maybe if she had, she could've stopped it all and gotten Addison to come home with her. She'd tried, but Addison was being an idiot. And Dusty was Maggie's friend, too. How could she sit there and watch? All she'd been able to do was bolt from the bar to escape what was in front of her, to escape herself. She realized, now, that was impossible.

Dusty knew she was changing, that she had changed quite a bit already. The fact that she could even recognize herself in Victoria, could admit that they were one and the same, showed that change. But now what? Rebecca had been going on for years about how what we see in others is really just a mirror of ourselves and that what we do will always come back to us. After tonight, Dusty got it. She could see it, but what now? What happened next?

Even more curiously, *why* now? Why was all this coming back around to her home and her family at the very time she was changing her ways, at the very time she was losing interest in one-night stands and sexual conquests? Sure, she still acted the part because it was what everyone expected of her, but she hadn't actually gone home with a stranger in months. She hadn't wanted to. She'd made up a few accounts to share with Addison, who had begun asking more and more questions about her exploits, but…

Was that a part of all this? Had Dusty's experiences and stories been a lure for Addison, a temptation to look for something outside of her relationship with Maggie? No, it wasn't Addison who was seducing Victoria. It was the other way around. Dusty heard her own words to Addison, *you get back what you put out there*. She winced. *Damn it, Addison. We were talking about the vibes you put out about being committed. Not this.* Addison had to be putting out some of *those* vibes of her own, though, and what if Dusty had made it worse with her stories?

Recently, though, stories were all they were. She was beginning to know the thrill of being with the same woman more than once, more than twice. She now knew what it felt like to *want* only one woman. She finally fully understood the difference between just having sex and making love. Yes, she was definitely changing, and as she stepped through the doorway of her home, she found the reason for that change waiting for her. She paused.

In the low wattage from the lamp that dimly lit the living room and entryway, Tess stood several steps up from the bottom of the staircase, silent.

Dusty's gaze traveled up the smooth, olive skin of her bare legs that disappeared beneath the tails of a powder blue cotton shirt. The long sleeves, rolled to her elbows, fit loosely, and the top two buttons of the neckline remained open to reveal the soft hollow of her throat. Her long hair, usually bound tightly in some type of braid, flowed freely to frame her sculpted features and delicate shoulders.

Arousal stirred in Dusty's abdomen. Her breath held. "Whatcha doing, Tess?"

"I came down for some orange juice, and I heard your motorcycle." She hesitated, drawing her lower lip between her teeth. "I wanted to wait and go upstairs with you."

Surprised, Dusty studied her. It was subtle, but she'd learned that with Tess subtle was the same as a promise. This was strange, though. It hadn't been that long since the last time. In the past few months, the frequency of their encounters had increased, but usually Tess didn't need her again this soon. It'd only been a little over a week—not that Dusty minded. "Are you okay?" she asked. "Did something happen?"

Tess's expression was hard to read. "I'm fine. I just…" She averted her gaze.

Dusty set her helmet on the antique cabinet near the stairs and climbed the steps to the one just below Tess. She stared up into her sultry, brown eyes and slid her hands beneath the thin fabric of the nightshirt. Bare flesh raised in goose bumps under her palms, a kind of sensual Braille against her fingertips.

Tess's eyelids lowered, and she exhaled a slow breath. She wrapped her arms around Dusty's neck and pulled her close.

Dusty inhaled the light scent of vanilla wafting from Tess's warm skin. She loved the way Tess smelled, the way her soft body felt in Dusty's arms. She loved everything about making love to this beautiful woman.

Tess laced her fingers through Dusty's hair then coaxed her head back. Her mouth captured Dusty's in a kiss that demanded an answer.

Dusty answered. She parted her lips and met Tess's tongue with her own. She swept hers across it, toyed with it, resisted Tess's claim for the briefest of moments. Then she accepted it fully into her mouth.

Tess moaned softly, pressing harder against Dusty.

The leather barrier of Dusty's jacket denied her the pleasure of Tess's breasts cushioned against her, prevented her from feeling the taut points that she knew Tess's nipples had become by now. Moisture pooled between her thighs at the thought.

Tess broke the kiss. "Come to bed with me," she whispered, a plea in her voice as if Dusty might really say no.

Without a word, Dusty tightened her grip around Tess's waist and lifted her from the step. She carried her to the top of the stairs and set her back on her feet. Still a little confused by the timing, she paused. "You're sure?"

Tess smiled and kissed her again before she led her down the hall.

They always used Tess's room, maybe to put her more at ease, maybe because they felt less conspicuous if they heard Maggie or Addison moving on the stairs. Whatever the reason, after the first time, Dusty would never have had it any other way. She loved the scent of Tess's bed, the feel of the sheets that touched Tess's flesh every night, the fact that she was not only accepted but actually invited into her most private space.

At the side of the unmade bed, Dusty sat on the edge and unlaced her boots.

While she waited, Tess ran a fingertip down the nape of Dusty's neck, then played with her hair. She leaned down and caressed her earlobe between her warm lips.

Dusty shuddered, her movements quickening. Barefoot, she rose and pulled Tess against her.

Tess grabbed the edges of Dusty's jacket, yanked it open, and shoved it off her shoulders. She looped her arms around Dusty's neck and crushed their breasts together.

Dusty's desire surged. She held Tess tightly and bent her head, kissing Tess's neck. It wasn't enough. She wanted her bare skin, the feel of her nipples with no obstruction. She shifted slightly and slipped her hands between them then worked the buttons of Tess's shirt. She urged her back toward the mattress as she slid the garment off. Dusty gazed down at Tess's body clad only in a pair of white satin panties. Her breathing quickened. No matter how many times she was gifted with this sight, it always affected her the same way. She flushed with need.

Tess eased back into the soft pillows and guided Dusty over her. Her eyes smoldered. "Let me feel you," she whispered.

Dusty conceded eagerly. She moved up Tess's body and brushed her lips across Tess's. She slipped a knee between Tess's legs, pressing into her.

Tess groaned and tightened her thighs. She slid her hands across Dusty's shoulders, over her breasts, down her stomach and tugged at the bottom of her T-shirt. She freed it from the waistband of her jeans and pulled it off, bringing the sports bra along with it and tossed the garments aside. She cupped Dusty's breasts, squeezed her nipples.

"Mmm." Dusty arched, pushing hard into Tess's caress. She thrust her hips, enjoying the pressure in the confines of her tight jeans. "You make me so hot."

"Shhh." Tess pulled her down hard and seized her mouth in a fervid kiss.

Dusty groaned, the full weight of her body pressing down on Tess. Their breasts, abdomens, thighs, all molded to one another with the heat of their desire. Dusty ground her pelvis into Tess's. Her tongue probed deeply, desperately, and she flamed at the rake of Tess's nails down her back.

Their kisses grew hotter, more urgent, until finally they weren't enough.

Dusty tore herself free and moved lower. She sucked one of Tess's stiff nipples into her mouth and stroked the other between her fingers.

Tess gasped and raised her torso into Dusty's grasp. She spread her legs, wrapped them around Dusty's hips. With a slow rhythm, she began to rock.

Dusty met each thrust with one of her own, but she knew there wasn't enough contact to give Tess any release. She ran the tip of her tongue around the hard nipple that stood erect between her lips and teased the other with a gentle caress of her palm.

A whimper escaped Tess's throat, and she grabbed Dusty's shoulders. She shoved her lower. "I want your mouth on me," she said with a gasp. "Please put your mouth on me."

As much as Dusty would've enjoyed making Tess wait just a little longer, she lacked the strength to resist the taste of her. It was like liquor to the alcoholic, heroin to the addict. Without hesitation, she slipped down to the vee of Tess's thighs.

She feathered her lips across the satin panel that covered Tess's dark curls, inhaled her scent through the shimmering fabric. She pressed her mouth firmly to Tess's mound.

Sucking in a long, shuddering breath, Tess lifted her hips and thrust herself against Dusty's face.

Dusty couldn't wait any longer. She gripped the panties and yanked them down Tess's quivering legs. She buried her tongue in her deep, wet center and drank in the flavor, breathed in the fragrance.

Tess stiffened. She grabbed the back of Dusty's head and ground against her. "Yes," she whispered. "Make me come, Dusty. Please make me come." It had taken a long time before Tess had been able to say what she wanted, but once she'd mastered it, there was never any doubt.

Dusty groaned and ran her tongue up Tess's soft folds. The silken flesh caressed her lips, and the wetness collected in her hungry mouth. Her own body ached for attention, but her focus remained on Tess's pleasure.

Tess's breathing grew labored, and her fingers tightened in Dusty's hair. She opened her thighs wider, as though reaching for every last sensation, every flick of Dusty's tongue. With a sudden surge, her body shook, her legs trembled. A choked cry escaped her clenched teeth, but she managed to stifle most of it.

Dusty held her mouth still while Tess's body pulsed against her lips. Then, softly, more slowly, she began caressing the sensitized flesh. Sometimes she fantasized about taking Tess someplace where she could cry out as loudly as she wanted with no concern of who might hear, who might know. What Dusty wouldn't give to hear that unrestrained release from this woman who affected her so deeply. She brought Tess down unhurriedly, with tenderness, with love.

As Tess's body calmed, she reached down and once again guided Dusty up over her. By now, she knew Dusty's body and responses well enough to know that Dusty wouldn't be able to wait long. She gazed into her eyes. Her skin still flushed from her own arousal, she unfastened Dusty's jeans.

Dusty wriggled out of them and kicked them to the floor, but before she could change position, Tess took a breast in each hand and raised her thigh, pushing it firmly between Dusty's. Dusty groaned and closed her eyes as she began to thrust against Tess's leg. Tess matched Dusty's quickening rhythm and caressed her nipples, driving her mad with desire. Each time Dusty opened her eyes, she found Tess smiling up at her, watching her intently. With a sudden rush, Dusty's release flooded her and she came hard and fast. She collapsed on top of Tess, gasping for breath.

Tess took Dusty in her arms and caressed her back. "Thank you," she whispered.

"Oh my God." Dusty panted. "Are you kidding?"

Tess laughed quietly.

She always thanked Dusty when they were finished, as if she believed it was some big sacrifice on Dusty's part to share this intimacy with her. Dusty wanted to talk to her about it, but they didn't really talk about those kinds of things. They didn't really talk about anything at all during these times together. It was like they were two different people in this sanctuary from the ones who lived together in the house with other women, and when they were with everyone else, it was just group stuff that went on. Dusty shifted her weight off Tess and eased down beside her.

Tess moved gently into her arms as she always did.

Maybe that could be different, Dusty considered, breathing in the fresh scent of Tess's hair. Maybe they could start sharing more with each other, actually get to know one another more deeply than just on a sexual level. Dusty wasn't sure she knew how to do that, though—or maybe, more accurately, she wasn't sure she really *did* want to do it. She wanted to know everything there was to know about Tess, but then she knew she'd have to tell everything about herself. Wasn't that the way it worked? If she did that, however, there was no way a woman like Tess would want to have anything to do with her.

She wanted to talk to Tess about what'd happened earlier at Vibes, but what if the conversation then led to her having to reveal her realization about herself being like Victoria Fontaine? It was one thing for Tess to know in general that Dusty was a player, but it was something else for her to actually hear about all the women Dusty had used and toyed with all her adult life. She felt her heartbeat quicken with the fear of Tess's reaction.

Tess wasn't like that, though. Dusty had never heard anything judgmental out of her mouth. She was one of the most accepting people she'd ever known. Maybe that would actually apply to the reality of who Dusty had been, too.

"Tess?" Dusty said softly. "Can we talk about something?"

"Mmm." Tess sounded sleepy. "What would you like to talk about?"

Dusty froze. Now that the door was open, what *did* she want to talk about? What was her priority? The incident at Vibes seemed less important now that she could talk about anything at all. She could talk about how she thought she was falling in love with Tess, how Tess was the one changing her, how she was afraid everything would be ruined if she talked about anything at all. She could bring up how she wanted to know where Tess grew up, if she had brothers and sisters, if the woman who'd died had been her only partner in her life and how long they'd been together. She could tell Tess how she wanted to be the one to never let anything hurtful happen to her again.

"Uh, I dunno. I just want us to talk. I want there to be more to us than just sex. I mean, not that I mind the sex. I love sex with you. But I don't think it's just sex anymore." Dusty paused. "You know what I mean?"

Tess remained quiet, her breathing even.

Dusty tensed. What was Tess thinking? Was she upset? She rushed on to explain. "I mean, I know we kinda agreed without really saying it that this would be just sex and that we wouldn't tell anyone about it, but now…I think…Now, I…I think I might be in love with you." There, she'd said it. She waited, her heart beating so furiously, like the wings of a frightened bird, she thought it might actually take flight right out of her chest.

Still no answer.

"Tess?" Dusty said finally. She eased back and looked down into Tess's face.

Her eyes were gently closed, the hand resting between Dusty's breasts, relaxed. She slept peacefully.

Dusty watched her. This was probably better anyway. Tess wouldn't want to know how Dusty felt. Feelings weren't part of their arrangement. They were too different. What could possibly come of Dusty being in love with her? Besides, Dusty thought she loved Tess beyond words—it was just as well she couldn't talk about it, to Tess or anyone else.

Maybe this was part of that *Law* of Rebecca's, too. Along with possibly having her home and family torn apart by someone like Victoria Fontaine—someone like herself—did she also have to be unbearably in love with a woman she couldn't ever have? She'd certainly *been* the one no one could ever have. She pressed her cheek to Tess's hair. Until now. Was it punishment, retribution? No, Rebecca called it something else. Whatever it was, maybe it was Dusty's turn. She'd have to ask Rebecca more about that *Law*. It was starting to tick her off.

As for her and Tess, it was better to leave things as they were between them, to just continue with the sexual thing and keep it in the dark. As long as they kept themselves hidden, Tess would never know all those things about Dusty, things that would make her see Dusty the way she really was, instead of the way she desperately wanted Tess to see her.

Reluctantly, she eased out from under Tess and slipped into her clothes. She looked at her sleeping lover one last time, pulled the covers up over her, kissed her gently on the lips, then quietly left the room. With her boots and jacket in hand, she pulled the door closed behind her and glanced up just as Eve was coming out of her own bedroom. Dusty froze, as though if she stood still enough, maybe Eve wouldn't notice her.

Eve's gaze flickered from Dusty, to Tess's door, then back to Dusty.

"I, uh, was just—"

Eve held up a hand. "None of my business."

In the illumination of the two nightlights at either end of the hallway, Dusty could just make out the redness of Eve's eyes. "Something wrong?"

Eve straightened a bit. "No. I was just going out for a walk. I can't sleep." She hesitated, then added, "I wouldn't mind some company, though. Would you like to join me?"

Dusty considered the invitation. Eve obviously could use a friend, though Dusty still had no idea why. She remembered Maggie's warning. *You stay away from her*. "Uh, no. I gotta..." Absently, she raised the hand that held her boots, then awkwardly tucked them behind her. "You know..."

Disappointment flashed in Eve's expression. "Sure. That's okay. I'll see you later." She ducked her head and moved past Dusty, around the stair railing, and down the steps.

Dusty listened as the chimes in the entryway sounded and the front door closed. She felt like an absolute jerk. Eve had obviously been reaching out for some comfort, and she had been making an effort toward Dusty in the past few days since she'd moved in. All that weirdness from the first day they'd met was gone, and although Dusty would've liked to return the gesture, there was no way she was going against Maggie.

Conflicted about the whole evening—Addison and Victoria, herself and Tess, and now Eve—Dusty headed to the tranquility of her own room.

Chapter Nine

Maggie stood in the lobby of the Cineplex Theater at Universal CityWalk and glanced at her watch. She had her ticket. She had popcorn. She had sodas. All she needed was her date. Silly as it was, she had been excited about this all week.

It was their first official date since they'd had their talk the previous weekend. Addison had actually called Maggie from work on Monday morning and asked her out to a movie this afternoon, to be followed by a romantic dinner at a restaurant of her choosing. They had made love Tuesday night, and flowers had come on Wednesday. Then Addison hadn't gotten home from dinner with a client that night until after Maggie had gone to bed. She had gotten up the next morning before Maggie woke, and they had seen little of each other since. Now she was late.

This wasn't how Maggie had envisioned their date beginning. She had seen them meeting in front of the theater and sharing a kiss. She would slip her arm around Addison's waist while Addison bought the tickets and refreshments, and they would walk hand-in-hand into the darkened theater to snuggle together and watch the romantic comedy they'd chosen. Again, silly.

Maggie had been excited about a fresh start after so many years, a kind of renewal of commitment to make their relationship a priority. She hadn't expected them to slip back into old habits so quickly. She hadn't expected that today she would, once again, be purchasing her own ticket so she would have time to get the food as Addison rushed in from work as she had done so many times. But there she was. So, as *she* had done so many times, she walked into the theater alone.

The previews began as Maggie fitted a drink in the cup holder of the empty seat beside her, but the images flashed across the screen sans her interest. Instead, she wrestled with quelling her irritation lest she start an argument before their date ever began. *This will take some adjustment. Habits will need to be broken on both our parts. Addison will, perhaps, be needin' some time to shift her thinkin' more frequently from work on weekends, and I'll be needin' some practice lettin' each moment be fresh, not holdin' us in the past.* Besides, Addison had said she'd gotten two new accounts this week, and start-ups were always more time consuming.

Ten minutes into the movie, Addison slipped into the chair beside her. "Did I miss anything?" she whispered. She took a huge gulp of her soda.

Maggie smiled. "Just the leadin' lady throwing a drink in someone's face. And my kiss hello."

Addison hesitated, then leaned over the armrest and brushed her lips across Maggie's. Her expression was difficult to read, and she sat back and slouched down in her seat after the perfunctory greeting.

Something was wrong. Maggie could feel it. Her *spidey sense was tingling,* as Dusty would say. Was it that air, that cloud, that Addison had been drifting around in for the past couple of months? Was it back? Maggie shifted uneasily. No, this was different. This was stronger, maybe darker. She passed the bag of popcorn to Addison, and their fingers touched.

Addison drew away, subtly, but definitely.

Maggie knew Addison, sometimes better than Addison knew herself. She had been with her—been her partner, her lover, her best friend, sometimes even her therapist—for twelve years. She knew when Addison was struggling. Whatever this was, Maggie intended to see her through it. They had broken through something last weekend and connected, deeply and intimately, and she didn't doubt the authenticity of what they had shared. *If that's what she needs, then that's what I'll give her.*

Maggie raised the armrest between them and pressed lightly against her. She slipped her hand over Addison's thigh.

Addison stiffened slightly, her eyes fixed on the screen. She held the bag of popcorn so Maggie could get some.

Maggie took several pieces into her own mouth, then held up a couple to Addison's lips. "Want a bite?" she whispered, blowing warm breath into Addison's ear. She felt Addison's sharp gasp.

Addison opened her mouth, the tip of her tongue grazing Maggie's fingertips as she accepted the popcorn.

That's more like it. Maggie grazed Addison's lower lip with her nail.

Addison shuddered and closed her eyes.

Maggie eased back. She rested her head on Addison's shoulder and smiled.

As they watched the movie characters maneuver through the antics of falling in love, Maggie began tracing tight circles along Addison's inner thigh. Feeling her begin to surrender to the caress, she deepened her touch, massaging with longer strokes.

Addison tipped her head back against the seat.

Maggie knew her eyes were hooded. In their early days, before their time together became commonplace and their joined lives got busier, she would tease Addison, slowly and at length. Her hands had always been somewhere on Addison's body, moving, exploring, tantalizing—just like now. Then, when they would finally be alone, Addison would go wild. She would take Maggie in pure need. Maggie *loved* it. She grinned in the dark. *Yes, it's time for some renewal. And if Addison needs some help with it, so be it.* She strengthened her touch and began a languid massage just below the apex of Addison's thighs.

Addison's body thrummed with desire. She'd been aching for release all morning—in truth, since Wednesday night. She'd been able to think of little other than the memory of Victoria dancing, moving against her. The ride back to the inn, the heat emanating from her body warming the ambiance in the car. Her distraction as Victoria talked on about how much she loved to dance and how grateful she was for Addison's willingness to spend the evening with her. And finally, that long moment when Victoria hinted with the closeness of her body and the slight parting of her lips that there might be a kiss, before she turned away with a wave. Addison had been desperate—desperate with need for Victoria's mouth on hers, desperate with relief that it hadn't happened. She wouldn't have been able to say no, and yet, even in that moment, she knew she had to.

Maggie's hand inched closer to the throb between Addison's legs. Her strong fingers worked the taut flesh of her inner thigh, tugging the seam of her jeans tightly against her clit with each movement. She knew Maggie wouldn't actually go there in a public place—well, she knew Maggie knew *Addison* wouldn't go there in a public place and would respect that—but she also knew Maggie had no idea just how on the edge she was. She could easily come right then and there, but she wouldn't do that to Maggie. She couldn't.

Addison's need right then, her need for the past three days, wasn't for Maggie. Sure, it *was* in the sense that she always desired Maggie and had since the day they met, but the ache in her clit, the hardness of her nipples, the burning need for release in this moment was all for another woman. Addison had come home Wednesday night wanting nothing more than to crawl into bed with Maggie and take her like she'd done the previous weekend, like she used to do all the time. She'd awakened the next morning aching to roll over and let Maggie feast on her as she so enjoyed doing in the early hours before dawn. Instead, she'd forced herself out of bed and gone for a run, unwilling to have Maggie's mouth on her while she imagined it as someone else's. She'd thought the cool air, the exercise, and a cold shower would calm her senses and drown the craziness of her mind and body, but that hadn't happened. Instead, she'd spent the past three days fighting off images of Victoria, trying to escape the memories of her by burying herself in work, but all efforts had failed. Even her attempts to bring herself release only left her aching for more, aching for Victoria.

And she couldn't take this need to Maggie. She couldn't make love to her with visions and fantasies of another woman spurring her desire. She had to get control, and she had to dissuade Maggie's obvious intentions until she did.

Maggie snuggled closer, her breast pressing against Addison's arm. She continued her teasing caress.

It felt so good. *Maggie* felt so good. Her knowledge of Addison's body, the mixture of love and torment in her touch, this *was* Maggie. No stranger, no one new could know exactly where and how to touch her. But Victoria's image crowded in, filling her thoughts, forcing all others out.

Addison gently grasped Maggie's wrist and slowed her caress to a stop.

Maggie looked up at her, an eyebrow arched.

She brought Maggie's hand to her lips and kissed her fingers, then smiled and slipped her arm around Maggie's shoulders, holding her close, but motionless.

When the movie ended, they walked out hand-in-hand. Addison's body had settled back into that ever-present yet still comparatively merciful hum of desire, and she was grateful they'd soon be in a restaurant on opposite sides of the table. "Did you decide where you want to go for dinner?"

"I was thinkin' Miceli's," Maggie said, smiling up at her. "We've not been there for a while, it's close to home, and Italian is always romantic."

Addison looked into Maggie's eyes, noting the spark of anticipation and desire. Addison loved her so much it hurt. She'd been so excited about their agreement to put more focus on the two of them, and she still was. Even though…*God, what am I doing? What the hell's wrong with me?* "Okay," she said with a soft stroke across Maggie's temple. "I'll follow you there."

As the hostess seated them at a cozy table in the back, Maggie excused herself to use the restroom. "Will you order me a glass of merlot, luv?" She trailed her fingertips over Addison's shoulder as she passed her.

"Sure." Addison touched her hand gently. She sighed. She knew already how disappointed Maggie would be later when Addison told her she wasn't up to making love. She winced at the thought of having to face that look in her eyes.

"Well, well, who do we have here?" A waitress stepped up to the table, the voice familiar.

Addison looked into the face of the woman from the gas station the previous week, the same day she'd met Victoria. *Christ! I am in hell. That has to be it. I've died and no one told me, and I'm in hell.* The thought actually brought her some comfort. At least if that were true, she wouldn't have to look at what a mess she could possibly make of her life.

"Did you change your mind?"

"Hi. No," Addison said quickly. She'd forgotten the woman worked here. She'd actually forgotten her completely. "I didn't change my mind." She glanced toward the bathroom. "And I'm here with my partner, so can we please not mention our conversation?"

The waitress smiled. "Sure, sweetheart. No problem. You look kind of pale, though. You might want to pat your cheeks a little bit." She demonstrated on herself.

"Yeah, thanks."

"Would you like to start with any drinks or an appetizer?" With a trace of laughter still in her eyes, she took out a pad and pencil.

"Please," Addison said. "Two glasses of merlot."

"You got it."

Addison's thoughts returned to the evening ahead, to Victoria's ongoing domination of her mind, to Maggie's inevitable disappointment, to the torment of lying next to her all night. Maybe she could just drink herself into oblivion. It wasn't her usual way of dealing with things, but then, there was nothing usual about her situation. "On second thought, make mine a dirty martini," she said. *The more alcohol, the better.* "And keep 'em coming."

Chapter Ten

Tess climbed out of her Sunbird, balancing her latte in one hand as she adjusted her purse and briefcase with the other. She'd had trouble sleeping the previous night—in fact, she'd had trouble sleeping all week, ever since the last time she had shared her bed with Dusty—and she was thankful for her early office hours today. The faculty parking lot was barely a third full at seven thirty, and the morning breeze carried the remaining fragrance of the night-blooming jasmine that filled the cement planters surrounding the quad at this end of the campus.

She began a casual walk across the lot toward the administration building that housed the English department. She never locked her car, always believing that if someone wanted what was inside badly enough, they would get in anyway and do damage in the process. If they wanted the car itself enough to steal it, well then, they probably needed it more than she did.

Dusty's friend Rebecca had told her at last year's Christmas party that if someone wasn't a thief in life, they didn't need to worry about anything being stolen from them. Tess had been fascinated by the concept. She had thought about it a long time until finally she realized that what she was actually thinking about was how odd she found it that a woman of such depth and wisdom would be close friends with someone like Dusty. It had been the catalyst to her watching and listening to Dusty more closely.

At the time, Tess and Dusty had slept together once—a pity shag, as Maggie might have called it, on Dusty's part. It had happened one night when she and Dusty were alone in the house, and Tess had finally thought about leaving her grief behind to consider the possibility of another relationship. The thought of it, though, had terrified her so badly she had ended up in tears, curled up on the living room sofa. Absorbed in her emotions, she hadn't heard Dusty come downstairs.

"Tess?" Dusty's voice had been soft, her touch gentle as her fingers grazed Tess's shoulder.

Tess jumped and sat up, trying to stifle her sobs.

"Are you okay? Is there something I can do?"

"No. No, I'm fine." Tess had run her hands down her face to wipe away the stream of tears.

Dusty grabbed the box of tissues that lived on the credenza behind the couch. She offered it to Tess and sat beside her. "Are you sure? You don't look fine."

Tess glanced at her.

Dusty's eyes were wide. She actually looked more frightened than Tess felt. She was obviously uncomfortable dealing with crying women. Her attempt touched Tess's heart.

Tess inhaled deeply to get control of herself. "No, really, I am. You don't need to worry."

Dusty released a sigh, and her body relaxed.

Tess dried her eyes and blew her nose into a tissue. "I'm sorry. I didn't realize you were home."

Dusty shifted on the edge of the cushion. "Well, yeah…that's okay." She fidgeted. "Are you sure there's nothing you need?"

Calmer, Tess had reflected on the question, and a crazy thought entered her mind. She'd known at the time it was crazy, and yet, she considered it anyway. Maybe she wasn't ready for another relationship, or even ready to date, but what about just sex? She had never done that before, but she missed being touched. She missed the feel of a woman's arms around her, of silky skin against her own, and Dusty wouldn't mind. Would she? Dusty did that all the time.

"Tess?"

Dusty interrupted her thoughts, and she realized they had been staring at one another. "Dusty…"

"Yeah?" Dusty looked wary again. She really was cute.

Tess ran a fingertip over Dusty's lips. They were soft, warm. Tess pressed her mouth to Dusty's.

And that's how it had begun.

In the eleven months since, Tess had learned without a doubt that Dusty ran much deeper than she revealed to anyone. Without ever saying a word about it, she had continued, in *her* way, what Maggie had begun in helping to bring Tess back to life. Dusty always allowed her to set the mood, the pace, and the frequency, and then always gave her exactly what she needed. It was tender when she needed tenderness. It was red hot when she needed heat. Dusty let her be romantic or lustful, in charge or submissive. Tess had explored parts of herself with Dusty that she had never been able to broach with Alicia, and all because it was never spoken. It was simply done. Tess had never felt so unconditionally accepted as she did with Dusty.

It was all only in the bedroom, though. Tess sometimes wondered if Dusty would be like that in all areas of a relationship, but then reminded herself—Dusty didn't have relationships. She had sex. And she was very good at it.

Even if Dusty were to have relationships, she would most likely have them with women far different from Tess. She would have wild, adventurous involvements with women who lived on the edge, women who explored things beyond the scope of Tess's imagination and comfort zone. No, Dusty would never be interested in someone like her in any kind of real way.

"Good morning, Dr. Rossini," a voice called.

Tess followed the sound and saw Randy Ortega jogging around the outside of the quad. "Good morning. How is your dad?"

He headed in her direction. "Better. The doctor says he'll probably make a full recovery if he follows orders." Randy jogged in place in front of her, his breathing barely above normal. "Thank you again for all your help."

"You're welcome, but you've thanked me enough." Tess smiled.

Randy had shown up for the school year a week late because his father had a heart attack. The college's policy mandated that if a student didn't attend the first day of class, the spot was lost, but when he had come to her with the explanation of his circumstances and begged to be allowed to take her course, she couldn't say no. He was a good student who had been in several of her previous classes and promised to catch up on the material he had missed. Because she trusted him, she had even gone so far as to convince JoAnn Bennett to go to bat for him with his remaining classes in the psych department, though she knew JoAnn's willingness to do so had far more to do with Tess than Randy.

"I'm just grateful I didn't have to miss a whole semester. Can I carry your briefcase, or get you anything from the cafeteria, or wash your car while—"

Tess laughed and began to walk again. "Don't be ridiculous. You're not my slave. Just finish your run and be sure you're ready for today's class."

"Okay." Randy chuckled. "Have a great day. I'll see you later."

As Tess heard his footsteps fade, the thought of JoAnn lingered in her mind as a contrast to her earlier musings about Dusty. JoAnn was far more the type of woman about whom she should be thinking. She and JoAnn worked in the same field, had the same level of education, and shared similar backgrounds in the areas of relationships and family. Tess realized that she didn't actually know anything about Dusty's family. Did she have siblings? Were her parents living? Was she even from Southern California? As she thought about it, in the three years they had lived in the same house, she had never known Dusty to visit family for holidays or at any other time. How could she know so little about a woman she knew so intimately in other ways? They could have far more in common than she knew…

Could she ask Maggie? That was absurd. Was she eleven? If she wanted to know something about Dusty, of course, she should ask Dusty. What good would that do, though? Knowing more about Dusty would most likely only deepen the already intense feelings Tess had developed for her. The last several times they had slept together, Tess had been left wanting so much more, and not just more sex or another orgasm. As she had felt Dusty leave her bed, she'd had to restrain herself from pulling her back into her arms to hold her through the night. Once, she had even gone so far as to allow herself to fantasize, while Dusty's strong fingers thrust into her and her soft lips suckled her nipples, that she was all hers—to sleep with every night, to wake with every morning. *Frightening.*

What was she thinking? Dusty belonged to no one.

She sighed and unlocked her office door. She forced her thoughts to the day ahead. She had morning office hours, a department meeting, and her Victorian lit class in the afternoon. Somewhere in there, she also needed to finish grading the essays from her freshman comp class.

She knew she should focus on now, this moment, and the reality of life, but Dusty still lingered at the edge of her mind. She leaned back in her chair, sipped her coffee, and allowed herself to once again close the distance between them.

A soft knock sounded on Tess's open door, and she started. She felt the heat flood up her neck and into her face as she pressed her thighs together to stem the ache caused by her inappropriate workplace fantasies.

"Dr. Rossini?" Sandra Jenkins said from the hallway. "Can I talk to you?" Sandra was a student from the Psychology in Literature class Tess was team-teaching with JoAnn.

Tess cleared her throat. "Of course. Please come in and have a seat."

❖

Afterward, Tess considered their conversation. Though Sandra had initially said she wanted to talk about her paper, in fact, she'd wanted advice on girls. One girl, the one she really liked, she felt was out of her league, and the other more *suited* to her was nice but didn't do it for her. Tess had told her to pursue the one that made her face light up. If she didn't, she would never know what might have been.

Tess settled back into her chair and thought about her own advice. Would she always regret it if she didn't speak to Dusty about how she felt? Would she always wonder? That *is* what she had said to Sandra, but that was different. Sandra was young, and youth was the time for adventurous decisions, experimentation. She hadn't already been through the loss of a partner, the loss of a life. Besides, she didn't yet know the girl she was attracted to, didn't truly know if she was correct in her assumptions about her.

Tess knew Dusty, to a degree, and had watched the way she lived for the past three years, had heard her stories that she shared with Addison. She'd heard Dusty talk about the women who had tried to get her into a relationship, and that discussion always had the same conclusion. Plus, Tess and Dusty shared the same home. If Sandra asked out her new interest and it didn't work out, they could go their separate ways. If Tess approached Dusty and it didn't work out, things could become so uncomfortable that someone could lose her home. Yes, Tess's situation was definitely different.

So, what was that whole conversation about for her? What should she be hearing in it—the part about the other girl, the one with whom she had so much in common? JoAnn?

JoAnn seemed sweet, dependable, and she shared some similar interests with Tess, reading and foreign films, among others. Tess had also found herself enjoying some of Dusty's picks for movie night at the house, though. She had loved *Groundhog Day* so much that she watched it by herself periodically. Mostly what she loved about the movies Dusty chose, however, was how hard Dusty laughed at them. Tess smiled.

Stop this. Deep down, she knew that any decision about talking with Dusty about her feelings had already been made. She knew she had to get control of her thinking, her emotions. No good for anyone would come of it if she didn't.

The one thing all of this did tell Tess, however, was that even if pursuing an involvement with Dusty wasn't realistic, she *was* thinking about being in a relationship again. That was something she hadn't done since Alicia's death. Maybe she was ready, at least for a date. With resolve, she opened her briefcase and started grading essays while she finished her office hours.

At eleven o'clock, Tess pulled her door closed behind her and walked across campus to Gregg Hall where the behavioral science labs and faculty offices were housed. She had written a note to leave in case JoAnn was not in, but as she rounded the corner of the corridor, she saw the door ajar. She knocked and eased it open.

JoAnn sat at her desk, the telephone receiver to her ear. Her light brown, close-cut hair shone under the fluorescent lighting. She smiled and waved Tess inside. "Yes," she said into the mouthpiece. "I'll be there…Okay…I'll see you then…Bye." She hung up and turned to Tess.

"Hi," Tess said. "Did I catch you at a bad time?"

"Not at all. Please sit." JoAnn's office was bigger than Tess's and accommodated a small sitting area that held a loveseat and an upholstered chair, arranged around an oval table.

"How is your morning?"

"Much better now." A broad grin lit JoAnn's eyes. She settled onto the loveseat across from Tess. In her early forties, she held herself with a light air that belied her more serious nature. Her once-athletic build now carried a few extra pounds, but they suited her, giving her the feel of an enticement into comfort, a soft place to land at the end of a long day. She continued to smile at Tess. "What's on your mind? Something I should know about class?"

Tess warmed under JoAnn's concentrated attention, knowing what she was there to do. "No, nothing to do with class. I've been thinking about your invitations over time, and I was wondering if you'd like to have lunch."

JoAnn blinked. "Really?"

Tess smiled. "Yes."

"Not a lunch as colleagues? But a lunch *date*?"

"Yes, a lunch *date*." Tess felt a twinge of excitement at the confirmation, but at the same time, there was something disappointing about it. Deep down, there was a part of her that wished it were Dusty she was asking out. She put the thought aside. It was time to begin to move on, and Dusty, as good as she had been for Tess, wasn't looking for the same things in life.

"You know I would love to have lunch with you, and anything else you want," JoAnn said.

Tess allowed herself to feel the pleasure of JoAnn's interest though, as usual, she remained cautious. "Just lunch for now. I'm hoping we can take it slowly?"

"Certainly, whatever you need." JoAnn reached across the table and took Tess's hand in hers. "You set whatever pace makes you comfortable."

"Thank you." Tess squeezed JoAnn's fingers, then gently pulled her hand away. "I thought maybe Saturday might be nice. If you're free, of course. That way we could get completely away from campus and anything that could resemble work."

"Sounds great." JoAnn grinned. "Where would you like to go? Anywhere. You name it."

"Why don't you surprise me? I picked the day. You pick the place."

❖

As Tess opened the front door and stepped into the foyer, she heard voices from the TV room.

"Who's there?" Dusty called over the back of the double rocker-recliner she sat in watching the big screen television.

"Only me." Tess set her briefcase and purse on the table just inside the doorway. Baxter lay sprawled out on his side on the floor next to Dusty. He barely raised his head to look at Tess. On the screen, two children huddled together while a man threw things around a darkened room.

"Hey. How's it going?" Dusty asked.

Tess moved around to sit beside her in the empty half of the rocker, stopping to scratch the Rottweiler's ear on her way past him. "Pretty well. What did you do to Baxter? I've never seen him this subdued."

"We went on a hike in the hills. He's worn out."

"I'll say. What are you watching?"

Dusty sat with her feet up, with a half-empty box of chocolate-covered cherries on the arm of the chair, the box Tess had seen Addison bring to Maggie when she had come home late the night before. "Some Lifetime thing about foster kids."

Tess watched the movie while she removed her shoes and dropped them to the floor. This room, decorated in the warmth of earth tones, always soothed her, and she felt the tension of her emotionally charged day begin to drain away. She pulled the lever that lifted the section beneath her feet. "What's happening?"

"I dunno. I just turned it on. It's Lifetime, you know? I'm just grateful no one's dying of leukemia yet."

Tess smiled, knowing Dusty's opinion that the women's network aired too many shmaltzy, sad stories. "Is anyone else home?" She began rubbing the sole of her foot.

Dusty shook her head in answer to the question. "Man, I dunno how you wear those things all day," she said, indicating Tess's high heels. She gently took Tess's foot and eased it into her lap. She began massaging the arch.

"Ooooh." Tess closed her eyes, shifted sideways, and stretched out, resting her other foot on Dusty's thigh. Dusty's hands always felt so good, no matter what part of her body they were touching. As she enjoyed the sensations, she listened to the dialogue of the movie. The children wanted their real parents. Tess's thoughts returned to her questions about Dusty's family from earlier that day. She opened her eyes and looked at her. "Dusty?"

"Hm?" Dusty switched feet and began rubbing Tess's toes.

"Mmmm." Tess had to concentrate. "Do you ever see your parents?"

Dusty looked up, surprise evident in her eyes. Her fingers moved down the sole of Tess's foot. She considered Tess briefly then returned her gaze to her task. "I never knew my dad, and my mom died when I was little."

Tess studied her. There was no emotion in her expression or her voice. "Who raised you?"

"My gramma." An almost imperceptible smile touched the corners of Dusty's lips. "She's the one who taught me to laugh. She always said, 'If you're not having fun, there's something wrong with you.'" Dusty grinned. "She was a kick."

Tess felt Dusty's fingers work their magic around the back of her heel as she listened. She was so forthcoming. Would it have always been this easy to learn more about her? "What happened to her?" Tess asked finally.

"She died of cancer when I was sixteen." A tinge of sadness tempered her tone.

"Oh, I'm so sorry."

Dusty looked up at her and grinned. "Thanks. But she told me right before she died that anytime I thought of her, I'd better be smiling. And she's not someone you'd wanna mess with."

Tess's heart softened. "Where did you live after that?"

"Well, I already had a good job with the city parks, so I took the GED, got emancipated, and found an apartment." Turning her attention back to her hands, Dusty increased the pressure of her thumb as she rubbed the inside arch of Tess's left foot.

Pleasure shot straight up Tess's inseam, finding its home in the apex of her thighs. She moaned softly, and her body tensed.

Dusty gave her a sideways glance and raised an eyebrow.

Tess let her head fall back. She closed her eyes again. "How do you know exactly where to touch me?" It was a question she had always wanted to ask but had never felt comfortable enough—until now. Why now?

"You always tell me," Dusty said softly, continuing her tantalizing massage.

The bells on the front door chimed. Baxter let out a low groan, or maybe it was a growl. Either way, it lacked conviction.

Tess flinched but had no time to move.

In an instant, Eve was in the room. "Hi there," she said, glancing down to Tess's feet in Dusty's lap then up to the two of them. "Boy, what a day." She stepped around the dog and flopped down on the couch against the side wall.

"Was it a long one?" Tess asked. With as much nonchalance as she could manage, she eased herself around to sit forward in the chair.

Dusty kept her hold a second longer then released it with obvious reluctance.

"Yes. And busy. I didn't even get lunch."

Tess had been gradually getting to know Eve over the past couple of weeks, and she liked her. Eve had a youthfulness to her, but at the same time, she already knew what was important in life. The struggle she was feeling between being a mother and possibly being a lesbian touched Tess. She didn't fully understand it, since she saw no division between the two, but she could identify with Eve's inner conflict. After all, many people wouldn't comprehend her own ambivalence regarding moving forward into a new relationship, but it had been, and continued to be, a battle for her.

"Do you have any plans for the evening?" Tess asked.

"Just to change clothes and relax." Eve stretched.

"That's it for me, too," Tess said.

"What about you, Dusty?" Eve asked.

"I dunno yet. It depends on what's for dinner."

Tess smiled as she watched Dusty fix her mask back into place and stare at the television screen as though she had been deeply engrossed all along.

The front door opened again, and Addison's voice carried into the room. "I didn't say I didn't want to. I just said I'm kind of tired."

Baxter scrambled to his feet and trotted off.

"I know, dawtie. You're *just tired* a lot lately. Is there somethin' I should be worryin' about?"

At the sound of Maggie's voice, Dusty jumped, grabbed the box of chocolate-covered cherries, and shoved it under the footrest of her recliner.

Maggie stopped in the doorway of the room. “Isn’t it nice to have everyone home this evenin’? Is everyone stayin’, or do you have other plans?”

“I’ll be here,” said Tess.

“Me, too,” said Eve.

“What’s for dinner?” asked Dusty.

Maggie frowned. “If you haven’t already filled up on junk, maybe we could order pizza, I’ll make a big salad, and we could watch a movie.”

Dusty’s expression brightened. “All I’ve had is fruit, Maggie Mae. Pizza sounds great. I’ll even treat.”

“All right, then. We’ve a plan. I’ll start on the salad. Addison, will you be a love and call in the pizza?” The couple moved out the doorway in mid-conversation, Baxter at their heels.

Tess eyed Dusty. “You know, you’ll probably go to hell for lying to Maggie.”

Eve let out a giggle.

“I didn’t lie. Cherries are fruit.” Dusty reached beneath the chair and retrieved the box.

“I don’t think they count as fruit once they’ve been dipped in chocolate.”

“Augh, you’re so analytical. Can’t you just *be*?” Dusty drew out the word in exaggerated serenity.

Tess laughed. “You’re going to just *be* sorry when Maggie finds out you ate the candy her sweetheart gave her out of the blue.”

Dusty’s expression looked momentarily serious, but she covered it quickly. “Well, unless you tell on me, she’ll never know. I’ll buy her more tomorrow.” Her tone still held a playful note, but her mind had clearly followed another thought.

Chapter Eleven

Eve stood in Maggie's kitchen, waiting for the kettle to boil. She plucked a tea bag from the Good Earth box and dropped it into the mug on the counter. Her emotions were raw after the night she spent with the boys in the home she'd shared with Jeremy for so many years. She'd wanted some extended time with them, so Jeremy had gone to the Friday night Angels game with friends and crashed on a couch afterward, while Eve and the boys went out for burgers and spent the rest of the evening watching *The Lion King* for the hundredth time over a bowl of popcorn. They'd laughed and snuggled, worked on Christmas lists for Santa, and cuddled up to sleep in Jeremy's and her king-sized bed. Overall, the boys seemed at ease with Eve's absence, as they were accustomed to her being away at conferences and training seminars for work several times each year. Only once had Daniel asked, as he always did in their telephone conversations while she was traveling, when she'd be home. She'd responded that she'd be with them again soon, and they had appeared reassured by the same answer she'd always given, but Eve's heart ached as she wondered if it were true this time.

Her plan had been to take the room at Maggie's for a while to give herself a little distance to find the answers she needed. Now that she'd been here a couple of weeks, she definitely could say she'd done the requisite thinking—thinking was all she'd done—but she felt no closer to any new answers than when she first arrived, nor had she made any attempt to meet any women other than those who lived with her. She hadn't been able to figure out why until she sat and watched her children sleeping in the big bed. The one answer she was certain of was that she couldn't leave them. How could she reconcile that with the rest?

What she'd managed to figure out was that she did love her family. She loved those beautiful boys, and Jeremy. But she'd also realized that she felt a distinct draw to the intimate interaction and connection between two women. Watching Maggie and Addison as they shared their lives with one another, as they maneuvered through whatever troubles they seemed to be having, and seeing the tenderness between Dusty and Tess, whatever the heck was going on there, stirred a longing in the depths of Eve's soul, a smoldering heat that she now had to admit she'd never felt with Jeremy. With him, she felt a strong connection, a commitment to his well-being, a safety in the structure of their life together. For him, she felt deep caring, even love, but now that she was being more honest, not the kind of love a woman would expect to feel for the man she married. She wasn't *in love*, although she wasn't sure what that actually meant.

The kettle whistled and Eve poured water into her cup and allowed the tea to steep as she made her way with it into the living room. She settled into one of the swivel chairs and gazed out the windows at the lush mountainside.

The love she held in her heart for Jeremy was the kind that grew and strengthened between intimate friends who were always there for one another, who couldn't, wouldn't, go a day without at least checking in and sharing some small piece of life, who had collected so many inside jokes and so much knowledge of one another they, many times, didn't even need to speak to share a thought. He was her best and dearest friend.

Even Jeremy, however, had said that wasn't enough, not for a marriage. She'd told him the truth, that she always felt something was missing for her, felt an emptiness deep within her. He had said that he never wanted to be the cause of anyone, most of all her, living an unfulfilled life.

"I've seen you watch other women," he confessed to her one night. "Sometimes you watch them the way a man does. I think I've always known there was an attraction there for you and that maybe someday you'd need to explore it."

That'd made it easier for her, at least where Jeremy was concerned. She knew he'd be fine. She knew they'd remain close friends. She even knew they'd continue to parent well together, and she had no doubt that some other woman, one who'd be able to love him the way he deserved to be loved, would come into his life.

But what about the boys? How would her decision to find love with a woman affect them? Would it confuse them, hurt them, even damage them? Would they be teased for having two moms—if it ever came to that? Weren't all kids teased, though, really? Daniel had been already. By the beginning of first grade, he'd been dubbed *gimpy* because of a slight limp left over from a surgery during his infancy. And Enos…what awaited him? At the time, she and Jeremy had thought it sweet to name their children after ancestors from both families, but on the playgrounds of the future, the only consideration of Enos's name would be the ease at which it could be made to rhyme with penis. What had they been thinking, for God's sake? Who could even imagine what stigmas might lay ahead for them without her throwing a lesbian mom into the mix? She could always just stay in her marriage until the boys were grown. Or stay single, so at least Jeremy could be happy.

Jeremy seemed to think, however, the decision had already been made. He knew something was missing for her with him, and he didn't want a pretense for a marriage any more than she did. She'd gotten the feeling he was not only resigned, but already moving forward.

Eve sighed and took a swallow of tea. Somewhere a door closed and some footsteps sounded on stairs. Another door opened.

"Hey, I'm glad I caught you." Dusty's voice traveled down to Eve.

She couldn't hear the response, but she identified Addison from the tone. She savored the comfort of her drink as she tried not to eavesdrop. She gazed out the window.

"It's none of your business." Addison's voice rose.

"Think about what you're doing. What you'd be throwing away."

"I haven't done anything."

"You have in your mind, and there's only one thing after that. And you're not gonna be able to fix it with a box of chocolate-covered cherries or a bunch of roses."

Addison's answer was hushed but fervent, then a door slammed on the second floor. As the conversation continued in muffled, unintelligible words, Eve returned to her own reflections. Whatever drama was going on in the house, it wasn't her business.

Had she made a mistake by telling Jeremy her thoughts and emotions before she had figured them out and come to some kind of conclusion? He had said he didn't want to be in a marriage that was a lie, and of course, neither did she, but nor did she feel ready to be pushed out into the world, especially without her children.

She set her tea on the coffee table and pressed her face into the warmth of her hands. Tears burned her eyes. If she followed what she thought was in her heart, how badly would those she loved be affected? Even though Jeremy obviously did, would Daniel and Enos understand what it meant to follow one's heart—if not now, ever? How could she explain it to them?

Eve heard an upstairs door open and close once more, and footsteps were coming her way. She sucked in a soft sob that was already halfway out and managed a hurried swipe across her wet eyes and cheeks before Dusty strode into the room, her motorcycle helmet under one arm.

She froze in mid-step. "What's the matter? Jeez, is this whole house coming apart?" she muttered.

"Nothing's the matter." Eve continued to wipe at her tears.

"Oh, right. You're just sitting here crying for no reason?"

Eve swallowed. "It's nothing. You wouldn't understand."

"Well, which is it?" Dusty shifted her weight. "Nothing? Or something I wouldn't understand?"

Eve thought about the discretion with which she'd been tiptoeing out of Tess's room the previous week, the ease with which she'd forgiven Addison for whatever had taken place between them the day Eve moved in, and the gentleness Eve had felt between Dusty and Tess the night they'd all ordered pizza. But she also recalled Dusty's arrogance at their first meeting and feeling mocked by her over the *Lesbian Sex* book. What did she have to lose, though? Dusty was a full-fledged lesbian through and through, after all. Maybe she would have some insights that could help. She was certain she couldn't feel any more lost than she did right now, no matter what Dusty's reaction might be. "I'm afraid of losing my children," she blurted before she could change her mind.

"What?" Dusty stared. "I didn't know you had kids."

Eve blew out a deep sigh. "Never mind."

"No, wait," Dusty said, still standing just inside the doorway. "Give me a minute to catch up. So, you have kids? Where are they?"

"They're with their dad."

"Oh, okay. And you're afraid of losing them." Dusty hesitated. "Have you ever lost them before?"

"What?" Eve blinked. "No, I'm not afraid of losing them like in a grocery store. I'm afraid of…you know…losing them. Not being able to be their mother, anymore."

Dusty had been nodding as she listened, but she stopped and her brow furrowed. "Why wouldn't you be able to be their mother? They're your kids."

"You know. Maybe being with me wouldn't be good for them."

"Why not? Are you a druggie, or a child molester, or something?"

Eve glared at her. "Of course not."

"An alcoholic? Mental patient? Ooh, a bank robber."

"Stop it."

"What, then?"

Eve considered Dusty in her black leather jacket, tight jeans and boots, her soft blond hair dipping down across her smooth forehead. The same pang of arousal she felt whenever she looked at Dusty for too long clutched at her abdomen. She sighed. "You, of all people, should know."

"Well, I don't." Dusty mimicked Eve's tone. "Why don't you tell me?"

She was going to make Eve say it—the L-word. She took a deep breath. "I might be a…lesbian."

Dusty blinked. "Might be? I thought you were. I mean, are."

Eve lowered her gaze. "I don't know what I am. I've been married for eight years, and I should be happy. Jeremy's wonderful. We have a great home, a nice life. But something's missing. There's this emptiness inside me. Do you know what I mean?" She looked up at Dusty.

Dusty stared at her with a vacant expression.

Eve knew she didn't, but continued anyway. "I keep getting too close to my women friends, wanting something I can't have. I wasn't even sure what that something was until recently. But then there are the boys, my sons." The image of their smiling faces flashed in her mind. "If I let myself have that something, I could lose them."

"Wait a minute." Dusty shifted her helmet to her other arm. "Are you saying you think if you're a lesbian, that for no other reason, you can't be a good mother?"

Eve sniffed, tears pooling in her eyes again. "Maybe. I mean, how could I be? I'd be sleeping with women. How could they understand that? They're so young. How could they understand my living…you know…an alternative lifestyle?"

Dusty burst out laughing. "Babe, you've been listening to too much Dr. Laura."

Eve's anger flared, replacing her self-pity. "This might be funny to you, but this is my entire life—everything I cherish."

Dusty cleared her throat and gained control of herself with obvious effort. "Okay, I'm sorry." She extended her free hand in a gesture of openness. "It's just that…That's the stupidest thing I've ever heard." She dissolved once more into a fit of giggles.

"All right, fine. Go ahead and ridicule me. I need just one more emotion today to fully flush out the degree of humiliation and terror I feel." Eve swiveled her chair away from Dusty. "I'm glad I've been able to amuse you." Pressure built in her chest. A tear spilled onto her cheek.

Dusty watched her for a long moment.

Eve grew uneasy.

"Hey, I'm really sorry." This time Dusty's tone held sincerity. She moved a little farther into the room. "Just cuz you sleep with women and live an…" She faltered, then said quickly, "an alternative lifestyle, doesn't have anything to do with what kind of mom you are to your kids. You know, unless you're some kind of slut-puppy who's out partying all the time, which I haven't seen any evidence of. Hell, you never go anywhere. You walk around here like Boo Radley, peeking out the windows and stuff. Do you even know any lesbians besides me, Maggie, Addison, and Tess?"

Eve found Dusty's words oddly comforting, or maybe it was the change in her manner. She sniffed again. She did think it strange that Dusty knew who Boo Radley was, but she chose to ignore it. Was she right? Eve couldn't think. "Look, just forget it. Get on your *hog*—isn't that what they call it—and go do whatever it is you do."

Dusty's eyes widened. "Hey, you know what? I've got an idea." She held up her hand. "Wait right here." She ran back upstairs.

Eve rolled her eyes. She wished she didn't find her so intriguing. She swore half the time Dusty was insane.

Within minutes, Dusty raced back down the steps and into the living room doorway. She carried a leather jacket. "Here, put this on. It should fit well enough. I've got an extra helmet down in the garage."

"What?" Eve asked in surprise, but she found herself rising and slipping her arms into the jacket Dusty held for her.

"I want to take you somewhere. It'll be great. It's just what you need."

❖

Forty-five minutes later, Eve climbed from the back of the motorcycle, her legs shaking from the vibration of the bike and the exhilaration of the new experience. Or maybe it was from the feel of her body pressed against Dusty's back, her arms around her waist. She'd never been so close to a woman for so long before. She pulled off her helmet and scanned the parking lot and the adjacent park. Families picnicked, children played, a dog chased a squirrel up a tree. Nothing appeared so out of the ordinary that it would hold the solutions to Eve's questions.

A child squealed. "Dusty!"

Other excited yelps followed.

Eve looked across the grass to see a group of children running toward them. She smiled. "Your motorcycle gang?"

"Very funny." Dusty fastened the strap of her helmet to the handlebar, then took Eve's and did the same. She squatted just as the children reached them, and one little boy threw himself into her arms. She scooped him up and lifted him high into the air before she settled him onto her hip. "Hey, how's the birthday bud?"

"Didja bring me a present?" The boy's rich brown eyes sparked with excitement.

"I sure did, but you're gonna have to wait till your mom says it's okay to open it." Dusty turned to Eve. "This is my friend Seth. He's four today."

Seth thrust out his chest and nodded.

"Seth, this is Eve." Dusty finished the introduction.

"Hello, Seth," Eve said, more than a little amazed. She never would've thought Dusty the type to have any children in her life. "It's very nice to meet you. And happy birthday."

"Hi."

"And this is Danny." Dusty pointed to each child in front of them in turn. "Rachel, Josh, Stewart, and Melissa." She pronounced the last name with an air of prissiness.

The little girl curtsied in her light yellow party dress.

She reminded Eve of Enos's latest crush at preschool. "It's nice to meet all of you."

Dusty shifted her attention back to Seth. "Eve comes from a place far, far away where nobody has two mommies."

His eyes rounded, and his mouth dropped open. The other children ooohed. Slowly, he turned and gaped at Eve. "Are you an alien?"

A blush heated her cheeks. "No, Seth, I'm not," she answered softly. She shot a glare at Dusty.

"I thought maybe you could help her out," Dusty whispered into Seth's ear.

He pursed his lips and nodded.

"Anyone ready for balloon games?" a woman's voice called out.

The children on the ground cheered in unison, and Seth hooted and wiggled in Dusty's arms.

She quickly lowered him, and he chased after the others in the direction of a group of women standing beside some shaded picnic tables. Several of them waved, and Dusty grinned and raised her hand in return.

"Is that why you brought me here? To tell everyone what's wrong with me?"

Dusty turned to her. "No, I brought you here so you could see all these kids who have lesbian moms. And so you could see that they play and laugh and sometimes throw fits and just live normal lives with parents who love them. So you can see how crazy you're being." Dusty unzipped a compartment beneath the backseat of her motorcycle and retrieved a beautifully wrapped birthday package. "Ready to party?" she asked with a smile.

As Eve and Dusty approached the group of women near a table piled high with gifts, several others supervised the beginning of a water balloon game off to the side. One woman in a flowered smock took the present Dusty carried before she hugged her with a warm hello. Two others dressed more like Dusty slapped palms with her, and the remainder took turns greeting her with hugs and friendly touches.

"Everyone, this is Eve," Dusty said, pressing a hand to the small of her back and coaxing her forward. "She just moved into one of the rooms at Maggie's, and she didn't have anything to do this afternoon, so I thought she'd like to come to one of the hottest parties in the Valley."

The group laughed, Eve included.

Dusty continued with the introductions, rattling off a list of names Eve knew she'd need to hear again before remembering many of them. She found herself deeply grateful for Dusty's tact at not mentioning the real reason she'd brought her.

They all smiled and greeted her.

"Welcome, Eve. Would you like a soda or water or anything?" one woman offered. She wore her hair in a short ponytail out the back of a Dodgers cap, and the fit of her blue baseball jersey tucked into white shorts flattered her curvy build.

Eve remembered *her* name. Sammi. She smiled. "Water would be great. Thank you." She noticed that even though most of the women had moved to watch the children race to fill buckets by tossing water balloons into them, they still kept a conspicuous degree of attention on her. She fidgeted under the scrutiny and leaned close to Dusty. "Why are they staring at me?"

"I dunno." Dusty shrugged. "Maybe they think you're cute. You do look kinda hot in your jeans and leather jacket with your hair all messy."

Eve's cheeks and ears flamed, but before she had to come up with a response, Dusty tapped her arm.

"Be right back," she said and jogged over to a woman who seemed to be in charge of the game.

She was a tall African-American in khaki shorts and a green tank top. Her mid-length curly hair was pulled back in a loose tie. She enveloped Dusty in an all-consuming hug then eased her back and placed a chaste kiss on her lips.

Sammi returned with a bottle of water and handed it to Eve. "Here you go," she said with a grin that deepened the tiny lines around her eyes. "We'll be having hotdogs a little later, but if you're hungry, there's chips and some dip on the other table."

"Thank you. This will do fine for now." Eve twisted the top off the bottle, trying to concentrate on something to steady her nerves.

"So, what do you do?" Sammi asked.

"I work for National Electronics, in HR." This was casual enough. "You?"

"I'm an RN. I have a cousin who works at National. Debbie St. John?"

"Sorry, I don't know her. It's a big company." Eve hesitated then decided since she was here, she might as well dive right in. "This looks like a great party. My sons would love it."

Sammi arched an eyebrow. "You have kids?"

"Mm-hm." She swallowed. "Two sons. Four and six."

"Where are they today? You should've brought them along."

"They're with their dad."

"Ah, the every-other-weekend scenario."

"Well, no, not really." Eve paused. "He's still in our house with them."

Sammi studied her. "Really? You don't have custody?"

Eve shifted uncomfortably. She wondered if there was a graceful way out of this conversation. Was she ready to talk about this with a total stranger? At least Maggie was friends with Aunt Carolyn, and Tess was part of Maggie. And Dusty? Well, Dusty had caught her off guard, that was all. But then, Dusty had brought her here, and Eve now realized she'd done that so Eve could recognize she wasn't alone in the decisions she was facing. She glanced around her. Surely, at least some of these women had had their children with husbands and had needed to come to terms with a change in lifestyle. She thought of Dusty's reaction to her comment about living an alternative lifestyle and smiled. There certainly didn't appear to be anything *alternative* about this birthday party. It looked and felt like any other birthday party for a four-year-old. Eve took a deep breath. "We haven't gotten to all of that just yet," she said.

Sammi smiled softly. "I've probably been where you are, so if you want someone to talk to, I'd be happy to offer what I can."

"You were married?" Eve asked.

She nodded. "Melissa's dad and I split up three years ago." She gestured toward the children and pointed out the little girl in the party dress. "She was two. It was a scary time for me, but exciting, too." She stepped back and sat on the bench beside the picnic table.

As Eve watched the children, she noticed another group of three women looking at her. She averted her gaze and took another drink of water. She glanced at Sammi, then back to the women. "Can I ask you something?"

"Sure."

"Is there something weird about me?" Eve asked in a hushed voice.

Sammi leaned on her elbows on the edge of the table. She ran her gaze over Eve from head to foot, then back, and raised an eyebrow. "Not that I can see," she said with a hint of suggestion. "Why?"

"Some of your friends keep staring at me. It makes me think I've wet my pants or have something stuck in my teeth."

Sammi laughed, a warm and genuine sound. "We're all just dying to know how you ended up with Dusty. She's never brought anyone with her before."

"Oh," Eve said. She found herself disappointed that the answer wasn't Dusty's earlier explanation. "It's just what she said. We both live at Maggie's. I've been a little upset…" She downplayed the reality, unwilling to admit to sobbing into her tea. "About what me being a lesbian might mean for my sons, and Dusty brought me today, I think…" Eve looked toward the game and saw Dusty holding one of the smaller children and running with him toward the bucket. "To show me how stupid I'm being." Her heart warmed as she realized the enormous gift she'd just received.

Sammi grinned at her. "You're not dating Dusty?"

Eve blinked. "Oh! Oh, no. Not at all." Eve felt herself blush yet one more time.

Sammi gazed up at her, still smiling. "Oooh," she said, drawing out the word. "That's really good to know."

Eve felt the slow stirring deep within her that she experienced watching Maggie and Addison or Dusty and Tess—that arousal at the thought of what went on between women. She let herself feel Sammi's soft gaze, her inviting smile. She wondered what Sammi's touch might do to her. She smiled but could think of nothing to say. She'd have to get better at this.

In the pause, Sammi turned toward a group of women and shook her head, clearly knowing that they'd all been waiting. They all returned their attention either to each other or to the children.

Eve felt awkward, then opted to bring the conversation back to the previous topic. "So, how does Melissa handle you and her father not being together?" she asked, sitting beside Sammi.

"She's fine with it. She was so young when we split up, she really doesn't know anything different. All she knows is that everyone in her life loves her—me, her father, everyone here, her grandparents."

"I know Daniel and Enos already know both Jeremy and I love them. And that will never change. And Jeremy's been so great with all this, taking care of the boys while I take some time to work out what I'm feeling."

"He already knows you're gay?"

Eve nodded.

"And he's okay with it?"

"He says he will be. He says he wants me to be happy, and if that can't be with him, then he doesn't want to stand in the way." Eve fingered a metal stud on the leather jacket she wore.

"Wow, that's really something. I haven't heard a story like that very often."

Eve looked up into Sammi's eyes. "Really?"

"No." Sammi laughed. "I mean there are some congenial breakups, but a lot of men take it personally when their wives prefer women."

Eve chuckled. "I suppose that'd be true." She considered the thought. "How do they work it out with the kids in those cases?"

"Some guys are jerks about it and try to take the kids, and some even succeed. But mostly, those cases are why God created joint custody." Sammi laughed. "But it sounds like you and Jeremy could agree on all of it anyway, which lets you keep it flexible. Me and my ex-husband had to spell out every detail, and he holds to every dotted 'i' and crossed 't' with a vengeance. He was really mad."

"You realized you were a lesbian while you were still married?"

"Oh, yeah. A lot of us did. Well, maybe not a lot, but me, Jen, Barbara…" Sammi pointed to different women around the picnic area. "Believe me, you're far from unique. At least in that way." She turned her attention back to Eve, flirtation in her smile.

Eve felt that stirring again. Heat rose all the way up into her cheeks.

Sammi's expression softened. "I'm sorry. I didn't mean to make you uncomfortable."

"You didn't." *If this is discomfort, bring it on.* "This openness is still all a bit new to me, but it feels so freeing." Her gaze met Sammi's silvery stare. "Is your ex-husband still mad?"

"Oh, yeah. Not quite as much, though, since he started dating a woman he likes. I think ultimately he's been mad at himself since he's the one who wanted me to watch girl-on-girl porn with him to *get him in the mood.* I've got to tell you, it definitely got *me* in the mood." Sammi laughed again. "And the rest just unfolded—or, as he would probably say, unraveled—from there."

A burst of laughter erupted from Eve, and she covered her mouth. "That is so funny. I can see where he might have some regrets."

The balloon game ended, and the winning team received their prizes—R2D2 Pez dispensers filled with candy. The rest of the participants seemed just as happy with their gifts of *Star Wars* coloring books and crayons. As Eve and Sammi continued their conversation, other women drifted in and out, adding their comments to whatever topic was being discussed and sharing their own stories. Eve was struck by the ease with which the entire group interacted, the evident love and friendship between the women, the village-like approach they all took with one another's children. As two women threw several packages of hotdogs onto a nearby grill and Sammi invited Eve to help her with the buns, condiments, and paper goods, Eve saw Dusty lead a charge of the kids to the playground and leap onto the merry-go-round.

"How did Dusty end up in this group?" she asked.

Sammi glanced at her, then followed her gaze to Dusty. "She was best friends with Emily's ex," Sammi said. "Seth's mom." She paused, looking at Eve as though checking to make sure she was making the connection.

Eve nodded. She had met Emily earlier, a petite black woman with a mild accent Eve couldn't place.

"Dusty was around the whole time Emily and Kris were dating and was right there when Seth was born. She just became part of the family, and then a part of us." Sammi set plastic knives beside the condiments. "When Kris left a couple of years ago, Dusty kept the connection with Emily. She's been really good to Em and Seth, and she's great with all of us. All the kids love her. She really is one of us."

"Was she ever involved with Emily?" Eve asked. She knew it was none of her business, but Dusty intrigued her.

"Oh, no. Dusty doesn't get *involved* with anyone. She's a player. That's why everyone was so curious when she showed up today with you."

What was she doing with Tess, then? She and Tess seemed pretty *involved.*

"Finally, I get to catch my breath and come over here to meet you," someone said in a rich voice that flowed like thick maple syrup.

Eve turned to meet the glittering gaze of the woman who'd been leading the water balloon game, the woman who'd greeted Dusty so warmly.

"I'm Rebecca." She took Eve's hand between both of her own.

Her touch was…what? Comforting? No, more than that. Peaceful. Her touch was pure peace. Eve felt it wash through her like a wave gently breaking onto sand.

"Rebecca's our fearless leader." Sammi's grin lit her features as she slipped an arm around Rebecca's waist and snuggled into her.

Rebecca laughed, that rich flow again. "Don't be silly."

Eve smiled and basked in the love between the two women. It was the same feeling she experienced when everyone was home and together at Maggie's house. "It's nice to meet you," she said, squeezing Rebecca's slender fingers. "I'm Eve Jacobs."

"Yes, I know. Dusty told me. I'm so glad she brought you today." She released Eve's hand and shifted in Sammi's embrace. "Sammi, sweetie, will you go see if the veggie dogs are ready yet, and bring plates for Eve and me?"

Sammi stepped back. "Uh-oh. Watch out," she said to Eve. "This means she has something for you." She picked up several plates. "I'm out of here."

Eve laughed, bemused. "What is she talking about?" she asked Rebecca.

"I don't have the slightest idea." As Sammi walked away, Rebecca shook a finger at her.

"Oh, Eve," Sammi called over her shoulder. "Veggie or regular dogs?"

"Veggie, please."

Rebecca sat and patted the space beside her. "Dusty tells me you're facing some big decisions in your life."

Eve eased down next to her. She felt a mild annoyance that Dusty would share that information, mixed with gratitude for not having to repeat it all again. "Yes, I guess I am. But being here today has let me know that what I was afraid of doesn't have to be." She looked around her. "I mean, with all this support, I'm sure my boys and I can work through it."

"The truth is that once you aren't afraid and are comfortable with who you are, your boys will be, too. They'll always reflect what you're feeling. Ultimately, they just want to know you love them. Is there a woman in your life at this point?"

"No. That's the other thing that seems ridiculous about all this. What if I make the decision to leave my marriage, then find out I don't really want to be with a woman? I mean, I've been attracted to women before, but I've never acted on it."

Rebecca studied her. "Are you attracted to anyone in particular, now?"

Eve felt herself blush. "I'm a little attracted to Dusty." She glanced over at Dusty, who was in a huddle with Seth and Josh beneath a nearby tree.

Rebecca chuckled, the sound low and throaty. "Everyone is at least *a little* attracted to Dusty. She just has that way about her, and she has a huge heart. But she's for someone else."

"Tess?" The name leapt out of Eve's mouth before she could stop it.

Rebecca arched an eyebrow. "You have some intuition."

"It's more just observation. It seems obvious to me, just by watching them."

Rebecca laughed softly. "It's apparently more obvious to you than it is to Dusty. But she'll find her way. She may be able to help you through some of your questions, however, if she listens to her own voice instead of Maggie's."

Maggie? What's Maggie have to do with this? Eve wanted to pursue the question but allowed herself to be self-absorbed. She had the distinct impression that this woman did—as Sammi had indicated—have something for her, and she wanted to know what it was. "Dusty scares me a little, though."

"She scares you because you see yourself in her."

"Myself? In Dusty?" Eve stared at Rebecca. "I don't see that Dusty and I are alike in any way."

"That's because you're just looking with your physical eyes. You have to look below the surface. We're all here to learn a lesson, or to heal something, if you will. You and Dusty have the same lesson, and since you're still learning it, it makes you uncomfortable to see it in someone else."

"What's the lesson?" Eve asked, intrigued.

"You both are here to learn to follow your hearts. It shows up for each of you in different forms, but it's the same lesson, nonetheless."

Eve considered Rebecca's words. She could see it, to some degree. She was trying to move through her fears of leaving the safety of her marriage to follow her heart into an unknown world of relationships that many people judged, and the legal system didn't recognize. And Dusty, if she was in love with Tess…Wow, Eve hadn't considered it before now, but if Dusty was in love with Tess, she had to have some fear about the differences between them, not to mention for Dusty to be *in love* with someone and in a relationship, she'd have to leave the world she knew as well.

"You see it, don't you?" Rebecca's fluid cadence brought Eve out of her realization.

She met the steady gaze that watched her, the radiant smile. "Yes," she said, the word barely a whisper.

"Okay, ladies, I hope the private talk is finished because everyone is heading this way for lunch." Sammi stopped in front of them, holding three plates with hotdogs on them.

Rebecca slipped an arm around Eve's shoulders and squeezed. "We'll talk more soon, if you'd like."

"I'd like that." Returning fully to the moment, she looked up at Sammi. Eve already felt a connection with her. "If everyone has a lesson to learn, what's hers?" she asked Rebecca, still gazing at Sammi teasingly.

Rebecca laughed. "Sammi's is patience," she said flatly.

"Augh, she tells me that all the time. I hate it."

"And what else do I tell you about it?" Rebecca asked.

Sammi looked thoughtful. "That it'll be worth the wait," she said, eyeing Rebecca questioningly.

Eve glanced at Rebecca and thought she saw a slight tilt of her head toward her.

"All right, everybody out of the way. We have a hungry birthday boy." Dusty strode up to the table carrying Seth on her shoulders.

Eve smiled up at her. "You said you'd be right back, and you abandoned me." She tried to look mournful but knew she failed.

"I did not abandon you," Dusty said. "I left you in the very capable hands of Sammi St. John. And she, in turn, passed you over to this beautiful and wise woman." She stroked Rebecca's cheek.

Rebecca feigned a swoon and laughed.

Eve giggled. "Okay. You have a point. I was definitely well taken care of."

As the rest of the group swarmed around the table, Eve began helping some of the children prepare their hotdogs.

Later, as she said good-bye to new friends, she watched Dusty buckle a sleepy Seth into his car seat.

He clutched the Game Boy Dusty had given him to his cake-smeared chest and grinned up at her.

Dusty stood beside Eve, waving at the cars leaving the parking lot. As the last one turned onto the street, Eve leaned over and kissed her on the cheek.

Dusty flinched and drew back. "What was that for?"

Eve smiled. "Thank you." She gazed into Dusty's eyes. "Thank you for bringing me today." She barely controlled the emotion in her voice.

Dusty shifted. "Yeah, well, I couldn't just let you sit at home and be stupid."

Eve pondered the statement. "Yes, actually, you could have. But you didn't."

A deep blush crept up Dusty's neck and into her face. "Just don't tell Maggie you were with me today."

"Maggie? Why not?" Eve couldn't even imagine why Maggie would object.

"Because." Dusty averted her gaze. "She thinks I'd be a bad influence on you."

"What? Why? You're so sweet once you get past all that bravado."

Dusty's flush deepened and she frowned. "I'm not really sweet, Eve. And if you *do* want to thank me for today, do it by not saying anything to Maggie. Okay? If you wanna talk about it, tell her you knew someone else here. I don't want her mad at me. Besides, she has enough to worry about right now."

CHAPTER TWELVE

Maggie pressed the button on the remote to the garage door opener as she pulled her '67 Mercedes convertible into the driveway. With her habitual check of the parking spaces, she determined that Tess and Eve were home and Addison and Dusty weren't. She sighed. She had picked up a message from Addison on the machine earlier saying that she had, once again, gone into the office on this beautiful Saturday to catch up on some work. Maggie had tried to return the call, but there had been no answer on Addison's private line at the firm. Sometimes, if she was absorbed, she turned off the ringer.

In the garage, Maggie leaned into the space behind the seats and retrieved the bag of groceries she had picked up at the market. As she turned, she noticed the extra helmet that usually sat on the workbench beside the empty spot for Dusty's Harley was gone. She remembered Dusty mentioning having a birthday party to go to this afternoon and wondered if she had taken someone and whose party it was, for that matter. Whoever enjoyed the celebration, though, Maggie celebrated with them in her heart. She had spent the afternoon talking and reading to Pete, an AIDS patient entering into the final stages of the disease. His partner, Ricardo, had gone to see a movie with some friends. She knew the hardest part still lay ahead for the two young men.

Spending the afternoon with Pete, listening to his stories of his years with Ricardo, had created in Maggie a longing to feel Addison's arms around her, to taste her lips, breathe in the scent of her skin. She wanted to make love, to feel alive—but Addison was working.

She brushed the thought aside and headed into the house. As she put away the groceries, she saw Tess sitting outside at the patio table reading, her bare feet propped on another chair. When she finished her task, she stepped out the sliding glass door into the late afternoon sunshine. “Hello,” she said, easing the door shut behind her. “Would you mind if I join you?”

Baxter sprang up from where he lay beside Tess and raced to Maggie, snatching up his ball on the way.

Tess looked up and smiled. “Of course not.” She closed her book, holding her place with a finger. “I was wondering where everyone was when I got home. Baxter acted as though he hadn’t seen anybody in days. I had to appease him by playing ball for a while.” She laughed.

Maggie chuckled and lowered herself into the rattan chair beside Tess’s. “Well, you know how he is. He’ll put on any kind of show to get someone to play with him.” She took the ball and threw it across the yard.

The dog chased after it.

“Isn’t Eve home?” Maggie asked. “Her car’s out front.”

“I haven’t seen her. Maybe she’s in her room.”

“Was Addison here when you got home?” Maggie hated sounding like she was checking up on her, but in truth, she supposed she was.

“No. She was still here when I left, though,” Tess said in a light tone, an obvious attempt to ease Maggie’s mind. “She’s still acting strangely?”

Maggie nodded. “It’s almost like she’s avoidin’ time with me,” she said, leaning back in her chair. “But time with just me. She still comes home and spends the evenin’s with everyone, but only goes upstairs when it’s late enough for sleep. As soon as she wakes up, she’s dressed and out of our bedroom, even if all she does is come downstairs to talk with everyone. It’s the oddest thing. I’d think she might be havin’ an affair, but she isn’t gone enough.” *Except for the evening last week when she came home from work late, and on days like today.* That suspicious voice in the back of her mind niggled at her.

“That *is* strange,” Tess said. “I wish I had something more helpful to offer you for all the times you’ve helped me find answers.”

Maggie smiled and patted Tess’s hand. “You just listenin’ helps a lot, luv. Addison and I will work it out.” She sounded more confident than she felt. “How was your lunch date with JoAnn?”

Tess watched Baxter run back across the yard. “It was nice.”

Maggie waited for her to continue, but the only sound was the gurgle of the fountain.

Baxter dropped his ball at Maggie's feet.

She threw it again. "That doesn't sound very good," she said with a hint of humor.

Baxter dashed off.

Tess laughed. "No, it really was nice. I didn't mean to make it sound like anything was wrong with it. It just felt different." Her gaze remained fixed on the bougainvillea climbing the back wall.

"Different from what you had with Alicia?"

Tess turned to her, then looked away again. "Yes," she said with a sigh. "But I suppose it would have to be, right? They're two entirely different women."

Maggie offered her a reassuring smile and nodded. "What did the two of you do?"

Tess set her book on the table and leaned forward, her arms wrapped around herself. "We went to lunch at Barone's, then saw an indie film JoAnn had heard about."

"You can't go wrong with a meal and a movie for a first date, now can you?" Maggie chose to disregard her own experience from the previous weekend. Tess's really was a first date.

Baxter plodded up, made a circle, and flopped down beneath the table.

Tess smiled. "I don't know, Maggie. I know I'm ready to start dating, and JoAnn is really very nice. She's being so patient and understanding with me. We have a lot in common. I like her."

"I hear a definite *but* comin'."

"But…" Tess paused. "Shouldn't I feel excited when I'm with her? Shouldn't I be unable to wait for her to touch me? Or to not be able to keep from touching her?"

"That's one type of relationship, yes. Is that the way it was with Alicia?"

"Alicia?" Tess leaned back. "Maybe. It's hard to remember all the way back to the beginning."

"What are you comparin' this to, then?"

Tess hesitated and bit her lower lip. "I don't know. Maybe just the romantic myth."

"Did the two of you touch at all today?"

"Yes. We held hands in the movie. And we kissed good-bye. Just a short kiss."

"And how was that?"

"It was nice. Warm. Comfortable." Tess shrugged. "You know what they say—something I could get used to." She smiled.

"I know sometimes relationships start out with fireworks and flames, and sometimes they start with a spark that catches and takes a bit to burn hotter. Maybe this one is the latter."

Tess studied her in obvious contemplation. "Maggie," she said. "There's something I want to—"

"Hi, everyone," Eve called as she stepped from the house. "Am I interrupting?"

Maggie watched Tess. "Darlin'," she said to Eve, "could you—"

"No, it's okay," Tess said. "Come on out. We were just talking about our days. How was yours?"

Maggie's attention remained on Tess.

"My day was fabulous." Eve sat in one of the remaining chairs and rested her elbows on the table.

Maggie glanced at her.

Eve's cheeks glowed a rosy red. Her eyes shone with a light that hadn't been there before and her smile encompassed her entire being. This was most certainly not someone who had spent the afternoon in her room. Maggie looked back to Tess, concerned that she hadn't been able to speak about whatever was bothering her. Maybe they could continue their conversation later. "Well, you certainly look happy," Maggie said to Eve. "What happened?"

Eve beamed. "I got to see how ridiculous all my fears have been."

"Really?" Tess's eyes sparkled with the reflection of Eve's enthusiasm as she smiled at her. "How so?"

"I ended up at a little boy's birthday party this afternoon, and all the kids there were children of lesbians. I met and talked with all the moms. I spent some time with one woman whose story is very similar to mine in that she was married and had a child before she realized she was gay. I really liked her." Eve's smile turned a little shy.

"Wow." Tess chuckled. "So much can change in just a few hours. When I left for lunch, you looked pretty down. Now, you've abandoned all your fears, made some new friends, and have a possible love interest."

"I don't know about love." Eve shrugged. "But definitely interest."

Tess winked at her. "You go, girl."

Maggie watched the playful exchange. Her heart warmed. "So, how did you happen upon this party?" she asked with an inner appreciation for the way life worked.

Eve glanced at Maggie, then down at her hands. "Um, a woman I work with is the cousin of the one I ended up talking to. The one I like. Sammi." She looked up again. "The woman I work with knows some of what I've been going through, and she thought it might help me to meet her cousin and some of her friends."

Maggie listened, remembering how uncomfortable Eve had felt sharing about her situation that first day when she had come to see the room. She wondered how on earth she would have managed to discuss it with a coworker. She smiled, hiding her doubts. "Well, she certainly seems to have been right. Is that Sammi St. John you're talkin' about?"

Eve's eyes widened almost imperceptibly. "Yes, do you know her?"

"I've met her a few times. She's in the group that Dusty's friends Emily and Rebecca are close with. Did you meet them as well?"

Eve fidgeted in her chair. "Uh-huh. They were very nice, too." She glanced at Tess. "Rebecca said some interesting things."

Tess and Maggie laughed.

"She always does," Tess said.

"So, was Dusty at this party?" Maggie asked. She thought about the missing motorcycle helmet in the garage and began to get the picture. "I know she really likes all the children in that group."

Eve hesitated. "Yes. She was there. I didn't talk to her much, though. She was playing with the kids a lot."

"How did you get to the party? Did Sammi pick you up?" Maggie watched as Eve shifted again. She could see the wheels turning. It was like watching a little girl who's realized her story is about to conflict with itself. Maggie felt a bit guilty enjoying Eve's dilemma, but she indulged herself a moment longer.

Tess waited, eyeing Maggie with a knowing smile.

"Mm-hm," Eve answered finally. It was all she said.

"So, you weren't the one wearin' Dusty's extra helmet this afternoon? And she isn't your friend from work with the cousin?"

Eve stiffened. "Oh, Maggie, I'm sorry," she said in a rush. "Yes, Dusty took me to the party, but please, please don't be mad at her. She was so nice about it all, and I promised I wouldn't tell you it was her."

Maggie and Tess began to laugh.

"All right," Maggie said, reaching across the table and squeezing Eve's hand. "Shhh. I'm not mad at anyone. I was just kiddin' with you. You're right. It was very nice of her to take you."

Eve released a sigh. "It was wonderful. I haven't felt that free and relaxed in so long. It was like coming home after being lost in the dark woods all night. I could actually see my boys playing with all those kids and feeling just as at ease as I did."

"It's good that you've begun to find your way, luv. We all could've told you your fears were nothin' to be worryin' about, but you needed to be able to see it for yourself." As Maggie listened to her own words, she thought of her fears about Addison and what might be going on with her. Did she need to see for *herself* as well?

"Oh, I know. I don't think I would've believed anyone if I'd just been told. I was so wrapped up in all my assumptions. I'm so thankful to Dusty for just sticking me on the back of her motorcycle and taking me there. I didn't even know where we were going. I was so surprised she was taking me anywhere. I didn't think she liked me until today. She's always just ignored me or left the room when I came in."

Tess shifted her gaze to Maggie. Her expression held mild reproach.

"Well, that's most likely my doin'." Maggie said, feeling sheepish. "It seems I may owe Dusty an apology." She turned a soft smile to Tess. "Our little wildling might be growin' up, and I never even noticed."

"What do you mean?" Eve asked.

"Let's just say that perhaps I was bein' a bit over protective of you, and I apparently shortchanged Dusty in the process. I thought I detected an attraction between the two of you when you first arrived, and, well… Dusty…" She looked to Tess for help.

Tess stared down at her fingers, folding and unfolding the corner of one of the pages in her book.

"Dusty's been known to toy with women sometimes," Maggie continued, "and you seemed too fragile for that. I apologize. I shouldn't have meddled."

"Oh," Eve said. Her eyes turned thoughtful. "That explains something she said."

"What's that?" Maggie asked.

"She said you thought she'd be a bad influence on me and you'd be mad at her if you knew she'd taken me there."

Maggie's chest tightened, and a current of shame blew through her like a hot wind. She loved Dusty, and while she didn't understand her lifestyle, she knew Dusty's deep down sweetness. Maybe recently she had blamed Dusty for the changes in Addison, but now, in this moment of honesty, she also knew that no one was responsible for Addison's behavior but Addison. "I'll need to take care of that, now won't I?" Maggie said, her throat taut with emotion. "I can't have Dusty believin' I think badly of her."

Tess smiled.

"But I wasn't supposed to tell you all this."

Maggie chuckled. "Don't you be worryin'." She pressed Eve's hand beneath her own. "We've a way of doin' things in this house. It'll all be fine." Resolved, she settled back in her chair. "It seems you both have potential dates for the Halloween party comin' up."

Both women stared at her blankly.

"Sammi? JoAnn?" She allowed her incredulity to show in her tone and expression.

"Does Sammi come to your Halloween parties?" Eve asked.

"She's been the past two years. She might be even more inclined if she has a date."

"She mentioned the party, but she didn't ask me."

"Maybe you could ask her. After all, it's bein' held in your home."

Eve's face went pale. "*Me* ask *her*? On a date?"

"You said you liked her. Why not?"

"Oh, my God, I've never even thought about how scary men have it, being the ones who are expected to take the initiative." She looked at Maggie, wide-eyed. "I don't know if I can."

"Of course you can, darlin'. If she sat and talked with you all afternoon, you can be sure she likes you as well. The askin's just a formality."

"Do you really think so?" Some of the color returned to Eve's cheeks.

"I do. Besides, Sammi's pretty cute. Do you want to take the chance that someone else might invite her?"

Eve smiled. "Okay. She gave me her number in case I wanted to talk. I'll call her."

"Good." Maggie turned to Tess. "And what about you, luv? You had a nice lunch with JoAnn. Time for the next step?"

Tess inhaled a deep breath then blew it out. "Yes," she said. "I'll do it."

"You're dating someone?" Eve asked Tess.

"Yes. We just started today. Her name is JoAnn."

"Oh." Eve's expression seemed slightly confused. "That's nice. Where did you meet her?"

"I work with her," Tess said, her tone somewhat subdued. "She's been asking me out for a while, and I decided it was time."

"Oh." Eve watched Tess a moment longer as if she wanted to say something else. Finally, she said, "Well then, it's time for both of us."

As Eve and Tess continued the conversation, Maggie returned to the fears that had taken up residence in the back of her mind. Was Addison having an affair? Was she bored in their relationship and had she found someone with whom to bring some excitement into her life? Perhaps Maggie did need to see for herself just where Addison was when she wasn't at home—and what she was doing.

Maggie checked her watch. Four forty five. "Will you girls excuse me?" she said, rising from the table. "I just remembered an errand I need to run."

On her way through the house, she picked up her purse and keys. As she neared the door, she heard the television from the front room. She peeked in and saw Dusty's blond hair over the back of the double recliner. Maggie strolled in behind her and looped her arms around the front of Dusty's neck. She kissed the top of her head.

Dusty leaned back with her eyes closed. "Whatcha been doing all day?" she asked.

"More important is what you've been doin', today."

Dusty opened her eyes and looked up at Maggie over the top of her head, her surprise evident. "What do you mean?"

Maggie moved around the chair and sat on its arm. "It was very sweet what you did for Eve this afternoon."

Dusty tensed and gave her a cautious look. "What?"

"Don't play dumb. I know you took her to the birthday party." Maggie combed her fingers through Dusty's hair and brushed her bangs to the side. "It was the very thing she needed. And it was very thoughtful of you."

"You're not mad? I know you told me to stay away from her, but she was crying, and I didn't know—"

"You did exactly the right thing, darlin'. And I apologize for implyin' what I did about you not havin' anythin' to offer her. I love you dearly, and I don't think you're a bad influence on her."

"Jeez," Dusty muttered, blushing. "Did she tell you everything?"

Maggie laughed. "I figured out most of it."

Dusty grinned. "I should have known I couldn't slip anything past you, Maggie Mae."

Maggie kissed Dusty's forehead. "Are you goin' out tonight?"

Dusty flopped back in the chair. She sighed. "I don't think so. Man, those kids wore me out."

Maggie smirked. "You're nothin' but a big kid yourself." She moved to the doorway. "I'll be back in a bit."

Thirty minutes later, Maggie maneuvered her Mercedes into the underground parking garage at Addison's work. She had decided the only thing she could do was to look for Addison where she was *supposed* to be. As she steered down the ramp, she saw it.

There, all by itself in the vast space, sat Addison's Explorer. She really was here.

Maggie pulled into the slot beside the Ford and turned off her engine.

Now what? She felt foolish.

There was nothing saying, however, that Addison was up in her office alone. That damned voice in the back of her head twisted its suspicion into her brain like an ice pick. But there was no other car here, Maggie countered. Addison could have picked someone up. But Addison would never use her office to have an affair. The Milton and Ryan Agency wasn't exactly conservative, but such behavior would certainly be unacceptable. Addison wouldn't risk it.

As Maggie sat staring across the garage at the bank of elevators that ran up through the building, the light above one blinked on, indicating it was in use. She froze. Could she start her car and get out of there before it reached the parking level? She doubted it. Well, she had wanted to see for herself what Addison was doing. She steeled herself and waited.

A ding announced the elevator's arrival and the doors opened.

Addison stepped out—alone.

Maggie exhaled a breath, flooded with relief.

On Addison's third stride, she raised her hand, pointing the Explorer's fob at her car, and her eyes followed. Her gait caught as surprise registered in her gaze. She smiled. "What are you doing here?" she called over the short distance.

Maggie opened her door and stepped out onto the cement. She opted for the truth—the first truth. "I needed to see you. Pete's moved into the final stages, and I just needed to feel your arms around me. I tried callin' but your phone is off."

"Oh, yeah," Addison said as she reached Maggie. "I'm sorry. I was trying to stay focused. I'm sorry about Pete." She took Maggie in a warm embrace and held her close.

Maggie shuddered in relief. Addison had been alone. Maggie hadn't realized just how frightened she had been that she would find out otherwise.

"Hey, it's okay," Addison said, kissing Maggie's temple. "I'm right here. Everything will be fine. And you're being such a loving presence for Pete and Ricardo and their family."

Maggie wrapped her arms around Addison's neck and buried her face in her shoulder. Addison had learned early in Maggie's hospice work exactly what she needed to hear, and Maggie was always so grateful for how easily she offered it. Right now, however, all Maggie needed had just been given—the sight of her lover, alone.

Chapter Thirteen

Addison stared at the open e-mail on her computer screen as she stroked the polished wood of her desk with her fingertips. Every line of the grain, the slight ridge at the edge, even the small mar left from a too-hot coffee cup caressed her skin as Victoria's words caressed her desire.

I can't take much more of this, Addison. I can't wait much longer. You know I've wanted you ever since we went dancing. I've been on fire during the weeks in between.

Addison knew exactly what Victoria meant. Her own body vibrated with a constant thrum. She couldn't shake the erotic images she conjured of Victoria spread out naked before her on a bed, the floor, a table, her desk. The setting didn't matter. Only the throb deep in her center mattered.

The past two weeks had been hell. As if Addison's own torment weren't difficult enough, Dusty had been on her at every opportunity. And Maggie—Addison knew Maggie suspected what was happening, even if she didn't know the details. Two days earlier, when Maggie had shown up in the parking garage, Addison had no doubt about her real reason for being there. Still, with all of that, she couldn't get control of her mind and body.

Even now, in the middle of the afternoon in her office, she ached with need and lust. She was grateful Victoria had been in San Francisco since that night at Vibes, ever since Addison had been forced to admit to herself that she wanted her. Also since that night, however, there'd been the e-mails, the building fantasies that increased in intensity, detail, and arousal. Then there was her guilt—her conflict between her love for Maggie and this lust for Victoria.

Addison knew she loved Maggie, still desired her sexually, sensually. She had no doubt about that, but her body raged and yearned for Victoria, for the fulfillment of the promise of her words in her e-mails. They lingered in Addison's mind.

I want to suck your clit, lover. Suck it and lick it until you beg me to let you come. Then I'll suck it longer.

I'll fuck you, Addison. Shove my fingers deep inside you.

I want you to fuck me with a big cock. I can see you moving over me, coming down hard into me. Taking me. Fucking me.

Vivid images of all this and more dominated Addison's thoughts, consumed her dreams. In the mornings, she awoke, aching to roll over and take Maggie's warm, inviting body, make her come, and find her own desperate release. But she couldn't. She'd known that the very first morning, and she'd held to it. She knew it wasn't much, but it was the best she seemed to be able to do right now.

A part of her wanted for Victoria never to return to Los Angeles, never to become an actual, full-blown tangible temptation standing in front of her. She wanted to remain faithful to Maggie, but if Victoria was right there with her, she wasn't completely sure she would be.

Addison knew she'd have to face Victoria eventually, take a stand for her commitment to Maggie, and cut all ties. She'd made attempts in several of her e-mail responses, but she admitted they'd been weak. She knew, as she'd saved Victoria's messages and reread them over and over, she wasn't fooling anyone, least of all herself. She recalled her own words in the first e-mail she'd sent.

Dear Victoria,

Yes, I felt like you the night we went dancing. I can't deny that. But as you know, I'm in a relationship. I've made a commitment to Maggie that I value and can't break. If you and I had met under different circumstances, at a different time, I'd love to be able to explore the heat between us. But I just can't. I shouldn't.

Even at the time she'd written them, Addison knew her words were pathetic, that she wasn't sure she had the strength to back them. It was obvious Victoria knew it, too. Since then, her e-mails had grown more explicit, more erotic, and those were the ones Addison found herself defenseless against. Would she really sleep with Victoria regardless of Maggie? Maybe if she did it just once, she could get it out of her system.

A knock sounded at her office door.

She looked up and registered the sight of Michael's broad grin just as Victoria stepped through the doorway behind him. Every shard of arousal she'd been fighting for the past week and a half arrowed directly to her center. Her pulse quickened.

"There she is," Michael said. "I was pretty sure she was in."

"Hello, Addison," Victoria said. "It's nice to see you again. It's been a while." She smiled.

I want to suck your clit, lick it, was all Addison could think as she watched Victoria's full lips. She opened her thighs beneath the desk, trying to relieve the pressure between them before she stood. "Hello," she managed in a voice she thought sounded remarkably normal. "I didn't know you were back in town." She fumbled for her mouse and closed her e-mail program.

"I got in a couple hours ago. Just in time for my meeting with Michael."

"Hey, are you okay?" Michael asked. "You look kind of flushed."

"Yeah, I'm fine. Just a little warm." The heat rose in her body, and she was grateful for her tailored jacket. She could feel her hardened nipples straining against her sports bra and cotton shirt. "What's up?"

"Victoria wanted to meet with you and go over the markets you've come up with for the gay and lesbian community."

"If you're not too busy," Victoria added. The gentle swell of her breasts lifted the vee-neck bodice of the chocolate-colored dress that hugged the contours of her form. An amber teardrop pendant nestled in her cleavage.

Addison's thoughts spiraled back to watching Victoria's movements on the dance floor, to her nude body in the bathroom of her hotel room. *I have to get a grip.* She gave a silent word of thanks for Michael's presence. "No, not at all. We can go over it and see if it's going to fit the ads you already have or if you'd like us to put together something more specific to the market."

"Great." Victoria watched her.

Addison turned to retrieve the Fontaine file from her desk.

"Okay then, I'll leave you two to it," Michael said.

Addison spun around. "Where are you going?"

In the doorway, he paused. "I have another appointment." Amusement shaped his boyish face. "Don't worry, boss. You'll be fine. She doesn't bite." He turned to Victoria. "I'll see you soon."

"Thank you, Michael." As he stepped into the hall, her gaze remained on his retreat for a moment before she shifted it to Addison. A smile played on her lips, danced in her eyes. "I might bite *you*." Her voice was a sultry whisper.

A nervous chuckle escaped Addison. She held up the folder and started around the side of the desk. "I think you'll be happy with—"

"I don't care about that right now." Her eyes still on Addison, Victoria reached behind her and eased the door closed. "I'm here for you."

Addison froze. She felt a line of sweat trickle down her spine. The pulse between her legs intensified. She watched Victoria work the lock on the doorknob. *I'll fuck you, Addison. Shove my fingers deep inside you.* She released a soft moan, then caught herself. "I can't do this," she said as she ran her gaze over Victoria's voluptuous body. "I told you that."

Victoria sidled toward her, dropping her purse into one of the chairs. "Addison," she said with a sigh. "Let's not pretend we're not going to enjoy each other." She stepped closer.

Addison edged away. She felt the desk against her backside. Panic and excitement warred within her. "But not here." *Not here?* What was she saying? Not *anywhere*, she *should* be saying, but all of a sudden it seemed more important to stop what was happening *here*. *Now.* With her coworkers right next door, her employers down the hall, people right outside, passing by.

Victoria licked her lips. "Just a taste. We'll save most of it for tomorrow night."

Tomorrow night? Addison couldn't think.

Victoria slipped her hands under Addison's jacket, grazing her hard nipples through her shirt. "Oooh, you're so happy to see me." She squeezed them between her fingers.

Addison forgot her objections. She closed her eyes and groaned. Need throbbed through her. "Victoria, please." She had to stop this. She grasped her wrists.

"Please what, baby?" Victoria pinched a little harder.

Addison jerked and tightened her grip.

Victoria closed what little distance remained between them and pressed her thigh between Addison's. "Is this what you want, baby? Something there?" She thrust her hips.

"Oh, God." Addison lifted her own.

"Say yes."

"I—"

"Say yes." She pushed harder. Her fingers worked Addison's nipples, her breath hot on Addison's lips. "Say yes and let me feel how wet you are. Let me see what you have for me."

They were so close Addison's knuckles brushed Victoria's firm breasts through her dress. Their lips touched ever so slightly as Victoria spoke.

Addison's will broke. She surrendered. She opened her hands to cup Victoria's breasts.

Victoria grabbed them. "You have to say yes first."

"Yes." Addison groaned, a long, low, guttural sound.

Victoria's mouth curved into a smile against Addison's. "Say please," she murmured. She moved her thigh against Addison's mound.

"*Please*." It came out as a growl.

"Please what?" Victoria's breath came fast.

Addison's fingers clenched, her hips pumped. "Please let me have you."

Victoria released Addison's hands and captured her mouth in a hungry kiss.

Addison grasped Victoria's breasts. She thumbed the nipples roughly through the fabric.

As she threw her head back, Victoria closed her eyes. She straddled Addison's thigh and rubbed herself against it. "Yes." She moaned. With an urgency, she unfastened Addison's slacks and unzipped her fly. She pulled the shirt free and ran a hand up Addison's bare torso, adeptly maneuvering underneath the bra to palm an aching nipple. She eased back and slid the other into Addison's pants.

Addison breathed hard, reveling in Victoria's touch, in the sensation of her taut nipples under Addison's fingers. She shifted, loosening her slacks around her hips, making room for what she knew was coming.

Victoria's fingers parted her and slid into her hot, wet folds.

They both moaned.

But Addison had to have more. She had to have what she'd been craving. She spread her legs, aching for Victoria to find her throbbing center, and she did. She began a slow, firm stroke.

Addison whimpered with a combination of relief and deepening need.

While she kept a steady pace, Victoria pushed up Addison's shirt and bra. She lowered her head and her warm mouth took in Addison's swollen nipple.

Addison lost all sense of her surroundings, her concerns, her commitments, of everything except the waves of pleasure cresting in her body. She was wet. She was hot. She was hard. She ran her fingers through Victoria's hair, gripping her tightly, arching into her.

Victoria pushed her backward, easing her onto the desk.

Addison complied, shoving paperwork onto the floor.

Within seconds, Victoria lay beside her, sucking hungrily at her breasts, fingers pumping slowly but forcefully inside her, her thumb massaging her pulsing clit.

Head back, eyes closed, thighs open wide, Addison gasped for air. Her orgasm built, higher, closer. Her muscles tightened. She began to tremble.

Victoria's hand stilled. "Not yet, baby. I'm nowhere near done with you." Her voice held amusement.

Gritting her teeth, Addison clenched her fists in Victoria's hair. She groaned in frustration.

The intercom on the phone beside her head chimed. She stiffened and her eyes snapped open.

Victoria leaned over her, pressing her to the desk. "Don't answer it."

Conflict raged in Addison's mind, in her body. "The secretary knows I'm here." She still panted. "She'll come looking for me if it's important."

Victoria hesitated, then shifted her thumb on Addison's clit.

Addison jerked and moaned.

"Make it quick," Victoria said with a smirk.

Addison drew in a steadying breath. She pressed the button. "Yes?" she said, shooting Victoria a warning look.

"Maggie's here to see you," Peggy's voice was soft, but the words slammed into Addison like a brick shattering a windowpane.

She blanched. Her eyes went wide. She felt Victoria press down harder on her body, her lips near Addison's ear.

"You're with a client," she whispered. "You don't know how long you'll be. You'll see her at home." She rose and arched an eyebrow.

Addison struggled to find a rational thought, a coherent sentence, another option. She couldn't very well say send her in.

Victoria stared down at her, a command in her eyes.

"Addison? Are you there?" Peggy's voice cut the silence.

Addison swallowed. "Yes, Peggy, but I'm with a client." She kept her gaze riveted on Victoria. "I don't know how long I'll be. Could you tell Maggie I'll have to see her when I get home?"

"Will do." The line went dead.

Addison's heart pounded with a new force—terror. What the hell was she doing? Before an answer came, though, Victoria's fingers pushed deep within her. Her teeth scraped Addison's nipple. Addison was lost again in rampant sensations, debilitating pleasure. She gave herself over to it all, incapable of any other response in that moment.

Again, Victoria's skilled touch brought Addison right to the threshold.

Addison arched upward, meeting every thrust, pumping her hips with every stroke.

"Ooooh," Victoria whispered. "You're so hard and wet. Do you want to come?"

Addison gasped and clutched Victoria to her. "Yes. Please."

"Or do you want to fuck me?" Victoria asked, her hot breath caressing Addison's flesh. Her hand slowed. "I need to be fucked."

Addison's body clenched around Victoria's fingers. "Please let me come first," she heard herself plead, and a part of her knew shame.

Victoria laughed. "Oh, lover. I can't wait. Besides, I want you to fuck me like this. I want to feel your need, feel you ram into me." Then she was gone.

Addison was empty, alone on the desk. She whined in animalistic torment. She heard a rustling sound then felt her pants slide down her legs.

"I have something for you," Victoria said, desire evident in her tone. "Look."

Addison obeyed.

Victoria stood between Addison's knees, dangling a large strap-on from her fingers. She smiled. "Let's get this on you." She leaned down and manipulated the harness around Addison's feet then up her calves.

Within seconds, Addison stood with Victoria's long, toned legs draped over her shoulders, gripping her hips.

Victoria lay stretched out before her—just like in her fantasies—on the desktop, her dress pulled up to her collarbone, revealing her beautifully naked body waiting for Addison's plunge. Victoria's breasts heaved with every wanting breath, her nipples hard, her folds coated with her arousal.

Addison grasped the strap-on and slid the head through Victoria's wetness.

"Take me," Victoria demanded in a harsh whisper. "Take me now."

Addison slammed into her.

A silent scream of pleasure contorted Victoria's features.

Addison pumped, hard and fast, driven by her own need, her own desperation. She held tightly to Victoria's hips, those enticing, teasing hips, pulling her into every thrust. She watched, mesmerized, as Victoria pinched and tugged her own nipples.

"Yeah, baby. Yeah. Fuck me," Victoria commanded between gasps. Without warning, she climaxed, her torso rising up off the desk, her body jerking and writhing as it settled back down then lifted again. Her jaw clenched, she groaned and clamped down on her stiff nipples.

Addison's breath came hard. She eased Victoria's legs down and collapsed onto her, still deep inside her. She pressed her lips around one of her erect nipples and sucked, heightening her own desire. Her need throbbed and pulsed between her legs. She was desperate for release.

Victoria moaned. "If you keep that up, you're going to have to fuck me again. I want to go down on you." She grasped Addison's shoulders and shoved her away. "Get on your back."

The words surged through Addison. She wouldn't have thought she could be more aroused, more filled with lust and want, and yet here was more. Desire consumed her entire body. She ached. She needed. She could form only one thought—I have to come. She yanked the harness from her waist and took the spot on the desk that Victoria vacated. She spread her thighs wide.

Victoria knelt between them. She inhaled deeply and moaned and ran her tongue once along Addison's exposed sex, barely touching her.

"Please."

Another lick, this time with more pressure. "Mmmm, you taste so good," Victoria murmured. The movement of her lips caressed Addison's swollen flesh.

Addison could only whimper.

A slight pause, and Victoria plunged her tongue in deep.

Addison arched her body and grabbed the back of Victoria's head. She fought to keep from crying out, grinding herself against Victoria's ravaging mouth.

Just as she'd promised, Victoria licked and sucked. Just as she'd promised, she made Addison beg. Just as she'd promised, she sucked until Addison thought she'd go insane with need. Finally, she pushed her fingers into Addison and ran tight circles around her clit with the hard tip of her tongue. With one last flick, Addison exploded in wanton release. Her orgasm racked her body with waves of pleasure, shudders of much-needed relief.

When she began to calm and regain her senses, she realized Victoria no longer touched her. She lay on her desk with the sounds of the outer office filtering into her awareness. She heard movement in the room. She opened her eyes.

Victoria wiped off the strap-on with a Wet-Nap, her dress once again covering her sensuous body. She smiled at Addison. "Time to get dressed, lover. I have to be going." She slipped the toy into her purse.

Addison sat up and looked down at herself. Naked from the waist down, her bra shoved above her breasts and her shirt unbuttoned—*what the fuck*—she felt a hot blush flood her face and neck.

Victoria laughed. "You are so adorable." She ran a tissue over her mouth, then spread some gloss over her swollen lips with a fingertip. "I don't want to wipe all of you off," she said. "I want to be able to taste you for the rest of the day."

Addison managed a weak smile. She slipped her pants back on and buttoned her shirt. "I…I don't really know what to say."

"Just say see you tomorrow night."

"Tomorrow night?"

"Oh, yeah, lover. We've just begun. Come to my room."

Addison felt her arousal begin to build again. Any thought she'd had of being with Victoria once and getting it out of her system took flight like a kite in a cyclone. After what'd just happened, she wondered if she'd ever get this woman out of her system. "I'm not sure I can get away tomorrow."

"Really?" Victoria returned her makeup bag to her purse. "I suggest you try. I doubt very much you want me to come looking for you. Do you?" She arched an eyebrow.

Addison paled at the thought.

"I didn't think so." Victoria held out her hand. She offered Addison a sweet smile. "Are you ready to walk me out?"

Addison couldn't move. Her head still spun. "Give me a minute." She lowered herself into one of the chairs in front of her desk.

Victoria watched her for a moment before she picked up the files and papers that'd landed on the floor during their interlude. When she'd finished straightening them, she settled into the other chair.

They sat in silence, staring at one another.

Victoria smiled, a satisfied glint in her eyes.

Addison felt stunned, her mind inundated with questions. Who *was* this woman? Why did she have such an effect on Addison? Had she really just had sex in her office? How could she have had sex with her at all? A sense of powerlessness swept over her.

"You're thinking too much," Victoria said. "This doesn't require thought. Just desire and a willingness to have a good time."

Addison considered arguing that she couldn't do it again, but she knew she would. She'd cheated on Maggie. She'd risked her job by doing it in her office—two things she thought she'd never do. And yet, she knew she'd do both again. What else might she do that she'd thought she never would? She said nothing.

Victoria stepped close. She held her fingers beneath Addison's nose. "Smell that."

Addison inhaled and moaned at her own scent.

"That's right, lover. It was so good. Just let yourself enjoy it." She took Addison's hand. "Now walk me to the elevator."

As Addison opened her office door and Victoria moved into the hallway, the familiar sounds of her workplace flooded in on her—the voices of colleagues, the ringing of phones, all the reassuring sounds that said the world really hadn't changed in the last half hour. But Addison's world had.

"Thank you again, for all the time you've put into finding the best places for our ads," Victoria said as they walked into the reception area.

"No problem at all. It's been my pleasure." Addison hadn't intended the double entendre, but she caught it as it left her lips.

Victoria gave her a knowing smile.

From the corner of her eye, Addison saw Maggie rise from a seat in the waiting area. Her heart slammed into her ribs. She wanted to run but turned to face her partner. "Maggie," she said with genuine surprise. "I thought you headed home."

"I decided to wait for a bit. I was hopin' we could go out for an early dinner." Maggie's air was relaxed and cheerful. She glanced at Victoria.

"Oh," Addison said, her mouth going dry. "This is Victoria Fontaine, a client. Victoria, this is my partner, Maggie."

"Yes," Victoria said, holding out her hand. "I recognize you from the picture on Addison's desk. It's a beautiful photo."

"Thank you. Aren't you sweet." Maggie took Victoria's hand and held it between her own.

Addison flinched, remembering her scent on Victoria's fingers, the feel of them deep inside her.

"Addison's mentioned your restaurant," Maggie said. "I can't wait for the openin'."

"It's still several months away, at least. But I so hope you can make it. Addison's done so much for me in the ad campaign."

"Just doing my job." Addison averted her gaze. "So, what brought you out this way?" she asked Maggie.

"Oh, just some errands for the party. I was plannin' to pick up our costumes, but mine still needs some alterations."

"Costumes?" Victoria eyed Addison.

"Mm-hm," Maggie said. "We're havin' our Halloween party weekend after next. We have it every year. Would you like to join us? You're more than welcome."

Addison stiffened and her stomach churned. She fought back nausea.

Victoria smiled. "That sounds like so much fun. I'd love to. If I'm in town, that is."

"That's great," Maggie said, opening her purse. "I think I have an extra invitation right here. It'll give you all the details."

Tension tightened Addison's shoulders, and her temples began to throb. Surely, Victoria wouldn't really come to the party—not after what just happened.

Maggie handed Victoria the invitation.

Victoria studied it. "Oh, darn. I don't think I'll be in town that weekend. But look. Here's your address." She glanced at Addison. "Now I know where you live so I can pester you at home, too."

Addison winced inwardly, remembering Victoria's comment about not wanting her to come looking for Addison.

Maggie laughed. "You wouldn't be the first client to track her down at home. She takes very good care of her clients." She rubbed Addison's arm.

"Oh, I already know that. She's taken care of my every need." Victoria smiled at Addison, then back to Maggie. "It was lovely meeting you. I look forward to seeing you again sometime."

"You as well," said Maggie. "If your plans change, feel free to come to the party."

"Thank you. And, Addison, I'll see you soon. I'd like to take a look at the revised drawings as soon as possible. Maybe tomorrow?"

"Sure." Addison marveled at the ease with which Victoria inserted the subtext. "I'm sure we can work that out."

"Okay, then. You two enjoy your dinner." Victoria crossed the reception area with a little wave of her hand.

As Addison and Maggie began to walk back toward the hallway, Addison glanced over her shoulder.

Victoria stood in the elevator.

Their eyes met and held.

Victoria's sensuous lips curved into a salacious smile, and she slipped a fingertip into her mouth.

CHAPTER FOURTEEN

Dusty stood beside the small, makeshift karaoke stage, surveying the party guests gathered in the front room. The costumes varied from traditional witches and zombies to princesses and fairies all the way to what looked like an enormous Tic Tac, for God's sake. What was that about? Maggie had outdone herself on the decorations throughout the house and grounds, and everything had been perfectly planned and arranged until the caterer's van had ended up smashed into a guardrail on the freeway. The workers walked away uninjured, but the canapés, stuffed mushrooms, and spring rolls went to the great hors d'oeuvre tray in the sky. Dusty's job now was to make sure the guests had drinks and were entertaining one another while the caterer, Maggie, and Tess frantically threw together some deviled eggs and brochette, along with whatever else they could come up with from the contents of Maggie's kitchen and the nearest market. Dusty was in charge of the front room and the main living room while Addison covered the patio and backyard. Everything seemed to be going well, a good time being had by all.

She listened as an Arabian princess covered in veils belted out, a little off key, "Damn, I Wish I Was Your Lover" from the stage and felt grateful that her costume concealed her identity as she noticed one of her most recent, though still fairly long ago, one-night-stands come through the front door alone. It always went better if someone from her past came in with a date. Just to be on the safe side, she stepped back a pace, moving further into the corner.

Eve's laughter caught her attention from across the room, and she turned to watch Sammi flick the red plume feather of the headband that went with Eve's flapper costume. Decked out in bell-bottoms patched with hearts, a fringed leather vest over a psychedelic shirt, a bandana tying back her hair, and love beads draped around her neck, Sammi gazed at a flushed Eve with evident affection. The two women sat facing one another on the sofa, clearly intent on their own conversation. Their knees didn't quite touch, but it was only a matter of time before contact would be made.

Dusty smiled as she remembered how nervous Eve had been before the party started.

Dusty had been sitting on the edge of her rumpled bed, pulling on a sock, when someone knocked. "Yeah," she called, glancing at the door to the hall.

It was the bathroom door, though, that opened a crack. "Can I come in?" Eve asked.

"Sure." In the weeks Eve had lived there and shared the bathroom with Dusty, she'd never ventured into Dusty's room.

Eve stepped inside, her gaze moving over the contents of what'd been the house's original master bedroom before Maggie and Addison added the third floor.

Dusty took a quick survey of her own, making sure no dirty underwear or other embarrassing paraphernalia littered the space. "What's up?"

Eve hesitated. "This is your room?" It wasn't really a question. "It looks somewhat like I'd expected, but different somehow, too." She continued her study of the area.

Dusty tried to figure out the meaning of Eve's words—after all, they *were* English—but she failed. "So…what's up?"

This time, the question caught Eve's attention. She looked at Dusty. "Um, I was just wondering if I look okay."

Dusty considered the red sheath, fringed dress, sheer black stockings, and red feathered headband. "Turn around," she said, twirling her fingers in the air.

Eve executed a half turn then came full circle, finishing with a slight curtsy.

"A Roaring Twenties flapper?" Dusty stood and moved toward her.

"Mm-hm. I love that era."

"You look great except for one thing." Dusty stepped behind her and tugged on the string of the price tag, pulling it free from the dress. "Now you look perfect." She smiled and handed it to Eve.

"Oh, thank you," Eve said. "That would've been embarrassing."

"Maybe a little. Wouldn't have been the end of the world, though." Dusty sat back down on the bed and slipped on her other sock.

Eve remained where she stood but said nothing. She watched Dusty.

Dusty grabbed one of her running shoes and paused. "You okay?"

"Mm-hm." Eve squeezed her eyes shut. "Noooo." She flopped down on the bed.

"What's wrong?" Dusty asked, leaning back for a better look at her.

"I'm so nervous." She crossed her arms in front of her torso. "I don't think I can do this."

"Course you can." Dusty bent forward and pulled on her shoe. "It's just a Halloween party."

Eve eyed her. "You know what I'm talking about."

"I don't have a clue." Dusty tied the laces.

"It's my first date."

"You and Jeremy never went on a date? You just got married right after the introductions?"

Eve narrowed her eyes and pursed her lips. "With a woman. With Sammi."

Dusty laughed. "It'll be fine. You'll have a great time." She reached for her other shoe. "I've never been on a date with a guy, but I'm sure a date with a woman is better."

"That's not what I'm worried about." Eve straightened and looked at Dusty.

"What, then?"

"What do I do? I don't know what to do."

"What do you mean?"

"Well…how does it work with two women? I mean, who asks to dance, or who takes the lead? Or…who…initiates the kiss?" Eve's face turned a deep red.

"Ah, that's really what you want to know, isn't it?" Dusty stood and tucked her orange Monster Mash T-shirt into her black jeans. "You want the old lip lock with Sammi."

Eve exhaled in obvious exasperation. "Why can't you ever just help me without making fun of me first?"

"I dunno. I think it's a sickness." Dusty crossed to the chair in the corner and picked up her costume. She held it up, letting the cloth sides hang down from the plastic frame while the narrow set of mini blinds remained pulled tight.

"What is that?" Eve asked.

"It's my costume. C'mere and help me put it on."

"Only if you help me." Eve moved to where Dusty stood.

Dusty laughed. "Of course I'll help you. Here, hold this." She handed the frame to Eve and leaned over to stepped beneath it.

Eve pulled it away. "Without making fun of me anymore."

"Yeah, yeah. Okay, no more making fun. It's just that you make it so easy." She lifted one of the cloth side panels and slipped underneath. She fitted the bicycle helmet attached to the frame onto her head, then buckled the strap beneath her chin and tightened the whole thing into place. She grinned at Eve.

Eve stared. "What the heck are you?" she asked, her forehead furrowed.

Dusty pulled the string on the mini blinds, lowering them to her waist. She peered out the opening she'd cut in the plastic slats. "I'm Boo Radley," Dusty answered, laughing heartily. "You inspired me."

Eve glared. "You said you wouldn't make fun of me anymore."

As she pulled the cord and raised the blinds again so she could see more clearly, Dusty grinned. "I thought you just meant about Sammi."

Eve pivoted and took a step toward the bathroom door.

Dusty grabbed her arm. "Okay, I'm sorry," she said in a rush. "What's the problem again?"

Eve let out a long hiss and stomped her foot. "I don't know what to do."

"Look, if you want to kiss her, just kiss her. It's not complicated. It doesn't matter who takes the lead."

Eve eyed her. "So, if a woman likes you and makes the first move, you're okay with that?"

"Yeah. Why not?"

Eve studied Dusty for a long moment, then sighed. "I can't really take you seriously with that thing on your head. Are you sure?"

Dusty put her hands on Eve's shoulders. "Why did you ask me?"

"Because you go out with a lot of women. Because I thought you'd know." Eve looked at her seriously. "Because you were right before."

"Okay, then. Trust me. You're making too big a deal out of this. You'll know when it's the right moment. Or if you don't, Sammi will. And it'll just happen. I've heard you in your room on the phone till all hours of the night. I doubt you were talking to your kids. You and Sammi have been building something even if you haven't actually seen each other all that much. These things have their own movement, their own momentum. All you have to do is go along with it." She felt Eve's muscles relax in her grasp.

Eve's features softened, and she ducked under the mini blinds and gave Dusty a tight hug. "Thank you."

Dusty chuckled and returned the embrace.

"I like it better when you're nice," Eve said, drawing back.

"I'm not nice." Dusty straightened the red feather on Eve's headband. "Now, let's go downstairs and see if Maggie and Tess need any help."

A genuine yowl from the cat on stage singing "What's New Pussycat?" drew Dusty's attention back to the party where she still watched Eve and Sammi across the room.

Their knees were pressed together.

While she talked, Sammi gazed at Eve and tucked several loose strands of hair behind Eve's ear. She lowered her hand, resting it on Eve's stockinged thigh.

Eve laughed at whatever Sammi had said and glanced in Dusty's direction.

Dusty winked at her, then remembering she couldn't be seen behind the blinds, she gave a slight lift of her beer in salute to Eve.

Eve smiled and returned her attention to Sammi.

Out of the corner of her eye, Dusty saw Tess step into the doorway with a tray of food and motion to her.

She grinned. The sight of Tess, even frazzled from her hurried work in the kitchen, with locks of her hair falling from her braid around her shining face, and spots from dropped or splattered food staining her blouse, quickened Dusty's heartbeat. She knew she had to do something about this. She either needed to get over her feelings for Tess or tell her about them and see what happened. She made her way through the partiers to where Tess stood. "Can I take that?"

Tess laughed. "I love your costume," she said, handing the hors d'oeuvres to Dusty in answer to the question. "You've done a great job transforming yourself into a modern day Boo Radley."

Dusty felt herself blush behind the blinds, grateful for her invisibility. *To Kill A Mockingbird* was the first book she borrowed from Tess, and really she'd done so only to have an excuse to knock on Tess's door one rainy afternoon. She'd read it, though, and she'd loved it—and, in the process, she'd remembered how much she'd liked to read as a kid. Ever since, she'd continued borrowing Tess's novels and enjoyed not only the stories but the feel of something that belonged to Tess in her hands. "Thanks," she said. "I liked your idea about the mini blinds instead of just cloth curtains."

Tess smiled. "Will you make the rounds with the tray and tell everyone the rest of the buffet is in the dining room?"

"Sure." Dusty set her beer bottle on the nearby table and adjusted her grip on the tray.

"Thank you. I need to go change clothes." Tess crossed the entryway and hurried up the stairs.

Dusty watched, not wanting to take her eyes off Tess's backside. Then, breaking the trance, she turned and offered the nearest group of women fresh canapés. After making the rounds through both rooms and seeing everyone begin to gather in the dining room, she returned the empty tray to the kitchen and left it on the counter. She took a discreet position back in the entryway where the doors to the two living rooms met. The evening had a different feel to her than the Halloween parties in the past. Everyone else seemed to be having a great time, but she didn't feel all that festive. Something seemed to be hanging in the air.

A movement at the top of the stairs caught her attention, and she looked up. She forgot to breathe. Arousal ignited in every cell of her body.

Dressed as an Egyptian queen, Tess stood on the top step, gazing down at her. A slinky gown accentuated the lush body beneath that she knew so well. Dusty took in the deep plunge neckline of the black bodice and the high split of the gold silk skirt. A cape, fastened at her throat and wrists with black satin bands, fluttered like wings as Tess descended the stairs, reminding Dusty of the beautiful statue of an ibis she'd seen at Rebecca's house. Scores of colored beads and rhinestones cascading from the headpiece mingled with Tess's thick, dark hair that draped freely around her neck and shoulders.

She stopped in front of Dusty and spread her arms, opening the cape so the sequins flickered in the light like shimmering flames. "How do I look?"

Oh, my God. She swallowed. "Gorgeous," she managed, her voice low with desire.

Tess smiled. She peered into the opening in front of Dusty's eyes. "Thank you." She squeezed Dusty's arm. "I'm going to go spell Maggie so she can change, too."

Dusty made a sound that wasn't quite a word and watched Tess round the corner. She definitely had to do something. Maybe she'd talk to Tess tonight after the party. No, not maybe. She *would.*

As she began to regain her composure, she heard the front door open behind her and high heels on the wood floor. She turned and froze.

Victoria Fontaine stood before her in a black velvet and lace vampire costume, the skirt slit all the way to the hip and a high, stand-up collar framing her sleek, dark blond hair. At another time, in another place, Dusty would've found the vision seductive and maybe irresistible, but she hated this woman. For the old Dusty, that might not even have mattered, but now…

"Good evening," Victoria said with a bright smile. "Am I in the right place? Is this the home of Addison Rae-McInnis?"

Dusty hardened. All traces of the warmth and emotion from her encounter with Tess vanished. "It's the home of Addison *and Maggie* Rae-McInnis. What are you doing here?"

Victoria arched an eyebrow and laughed. "I would have thought a party would have a more inviting greeter." She eyed Dusty. "But then I doubt you're one of our hostesses. To whom do I have the pleasure of speaking?" she asked with mocking formality.

Dusty pulled the cord that raised the blinds and glared at Victoria.

"Oh, it's you." Victoria turned away and ran her gaze over the many occupants of the main living room. "What was your name?"

Dusty stepped in front of her, blocking her view, but mainly concealing her from either Addison or Maggie if they happened to be close. "I asked you what you're doing here. What the hell are you doing in Maggie's house?"

"I'm here to celebrate All Hallows' Eve, same as you, I suppose." Victoria fluttered her lashes. "Well, maybe not *the same* as you. After all, we all have our own ways of celebrating, don't we?"

"And you're here to celebrate with some bloodsucking?"

Victoria smiled and flicked her gaze down Dusty's torso. "And you're celebrating…how?"

"I thought vampires had to be invited in."

"I was invited. By sweet Maggie herself." Victoria's civility evaporated. "Now get out of my way unless you'd like me to create a scene that would require an explanation of your rude behavior."

Dusty hesitated. The bitch had her. The last thing Dusty wanted was for anything about Victoria to need to be explained in the presence of Maggie. She wasn't sure if anything had actually happened yet between Addison and this viper, though she suspected it had. Over the past two weeks, Addison had worked late a number of times, and the previous weekend she'd been unreachable the whole time Maggie had been with Pete and Ricardo. "Leave Addison alone," Dusty said. "I'm sure you can find someone else to play with."

"I have no idea what you're talking about. I'm here by invitation to enjoy a party." Victoria stepped around Dusty. "If you'll excuse me."

Dusty sighed. She remembered comparing herself to this woman, but she'd never been this calculating, this deliberate. Did that matter? Was carelessness any better than callousness? She watched with a sense of dread as Victoria began to mingle.

Eve felt Sammi's hand slip around her own as they moved through the crowd of women and out the open sliding glass door. Her heartbeat quickened and she suppressed a burgeoning smile. She thrilled at the touch of Sammi's soft skin but didn't want to seem like an inexperienced schoolgirl. After all, she'd held hands before, been on dates, kissed, made love, all of it—she *was* an adult—just never with a woman. But, wow, did this feel different. She'd never been this excited at a mere touch, at the mere *thought* of a touch. Was she crazy? She laced her fingers between Sammi's.

Sammi grinned. "It's nice out here," she said, inhaling a deep breath. "I needed some air."

Eve looked up at the clear night sky and then turned to Sammi. "Would you like something else to drink?"

"Sure." Sammi smiled at her. "But a break from wine. Maybe just water."

"Okay, I'll be right back." As she crossed the patio, Eve considered that a bottle of water had been her and Sammi's first exchange a couple of weeks earlier at the park, and the connection they began that day had only deepened with their phone calls and a play date with the kids. She hoped Dusty was right, that the next step she wanted so much—their first kiss—would happen just as naturally. She returned from the ice chest outside the kitchen door and handed the water to Sammi.

Their fingers brushed again.

Eve's stomach fluttered. "I thought we could share," she said, realizing she sounded a little shy, and it felt like the boldest thing she'd ever said.

Sammi smiled. "I'd love to." She unscrewed the cap and handed the bottle back to Eve. "You first."

Eve took a swallow.

Sammi watched her. Then, with her eyes still on Eve, she took a drink of her own. "Your lips taste good," she said with a wink.

Eve felt herself blush. "And you're a flirt, but I like it."

"If you like that, you'll love my other talents."

"And what talents are those?"

"Well," Sammi said in a conspiratorial tone, "I make a mean bowl of oatmeal, and I can sing 'American Pie' all the way through."

"'American Pie?' Really?"

"Yep. I know all the words."

Eve giggled. "Actually, that *is* impressive. That's a really long song."

Sammi laughed. "Would you like to sit down somewhere?"

"That'd be nice."

They glanced around, taking in the occupied seats of all the patio furniture and extra chairs Maggie had set out then turned back to one another.

Sammi cocked her head and held out one hand toward the lawn. "Madam, would you care to join me on the grass?"

Eve giggled again. She had to stop that. "Lead the way." She followed Sammi to the far side of the yard and watched her take off her vest and spread it out on the ground.

"It's not an overcoat, but it's the best I have right now."

Eve sat on it and drew up her knees.

Sammi stared down at her, a soft smile shaping her lips. "I feel like I've waited so long for you."

Eve gazed up at her. "What do you mean?"

Sammi lowered herself to the ground. "Okay, I'm just going to say this." She inhaled deeply. "Three years ago, when I first came out and ended my marriage, I met Rebecca and all the girls in our group. I did some dating and some experimenting…" She paused and blushed. "You know?" Hesitation showed in her eyes.

"Of course." She didn't, really, but she could imagine.

"But even though I felt the excitement of being with women for the first time, I never felt any kind of real connection with anyone. It really upset me." Sammi looked down at the water bottle. "But all along, Rebecca kept telling me to be patient. That someone was on her way and it would be worth the wait."

Eve hoped she was right about where she thought this was going. She could tell that it was important to Sammi to be able to share her feelings, so she sat quietly, listening. She let her gaze travel down the curve of Sammi's neck, imagining the caress of the soft flesh if it could've been her fingertips or her lips making the journey.

"I hope this doesn't scare you, but I think I've been waiting for you." She looked at Eve, her expression genuine and nervous.

Eve's breath caught.

"Does it?" Sammi asked.

Not sure she could speak, Eve shook her head. It was only a little lie.

"I know this is all new for you, but I want to kiss you so bad." Sammi's voice was a mere whisper. "I know I should wait and let you—"

"No, don't." Eve heated with desire.

"Okay, I'm sorry." Sammi started to turn away.

Eve touched her cheek. "I mean, don't wait."

"Are you sure?"

Eve's heart pounded. She shifted her gaze from Sammi's eyes to her mouth.

The subtle movement seemed to be all the *yes* Sammi needed. She leaned in and feathered her lips across Eve's.

Eve gasped. Her lips were so soft, so sensuous. Arousal stirred deep in her center.

Sammi kissed her again, this time more certain, less restrained. Her mouth moved against Eve's. "You feel so right," she said, taking Eve into her arms.

Her hand still on Sammi's face, Eve stroked the smooth skin then combed her fingers into Sammi's hair. She sighed at the silken touch on her palm. She felt the gentle probe of Sammi's tongue parting her lips and opened to receive it.

The kiss deepened.

Need flared in Eve's body, engulfing every cell. She'd never felt so aroused. She slipped her arms around Sammi's neck and pressed against her. Sammi's breasts cushioned hers. For a moment, she lost all control. She kissed Sammi hard, demandingly.

Sammi moaned. She tightened her embrace and with an urgent thrust, found Eve's tongue with her own.

Eve's desire throbbed between her thighs, and her nipples ached as they grew harder with each passing second. She answered Sammi's moan with one of her own.

A peal of laughter from across the yard broke into Eve's awareness, reminding her where she was. She didn't want to stop, didn't want to let Sammi go, but if she didn't, who knew what would happen. Unless Sammi showed more control than Eve's libido was displaying, she'd have an embarrassing explanation to give Maggie and Addison as to how and why her first sexual experience with a woman became a party game. Reluctantly, she eased back, breaking the kiss. She gasped for air.

Sammi loosened her hold but didn't release her. "I'm sorry." She panted. "I didn't mean to get so carried away."

"Oh, my God," Eve said, still breathless. "That was incredible. I need a minute."

Sammi smiled. "Yeah, it was." She shifted around and settled behind Eve, easing her back against her. "*You're* incredible," she whispered in Eve's ear.

The sensation of Sammi's breasts like pillows against her back, and her thighs pressed around her hips, kept Eve's mind racing with thoughts of possibilities, and her body surging with arousal. She put her hands over Sammi's and leaned her head back against Sammi's shoulder. "I've never felt anything like this before."

"I know. It's something else, isn't it? The feel of a woman is like nothing I'd ever experienced either. But now that it's you…wow."

Eve wondered if that were true for her, too. Was the power of what she was feeling, her responses, just from the experience of being with a woman, or was it intensified because she really did feel a connection with Sammi? She guessed it was both, but how would she know for sure, or did it even matter? She just knew it felt so very right.

Sammi ran the tip of her tongue down the nape of Eve's neck.

Eve moaned and went weak. She tightened her thighs, feeling a flood of wetness between them. Could she take Sammi up to her bedroom without being noticed? She imagined Sammi on top of her, running that tongue between her breasts, around a nipple. As the vision became clear in her mind, she gasped.

Sammi caressed the curve of Eve's shoulder with her soft lips.

Eve wanted this woman, wanted Sammi's mouth on her breasts, parting her wet folds. But then what? Then…it would be Eve's turn. It would be time for her to reciprocate. Then what would she do? Her eyes snapped open, and she tensed. She didn't know how.

Sammi lifted her head and looked at her. "Are you okay?"

Eve sat forward to catch her breath. She nodded. "Yeah, I'm fine. Just a little overheated." She laughed. The need in her body raged against the fear in her mind. "Sammi," she said, "you feel so good, and I really want more, but I don't think I'm ready."

Sammi offered a sheepish smile. "I'm sorry. I didn't mean to push—"

"Oh. Please. Don't be sorry. I really want it. I just need more time." She shifted to face her and ran a fingertip across Sammi's lips.

Sammi kissed it. "Of course. The ball's in your court. We'll wait as long as you need to."

Even as she relaxed a little, Eve felt conflicted. What she really wanted was to create the reality of the picture she'd seen in her head—Sammi in her bed, Sammi touching, kissing, fondling her, Sammi bringing her to orgasm. Once again, the uncertainty of what would happen next shattered the fantasy. Dusty's words returned to her. *These things have their own movement, their own momentum. All you have to do is go along with it.* She wished she could, but she couldn't. She had to know more first. She traced Sammi's lips one more time then lowered her gaze. "Would it be too much for you to just hold me for a while? You know, like you were."

Tenderness shone in Sammi's eyes. "That'd be nice," she said.

Eve turned around and settled against her again. Aware of the heat of Sammi's body, of her own arousal, and wondering just how aroused

Sammi was as well, she decided to simply experience the moment, the feel of it.

Sammi wrapped her arms around Eve and sighed.

Eve felt the gentle breath touch her cheek. Everything about Sammi was soft, tantalizing. She definitely wanted more, more of what she'd already had and still more than that. She remembered the books in her room and set an intention to study. For now, though, she had to get her mind on something else.

She let her attention roam over the partiers in the backyard and those she could see through the windows. In the kitchen, she saw Addison and Maggie in their pirate and wench costumes refilling an empty tray. They talked as they worked and seemed to be enjoying one another's company tonight. She'd noticed since she'd moved in that wasn't always the case. Dusty, in her Boo Radley costume—Eve had to giggle inwardly in spite of herself—stood by the buffet in the dining room, chatting with a group of women. Eve suspected that many of them probably knew it was Dusty peeking through the slotted mini blinds and might be hoping for something more with her at the end of the evening. Eve also knew, though, that none of them had much of a chance. As she followed the trajectory of Dusty's body language, she confirmed that Dusty's only real interest was Tess, who stood at the other end of the living room, talking with a woman in an Elizabethan lady's dress. Was that JoAnn? Eve could understand Dusty's focus. Tess looked stunning, and from this vantage point, Eve could see just how many others thought so, too.

Another woman drew Eve's attention, though—a beautiful blonde in the sexiest vampire outfit Eve had ever seen. Her stare lingered. She would bet her life savings that *that* woman had no insecurities about how to please a female lover. She became aware, once again, of the need pent up in her body, of Sammi's embrace, her closeness. The excitement from their kiss and the delicious fantasy that still hovered in her mind rushed back in to claim her. She had to get control. She sat up. "Okay, I'm ready to hear 'American Pie.' Are you ready to sing to me?"

Chapter Fifteen

Addison finished rinsing out the kitchen sink and sighed. This Halloween party certainly was different from any of the others she and Maggie had thrown. She'd never fully realized how much work the catering crew did for these evenings. She intended to tip them even more generously come the annual Christmas party. As she grabbed a dish towel, she eased back against the counter and dried her hands.

She'd been in the kitchen or serving all evening so far and had little opportunity to socialize. Now, listening to the music, voices, and laughter filtering in from the other rooms and the open window, she remembered yet another of Dusty's quotes from her friend Rebecca. *We're always exactly where we want to be, doing exactly what we want to do, whether or not we realize it at the time*. Addison glanced out the window to where Rebecca sat at the patio table, laughing with a group of guests, and her partner, Jessica, leaning on the back of the chair and stroking Rebecca's hair. Addison had to admit that Rebecca was usually right. Maybe she was right about this, too. With everything going on between herself and Victoria—her guilt, her lack of control, the feeling that she was losing her mind as well as possibly the most important things in her life if she couldn't get a grip on herself—she didn't really feel like socializing tonight. So, here she stood in the kitchen.

She'd been with Victoria five times since that day in her office less than two weeks earlier, including the better part of the previous weekend while Maggie was supporting Pete and Ricardo through a rough couple of days. Even with all that, being with Victoria again was all she could think about. She was up in the Bay Area this weekend—something to do with hiring new staff—a fact for which Addison was eternally grateful ultimately, but even in her absence, the thought of her expert hands, full and supple lips, skilled tongue, and her tantalizing curves, kept Addison completely consumed with desire.

As her body responded to the thoughts, her gaze landed on Maggie. The now so very familiar pangs of guilt twisted through her. She wondered if they'd actually become a part of the arousal itself.

Hey, lover. She heard Victoria's sultry whisper in her mind. Instant need throbbed between her thighs. She squeezed her eyes shut. She felt her hand move from the edge of the counter toward the fly of her pirate costume. She caught herself. She wanted to touch herself, the way Victoria made her do while she begged for Victoria's strokes instead.

Go on, the voice in her head teased, now a murmur just above the whisper. *It'll be hot with all these people around.*

A soft moan rose in Addison's throat as she remembered the night she and Victoria had gone to a small, dimly lit restaurant and Victoria brought Addison to orgasm with her oh-so-experienced fingers while they sat at the table waiting for their meals. It'd felt so dangerous. It'd been so very hot. The pulse of her building desire pounded harder at the memory. She had to get some release. She opened her eyes and took a step toward the back entrance to the kitchen. She froze.

Victoria stood against the cabinets, a salacious curve to her delicious lips, amusement shimmering in her eyes. "Come on, lover. I know what you need."

Addison felt herself pale. Her worlds collided. Her needs, desires, wants, warred within her. She glanced out the other doorway at Maggie still chatting and laughing, then back to Victoria, a seductive vampiress clearly looking for prey. In any other circumstance, Addison would've dropped to her knees and given herself, but this was too much. Her mortal life she might've offered in exchange for the release she craved, but her life here in this house—her life with Maggie? "What are you doing here?" she whispered.

Victoria's smile broadened. "I was invited. Remember? You were there."

"But you said—"

"I realized it's my manager's job to hire waiters." Victoria grabbed Addison's hand and pulled her across the short distance between them.

"I don't want to talk about it. I like what you were thinking." She pressed her fingertips to the apex of Addison's thighs.

Addison gasped in both arousal and in fear. "Not here." The words came out in a hiss.

"Then take me someplace where I can." Victoria began a slow massage.

Addison's knees went weak. She grabbed her wrist. "Not *here*. Not in this house." She moved forward, pushing Victoria back so they were no longer visible from the dining and living rooms. They stood in a nook of the hallway just outside the bathroom.

Victoria slipped her fingers between Addison's thighs and leaned closer, her lips closing in on Addison's with the bearing of someone who hadn't heard a word.

"Victoria, no." Addison eased her back more. They broke contact.

Footsteps sounded on the teak floor, and a smiling Snow White passed them and went into the bathroom.

Addison gave her a polite nod, grateful she didn't know her. When the door closed, she grasped Victoria's arm and pulled her across the hall into Maggie's darkened office. Before either one could say anything, a low moan sounded from the corner, then a giggle. Two women emerged into the pool of light shining through the doorway.

Addison's florist, Monica, blushed. "Sorry," she said. "This is Jen, my new girlfriend I told you about. We're still in that glorious can't-keep-our-hands-off-each-other stage. Jen, this is Addison, our other hostess."

They exchanged pleasantries, all the while with Addison's awareness acutely honed in on Victoria. She flipped on the light. "This is Victoria, a client of mine. I was just giving her a tour of the house."

Victoria smiled and shook hands with the women.

The four of them made their way back into the hall and toward the entryway.

"We're really sorry, Addison," Monica said, her face flushed once again.

"No problem. I'm glad you're enjoying each other." Addison envied them the luxury of being able to do it without guilt. She smiled, thankful to be back out in the mix of her guests. She knew Victoria wouldn't do anything in the middle of the party. Would she?

As Monica and Jen moved away, Victoria grinned. "I like the idea of a tour of your house," she said. "I've seen everything downstairs. What's up here?" She danced up the first few steps.

"That's not funny. Come back down," Addison said, glancing around to see if anyone had noticed.

"But I really want to see. Your house is so beautiful." Victoria edged up two more steps, out of reach.

Addison's throat closed. She shut her eyes. "Victoria, please."

"Mmm. You know what begging does to me."

Addison flinched, her eyes snapping open. She had to get Victoria out of here. With feigned nonchalance, she moved toward the stairs.

Victoria turned and strode up to the second floor.

Addison's heart pounded. Victoria was playing her. Should she just let her go? What if Maggie found her wandering around up there, though? How would Victoria explain it? There was the other bathroom that was used by those who were more familiar with the house, Tess's bathroom, but what about the third floor? What if Victoria ended up there? Addison grimaced and hurried after her.

As Addison rounded the top of the railing, Victoria's arms slid around Addison's neck, and she kissed her full on the mouth. She snaked her tongue adeptly between Addison's lips.

Addison grabbed her shoulders and pushed her away. "Will you stop it?" she said, her voice almost a growl. She held her at arm's length.

Victoria smiled and softened in Addison's grasp. "You're not having fun?"

Addison sighed, a deep, exasperated sigh. "No, I'm not."

Victoria studied her. "I'm sorry. This must be difficult for you, having me here where you live with Maggie."

Finally feeling like Victoria was listening, Addison relaxed. "It is. So could we please go back to the party? And could you just mingle with the other guests?"

"Of course, baby. I'm sorry."

Addison stepped back to the top of the stairs and gestured for Victoria to go first. Her heartbeat began to slow. Her body still ached with desire, but at least her tension and fear were diminishing. She just needed to make it a little longer and everyone, including Victoria, would be heading home. Maybe she could convince Victoria to leave now. She opened her mouth to make the suggestion.

Once again out of Addison's reach, Victoria grinned. "What's up there?" she asked, darting across the corridor to the flight of steps leading to the third floor.

Before Addison could react, she saw Maggie round the corner below. She stiffened.

"There you are, dawtie." Her smile radiated with her inherent warmth. "What would you be doin' up there?"

Addison's mind raced. "I just have to use the bathroom. I thought I'd leave the one down there open." She was getting way to good at this lying thing.

"Okay, luv, but hurry. People are startin' to leave and wantin' to say good-bye."

"I'll be right there."

Still smiling, Maggie moved into the living room.

Addison returned her attention to Victoria just in time to see her dash up the steps. She swore and followed. She reached the top landing as Victoria stepped through the double doors of the master suite.

Victoria let out a low whistle. "Very nice, daw-tie." She drew out the endearment in mocking exaggeration.

Anger flared through Addison. She was surprised to realize how much she hated Victoria knowing anything intimate about herself and Maggie. She wanted her out of their bedroom. "Come on, let's go," she said, her voice hard.

"Ooooh, I like that. You're so forceful."

"I mean it."

"Come here and show me how much you mean it." A teasing glint flashed in Victoria's eyes. She backed further into the room. As she swayed, one leg slipped from the long slit in the skirt of her costume, revealing smooth skin all the way to her upper thigh.

Addison's abdomen clenched. Her breath came fast. She knew this sudden surge wasn't simply a response to the bare flesh. It was the whole package—the seductress, yes, but also the teasing, the risk, even her own anger, her desire to control Victoria, to put her in her place. She strode forward as Victoria continued backing away until Victoria's shoulders pressed against the armoire on the opposite wall.

Victoria grinned as Addison approached, a dark, dangerous flame smoldering in her gaze. She grabbed the front of Addison's shirt and spun them both around, slamming Addison against the wooden cabinet. She took Addison's mouth in a bruising kiss.

A part of Addison wanted to fight, wanted to push Victoria off her and out of her bedroom, out of her house, but her need raged, consuming all her willpower. Her anger and desire intertwined, combining to create something new, something dark. She surrendered to its force. She gripped Victoria's hips, flipped her around, and pinned her. She found the slit in Victoria's skirt, tore away the black lace panties, and sank her fingers deep into Victoria's center.

Victoria cried out and opened herself to Addison's thrusts.

After saying good night to Rebecca and Jessica and seeing them out onto the stoop, Maggie stood just inside the front room, watching Sammi sing the many verses of "American Pie." The girl not only knew all the lyrics flawlessly, but she also performed them with accompanying expressions and gestures that entertained the entire room. Those who weren't dancing on the folding wooden floor that covered the carpet for the evening sang along and cheered her on, but Sammi clearly sang only for Eve. Maggie smiled. *Young love.*

As Sammi continued, Eve simply watched. She appeared to be beyond the dancing, far past the amusement. Her shining eyes and beaming features held the fresh and tender sprouts of budding romance. In contrast to the first day Maggie had met her, she seemed completely at peace with her new knowledge of herself.

A hand rubbed Maggie's shoulder, drawing her attention.

"We're going to take off," Monica said, her arm around Jen. "Thank you so much. We had a great time. You and Addison are such a gift to give these parties every year for all of us."

"You're welcome. It's always our pleasure. If you wait just a second, Addison should be down." Maggie gestured toward the stairs.

"Oh, that's okay. She was still on the first floor of the tour when we saw her. She might be a while." Monica glanced to Jen. "We want to get home."

"Tour?"

"Uh-huh, she was giving one of her clients a tour of your house." Monica's answer was distracted.

Maggie tensed. Is that why Addison had been on the second floor? Why would she have lied about that? "Oh," she said with a casual air. "That explains where she is, doesn't it?"

Monica smiled. "Just give her a hug for us."

"I will." Maggie enclosed both women in a loose embrace. "Jen, it was so nice meetin' you."

As the couple made their way out, Maggie's gaze drifted to the top of the stairs. Had Addison been with someone when Maggie saw her? A client? She remembered Victoria Fontaine. Maggie had greeted her earlier after changing into her costume and returning to the party, but she hadn't seen her with Addison. In fact, Addison had spent most of the evening in the kitchen, keeping the serving trays filled. She had been a sweetheart. On the other hand, her lack of interest in interacting with their friends all evening fit with the general manner of reclusiveness she had been displaying for a while now. *Victoria Fontaine?* Could *she* be the reason—the one Maggie had suspected for several weeks? She was so young, though, practically a child. How could Addison…? An image of Victoria in her vampiress costume flashed in Maggie's mind. No, she was no child—and Maggie had invited her into their home.

She stiffened and heated with anger—but anger at whom? Victoria? Addison? Herself? She looked up the staircase. If they were up there, what were they doing? Surely, Addison wouldn't violate the home they had created together. Her jaw tight and her fists clenched, she started up the steps. Halfway to the second floor, she halted. Did she want to see it? Did she want to know? Right now, it was still a suspicion—a strong one, perhaps, but a suspicion all the same. Addison could still be her faithful partner. Schrodinger's cat came to mind. Until she opened the box, the cat could be alive. But *this* box was already open, she had to admit, this cat already dead. Addison had been lying to her for several weeks, and as much as she had tried not to know, deep in her heart, she did.

Slowly, calmly, she ascended to the second floor. Outside Dusty's room, she paused, listened. She took hold of the doorknob and turned it. She had seen Dusty downstairs moments earlier, so she knew she wouldn't be interrupting one of her trysts. Besides, to her knowledge, Dusty didn't conduct that faction of her personal life at home. But then, Maggie scoffed to herself, what did she know? The room was empty.

Maggie looked down the hall toward Eve's and Tess's rooms. Both doors stood ajar. The bathroom door was closed. As she took a step toward them, she heard a soft thud from overhead. She looked up in surprise.

Our room?

She went numb. Did she know Addison at all, anymore? Seemingly of their own volition, her feet carried her to face the truth.

Maggie stood silently in the doorway of their bedroom and watched. The scene seemed surreal—a sexy blonde kneeling before her enthralled lover. Maggie would have thought it beautiful if the enthralled lover were not *her own*, her life partner, the woman she had loved for so long. Addison stood still, her head thrown back and eyes closed, her shirt unbuttoned and Victoria's hands pleasuring her breasts. Her fingers twisted in Victoria's hair as she gripped her head and thrust her hips in an obviously desperate rhythm.

Maggie cleared her throat.

Addison's eyes flew open and she blanched.

Victoria looked over her shoulder and sat back on her heels. She wiped her mouth with the back of her hand. The antithesis of Addison's, her expression was cool, maybe even smug.

Maggie stared at the tableau. She had wanted to know, needed to know, and so…now, she did. Here it was, what she had always feared—Addison with another woman. Now what?

Well, she didn't have to be afraid any longer. The fear twisted, wriggled, morphed into anger. Suddenly, it didn't matter that she was older or that Addison hadn't gotten to play the field when she was younger. What mattered was that they had built a life together, one that Addison had wanted. What mattered was that when she had started feeling differently, she hadn't trusted Maggie enough to talk to her. What mattered was that she had brought her lover into *Maggie's* bedroom and violated that intimate space. A wave of rage threatened to engulf her.

She wanted to scream, maybe throw something, to set loose the fury within her—but she wouldn't. She wouldn't give this other woman the satisfaction. She would hold on. She steadied herself. "I don't really know the fittin' thing to say, but I *would* like to speak with my partner in private." Her tone was icy. Her gaze never left Addison.

Without a word, Victoria rose and moved toward the door.

Maggie pointed to the torn panties on the floor.

Victoria bent to retrieve them. "I—"

"Please leave my home," Maggie said, her anger seething just below her surface. She was mildly curious as to what Victoria could possibly have to say, but she was more interested in speaking with Addison.

Victoria left, almost sauntering.

Maggie found it more pathetic than irritating. When they were alone, she watched Addison for a long moment.

She had looked away when Victoria had risen, and now she just stared at the floor in front of her. She rearranged her clothing and buttoned her pants and shirt.

Maggie crossed the carpeted floor and sat on the end of the bed. She sighed. "Are you in love with her?" She knew the answer to this question would determine the rest of the conversation.

"No," Addison said without hesitation. "I don't think so."

Maggie nodded. "But you aren't sure?"

Addison raised her hands, looking helpless. She shoved her fingers into her hair and leaned forward. "I don't know anything right now, Maggie. I'm so screwed up."

"I can see that, dawtie." Maggie's heart ached. She had wanted to hear *No, I don't love her. It was just a fling, and it's over. I love you.* Wasn't that what happened in the movies? "But you are goin' to have to figure out what you want."

Addison straightened and met Maggie's gaze, her eyes filled with tears. "I know. I can't imagine my life without you, though."

Maggie felt a wry smile shape her lips. "I can't imagine mine without you, either, but sometimes we make different choices in spite of our feelin's."

With a pained expression, Addison knelt in front of her. "I don't know what to do. You've always been my rudder, my North Star. I couldn't talk to you about this, and that's why I got so messed up. I love you, but I know I can't promise to never be with Victoria again. I'm crazy with her. I think one thing, but do the opposite."

Maggie's stomach churned. "I can't help you with this, luv. I'm not willin' to. Find a therapist, a friend, a bartender. Just don't expect this of me." Her throat closed. "I'm hangin' on by a thread here."

Addison laid her head in Maggie's lap. "I'm so—"

"Don't," Maggie snapped. "Don't tell me you're sorry when you've just said you can't promise not to be with someone else. If you can't promise that, you need to leave until you can. And after doin' it in our house. In our room…"

Addison gripped Maggie's knees. She began to sob.

Resentment reared up in Maggie at the desire she felt to comfort Addison. She had never been able to see her in pain without wanting to console her. She fought the urge, then relented. She combed her fingers through Addison's hair. "Actually, luv, I *will* make this easier for you. I can't be with you while you're doin' this. I've been down this road before, and it isn't for me. I'm a one-woman woman, and I want the same. So, you go do whatever it is you need to do." She choked on the words. "And you decide what it is you want. If that's me, we'll see where we are. If it isn't…" Her voice almost broke, but she managed to keep it firm. "I'll always cherish the life we've shared."

After a bit, Addison's sobs softened and she lifted her head. She gazed at Maggie as though studying her features to remember them.

Maggie steeled herself. She didn't want to break down in front of Addison—she wouldn't. Her heart had already taken a huge hit, and she felt like a fool for ignoring the signs and her intuition. If nothing else, she would make sure her dignity remained unscathed.

After another moment, Addison rose.

Maggie watched in silence as she pulled some things from the armoire and closet and shoved them into her duffle bag, then disappeared into the bathroom to retrieve some toiletries.

When she emerged, she stared at Maggie until Maggie finally averted her gaze.

She heard the bedroom door close behind Addison, listened to her footsteps as she crossed the tiled landing to the stairs, and waited long enough to imagine her walking out the front door. She fell onto the bed and clutched a pillow to the ache in her chest, a hurt so deep it felt like her heart might actually stop beating altogether. Her stomach roiled as anger, devastation, and betrayal spread through her like poison. Her eyes burned with tears. She surrendered to the pain, and a sob tore from her throat.

❖

As Tess walked JoAnn up the hill to her car, she listened to a joke someone at the party had shared. She really did enjoy JoAnn's company, her sense of humor, her intelligence. In fact, if Dusty hadn't been so present this evening, she would have been content to spend the whole time with only JoAnn.

"And her partner whispered back, 'Honey, I think you need to change the batteries in your hearing aids.'" JoAnn delivered the punch line.

Tess burst out laughing. "Oh, that is so bad, I wish I didn't find it funny," she said, holding her hand to her mouth.

"I know." JoAnn chuckled. "I'll keep your secret if you keep mine."

"It's a deal."

They stopped beside the car, and JoAnn gazed into Tess's eyes. "I really enjoyed tonight."

"So did I."

"No, I mean it. I enjoyed seeing where you live and meeting your friends." JoAnn took Tess's hands in hers. "Thank you for inviting me as your date. I was the luckiest woman there."

Tess felt the heat rise into her cheeks and hoped the street was too dark for JoAnn to see the blush. "You're welcome. Thank you for coming."

"Oh, Tess." JoAnn sighed, her eyes closed. "You have to know I'd go anywhere with you." She slipped her fingers into Tess's hair and grazed her lips with her own. She paused and met Tess's gaze, then covered her mouth more firmly. Tess parted her lips, accepted the kiss, accepted JoAnn's tongue. She moved her own against it. The kiss was long and tender. She felt a slow arousal stir within her, but JoAnn's more ardent passion was evident in her soft moan.

Finally, JoAnn eased away, her breath slightly ragged. "I know," she said. "Slowly. I haven't forgotten."

Tess smiled and placed another light kiss on JoAnn's lips. "Thank you for that. And for a lovely evening."

As JoAnn pulled away from the curb and headed down the hill, Tess hugged herself in the night breeze. She knew she was being unfair, that the main reason she wanted to take it slowly was that she still wanted to hold on to what she shared with Dusty. If she was going to start something real with someone else, she had to let go of any fantasies she had, as well as the sex. No matter how good it was.

She sighed and began the walk back to the house. It could be over right now. In fact, it should be. All she had to do was not sleep with Dusty again. How difficult was that? It was entirely in her control. She had been on two dates with JoAnn. She shouldn't be sleeping with someone else. *Other women still sleep with other people if they aren't exclusive, though, right*? She would only be fooling herself, and she knew it. She would never fully give herself and JoAnn a chance as long as she still held on to her feelings for Dusty. Could it be over with Dusty, right now? That would make their last time together the night she had heard Dusty's motorcycle and met her on the stairs. That was a nice night. She had fallen asleep in her embrace. But she wanted to know that the last time was the last time while it was happening. She wanted to savor every moment of it. As she ascended the cement steps to the front door, she decided. There would be one more time—maybe tonight.

As she moved through the house, she noticed that very few people remained. Eve and Sammi were snuggled together on the sofa in the front room while another couple talked quietly in a corner. A few guests still mingled in the living room, and Tess saw the woman who owned the catering company stacking trays and other supplies to carry out to her car. She smiled and waved. Neither Addison nor Maggie were anywhere to be seen, which was unusual. Maybe they were upstairs. She stepped through the open sliding glass door and into the backyard and found Dusty with a large trash bag picking up bottles, plastic glasses, and paper plates.

Tess watched her.

With her costume no longer concealing her torso, a tight orange T-shirt hugged her lean frame and the soft curves of her breasts. Black jeans covered her narrow hips and the thighs Tess knew to be so firm. She felt the familiar burn of her attraction begin to simmer. She realized she would need to create some distance between herself and Dusty if she were to have any chance of getting over her feelings for her because it wasn't just the physical draw that kept her so fixated. It was Dusty's gentleness, her kindness, her generosity. It was the fact that she was out here cleaning up while everyone else was doing whatever they wanted to do, the fact that she would take Eve to a child's birthday party to show her the truth about her fears, the fact that she had kept Tess's secret for so long, when everyone expected nothing but bragging from her. Tess's feelings crested within her, and as she watched Dusty, she knew she had fallen in love. Maybe one last time wasn't such a great idea after all.

Dusty turned and caught Tess looking at her. They stood staring at one another for a moment before Dusty grinned. "Really?"

Tess blushed. "Really, what?" she asked, but she knew Dusty had seen her desire. Dusty knew her in that way better than anyone ever had, and maybe ever would.

Dusty laughed and glanced at the open kitchen window. "You want to help me clean up?" she asked, her tone low. "There's a lot of trash over here." She edged toward the dark corner of the house.

Tess hesitated. Was Dusty actually suggesting…? They had always had sex only in Tess's bed when everyone else was asleep or not at home—where it was safe. If this was going to be the last time, however, maybe she should be more adventurous, make it truly something to remember. She did want to end up in bed, though, to fall asleep one last time in Dusty's arms. Tess offered a playful smile and walked toward her. "Well, if you really need my help…"

With every step Tess took, Dusty's eyes grew hungrier. She licked her lips. "Oh, yeah. I definitely need your help," she whispered. When Tess finally reached her, Dusty coaxed her around into the darkness of the side yard.

Tess entwined her arms around Dusty's neck and allowed herself to be taken in a deep, sensuous kiss. Her body ignited in instant response. She recalled her slow, placid reaction to JoAnn's kiss and quickly pushed the memory from her mind. Passion would grow in time. With Dusty, she already knew what was coming, what to expect from her fingers, her mouth, her knowledge of Tess's body. The mere thought made Tess ache. She crushed herself to Dusty as she felt the hard wall against her back. She raised one leg, feeling it slip through the high slit of her skirt, the cool night air caressing her skin. She wrapped it around Dusty's hips and pulled her in more tightly.

Dusty moaned and tore her mouth from Tess's. She lowered her lips to Tess's neck and began an excruciating trail of nips and kisses down to her shoulder, slow and teasing. She slipped one hand down to where their mounds met and slid it beneath Tess's skirt. Her fingers brushed Tess's center through her silk panties.

Tess gasped. "I don't want to come here," she murmured into Dusty's ear. "I want you in my bed."

"Mmm. Yes." Dusty groaned against Tess's neck. "Anything. Anything you want." She stroked Tess's sex through the soft panel that covered it, then pushed the fabric aside. Her fingers moved through Tess's wet, hot folds to caress her hard clit.

Tess bit back a cry, but she knew Dusty wouldn't take her over the edge.

"Tess," Dusty murmured against her skin. "Oh, God, Tess." Her voice sounded as though it broke. "I have to tell you something."

"Ooooh." Tess arched into Dusty's caress. "Tell me."

Dusty ducked her head and pulled Tess even closer. "I'm in l—"

"Excuse me. I'm *really* sorry to interrupt."

Eve's voice barely reached Tess's awareness. Her arousal, Dusty's touch, the anticipation of her words…they were all too much.

Dusty groaned. Her hand slowing, she lifted her head. Her eyes met Tess's. "What is it?" she said to Eve. She even managed to sound polite.

"It's Maggie."

Dusty lowered Tess's leg and looked at Eve. "What about Maggie?" she asked with evident urgency.

Now fully present, Tess also took in Eve, who stood with her arms wrapped around herself, her shoulders drawn up tight.

"I don't know. Something's wrong. I think she needs you guys."

CHAPTER SIXTEEN

Dusty jumped at the knock on her door and shoved the book she was reading under the rumpled covers of her bed. A gentle rain kissed the windowpane beside her, a soothing sound that had allowed her to sink into the story, but after Addison's move to a hotel, following Maggie's discovery of her and Victoria the previous weekend, Dusty had a hard time believing that Rayann and Louisa, the characters of the romance novel, had much of a chance at love anyway. "Come in," she called.

"Can you open the door?" Eve's voice carried from the other side.

Irritated, Dusty swung her bare feet to the floor. She'd felt grumpy all week. She was so mad at Addison. She'd warned her repeatedly, and still she'd gone and been stupid. She opened the door and peered into the hallway.

Eve stood in jeans and a lavender sweatshirt, her long, chestnut hair damp as though she'd been outside. She held two large mugs of steaming brown liquid. "I made us some cocoa," she said with a hesitant smile.

"Why?" Dusty asked. She really just wanted to be alone.

Eve's smile faded. "I don't know. It's raining, and I thought it would be nice and cozy and…" She faltered. "I wanted to talk, okay? Can I just come in and talk to you?"

Dusty paused, then with an inner sigh, she stepped back and opened the door. Living with Eve was getting to be like having a kid sister who always wanted to hang out. What'd happened to the days when being at home meant having time to herself and no one wanting anything from her?

For the first few years, Maggie and Addison had been only her landladies, the other tenants people she didn't know who came and went with no disruption to her life. But then she'd let people in, she'd opened herself up, allowed herself to care—and what'd it gotten her? Addison, the one person in her life since her gramma who'd been a role model for what Dusty ultimately wanted to be, had turned out to be just as flawed as Dusty. Maggie, whom she loved like the mother she'd never known, though putting up a brave front, was sad, her strong spirit not broken but certainly suffering from a hard hit—and Dusty had failed her just as surely as Addison had. She'd known about Victoria and hadn't been able to do a dammed thing to stop it. And the one person Dusty would've wanted to be with right now had all but vanished. Tess was either with Maggie, which, of course, was understandable, or she was gone or locked in her room, working. Now here was Eve, settling onto Dusty's bed, handing her a cup of hot chocolate and wanting…what?

Eve stared at her.

"Okay, what?" Dusty's tone was sharper than she'd meant it to be.

Eve pursed her lips. "Are you mad at me?" she asked, her eyes wary. "Did I do something wrong?"

Dusty called herself into check. "No." She looked out the window at the wet day. Of course she wasn't mad at Eve—almost everyone else, but not Eve. She was mad at Addison, Victoria, herself, even maybe a little at Tess for being so absent right now. She knew, deep down, that Tess had no obligation to her, no reason to be doing anything other than exactly what she was doing. Dusty remembered her plan to tell Tess how she felt, that she was in love with her. How close she'd come that night. What a farce that'd been. If Maggie and Addison couldn't make it, she had about as much chance of having anything with Tess as a cat had of winning a dog show. Disappointment swelled within her. She rubbed her hand over her eyes to stop the burn of tears that threatened. "I'm sorry." She turned back to Eve. "What do you want to talk about?"

Eve glanced down into her mug. "I just feel so bad for Maggie. How could Addison do that to her? She loves Addison so much."

"I dunno." Dusty shrugged and took a sip of cocoa. She knew what Rebecca would say, *had* said at other times like these. *We're all here for the same reason, just to work out whatever it is we're here to work out. There is no right or wrong.* Dusty pushed the words away. She didn't want to hear Rebecca right now. She wanted someone to be wrong. She wanted to blame Addison. That way she could stay mad and avoid whatever was nagging at her underneath. "She's just being stupid."

Eve frowned. "I think it's awful what she did. I thought she was so nice and that her and Maggie's relationship was so strong. I never would have thought…"

Dusty stopped listening. She watched Eve's lips move but remained focused on her own musings. She was mad at Addison, yes, but still, Addison was her friend. It felt wrong to sit here and bash her. Of all people, shouldn't Dusty be the one to cut her some slack? She had no explanation for Addison's behavior, or for her decisions, given what Addison was throwing away, but Dusty had done her share of… what was the word…philandering? What a weird word. It sounded like such a happy word, but if this were the result, there was nothing happy about it.

"…she made a commitment." Eve rambled on.

Dusty recalled the first night she'd seen Addison with Victoria at Vibes and remembered her realization that she had done exactly what Victoria was doing, numerous times. Her guilt began to creep in again. As she felt it worm its way through her, she became aware there was no difference between being on Victoria's end and being on Addison's. Cheating was cheating, and wasn't cheating wrong? *There is no right or wrong.* It seemed to Dusty, though, that just made them both wrong, so she still had to be mad at Addison—and as much as one part of her wanted not to be, another part wanted to be. Jeez, she was confused. Eve's voice filtered in. She looked up and studied her. Why was *Eve* so mad? An idea struck her. "Hey," she said.

Eve's rant halted. She looked startled. "What?"

"Do you feel guilty for leaving Jeremy?"

Eve blinked. "Guilty?" She paused. "You think what I did is the same as what Addison did?" Her eyes narrowed and her anger now seemed directed at Dusty.

"No." She wondered if a less direct approach might've been better. "I don't think it's the same. I just wondered if you feel guilty."

Eve sat quiet for a moment. She pursed her lips. "Yes," she said finally. "I do." Her voice softened. "I made promises to him, and he believed me. And now it looks like I'm not going to keep them. So, yes, I feel guilty."

Dusty nodded. Okay, both she and Eve felt guilty.

"I thought at the time I'd be able to. I just didn't know myself." Eve sounded defensive. "Do you think Addison didn't know about this part of her?" Her expression seemed to beg for an answer.

With sudden understanding, Dusty knew she was no longer the baby of this family. She really did have a kid sister, someone who now looked to her the way she'd always gone to Maggie or Addison. She fidgeted. "I dunno. Maybe. I don't really have any idea what Addison's thinking, and I can't make myself care because I'm just so mad. So, I'm trying to figure out why I'm mad. Why I just want to judge her."

"Well…" Eve tilted her head thoughtfully. "What she did was pretty awful."

"Really? Was it?" Dusty watched the rain trickle down the window. "I mean, was it any more awful than anything I've done?" She felt herself flush. "I've slept with all kinds of women who were in committed relationships without caring who it might hurt. How do you think the partners of those women felt? But at the time, it never even occurred to me. I was just doing what I needed to do to feel better. I know more now, but then I didn't. And what about you? You're just doing what's right for you, what you need to do in order to work through your stuff and live a happy life. And, yeah, Jeremy's being great about it, but he has to be hurting some, don't you think?"

"Are you just trying to make me feel bad?" Eve started to turn away.

Dusty grabbed her arm. "No. I'm trying to figure out what I'm feeling, why a part of me wants to be mad at Addison, but another part thinks I shouldn't be. Maybe because I feel guilty for what I've done, I'm mad at her, but not really for what she's doing, but for showing me how what *I've* done looks and feels. Does that make sense?"

Eve furrowed her brow and tightened her lips. "I'm not sure. When you put it that way, it sounds like we're all just horrible, selfish people."

Dusty sighed. "Yeah, it does kinda, doesn't it?" She knew there was more to it, though. Something else, some other piece niggled around inside her, peeking out here and there. She needed help, she decided. She stood. "I gotta go."

Eve jumped up too, and a splash of her hot chocolate landed on Dusty's sheets. "Oh, I'm sorry." She dashed to the bathroom. "Go where?" she called over her shoulder. She returned with a towel and began patting the spill.

"Rebecca's," Dusty said, rifling through her sock drawer. "I need to talk to Rebecca."

Eve watched her. "Can I go?" she asked in true kid sister fashion.

Dusty chuckled. "Sure," she said, kind of liking her new role. "Can we take your car? Otherwise, we have to mess with rain gear."

❖

A half hour later, Dusty knocked on the front door of the condo where Rebecca and Jessica had lived for the past four years. Their relationship had seemed to appear out of nowhere. No one knew where it came from, except for them, of course. One minute Rebecca was still long-single, and the next, she was living with Jessica, a woman no one else had even seen before. That was how Rebecca did things, though. When she said yes to something, it was instant and sure, and it was lasting.

"Ya got that, Becca?" Jessica called from somewhere within the condo.

"Got it." Rebecca's answer came just as the door swung open. She greeted Dusty and Eve with her customary warm and inviting smile. "Look at the two of you. Getting to be good friends?" Her deep yellow lounge wear glowed gold against her dark skin.

Dusty glanced at Eve, feeling a little bad for her earlier irritation.

"Come on in," Rebecca said, not waiting for a response. She ushered them through the foyer. "Excuse the mess. Jessica's redecorating again." The smell of fresh paint thickened the air, and clear plastic covered the furniture, artwork, and hardwood floor of the living room. "She does it every six months," she said to Eve.

"Lies!" Jessica's voice sounded from behind the baby grand piano in the far corner.

"But it always looks beautiful," Rebecca said loudly. She raised an eyebrow at Dusty. "Kitchen," she whispered.

As Dusty and Eve settled in the tall chairs around the high table, Rebecca poured three cups of hot water from the kettle on the stove and placed them on a tray with a small basket holding a variety of herbal teas. She eased herself into one of the remaining seats. "What can I do for you ladies today?"

Dusty and Eve exchanged glances.

Eve dropped a tea bag into her cup.

"Nothing's right at home." Dusty blurted it out without realizing the words were on their way. She sounded like an eight-year-old, but then that's exactly how she felt—like a child whose home was falling apart. "Addison's gone. Maggie's hurt. The house is too quiet."

Rebecca reached across the table and squeezed Dusty's hand. "First of all, I've spoken with Maggie, and she's working out her feelings. She'll be fine. Secondly, nothing is actually wrong at home. Things are simply different."

Dusty's tension eased. She'd known that's what Rebecca would say. She'd just needed the reassurance of hearing it. Rebecca had a way of seeing things that made sense out of a world that seemed senseless. Dusty sighed. "I just wanna kick Addison's ass. Why am I so mad at her?"

"Why are you?" Rebecca asked. She took a sip of her tea.

"It was just such a stupid thing to do."

"Why was it stupid?"

"Because." Dusty stared at Rebecca. "She has Maggie and their life together. Why would she throw all that away?"

Rebecca rested her forearms on the edge of the table and held her cup in front of her. "Who says she's thrown it away? Perhaps Addison needs to experience this in order to learn something about herself or the life she's created with Maggie. Perhaps once she learns it, she'll be back. And if it turns out that life as it has been changes, then it's time for it to change—by Addison's and Maggie's decisions together. Neither one is a victim."

"What did Maggie do?" Eve asked, clearly confused. "Is she having an affair, too?"

"Not to my knowledge," Rebecca said. "But for her to be experiencing this, there would have to be a time in her life that she did something similar to someone else, and she must still feel guilty about it."

"I don't understand," Eve said.

Rebecca set down her tea. "Do you think the events of our lives take place at random? What we experience comes from what we believe and what we think. If we believe something will happen or we are afraid it will, we ultimately create it in our lives. If we fear something will happen, it is the result of guilt from when we did it, and we are afraid then it will happen to us. This isn't usually on a conscious level that we're aware of, but if you think about it—look at your own life—you'll most likely see an example of it. We do something. We feel guilty for it. Out of that guilt comes a fear it can happen to us, and from the guilt and fear, we create it. In essence, we project the guilt out and create the same circumstance for ourselves so we can see it and know what it feels like to be on the other end. Maggie has held on to some guilt and fears for years that now have come to fruition. So now she can choose to forgive the guilt. She can see there is really nothing to fear. That she'll be fine and *is* fine, no matter what, and that anyone she's done this to in the past must also be fine."

"Wow, I never would've thought of that," Eve said, her tone pensive.

"Maybe I'm just mad at myself," Dusty said.

"Ah, now we're getting to the heart of it." Rebecca smiled. "Why do you think you're mad at yourself?"

"For when I did things like this. Besides, I knew. I saw Addison with that woman at the bar. I knew what was happening, but I couldn't stop it."

Rebecca took Dusty's hand and held her in her loving gaze. "Of course you couldn't, sweetie. It wasn't yours to stop."

Dusty searched Rebecca's eyes. She relaxed into their tenderness, grateful to be told it wasn't her fault.

"This is just something Addison needs to do. There's something about it she needs to experience, something she needs to know that she can't know any other way. We don't have any idea what that is, and we don't need to. Our part, as her friends, is to love her through it and let her know she isn't alone. It's not to judge her. Don't you think she may need a friend right now, too?"

"Yeah," Dusty said slowly. "I thought of that, but a part of me wanted her to feel alone, like I think Maggie feels."

"That isn't your place. Besides, Maggie isn't alone. She's surrounded by loving friends, the two of you included. So *be* loving friends—to both of them."

Dusty looked at Eve and saw her own regret reflected in her eyes.

"And," Rebecca said, tapping Dusty's teacup. "You're actually mad at yourself for the first reason you tried to gloss over."

Dusty shifted her attention back to Rebecca. "I am?"

"Mm-hm. You're mad at yourself for doing the same thing, but you want to judge her instead of facing that. I'm going to take a wild stab here and guess that maybe it's all your own promiscuous behavior over the years that you feel guilty about, now that you've experienced something different. Addison is just showing you who you've been."

"Hey." Eve perked up and looked at Dusty. "That's what you said."

Rebecca laughed. "I'm glad to see you've been listening over the years."

Dusty frowned. "I've been listening. I just don't like it."

"And now I see what you were saying about me and Jeremy." Eve turned to Rebecca. "I was being really judgmental of Addison earlier, and Dusty asked me if I felt guilty about leaving Jeremy, which I do, to a degree. I feel guilty about leaving him, so I'm critical of Addison for not valuing her relationship with Maggie. Is that right?"

"Exactly."

Eve looked pleased, then hesitated. "So, what do we do?"

"Recognize you aren't doing anything wrong. There's nothing to feel guilty about. You're doing what you need to do in order to live an authentic life. You didn't know you're gay when you married Jeremy, did you?"

"No."

"How could you have done anything wrong if you didn't know?" Rebecca's tone was gentle. "Even if you had known, if you could have done it differently, you would have. We always do the best we can with what we know at the time. And, Dusty, we've talked before about you needing all those women in order to feel connected because you weren't ready yet for any kind of real emotional connection. You were just doing the only thing you knew at the time. Addison's doing the same."

"But didn't Addison know better? She knew she promised to be faithful to Maggie. She knew better, but she cheated on her anyway."

Rebecca looked thoughtful. "If you mean she knew the promise she made to Maggie and that she was breaking it," she said, "then, yes, she knew better. But if you take into account that sometimes we have to experience things in order to learn what we need to learn from them, and that often we don't know what that is until after the fact, then perhaps she didn't, actually, *know better*."

"But she did it in Maggie's bedroom," Dusty said.

Rebecca smiled softly. "That certainly upped the emotional charge and got everyone's attention, didn't it? We don't know how they ended up there, but knowing Addison, I doubt very much she deliberately set out to violate her and Maggie's private space. Do you think so?"

Dusty thought of the Addison she knew. *Of course not.* She shook her head.

"Sometimes that level of emotional charge forces us to look at things we were happy avoiding. The bottom line is that there might be a lot of things about it we might never understand, and we don't need to, as I said before. Maggie and Addison certainly have some things to look at, and they're both doing the best they can with it. And you two, given your closeness to the situation, also have the opportunity to let go of your own guilt for things you feel you've done. The most important thing you can do is just love everyone involved."

Dusty nodded.

"And when you recognize that and let go of the judgments of yourself, then, and only then, can you see Addison differently. I want to add, though," Rebecca said, the timber of her voice lowering. "You're also mad at Addison because she's doing what she set up for herself to do and you're *not*, at the moment."

"What do you—"

"You know what I mean." Rebecca gave Dusty a pointed look.

Tess flashed in Dusty's mind. She flinched. "You mean Te—" She glanced at Eve.

"Oh, who do you think you're fooling? I know about you and Tess." Eve laughed. "I saw you coming out of her bedroom the first week I was there. Remember?"

"You haven't spoken with her yet, have you?" Rebecca asked.

Dusty shifted in her seat. "Well, no. I've tried, but every time—" A smirk from Rebecca cut her off. "No, I haven't."

"And yet, even as difficult as it is for Addison and Maggie to move through what they're doing, even though it's a huge risk for Addison…" Rebecca paused and raised a questioning eyebrow.

"Yeah, yeah, I get it. She's at least doing something, and I'm not. And that's really why I want to be mad at her."

"Wow," Eve said as though she'd just been shown the way to Eden.

"And you're in the same boat, little missy." Rebecca pointed at Eve with a teasing grin. "What is all your feet dragging about with Sammi?"

Dusty snorted.

"I—" Eve blushed. "I just don't—"

"Mm-hm," Rebecca said, leaning back in her chair. "You just don't. Both of you girls need to get busy with your own paths, and believe me, you'll have a lot less time to be judging someone else who's actually walking hers." Her tone was loving but still drove home her point.

After sharing tuna sandwiches and fruit salad with Rebecca and Jessica and helping with the clean up of the brushes, rollers, and drop cloths, Dusty and Eve said their good-byes and stepped out into the afternoon. The rain had stopped, and the sun peeked out from behind the remaining gray clouds.

Dusty felt as cleansed as the crisp air and took a deep breath. She could always count on Rebecca to clear things up. She made up her mind to call Addison as soon as she got home.

CHAPTER SEVENTEEN

Eve stepped into Sammi's arms and returned a long, languid kiss.

"I've been thinking about that all week," Sammi whispered when their lips parted. "The first kisses are great, but after that, you always know exactly what you're missing."

Eve smiled. She slipped her fingers into Sammi's thick, hair. "Can I show you again what you've been missing?" She was no longer uncertain about this part.

"By all means." She pulled Eve close.

They stood in Sammi's living room, exploring each other's lips and tongues, their mouths making love the way Eve hoped—no, knew—they would do with their bodies someday. In Sammi's embrace, she lost all sense of time.

Sammi drew away. "I need to stop or we're going to have scorched zucchini soup for dinner."

Eve looked into Sammi's gray eyes and saw her own desire reflected back to her, but she accepted the graceful segue into the evening ahead. "Is there anything I can do to help?" she asked.

"You can chop vegetables." She took Eve by the hand and led her into the kitchen. "I meant to have the salad already made, but Nick was late picking up Melissa, so I'm running behind."

"I'd be happy to." It would give her something to focus on besides everything she wanted to do with Sammi but was too afraid. She took in the soft contours of Sammi's body beneath her charcoal gray cashmere sweater and blue jeans. The heat from their kisses continued to simmer.

Sammi stepped around her and set a bag of ingredients for a green salad on the counter. She pressed her lips to Eve's neck. "Thanks. The knives are right there." She pointed to the block in front of Eve.

Before Eve was halfway through a head of romaine lettuce, Sammi set a wooden bowl beside her and returned her attention to the pot on the stove. They worked side-by-side comfortably, and Eve began to relax.

"How was your time with the boys?" Sammi asked, stirring the soup.

"It was fun. We went to Chuck E. Cheese's for dinner," Eve said. "They love it there."

Sammi's eyebrows shot up. "On a Saturday night? Wow, you get Mom of the Year for that one." She laughed.

"Yeah, it was a little crazy." Eve smiled. "But as soon as I got to the house, Daniel turned on the charm, and Enos put on his pleading puppy-dog face. I never had a chance."

Eve had spent the previous night and all that day with the boys until it was time for her date with Sammi. It always felt so right to be with them for those extended periods, and she no longer worried about whether she would ever live with them again. It was just a matter of figuring out where and working out the logistics with Jeremy.

They'd had a little time to talk that afternoon when he'd returned home and the boys were busy playing video games. Eve could tell that something had shifted. At first, she thought it was between them, but after a while, she realized it was simply within her. She felt at peace—with the direction her life was taking, with the awareness she would never share a home with Jeremy again, and with the ending of their marriage. Discovering and admitting that she'd been feeling guilt had allowed her to release it, to acknowledge to herself she truly wasn't doing anything wrong. She'd simply learned more about herself and was doing what she needed to do to live honestly. She'd always be so grateful for her conversation with Rebecca the previous afternoon and for everything that'd had to come together in order for it to take place—Aunt Carolyn introducing her to Maggie, meeting Dusty through that, Dusty taking her to Seth's party…She was beginning to marvel at the way life worked, the way it conspired for everyone's good. She trusted this next part would go just as naturally if she kept out of her own way.

She'd been leaning against the tiled counter in the kitchen she and Jeremy had remodeled together, watching him work beside her.

"What's up?" he'd asked. He pushed the bicycle inner tube he'd just inflated into the sink full of water. The blue and gold UCLA T-shirt he wore stretched across his swimmer's shoulders, reminding her of the strength of his embrace.

"You know, don't you?" she asked, already certain of the answer. "You've known all along."

There was the slightest hitch in his movement as he ran the tube through his fingers, searching for the leak. "Know what?"

"That we're…" Eve hesitated. "That you and I are over."

Jeremy stilled, gazing down into the sink. When the bubbles broke the surface of the water, he smiled.

Eve retrieved a towel from the drawer behind her and handed it to him.

He began to dry the inner tube. He turned to face her. "I hope we aren't over." The lenses of his steel-rimmed glasses magnified the brown flecks in his green irises. "I hope we're just…" He shrugged.

Eve remembered Rebecca's comments about Maggie and Addison. "Letting our relationship be different?" she asked.

"Yeah." He nodded. "That's a good way of putting it."

Eve sighed. "I just can't help but wonder why you don't hate me. I've talked to other women in similar situations, and their husbands—"

"If I hate you, I lose my best friend in addition to my wife, and I don't want to lose you as my best friend." He brushed a few strands of hair from her forehead. "But mostly, I really want you to be happy. And, yes, I've known for a while that I'm not the one who can do that for you."

"You really are my best friend, too. You know that, don't you?"

"I do," Jeremy said quietly. "And because we're friends no matter what else happens, and because of those two great boys in the other room, we're going to be fine."

Eve nodded and squeezed his hand. "I believe that."

"And now, I've lost the leak again, so I have to start over." He shook the inner tube at her.

Eve laughed. "And I need to run. I—" Eve stopped herself. Could she tell him she had a date? He *was* her best friend, and she'd wanted to tell him about Sammi, but she thought it too soon—for both of them. She didn't even know where Sammi's and her relationship might end up, and Jeremy…Was he ready to know she was already dating someone?

"Daniel told me about Sammi," he said, as if reading her mind. His hands were back in the water.

"Well, that certainly hasn't changed," she said, embarrassed. "You still know everything I'm thinking. When did he tell you?"

"A few weeks ago, after you took them to the park with Sammi and Melissa. It's actually Melissa he couldn't stop talking about, but I put the rest together." Jeremy lifted the inner tube from the sink, this time holding his finger over the hole. "I'm not ready to hear a lot about it, but I'm glad you've met someone you like."

That was Jeremy, genuine and to the point.

With an inner smile, Eve brought her thoughts back to the present. She glanced at Sammi. "What did you and Melissa do today?"

"Since I'm working twelve-hour shifts the next three days and she's with her dad until Thursday, she got to pick how we spent our day." Sammi's cheeks turned red. "We played princess dress-up."

Eve grinned. "I would've loved to have seen that." She knew it was Melissa's favorite game, one that Sammi consistently tried to dissuade, but Melissa usually won. "Which princess were you?"

"Snow White, of course." Sammi fluffed her dark brown hair. "Lissa's very picky. I wanted to be Cinderella this time, but she says I have the wrong coloring."

Eve laughed and sliced a cucumber onto the lettuce. "I think it's so funny you ended up with such a little girly-girl."

"My mother says it's Karma for me being such a tomboy when she wanted me in all the frilly dresses that she loved." Sammi added some basil to the soup. "At least it gives the two of them a common bond. You should see my mom all decked out. She makes a great Fairy Godmother."

"She doesn't get to be a princess?" Eve asked in surprise.

"Oh, no. Lissa told her she was too old," Sammi said, imitating Melissa's serious tone.

"Ouch." Eve giggled. "That's so harsh."

"Yeah, I guess I should consider myself fortunate." Sammi chuckled. "I have a plan, though."

"What's that?" Eve reached for a tomato and cut it in half.

"As soon as she's a little older, I'm going to introduce her to Xena." Sammi raised her eyebrows. "*That's* the princess *I* want to be."

Eve looked at her, intending a humorous response, but her mind went blank as she pictured Sammi in the tight, low-cut bodice, short skirt, and wrist cuffs the warrior princess wore, a sword and shield in hand. Her simmering desire rekindled. "I could see that," she said softly.

Sammi flashed a sexy smile. "I can see you'd *like* that." She stepped forward and held a spoon to Eve's mouth. "Here. Taste."

Eve parted her lips and took in the thick, hot soup, her gaze locked on Sammi's. Flavor exploded on her tongue. "Mmm, that's good."

"Maybe I'll go to next year's Halloween party as Xena for you."

Next year? Would they be together next year? Eve swallowed the soup. Its warmth mingled with the heat already stirring in her belly. She didn't want to have to wait until next year. Ever since she'd begun reading on the subject of lesbian sex, her fantasies had gone berserk. In this very moment, she could see Sammi in the costume, coming toward her, grabbing her, taking her. She had a flash of Sammi pushing her down on the bed, pinning her, and moving over her, but it vanished when it was replaced by the reality of Sammi's lips on hers, her tongue moving in Eve's mouth. Eve dropped the knife she'd been using onto the counter and turned fully into Sammi's arms. She pressed her body against hers and lost herself in the flame of both their need.

Eve moaned and slid her hands over the small of Sammi's back. The sweater slipped up, and her fingers grazed soft flesh.

Sammi gasped, then deepened their kiss.

Eve couldn't stop touching her. She slid her hands underneath the cashmere and stroked warm skin.

Sammi thrust her hips and tightened her hold.

Eve felt a hand slip beneath the tail of her cotton blouse. It was as though time stood still as she waited…waited…waited…for that first touch of Sammi's fingers on her bare flesh—the first time a woman would touch her there. When it came, Eve cried out into Sammi's hungry mouth.

They kissed hard, ground their bodies together, moaned and panted as each caressed the other.

Eve's hands moved upward, her fingertips grazing the hooks on Sammi's bra. It was surreal, so very different from anything she'd ever experienced. Her own nipples hardened as she thought about Sammi's breasts. She ran her fingertips over the strap, tracing the edges. She stroked between Sammi's shoulder blades, feeling the play of firm muscle beneath the delicate flesh. She felt tears burn her closed eyes. A soft whimper escaped her throat.

Sammi's hands explored Eve's back, more boldly, but gentle in their strokes. She bit Eve's lower lip while her fingers trailed up Eve's sides, inching close to her breasts then retreating. With a groan, she wrenched her mouth from Eve's. "God, I want you," she whispered in a rush.

"I want you, too. Now." She thrust her hips into Sammi's.

Sammi's eyes widened. "Really?"

"Yes." Eve captured her mouth again.

"Are you sure?" Sammi murmured against Eve's lips.

"Yes." Eve moaned. "Yes. Yes."

Sammi's body lurched, and she crushed Eve between herself and the counter. She moved to Eve's neck and kissed and nipped.

Eve threw her head back, aching for more.

Sammi's tongue, her lips, her teeth blazed a trail down to the hollow of Eve's throat before she moved along her collarbone. Her blouse inched open. Need throbbed between her thighs in rhythm with the hard pulse in her temples.

Sammi's fingers worked the buttons of her shirt. As her mouth moved lower, cool air caressed the moist skin it left in its wake.

Eve imagined that hot mouth on her stiff, aching nipples. What she had been waiting for, without even knowing it, was about to happen, was already happening. A woman was making love to her. Her body raged. It burned. She released a deep sob of exhilaration. Tears flooded her eyes.

"Oh, my God." Sammi gasped, her mouth suddenly gone, her hands still. "I'm so sorry."

"Noooo." Eve pulled her back. "Don't stop."

"But what's the matter? You're crying." Sammi wiped the wetness from Eve's cheeks.

"Please don't stop." Eve grasped Sammi's face and pulled her mouth back to hers. "Kiss me. Please. Don't stop. It's just so incredible."

"You mean you're crying because it's good?" Sammi sounded bewildered.

"Yes." Eve moaned, her pulse still throbbing, her nipples still aching. "So good." She slid her tongue between Sammi's lips. She wanted Sammi's mouth where it'd been, doing what it'd been doing, going to where it'd been going. She guided Sammi lower.

"Wait a minute," Sammi whispered just as her lips were about to touch the swell of Eve's breast.

"I don't want our first time to be up against a counter."

Why not? Eve's body screamed. Up against a counter, on the floor. Who cared? "Just do it, Sammi. Please. I need you."

"Come to my bed with me?" Sammi's voice was husky, filled with lust. Her eyes burned into Eve's.

"Yes," Eve said, but in that briefest of pauses, her doubt reared its slimy little head. What if she didn't do it right?

Sammi smiled. She took Eve's mouth in another deep, thirsty kiss.

Eve's mind went blank.

Sammi reached over and turned off the burner beneath the soup, then wrapped an arm around Eve's shoulders and guided her out of the kitchen. As they crossed the living room, the doorbell rang. Sammi froze. She looked at the front door, clearly thinking about ignoring it.

A tall blonde waved through the glass panel beside it. Her smile lit her face.

"I knew I should've taken those windows out when I bought this place," Sammi grumbled. She looked to Eve. "I'm sorry."

Eve smiled and gave a small shrug. While her body still thrummed with arousal, she couldn't help but wonder who the woman was.

Sammi opened the door. "Hi there," she said with a casual air.

"Oh," the blonde said, her smile dimming. "I know that look." She glanced at Eve. "I'm sorry. I didn't mean to interrupt anything. I left you a message on your machine. Did you get it?"

"No. I guess I didn't check it."

"Oh. Last time we talked, you said you had some things I left here and I could come by to get them anytime. I was out this way today, so I thought I'd swing by."

"Oh, yeah, sure." Resignation tinged Sammi's voice. "Come on in."

"It smells good in here," the blonde said, looking at Eve. "Isn't Sammi a great cook?"

Eve wouldn't know, she realized. She'd been in Sammi's life for about a minute and a half. And this woman, how long had she known Sammi? And who was she?

Sammi shifted her gaze to Eve. "Eve, this is Janet. Janet, this is Eve."

"It's nice to meet you," Eve said.

"Nice to meet you, too, Eve."

"I'll get your stuff," Sammi said to Janet. "Be right back," she added to Eve, her jaw muscles a little tight.

Alone with Janet, Eve flinched. "I'd better check the soup." She moved toward the kitchen. "Again, it was nice meeting you."

"Same here," Janet said as Eve retreated.

In the safety of the next room, Eve hugged herself. Her mind flooded with unwanted thoughts and questions. Was Janet one of the women Sammi had slept with? Why else would she have things that she'd left here? And if she had *things* here, it had obviously happened more than once. To have *things* here and to feel comfortable enough to just drop by without Sammi returning her call, she must've been pretty comfortable here. And confident. One of those women who was confident in bed as well, Eve was sure. She looked the type.

What'd she been thinking? She'd almost ended up in Sammi's bed. Sure, it would've been great as long as Sammi was fulfilling all of Eve's fantasies, thrilling Eve with her touch—she remembered Sammi's hands on her flesh—but sooner rather than later, Eve would've been expected to fulfill Sammi's fantasies as well. Then what? Eve had been an idiot, letting herself get so out of control. Now, without Sammi's hands, her lips, her tongue on her, without Sammi's body rubbing against her, she could reason again. She wasn't ready. She didn't know how. She didn't know if she'd ever be ready for her first time. She was falling in love with Sammi, she knew that, and she couldn't stand the thought of her being disappointed with their first time together.

She thought of Jeremy. She'd been a virgin when they met and they'd been so young. She hadn't known anything about pleasing a man when they'd first slept together, and that'd worked out fine. They'd learned together, though, she reminded herself. He hadn't known much more than she had, really. This was different. Sammi had been with other women, women like Janet.

Eve didn't want to screw this up. Maybe if her first time was with someone else, someone with whom it didn't matter so much, so she could learn some things, then she would have something to offer Sammi.

Eve heard soft murmuring from the living room. She moved a little closer to the doorway.

"I'm really sorry for interrupting," Janet was saying again.

How did she know she'd interrupted? She'd been with Sammi, that's how. She recognized that look that Sammi got when she was aroused—even Eve knew *that* look already. Janet had been here, right here in this house, in the same bed Eve and Sammi had been on their way to. Eve moved back to the stove and turned up the heat under the soup, then finished the salad. "I think we're all set," she said when Sammi came back into the room.

Sammi stilled. She studied Eve. "I don't suppose we can pick up where we left off?" she asked quietly. She ran her fingers through Eve's hair, pulling it back from her face.

Eve turned to her, offering an apologetic smile. "I don't think it's a good idea."

"It seemed like a really good idea at the time," Sammi said, but the look in her eyes revealed that she knew a crucial moment had passed.

Eve took Sammi's hand and kissed the palm. "Yeah, it did. But…"

Sammi sighed. "Okay then. Dinner it is."

Later, after they'd finished eating and had cleaned up the dishes, Sammi placed the VHS they'd planned to watch in the machine. It was one of her favorites she wanted to share with Eve.

Eve couldn't remember the name of it. She couldn't remember much of anything with her head still cluttered with the memory of how free it'd felt to be heading to Sammi's bedroom and thoughts of Janet and all the other women in Sammi's life like her.

Sammi eased down beside her. She looked at the remote in her hand. "Can we talk about earlier?"

Eve didn't know what she could possibly say about it. She was so embarrassed. "Which part?"

"All of it. I mean, what happened?"

Eve hesitated, hoping some words would come to her. "I just…I got carried away, ahead of myself. It just all felt so good, I couldn't stop."

"Then why did we need to? You're right. It felt so good. You seemed so ready. If we'd just started again after Janet left, we would've been there again in a minute."

Eve stared straight ahead. Could she tell Sammi the truth? If she did, she knew Sammi would promise her that it was okay, she knew it was Eve's first time, et cetera, et cetera, because that's how Sammi was. She'd be accepting, she'd be reassuring, and in the end, she'd be disappointed. She'd never say a word, though, and Eve wouldn't be able to face her.

"I'm not pushing you, honey," Sammi said when Eve remained silent. "I'm just trying to understand."

Eve turned sideways to face her and rested her arm on the back of the sofa. She drew her legs up under her. "I know you're not pushing. You're being so great," she said. "I'm just still not ready. I know it seemed like I was, and I really was physically. Believe me." She felt a flash of heat course through her body at the mere thought. "But emotionally, I'm still not."

Sammi released a deep sigh and the concern left her eyes. "So, it's not that you were upset about Janet?"

Eve tensed at the mention of the name.

"Because I'm not seeing her anymore, I swear." Sammi's words tumbled over one another like squabbling bear cubs. "It's been a long time since I saw her. I'm not seeing anyone but you."

Eve blinked. Sammi thought she was jealous. She supposed she was in a way—jealous that Janet knew how to satisfy her, how to give her pleasure. It'd never occurred to Eve that they might still be seeing one another. She smiled. "I didn't think that," she said, taking Sammi's hand in hers. "But was she…"

"Was she what?" Sammi's tone was tender. She relaxed against the back of the couch.

Good in bed? Eve wanted to ask, but she stopped herself. She couldn't ask that. What a tacky question. "Was she important to you?" she said finally.

A deep blush overtook the easy set of Sammi's features. She shrugged. "Not really. Not in the way you probably mean." She looked at Eve. "You know, I was pretty shallow when I first came out. No one I dated was very important to me for anything other than sex."

"You and Janet just had sex?" *Just?* Eve scoffed at herself. Who was she to diminish it? *She* couldn't *just have sex*.

Sammi nodded.

"How did that work with Melissa?"

"She never met Melissa. None of the women I dated met her. I only saw them when she was with Nick." Sammi coaxed Eve to her and cradled her head in the hollow of her shoulder. "I told you, you're the one I've been waiting for. You're different. I knew it was okay for you to meet Melissa."

Eve listened, knowing the weight of those words. They should've eased her fears, comforted her. Instead, she felt their pressure as they were piled one on top of another. She *had* met Melissa. Melissa had liked her. The boys had liked Sammi. Daniel, apparently, had really liked Melissa. And all of them could end up disappointed if Eve couldn't figure out what to do with a woman in bed. There had to be a manual somewhere.

Then she remembered her earlier idea—learn with someone else. After all, Sammi had slept with a bunch of women. That's how she'd learned. Eve only wanted Sammi, though. So she wouldn't sleep with *a bunch*. Maybe she could find just one, one who was experienced, good in bed. But she didn't know very many lesbians.

She felt Sammi's lips on her hair, her hands stroking her back. Eve's desire pulsed through her. It had to be soon.

One lesbian, Eve thought, who's experienced in bed. Someone she knew.

Dusty.

CHAPTER EIGHTEEN

Tess ran a brush through her hair and coaxed a few errant strands back into place. As she studied herself in the mirror of JoAnn's downstairs bathroom, she realized how much more often she wore her hair loose instead of in the tightly wound braid she had kept it in for so long. She noticed how its waves around her face softened her features and more fully brought out the lushness of her brown eyes—her mother's eyes. She knew this seemingly minor change in hairstyle reflected a more profound difference in how she expressed herself and knew she had Dusty to thank for this shift.

Dusty had given her that space to explore herself, the safety to let go, to decide who she wanted to be in any given moment. Tess now understood it was through that exploration of so many different possibilities that she had come to realize she didn't have to be just one way. She could allow herself to flow more easily, more fluidly, through life.

JoAnn was the one who had brought it to her attention. One afternoon when they had been strolling through CityWalk Mall following a long lunch at the Hard Rock Cafe, Tess had kicked off her shoes and run into the sidewalk fountain where a group of children were playing. She hadn't even known herself in that moment. She'd had no idea she was going to do it until she was standing in the midst of the shoots of water.

Three little boys squealed and pointed at her in evident surprise.

She splashed them then ducked their return assault. She spun and laughed. "Come on," she called to JoAnn.

JoAnn scoffed. "This blouse cost a hundred and twenty-five dollars. I'm not ruining it by running through a fountain."

It was only then that Tess remembered her own silk top and suede purse. She didn't care. They could be replaced. This moment with these particular children would never come again.

"That's one of the things I love about you," JoAnn told her later. "You're so free."

Me? Free? Tess had been stunned. That was the main complaint Alicia had voiced about her, that she never let go. Alicia had tried and tried. She had coaxed Tess, nagged her, even attempted bribery at times. "If you'll run with me out into the waves with your clothes on, we can go anywhere you want for vacation." Or, "Hey, that's our song," she pointed out one day in the grocery store. "Dance with me right here and I'll buy you that watch you liked."

Tess would never do those things, could never bring herself to do them. Now, she found herself doing things she never would have dreamed of before, and it was because of Dusty.

Dusty hadn't nagged or bribed, though. She had merely been herself and let Tess be the same. At first, Tess simply watched. One afternoon in the backyard when Baxter was just a puppy, Kristin, a previous housemate of theirs, had been scolding him and shooing him away from her. Without hesitation, Dusty had called the puppy to her, dropped to the grass on all fours, taken the other end of his tug toy between her teeth, and begun to growl. The first genuine laugh since Alicia's death found its way up through the layers of Tess's grief. Kristin rolled her eyes, frowned, and went into the house. Dusty hadn't seemed to notice anything.

Tess wondered if seeing Dusty be so free, in everything she did, had enabled Tess to muster up the courage for that first time she had kissed her. Even that was so unlike her, and yet, it was from there that connection between them had been created, allowing Tess the freedom to play and to explore sexually. It had built Tess's confidence, her comfort with herself. And now, in so many other ways, so many places in her life, she no longer felt the need to remain so controlled.

She returned to the moment and smiled at her reflection. She was a new woman in many ways. She had decided the night of the Halloween party it was time to move forward, and though she had been disappointed when she and Dusty had been interrupted, she took it as a sign. In the two weeks since, she and JoAnn had been on several more dates and were enjoying getting to know one another on a more personal level. Tonight, however, was the first evening they had spent in the privacy of JoAnn's home. Dinner had been delicious, the wine relaxing and seductive, JoAnn inviting. With all that, Tess still felt reluctant.

Her body was ready, no doubt. It tingled from the drink, the intimate setting, even the brush of fingertips and lips throughout the evening. Deep down, though, she still wished it were Dusty. In truth, even one month earlier, she would have invited Dusty into her bed tonight when she got home. A memory of those familiar lips, those skilled fingers that knew her so well, prowled the outskirts of her mind like a hungry wolf. She quickly banished it. That was over and those recollections a luxury she no longer permitted herself. She wouldn't sleep with JoAnn while she still wanted it to be Dusty, but she *would* keep her attention on the lovely woman who clearly cared for her so much. Surely, she would get over Dusty soon. After all, as much as she had enjoyed what they had shared and grown from it, Dusty wasn't someone she could have. With that final reminder, she dropped her brush back into her purse and left the bathroom.

She lingered in the living room doorway and watched JoAnn light an array of candles in an elaborate brass holder positioned in the center of the fireplace. The flickering flames cast the ambiance of warmth over the elegant white furnishings and the Persian rugs that covered the hardwood floor. Debussy's "Clair de lune" played softly on the stereo. JoAnn knelt before the hearth and touched a match to the last wick. She wore a loose-fitting caftan the color of night, and the cream-colored embroidery brought out the highlights in her light brown hair. It wasn't actual beauty that drew her attention to JoAnn, but there was something striking about the way her features enhanced one another and the poise with which she moved.

She turned to Tess. "You aren't leaving, are you?"

"No." Tess smiled. "I'm just admiring the scene."

"Why, Tess Rossini." JoAnn made a graceful shift to where a tray holding a bottle of wine and two glasses sat in front of the sofa. "I do believe this is the first time you've actually flirted with me." Pleasure danced in her eyes. She patted the floor beside her.

"That can't be." Tess closed the space between them and eased down into the crook of JoAnn's arm resting on the couch cushion. "I've flirted with you before."

"No. You've been kind. You've been sweet. You've even been playful at times, but you've never actually flirted." She leaned close and kissed Tess's earlobe. "I like it."

Tess's body responded to the warmth of JoAnn's breath on her neck. She tried to ignore it. "I still think you're wrong." She played it off, but she knew it was true. She knew how reserved she had been with JoAnn in that context. For so long, she had been aware of the feelings JoAnn had for her that she hadn't been ready to reciprocate in any way, and more recently, even as they had begun to date, she had still been sleeping with Dusty and hadn't wanted to give JoAnn the idea that she was ready to move their relationship into a sexual one. The mild flirtation that had just slipped past her lips had surprised her as much as it seemed to have surprised JoAnn. "But in case you're right, maybe it's time to remedy that."

JoAnn chuckled. "You certainly won't get any argument out of me." She nuzzled Tess's ear again then sat up. "More wine?" she asked, holding up the bottle.

Relief and disappointment mingled in Tess at JoAnn's withdrawal. "Maybe just one more glass," she said. "I do need to drive home."

"Hm." JoAnn glanced at Tess as she poured the light amber liquid. "I would say you don't have to, but you know that." She handed the drink to Tess. "But if you're going to insist on it, I'm going to stay just a little bit over here." She rested against the sofa again, this time keeping some distance between them.

Tess smiled. "Thank you. You're very sweet to me."

"Believe me," JoAnn said with a laugh. "It isn't for you." She took a sip of wine. "I knew being this alone with you would be difficult. I just wanted you to myself without waiters interrupting or strangers all around us."

"It's been a very nice evening." Tess took JoAnn's free hand in hers and traced the knuckles with her thumb.

"Yes, it has." JoAnn gazed at her then said abruptly, "And it isn't over yet. I still have you to myself a little longer. Tell me how Maggie's doing."

Tess sighed at the thought of her friend. "She's doing well. Better than I would be under the same circumstance, I think." She swirled the wine in her glass. "Maggie has a wisdom that most people don't have. She says she hopes Addison decides to come home, but she knows sometimes relationships aren't forever."

"I suppose that's true enough. Is she really that matter-of-fact about it?"

"She's pretty strong, but there are some mornings when it's obvious she's been crying." Tess remembered waking to the sound of Maggie's sobs through her open bedroom window one night and finding her outside at the patio table. When Tess sat beside her, Maggie had fallen into her arms. No words were spoken. Tess simply held her while she cried. She saw no reason to share that, though. "She's also been fairly preoccupied with a friend who's in the final stages of AIDS, so her emotions are fairly raw these days."

"That's a lot to handle all at once." Candlelight reflected in the shimmer of JoAnn's eyes.

Tess nodded. "Maggie's a hospice volunteer, so she sees her role with Pete as one of support for him and not about her own grief, but still…"

"Has anyone heard from Addison?" JoAnn turned her hand in Tess's loose grasp and caressed her palm.

"I've called her a couple of times and left messages. She called me back once and said she was well. It was awkward, though. I'm closer to Maggie than Addison, so I'm not someone with whom she'd probably share a lot about her activities or feelings these days."

JoAnn squeezed Tess's fingers. "I'm sure she has other friends."

"Of course." She had wondered if Dusty had been in touch with Addison. Dusty had been furious at her the night of the party when Eve had taken them up to Maggie's room and they found out what had happened. Had she and Addison spoken since then? That had also been the night Tess resigned herself to end her involvement with Dusty, so they hadn't been alone for her to ask. Who was she kidding? She had been avoiding Dusty because she didn't trust herself to be alone with her. "She does have friends," Tess said. "I'm sure she's fine. I do miss her around the house, though."

"It's nice you're not taking sides," JoAnn said quietly.

"There are no sides." Tess shook her head. "They're both my friends, and I want both of them to be happy. I'd like it if they can still be happy together, but if not…" She shrugged. "I have another friend who says we never know enough to judge."

JoAnn's eyes held Tess's. She seemed to be listening still, but her gaze shifted to Tess's lips. Without a word, she leaned in and pressed them to her own.

Tess drew in a sharp breath as the heat rose in her body. She felt JoAnn's tongue slip into her mouth. She tasted of chardonnay, citrus salmon, and desire. Her own arousal pulsed through her, pooled in her center. She had realized earlier that it had been over a month since the last time she and Dusty had truly been together, and it had struck her in that moment that Dusty had spoiled her. For almost a year, Dusty had been, for all intents and purposes, at her beck and call sexually. Whenever Tess wanted closeness, affection, or just release, all she had needed to do was send Dusty a look, meet her in the hall, or leave her a note under her door, and nothing had been asked of her in return. Now, here was JoAnn—kissing her, moving closer, slipping her hand around Tess's waist but also wanting more, wanting a commitment, wanting Tess's heart. Tess's heart, however, was not what was foremost in Tess's mind.

Just as suddenly as JoAnn had started, she pulled away. She took Tess's glass and set it, along with her own, back on the tray. Then her mouth covered Tess's again, this time more fervently.

Eyes closed, Tess lost herself in the kiss. Then Dusty was there—right there, kissing her, touching her, making her…

JoAnn moaned.

"Wait." Tess sighed against JoAnn's mouth. She pressed her hand against her shoulder. She pushed. "I can't."

JoAnn flopped back against the sofa, her eyes shut. "Okay."

Tess tried to get control of her mind and body. She wanted release—needed release—so badly. She liked JoAnn, was attracted to her, and JoAnn was right here, wanting her. Why couldn't she get Dusty out of her thoughts, out of her fantasies, out of her heart? And yet, she couldn't go to bed with JoAnn thinking of Dusty. She wouldn't. "I'm sorry," she whispered.

JoAnn waved a hand. "No, you've been clear. I'm the one who should be sorry." JoAnn smiled up at the ceiling. "But I'm not. That was incredible, feeling your passion. I know it's going to be so amazing."

"No, really, JoAnn. I shouldn't have. It's not you. It's—"

"It's Boo Radley," JoAnn said softly.

"What?"

"It's Boo Radley." JoAnn turned to face her. "It's the woman at the Halloween party dressed as Boo Radley. I don't know who she is, and I don't think I want to, but I know she's the reason you're holding back."

She knows? Tess stared at her. "Wh—what? How?"

"I saw the way you were looking at her. I know you're in love with her."

Tess felt the heat of a deep blush flood her face and chest, hotter than the arousal that had already claimed her. It was the heat of shame. She knew? Tess started to rise. "I'm so sorry."

JoAnn grabbed her hand and pulled her back down. "Please don't go. Not like this."

Tess averted her gaze. She wanted to run.

"Just relax. It's okay."

"It's not okay." Tess chided herself. "I should never have started dating you until I was completely—"

"No." JoAnn brought Tess's fingers to her lips and kissed them. "That's the last thing I want. Look, I don't know what happened between you and the Boo woman, and I'll be honest with you, I think she's a moron. She obviously has—or had—your love and either threw it away, or didn't know what to do with it or…something. And I'm grateful for her stupidity. Tess, I promise you, I am going to love you so well that someday you're going to look at me the way you were looking at her."

Tess was still stunned, confused, and embarrassed, but she had to say something. "JoAnn, I don't want you to think you have to compete—"

"I will. I'll do whatever I need to do to show you how happy you can be with me. I've been in love with you for a long time, and I know we could be good together. We *are* good together."

Tess heard the words, but they were too much. She wasn't ready for professions of love, not from JoAnn. Not yet. "I'm not going to deny it. Yes, I was involved with her. It was a strange thing, and somewhere along the way I fell in love. And no, she doesn't feel the same. I *am* working out my feelings, but it isn't really fair for me to date you—"

"I'm going to interrupt you every time you head in that direction," JoAnn said. "I don't want anything to change between us. Well, I do. But not in the way you're talking about. I just wanted you to know that I knew and that you don't need to hide it. I'm willing to wait." She brushed her lips across Tess's. "As I said, I know it's going to be amazing."

"JoAnn, she lives with me," Tess said. If all was being shared, she might as well truly let it be *all*.

"What?"

"Not *with* me, but in the house. She lives at Maggie's."

JoAnn hesitated. "Are you getting over her?"

Tess looked down to where their fingers intertwined. "It's been more difficult than I'm sure it would have been under different circumstances, but yes, I think I am." Was that true, or was it merely her intention to do so?

"I could probably help with that," JoAnn said, flirtation back in her voice. "If you'd let me."

Tess smiled, considering the thought. Perhaps it was true. Spending more time with JoAnn had helped Tess keep her feelings for Dusty at bay, had kept thoughts of a life with her from filling her mind. Maybe JoAnn's touch, her kisses, her responses to Tess's, could chase away her desire for Dusty. Who was to say, though, that her dates and time with JoAnn were really helping her free herself from her feelings, or if they just offered a distraction and kept her out of the same house? Besides, if JoAnn's caresses and arousal were enough to overcome Tess's desire, this very moment wouldn't have happened and the evening would already be ending much differently. But maybe soon. "Not yet," was all Tess said.

"But you thought about it." JoAnn flashed a grin of victory.

Tess laughed. "Yes, I thought about it."

"I take that as encouragement," JoAnn said, coaxing Tess into her arms. "I'm going to make you happy, Tess. I'm going to make you forget all about Boo Radley, I promise." She kissed Tess tenderly.

Later, as Tess walked up the stairs to her own bedroom, she remembered JoAnn's words and wondered about such a promise—wondered about promises, in general. Hadn't Addison promised to be faithful to Maggie? Tess had promised Alicia she would never let anything happen to her. Alicia had promised they would grow old together. Tess had promised herself she would only have sex with Dusty. All these, and many more, had been made in sincerity, and yet all had been broken. Now, here was JoAnn, promising she would make Tess forget.

At the top of the steps, Tess paused outside Dusty's door. Oh, that JoAnn's promise had already been fulfilled, or the one before it, or even the ones before that. If any of them had been, she wouldn't be standing here wanting so much to turn the knob and go inside, to slip into Dusty's bed, and just let herself love her.

CHAPTER NINETEEN

The doorbell sounded. "I Can't Get No Satisfaction."

Maggie stared out the glass wall of her living room and up the mountainside. Maybe she should change that. She had agreed to the Rolling Stones because they were Addison's all-time favorite band, but that particular song now brought up questions, the answers to which Maggie wasn't sure she wanted to know. How long had Addison felt unsatisfied? Was she getting satisfaction now? Clearly, the answer to the latter was yes. Maggie could keep the Stones until she saw how things would unfold, and maybe just change the song. Change it to what, though? "It's All Over Now?" That was worse. Maybe "Mixed Emotions." She didn't move.

It had been a long day and an even longer previous night. Pete had released his final breath at four thirty-seven that morning. It had been quiet, so quiet. Later had come all the usual activity, including the arrival of the funeral home personnel and the transport of Pete's body. And that had been followed by assisting Ricardo and the family with some cleaning up, the final arrangements for services, and sitting for a while just sharing feelings.

The doorbell chimed again.

This time, Baxter lifted his large head from her knee and cocked it to one side. He let out a soft whine.

Maggie sighed. "All right, laddie," she told him as she heaved herself out of the chair. "Are you expectin' someone?" *Who even rings the doorbell?* She tried to imagine. Everyone she knew simply let themselves in. "Maybe it's a package," she said to the dog. She shot a longing glance up the stairs toward her bath and bed as she stepped into the foyer.

The chimes sounded once more.

Maggie turned the knob and opened the door. "I'm right h—" She stared in disbelief. "Here."

Baxter rushed past her, wagging his stub of a tail along with his whole back end.

"I'm sorry," Addison said. She bent and greeted Baxter with a vigorous scratching of his ears. "I know sometimes it's hard to hear the bell from the third floor. Hey, Bax, how ya doin'?"

Yes, she would know that. She was the one who insisted on no doorbell extender up there. What was she doing here, and why was she using the bell, anyway? "You don't need to ring," Maggie said, thankful for *something* to say. "This is still your home, unless you've decided otherwise."

Addison hesitated. "It didn't seem right not to." She shrugged. "I'm not sure why."

Guilt, Maggie knew. "Would you like to come in?" Her heart pounded. Why was Addison here after two and a half weeks without so much as an e-mail? Maggie couldn't help hoping she had come home, but somehow she knew better.

A slight smile touched the corners of Addison's mouth. "I'd like that." When they were settled in the living room, she looked around her. Her body relaxed into the sofa cushions, and she released a sigh.

Maggie waited. She wanted Addison to speak first. She would have liked to ask her how she was doing, but if the answer involved anything to do with her affair, Maggie really didn't want to hear it. She did care how Addison was, though.

"I heard about Pete," Addison said finally, saving Maggie from her dilemma. It seemed Addison didn't want to open the subject of how Maggie was either. "How's Ricardo?"

"He's okay. He has some grievin' to finish up, but he's relieved it's over for Pete. That's such a cruel disease." She shifted in her chair and tucked one foot beneath her.

Addison nodded. "It is." She fingered the crease of her black slacks. "Were you there when he went?"

"Yes. I was holdin' his hand. I felt him go." Maggie remembered the intimacy of the moment. "He was peaceful."

"Are you okay?" Addison asked, her voice tender.

The question startled Maggie. She looked at Addison. "Of course. This isn't my first time. You know that."

"I know. I just thought since it was someone you knew, a friend, it might've been more difficult." Addison paused. "I was just concerned about you, that's all."

Concerned about me. Anger began to uncoil in her stomach like a waking dragon stretching its neck. *About whether or not I'm okay with a friend finally getting to leave his disease-riddled body and be free? Not concerned about how I might be doin' after findin' you in our bedroom with another woman between your legs and not hearin' from you since you walked out the door that night?* Even though those thoughts were in her head, that wasn't who she wanted to be. She commanded the dragon to settle again. "I'm fine," she said instead. "I'll miss him, but he's finally free, and I'm happy for him."

"Good." Addison glanced around. "I'm glad you're okay." She ran her hands down her thighs. "I was concerned."

"Yes, you said that."

Addison exhaled a deep sigh. "God, this is hard. I'm sorry. Maybe I shouldn't have come." She stared at the floor.

Maggie could see—could feel—Addison's discomfort, her struggle. She realized Addison had no obligation to come over this afternoon, and the fact that she had showed that she truly had been thinking of Maggie. She'd always been the one Maggie wanted to have hold her after one of her patients left this earthly plane. She'd always been the one to help Maggie get anchored once more into daily life, and here she was, in the midst of everything else, offering that again. Maggie softened. "Yes, it is hard, but I thank you for comin'. We had to face each other for the first time at some point."

"I suppose." She looked at Maggie. "Does that mean it'll be easier from now on?"

"From now on?"

"Yeah. You know. Next time?" Something that looked like hope flickered in Addison's eyes. "There'll be a next time, won't there?"

Would there be? It had taken a friend dying for this moment to take place. They had a lot of friends, but most of them were relatively healthy. In her fatigued state, the thought struck Maggie as humorous. She laughed softly.

"What's funny?" Addison asked, a questioning smile playing on her lips.

"Nothin'. I'm very tired. My thinkin' isn't right." Maggie watched as Addison absently petted Baxter. She considered how good it would feel to have Addison's hands massaging her neck and shoulders, stroking her back. She wanted so much to ask her to hold her, but it was all too confusing. She knew she would break down in Addison's arms and she wouldn't be able to control what came out—the dragon, the tears…or who knew what? "Of course there will be a next time. And yes, it will be easier."

Addison nodded then looked down at Baxter. "When is Pete's service?"

"Saturday." Maggie was relieved at the change of subject. "Ricardo's sister was still workin' out the time when I left."

Addison hesitated. "Would you like to go together?" Her voice was low, barely above a whisper.

Maggie wasn't sure she had heard correctly. "Together? You and me?" she asked.

"No, you're right," Addison said quickly. "It'd probably be too—"

"Yes," Maggie interrupted. "That would be nice."

Addison looked up and smiled. "Great. Just let me know what time, and I'll pick you up."

"I will. Thank you."

Their eyes met and for just an instant the characteristic ease of their relationship enveloped them. The next instant it was gone. An awkward silence stretched between them.

Addison looked back at Baxter.

"Are you goin' to your folks' house for Thanksgivin' next week?" Maggie asked, trying to sound light. She hoped the question didn't backfire on her and bring up any plans Addison might have with Victoria Fontaine, but she couldn't think of anything else to say that didn't have the potential for the same feared topic.

"No, they're cruising. Besides, I haven't mentioned…" Addison looked out the windows.

"Well, if you've no other plans," Maggie said in a rush to ward off any further confessions, "you're welcome to join us for Thanksgiving dinner." There, she had said it. She braced herself for the answer.

Addison squeezed her eyes shut. When she opened them, they shimmered with tears. "I'd like that. Thank you, Maggie."

"This is still your home, daw—" The sting of the endearment was too sharp for her to continue. Was Addison still her dawtie? She also wanted to add, *for now*, but she refrained. "We'll be havin' dinner on Friday rather than Thursday so Eve and Sammi can join us. They'll both be with their little ones on Thursday."

Addison raised an eyebrow. "That's going pretty well, I gather."

"Oh, yes. They seem quite taken with each other." Maggie felt a twinge of envy as she remembered the two of them giggling on the sofa one evening the previous week. "Things are movin' right along, from what I can tell."

"That's great." Addison studied Maggie. "What are you doing on Thursday?" she asked.

"Tess and I are goin' to the canyon in the mornin' for some time in the mountains and a walk up to the waterfall. Then we'll start on the pies when we get home." Maggie saw a flash of resignation in Addison's eyes. What had she been thinking? "Tess is considerin' invitin' JoAnn for Thanksgivin' as well."

"JoAnn?"

"Mm-hm. The woman she brought to the Halloween party? Remember?" The words flopped down between them like a dead bird out of the sky, the harbinger of the very moment they had both been working so hard to avoid.

"Oh." Addison shifted on the couch. "Yeah, I remember." She cleared her throat.

Maggie knew she was lying. She could probably count on one hand the things Addison remembered from that night and Tess's date certainly would not be among them. "She might join us, too."

"Is Tess getting serious about her?" Addison glanced around the room, her gaze landing anywhere but on Maggie.

"I think it's too soon to tell, but she is enjoyin' spendin' time with her." Maggie needed *this* time with Addison to come to an end. She was glad Addison had stopped by and that they had gotten their first conversation over with. She was especially happy they would be saying good-bye to Pete together and sharing Thanksgiving—both showed promise—but she had endured all she could manage for now. She needed some sleep and some distance.

Addison seemed to feel it, too. "I should take off and let you get some rest." She rose.

"I appreciate you stoppin' by." Maggie moved toward the doorway. "I'll let you know about the service as soon as I get all the information." She crossed the foyer and opened the front door.

Addison stepped outside. "Thank you, Maggie," she said softly.

Maggie knew it was for more than the time of the service. She nodded. She watched Addison descend the front steps then closed the door. She couldn't bear the sight of her driving away.

After filling Baxter's food dish and wiping a few Fruity Pebbles off the kitchen counter—remnants, she assumed, from Dusty's breakfast—she went upstairs, changed into one of Addison's over-sized T-shirts she wore for sleeping, and crawled into bed. The sheets were cool, the mattress soft. Baxter curled up at her feet. She expected sleep to run her over like a speeding truck, but it held back, tailgating, but never overtaking her. She tossed and turned, reliving Addison showing up at the door, remembering how badly she had wanted to feel Addison's arms around her, rehashing all of her conflicting thoughts and emotions about Addison's affair, their life together, and the numerous possible futures. Finally, she gave up and headed downstairs for a glass of milk or a cup of tea, something to help her sleep.

An hour later when Dusty came in from work, Maggie sat cross-legged on the sofa with a bowl of lime wedges, a salt shaker, a shot glass, and a bottle of tequila spread out on the coffee table in front of her. Four rinds lay in a row.

Dusty eyed her. "Hey, Maggie Mae, whatcha doing?"

Maggie looked up at her. "I think I'm gettin' drunk." She swayed.

Dusty steadied her. "Yeah, that's what it looks like to me, too." She sat next to Maggie. "What's the occasion?"

"I couldn't sleep," Maggie said. She realized now the loneliness of the empty bed had been too much for her. She missed Addison beside her. She leaned into Dusty.

Dusty put an arm around her. "Well, baby," she said with a laugh. "That's why they make chamomile tea. I think tequila is for other purposes." She rubbed Maggie's back.

Tears burned Maggie's eyes. "Addison came by." She sniffed.

"Ah, now I get it." Dusty sighed. "What'd she say?"

"She was concerned about me because she heard Pete died."

"Huh." Dusty grunted. "I guess that's something."

"But it made me angry that's what she was here for. I mean I'm glad she wasn't here to talk about the affair and that woman, but..."

Maggie sat up and looked into Dusty's eyes. "I know she has to do this for her own reasons and she has to find her own way, but I just wanted her to want to come home. I miss her so much." The words poured out as her tears began to flow. "I miss her laugh and her strength. I miss her touch and her kisses and making love with her. And I don't want to be without her. But I'm so damned mad at her." She punctuated her last statement with a slap of her hand against Dusty's sternum.

Dusty grabbed the box of tissues off the credenza and handed Maggie a couple. She took Maggie in her arms and drew her close. "I know. I feel the same way," she said. "You know…except for the touching and kissing and making love stuff."

Maggie chuckled and blew her nose. "You're a good friend," she said, patting Dusty's knee. "Here, drink with me." She pulled back and filled the shot glass. She slid it in front of Dusty.

Dusty laughed. "No, I don't think that's the answer."

"It is," Maggie said flatly. "Friends don't let friends drink alone." She picked up the salt shaker and held it out to Dusty.

"I thought it was friends don't let friends drink and drive."

"So, don't drive." Maggie shook the shaker at her.

"Maggie, really—"

"Okay." Maggie sat up straight. "I'll drink it then." She brought her wrist to her mouth.

"No, no." Dusty grabbed the salt. "I'll have one, but no more for you. Okay?" She licked her wrist, sprinkled on the salt, then sucked it up. She downed the shot and shoved a lime between her teeth. "Woo-hoo." She shook her head. "It's been a while since I've done that. Where'd this stuff come from, anyway?"

Maggie winced. "That damned Halloween party." If there had ever been a night she wished she could take back, that was it. She refilled the glass. "I don't ever want to have another one." She prepared her wrist and reached for the drink.

Dusty snatched the glass with one hand and Maggie's arm with the other. She licked up the salt Maggie had poured then threw back her second shot. After sucking the lime, she said, "Okay, no more. Let's go upstairs and get you to bed. I'll sit with you, and we can talk until you fall asleep."

Behind them, the front door opened.

"What's going on?" Tess asked as she walked into the room.

Maggie turned and grinned up at her. "Dusty'n I're gettin' drunk b'cause we miss Addison." Somewhere along the line her words had begun to slur, and she couldn't quite focus on Tess.

Tess looked at Dusty. "Really? Do you think that's the best thing to do?"

"I wasn't get—"

"An' Addison came over," Maggie continued, "an' I was'n okay, but I told her I was."

Tess turned back to Maggie. "Have you gotten any sleep since you called me this morning about Pete?"

"No." Maggie shook her head, making herself a little dizzy. "Tha's the other reason we're gettin' durunk, to help me sleep."

"Mm-hm." Tess glanced at Dusty again.

"I wasn't getting drunk with her," Dusty said. "I was keeping her from drinking any more. And we were just about to go upstairs and put her to bed."

"Okay, then. Let's do that," Tess said, her tone tight. "Let's get you to bed, Maggie."

"Okay." Maggie stood, and the room tilted. She stumbled and hit her knee on the coffee table.

Dusty caught her and pulled her close. "Easy, Maggie Mae. Let's take it slow."

As they moved toward the stairs, Tess slipped her arm around Maggie's waist from one side and Dusty from the other.

Maggie patted them both on their shoulders. "You're both such good friends."

"Really, Tess, I wasn't—"

"Not now. Let's just get her upstairs."

Maggie stopped halfway up the first flight of steps. "Are the twouv you fightin'?"

"No, sweetie, we're just taking care of you," Tess said, sounding nice again. "Just keep walking with us, okay?"

Maggie had to concentrate to get her feet moving. She placed one on each step then felt the muscles in her leg tighten as she pressed upward. She was fascinated by her awareness of the feeling in her body. She felt the solidness of the floor beneath her bare feet, the play of the fabric of her friends' shirts under her fingers, the warmth of being sandwiched between them. She noticed the carpet give way to tile as they stepped onto the third-floor landing. Suddenly, she remembered the conversation. "You two can't fight. We all havta love each other," she said, trying to focus. "I loved Addison, but I didn't do it well enough. I shouldna fought with her when she was havin' trouble." They passed through the doorway of her bedroom.

"Just a little farther, sweetie," Tess said.

"It wasn't your fault," Dusty said. "Addison was going through some stuff."

Tess and Dusty lowered Maggie onto her bed.

"There's no point in trying to talk to her while she's drunk," Tess said to Dusty. "Even if she hears you, she won't remember it."

"I'm not drun'." Maggie fell backward onto the mattress. She laughed. "Maybe I am. What was I sayin'?"

"*I* was saying it wasn't your fault," Dusty said. She coaxed Maggie to a sitting position, and Tess tugged the covers out from under her. "I tried to talk to Addison about what she was doing with Victoria, but she wouldn't listen to anything. Rebecca says she needs to do this to learn something."

Maggie gazed up into Dusty's eyes and stroked her cheek. "You're so sweet." Then she realized through the alcoholic fog what Dusty had said. "You knew?" Her hand stilled on Dusty's face.

"What?" Dusty tried to ease Maggie's legs onto the bed, but Maggie stiffened.

"You said you tried to talk to her about what she was doin'. You knew."

Dusty's eyes widened.

The dragon woke, this time not in a languid stretch but in full, flaming rage. All the anger Maggie had been stifling reared its head. "How could you've known and not warned me? You're *not* a friend." She raised her hand to strike at Dusty.

Tess caught it. "Maggie, it's okay. Calm down."

"She knew." Maggie pointed a shaking finger.

Dusty backed away. "I'm sorry. I was trying to help."

"Get out," Maggie yelled. Her head pounded. "Pack your stuff and get out of my house."

"What? You mean—"

"Dusty, just go," Tess said over Maggie's tirade. "Let me handle this."

"Yes, just go, Dusty Renee Gardner." Maggie's voice rose higher. "Get out."

Dusty left the room and closed the door behind her.

Maggie stilled. The silence crashed in on her. What had she done? She began to sob.

Tess eased down beside her and took her in her arms. "Shhh." She stroked Maggie's hair.

"I didn't mean that." Maggie cried shuddering sobs. She buried her face in the hollow of Tess's shoulder.

"She knows that," Tess murmured. "It will all be fine."

"No. I have to go apologize." Maggie tried to pull away, but Tess held her firmly.

"You have to get some sleep, Maggie. Dusty knows you didn't mean any of that. She knows you love her and would never kick her out. And I'm sure she knows not to listen to the tequila in anyone." Tess's voice was warm, her words soothing in their reassurance. "Please lie down and go to sleep. It will all be better in the morning."

A wave of exhaustion overtook Maggie, and she slid from Tess's embrace and onto the pillows. "I've made such a mess of things."

Tess brushed her thumb over Maggie's forehead. "No, you haven't, and you'll know that again in the morning." She continued the caress.

Maggie felt her eyes close. "You sound so sure."

Tess laughed softly. "I've had my share of drunken miasmas. Nothing we think during them is ever true the next day."

Maggie released a sigh of deep surrender. "Okay, I'll trust you," she whispered.

"I'll be downstairs if you need anything," Tess said quietly.

"No." Maggie opened her eyes. "You've got a date with JoAnn."

"I'm going to cancel it. She'll understand."

Maggie grasped Tess's hand. "No. I'd feel horrible if you did that on account of me. I'll be fine. I'm so worn out, I know I'll sleep till the mornin'. You go and have a good time."

Tess smiled. "Okay, but I'm not leaving until you're asleep, and I won't be late." She resumed her gentle caress of Maggie's brow.

Maggie closed her eyes again and within minutes found herself in a dream, kissing Addison at the waterfall.

Chapter Twenty

Dusty followed Baxter as he ran up the steps leading to the front door and readied herself to enter the house. She'd taken him for a walk around the neighborhood and let him drag her up into the pines and underbrush of the mountainside to keep herself out of Maggie's room. In her initial guilt and panic, she'd wanted so much to barge back in to make sure Maggie hadn't really meant what she'd said about Dusty packing her stuff and leaving. She was pretty sure it was the emotion of the day and the tequila speaking, but she wanted to hear it. Now that she'd gained some perspective, she trusted she was right, and though she still felt bad, she could wait until morning.

Tonight, she was more concerned about clearing things up with Tess. She didn't want Tess mad at her, believing she'd been getting Maggie drunk. Tess had been acting weird since the Halloween party, though, so who knew what was really going on there?

The sun had just set, and someone had flipped on the porch light, probably on their way out as was the habit of the household. She hoped Tess was still home. As she let herself in, she heard noise from the kitchen. "Tess?" she called, heading in that direction.

"No, me," Eve said as Dusty entered the room. She stood at the counter, spreading cream cheese on a cracker.

"Wow, you look great," Dusty said, taking in the low-cut, tight-fitting red dress and strappy, black, f-me shoes. "If you and Sammi have a date, she doesn't stand a chance if she's playing hard to get."

Eve turned and smiled. "Thank you. I'm glad you think so." Something in her tone wasn't quite right. "Actually, it's you I wanted to take out to dinner."

“Me?” Dusty opened the refrigerator and examined the contents. “Why?”

“I’d like to talk to you about something,” Eve said. “I have a favor to ask.”

“Can’t you just ask me here? I don’t really feel like going out.” She opened a Tupperware container and took out a fried chicken leg. She loved Maggie’s fried chicken. “I wanna talk to Tess.” She took a bite.

“Tess isn’t here.”

‘Mm.” Dusty chewed. “She say anything before she left?”

“Just that Maggie’s asleep. She was up all night with Pete and his family.” Eve paused. “Dusty, please? It’s really important.”

Dusty swallowed. “What is?”

Eve sighed. “The favor.”

“Ask me, then.” Dusty clutched the container against her chest and grabbed a carton of orange juice with her free hand.

“I don’t want to just ask you.” Eve’s voice tightened. “I wanted to…”

Dusty stepped to the cupboard and set the chicken on the counter. “Wanted to what?” She took another bite from the leg in her hand. “Why all the intrigue?”

“Will you stop eating? I want to take you to dinner.” Eve’s voice rose to the pitch of a discontented girlfriend winding up for a tantrum. The only thing missing was a foot stomp.

Dusty laughed. “But I don’t wanna go out to dinner. I wanna eat cold chicken and wait for Tess to get back. In the meantime, you can ask me anything you want. Why won’t that work?”

Eve folded her arms in front of her. “I had a plan.”

Dusty filled a glass with juice. “What kind of plan?” She took a long drink.

“I was going to seduce you.” Eve actually stomped her foot. “Okay?”

Dusty choked. Orange juice shot out her nose, and she bent over and began to cough.

“Oh, my God.” Eve pounded Dusty on the back. “Are you all right?”

Dusty’s eyes watered and she gasped for breath. “You were gonna *what*?”

"I'm sorry." Eve slumped against the counter. "See, that's why I didn't want to just tell you. I wanted to…you know."

"No, I don't know. What the hell are you talking about?" Dusty turned and got a second look at Eve's outfit. A new awareness seized her like a bad cramp. "Don't tell me you dressed that way for me."

"Well, yes, but—"

"No."

"Dusty, wait. It's not what you think."

Dusty turned on the water and rinsed off her face. "I don't even know what I think. You're crazy. We can't…no." She snatched a dish towel and dried herself off. She wiped up the juice that'd sprayed the counter.

Eve grabbed her arm. "Will you please just listen for a minute?" She pulled Dusty to the table and pushed her into a chair.

"There's nothing to listen to. I'm not gonna—"

"I don't know what to do," Eve said over Dusty's objection. "I want to sleep with Sammi, but I'm afraid to. I don't know how to…you know…please her. I thought you could…"

Dusty was stunned. She felt her mouth drop open, but the only word she could think of was no.

"I thought you could…teach me." Eve waved her hand in a vague motion, as though that explained everything.

"Teach you?" Dusty stared. "If you were gonna seduce me, you must already know something. And I gotta tell you, that outfit is a great start. Just go from there."

"It's the going from there I don't know how to do." Eve dropped into the chair across from her. "I'm afraid I'll disappoint her."

"You won't. She'll be thrilled just to be with you."

"I'll feel like a fool." Eve's expression grew serious. Her gaze held Dusty's. "I want to be good for her, and you could show me how, if you just would."

Dusty shook her head. "This is crazy. I'm not sleeping with you."

"Why not?" Eve looked stricken. "You sleep with Tess."

Yeah, and look where that got me. "That's different."

"Why?" Eve asked, genuine bewilderment in her tone.

Because she was in love with Tess. She hadn't been, though, the first time they'd slept together, or the second, or even the third. She didn't, in fact, know when it'd happened. All she knew was that it had, and since then, she hadn't wanted to sleep with anyone else. She couldn't say that to Eve, though. Could she? She'd told Rebecca, of course—or rather, Rebecca had told her—and she'd told Tess herself even though, as it'd turned out, Tess had slept through her confession, but she'd never actually said it to anyone else. Was there even any point in sharing it with anyone? For a while, she'd hoped maybe admitting her feelings to Tess could possibly lead to something more. She'd even thought she'd felt something from Tess in return, but for the past couple of weeks, things between them seemed to have gone back to how they'd been the first two years Tess lived there. They were just housemates whose paths seldom crossed—until today. Today, Tess had actually noticed Dusty once again and interacted with her, although not in a way Dusty wanted. She was so confused. She just wanted Tess. That was all. "I'm not sleeping with you," she repeated.

Eve slapped her hand down on the table. "Fine. I'll find someone else, then. Someone who *is* willing to teach me."

"Eve." Dusty exhaled the name in exasperation. "Just go to Sammi. She's the one you want, so it'll *be* good. I swear to you, you head over there right now, looking like that, and you're not gonna have to know a thing."

"You don't get to have an opinion anymore." Eve thrust herself to her feet. "I told you how you can help, and you said no, so just never mind."

"Fine," Dusty said, raising her hands in defeat. She leaned back in her chair. How'd this day get so messed up? One minute everything was great, the next, Tess was blaming her for Maggie being drunk, Maggie was telling her to move out, and now Eve was furious at her for telling her to sleep with the woman she truly wanted.

Eve stalked to the counter and began wrapping up the crackers and returning them to the box.

"Did Tess say where she was going?" Dusty asked, hoping the change of subject would calm Eve.

"She's on a date." Eve put the cover on the cream cheese and smacked it into place with the palm of her hand.

The statement took Dusty as much by surprise as Eve's plan of seduction. "A date?"

"Yes." Eve yanked open the refrigerator door and dropped the cream cheese onto the shelf. "With JoAnn."

Dusty blinked. "Who's JoAnn?"

"The woman she brought to the Halloween party." Eve's tone remained sharp. "They've been dating for weeks."

Weeks? Dusty didn't know what to say. The words hung in the silence as though they'd been skewered and tacked to the air itself. She'd heard them, could see them and, worst of all, felt them like a cold snake tightening its coils around her heart. All those opportunities she'd had to tell Tess how she felt, the times she'd let herself be interrupted and hadn't gone back to try again, all those *intentions*, and yet, she'd blown her chance. Or had she ever really had one? *They've been dating for weeks.*

"You didn't know?" Eve's question rang like a distant bell.

"What?" Dusty focused to find her staring at her.

"You didn't know." This time it was a statement. Eve eased the refrigerator closed.

"No." Dusty collected her thoughts. She didn't know. "But, hey… why should I?" Her voice threatened to break, but she steeled herself. Right, why should she? She wasn't anything to Tess. She got up from her chair. "I'm gonna go take a shower."

"Are you okay?" Eve asked.

"Yeah. Fine." Dusty replaced the lid on the container of chicken. She rinsed out her glass and put it in the dishwasher, trying to ignore the trembling in her hands and the churning in her stomach.

Eve watched her. "How strong are your feelings for her?"

"They're nothing," Dusty said, her tone flat. "We sleep together sometimes. That's it. And we haven't even done that for a while now. See? Everything's fine."

"It hasn't been that long. The night of the party, I—"

"Drop it." Dusty turned her back. She opened the refrigerator to put away the chicken and clenched her eyes shut. She remembered Tess that night—gorgeous, sexy, and, apparently, with a date—and afterward, she'd come to Dusty. She'd had a date that night, and she'd come to Dusty for sex. Dusty had almost said I love you, and Tess had just been there for sex. *Jeez, what a chump.* Why would that night have been any different, though? Sex was all they'd ever had. She held back the tears that threatened.

"Dusty?" Eve's tone was tender—too tender.

Dusty straightened and hardened her emotions. "I'm fine, Eve. Just leave me alone." She slammed the refrigerator door. "I'm fine. You're fine. Tess is fine. Tess's date—I'm sure—is fine. Everybody's fine, okay?" She stalked from the room and headed upstairs.

In the shower, her tears mingled with the flow of hot water washing over her face and down her body. How could she have been so stupid? But *how*, exactly, had she been stupid? Was she stupid for thinking that if she shared her feelings with Tess they might be able to explore a relationship together, or was she stupid for *not* sharing those feelings before Tess started seeing someone else? Regardless, she had a hard time believing that Tess would date someone while she was still sleeping with Dusty, not necessarily for Dusty's sake, but for that of the other woman. It didn't seem like something Tess would do, and yet, it seemed that'd been her plan.

What did Dusty know about Tess, anyway? She knew the roughness of denim against Tess's most tender flesh made her wet. She knew Tess could *almost* come from just having her nipples sucked if done just the right way. She knew the top of Tess's clit was more sensitive than the underside. She knew the exact amount of pressure and how deeply to apply it to make Tess come the hardest. But so what? What did all that matter when Tess could be with someone in her own league?

Dusty knew other things, though, too. She'd noticed Tess's favorite coffee was spiced butter rum with a splash of vanilla creamer and she liked it best on the patio in the morning sunshine. She knew Tess liked watching the movie *Groundhog Day* but switched the TV to PBS if she heard someone coming. She'd figured out that when Tess bit her lower lip, it meant she was unsure of herself. She even knew Tess had called 1-800-FUN-COLOR and voted for the blue M&M to replace the tan ones—Dusty had voted for purple. Evidently, though, none of that counted for anything, either. Dusty was just good for sex.

As she turned off the water and grabbed a towel, Rebecca's voice drifted into her head. *With all the women you've used sexually, if you hold on to the guilt you feel about it, you might need to experience how it feels to be on the other end in order to be free from it all.*

This was it—the other end—and, boy, did it suck.

"Do I have to?" Dusty remembered asking.

"Not necessarily," Rebecca had said. "You could forgive yourself right now and be done with it."

"Then I don't have to be punished?"

Rebecca laughed. "It isn't punishment. It's just the way the Law of Cause and Effect works. What you send out always comes back, but it comes back to where you were, or who you were, when you sent it. If you've moved on—forgiven yourself, grown, and changed—then you aren't in the same place when it returns."

Obviously, Dusty hadn't moved on. So, why bother, now? Life had been fine when she just had sex with women and kept her heart to herself, and there were always women like her who were just looking for a one-night stand, no strings, no complications, no commitments. She'd just stick to those and be careful not to hook up with anyone who wanted more. It'd been over a month since she and Tess had last been together. Maybe she could get into an anonymous encounter. One thing she was sure of, though, she couldn't just sit around at home and think about what Tess might be doing on her date. If it was time for Tess to move on, it was time for Dusty, too.

Dressed in her tightest black jeans and a tank top that'd proven popular in the past, she checked on Maggie, set a tall glass of water and two aspirin on her nightstand, left the bedroom door open for Baxter, and went downstairs. The house was quiet. The stillness, the emptiness, merely reinforced her decision to go out for the evening. The atmosphere that usually felt peaceful and soothing now held a lonely aura. She slipped into her leather jacket and closed the front door behind her.

As she stepped into Vibes, she took in the scene. The music's beat pulsed through her. It felt familiar and strange at the same time. When was the last time she'd been here? Had it been the night she'd seen Addison and Victoria? She shook the memory. Tonight was for now, for living in the moment with no yesterdays, no tomorrows. Tonight was for getting lost and getting—

"Hey, stranger," a voice called from a nearby table. "Where ya been?"

Dusty smiled and waved and greeted several other friends on her way to the bar. She slipped onto a stool and winked at the bartender. "Hey, Char, got anything for me tonight?"

"I got plenty for you, lover, but I don't get off till two." Charlotte arched a waxed eyebrow as she tucked the end of a towel into her back pocket. She planted her hands on her ample hips.

Dusty grinned. "I'd get you off way before two."

A slow smile claimed Charlotte's full lips. "Yeah, you would," she said, leaning forward and resting her elbows on the bar. The open top two buttons of her white shirt revealed generous cleavage. "But then you'd have to pay my rent."

Dusty laughed. "Okay, then. How 'bout a beer?"

"You got it, sugar." In a matter of seconds, Charlotte set a Corona in front of Dusty. "Where have you been?" she asked with a glint in her topaz eyes. "There's a pool going on for when your obit was going to show up."

Dusty took a long swallow. "It hasn't been that long."

Charlotte laughed. "It's been longer than ever before. Nobody's seen you. I even heard one rumor that some jealous cop husband got a hold of you."

Dusty smiled. She shook her head. "Do people stay awake all night making this stuff up?"

"Well, when one of our permanent fixtures disappears, we start to wonder." Charlotte held up a finger to a woman down the bar. "So everything's okay?"

You mean, other than feeling like my heart just got dragged over a cheese grater? Dusty nodded. "Yeah, everything's great."

Charlotte squeezed her arm. "It's good to see you."

"You, too."

As Charlotte went back to work, Dusty turned on her stool and watched the crowd. It was a pretty good one for a Wednesday night, and she knew it'd get bigger as the time got a little later. She'd have plenty of women to choose from. She nursed her beer and chatted with other friends and acquaintances that came over to find out what she'd been up to. She even joined a group at their table for a while. When her beer was gone, she returned to Charlotte and ordered another. As she took it, she heard a familiar laugh. She turned. She stared at Eve seated at the end of the bar sandwiched between Jodi Van something-or-other, a successful entertainment lawyer but weak in bed, and a leering Steph Brooks, a well-known Domme. Was this what she'd meant when she'd said she'd find someone who *was* willing? Dusty doubted Jodi could teach her much of anything, and Steph's classroom, Dusty was sure, was more specialized than Eve had in mind.

She rose and strode down the length of the bar. "Ladies," she said as she came to the trio.

"Well, if it isn't Lusty Dusty," Steph said. "I saw you down there earlier and was going to come see if you wanted to play, but I got distracted."

The old nickname felt oddly like an outgrown pair of shoes. She ignored it. "I see that." Steph had been trying for years to get Dusty to do a scene with her, and Dusty did occasionally enjoy some kink, but there was something about Steph that felt more sleazy than arousing.

"Dusty!" Eve giggled. She held up her drink. "Let's toast. Isn't this fun? I've never been to a lesbian bar before."

Dusty gazed at her. "How many of those have you had?"

"Several. And I plan to have several more, but it's okay because I've been dancing."

"Yeah, Eve's quite a dancer," Steph said with a hint of suggestion. "Especially in those shoes. Remember, later," she said to Eve. "I'd like to see you in *just* those shoes."

Eve blushed but smiled.

"Yeah, well, I don't think that's gonna happen," Dusty said, keeping her eyes on Eve. "This isn't the way to do this."

"Oh, really?" Eve asked. "Does that mean you've changed your mind? Are you going to help me?"

"No," Dusty said with as much patience as she could manage. "But I'm not gonna let you do *this* either. You don't know what you're getting into."

"You don't have anything to say about it." Eve downed the last swallow of her drink. "*You* weren't interested, so I'm making some new friends."

Dusty felt Steph watching them. "Eve, c'mon. Let's go." She took her hand and coaxed her off the barstool.

Eve stood eye level with Dusty in the spiked heels and slipped her arms around her neck. She pressed against her. "Are you going to teach me?"

Dusty grasped Eve's elbows and pulled her arms down. "No," she said firmly, setting her back a pace.

"Teach her?" Steph said, enjoyment lighting her expression. "What're you going to teach her, Dusty?"

"Nothing. We're gonna go."

"That's right, nothing." Eve pulled away and sat back down. "So, you go, and I'll stay here with my new friends, and maybe they'll teach me."

"Sure, honey. I'll teach you anything you want to learn." Steph's tone sounded more interested than before. "You could join us if you want, Dusty. Maybe I'll even give you some pointers."

"Hey, I'm going to head out," Jodi said with a nervous laugh. She'd been so quiet Dusty had forgotten she was there.

"Okay, see ya," Dusty said. One down, but not the persistent one. "No, thanks," she said to Steph. "And Eve's going with me." She reached again for Eve's hand.

"No, I'm not," Eve said. "You had your chance. I'm staying."

Steph laughed. "Are you two a couple?" she asked with obvious astonishment.

"No," they said in unison.

"Well then, I think Eve can make up her own mind." Steph gave Dusty a tantalizing smile. "Why don't you take off and let us get to know each other?"

"Yeah," Eve said, her voice hard. "I don't need your help, anymore."

Hesitating, Dusty looked from Eve to Steph and back again. She knew she shouldn't leave them, but she couldn't very well drag Eve off against her will. She thought of Maggie's initial concerns about Dusty being around Eve at all, about Tess being angry at her for the part she believed Dusty played in Maggie being drunk. They'd probably both have something to say about her leaving Eve drinking with a dominatrix, but why should she care about what they thought? Maggie had yelled at her, and Tess was on a date without so much as a word to her about it. And Eve…The only thing that would make Eve happy would be for Dusty to instruct her in Lesbian Sex 101. To hell with all of them.

"Fine," Dusty said. "Do whatever you want."

"Fine," Eve said. "I will."

Dusty ordered another beer and sat at the opposite end of the bar. She listened to the music, chatted with Charlotte, even checked out a few women who were checking her out, but she couldn't get into it. Between keeping tabs on Eve with Steph and imagining Tess kissing some woman named *JoAnn*, she lost her train of thought before she could act on it. The bottom line was she didn't want any of these women. She considered going home but still couldn't bear the idea of the empty house, and Tess's potentially empty room.

"Buy you a drink?"

The soft voice and words registered at the same instant as the warm breath in her ear and the cool touch on the bare skin of her shoulder. She turned to find herself nose to nose with a brown-eyed brunette. Tess. Her breath caught, but it wasn't Tess. She eased back and raised her bottle. "I have one. Thanks."

"I know." The woman smiled. "But I had to say something." She slid onto the barstool beside her.

Dusty forced a chuckle.

"Do you remember me?"

Dusty tensed. She hated these moments. Usually, she tried to fake it or come up with some clever response, but tonight, she had nothing. She shook her head. "Sorry."

"I'm Trena."

Dusty nodded. "It's nice to meet you. I'm—"

"I know." Trena smiled again, amusement in her eyes.

"Oh, yeah." Behind Trena, Dusty saw Steph move closer to Eve and slip an arm around her. Eve nestled against her. Steph met Dusty's stare and grinned.

"You look sad," Trena said, recapturing Dusty's attention.

Dusty picked at the Corona label. "I think I am," she admitted for the first time all evening, maybe for the first time in her life.

"Want to talk about it?"

Dusty regarded her. "Naw." She glanced back to Eve. "It's a long story."

Trena looked over her shoulder. "Is that who you're sad about?"

"Huh? Who? Eve?" Dusty laughed. "No. That's an even longer story." She took a drink of her beer.

"You know, the night I met you, I was really sad." Trena's voice was soft. "And lost." She paused.

Dusty turned to her, curious.

"I thought I was straight. Then I met this girl and I felt things for her I'd never felt before. I wanted to do things with her I never knew I wanted." Trena cocked her head to one side.

Dusty nodded. She knew those things.

"But when I told her, she freaked out. She called me a pervert and said I made her sick. She said…well, you get it." Trena gave a little shrug.

"Yeah. I got it." Dusty shifted to face her more fully.

"She told me she never wanted to see me again. I was pretty upset and confused. But, most of all, my heart was broken."

Dusty felt the pain of Eve's earlier words—*they've been dating for weeks*. She blinked against the burn of tears.

"And then one night, I came here," Trena said. Something flickered in her velvet brown eyes, Tess's eyes. "And I met you, and we left together. And you showed me a whole new world." Tenderly, she wiped away the moisture from a tear Dusty hadn't realized had rolled down her cheek. "You showed me how amazing those things I wanted could be, and you made sure I knew there was nothing wrong with them—or me. And I just wanted to say thank you."

Dusty drew in a breath. "I don't know what to say." She supposed she could've said that with all the ways she'd screwed up in her life, she'd really needed to hear that something she'd done had made a difference to someone. She knew she wouldn't get that out tonight without ending up a blubbering mess, though.

Trena smiled. "And my girlfriend…" She turned and looked to a table where a group of women sat, watching.

Dusty followed her gaze.

One of the women raised her glass to Dusty.

"She thanks you, too," Trena said. "I met her a few weeks after you, after you and I spent the night together, and I knew what I wanted was okay. And we've been together ever since."

Dusty raised her beer to the woman in return.

The woman smiled.

"So," Trena said. "I just wanted you to know how important that one night was to me and how important *you* were."

Dusty cleared her throat. "Thank you," she said. "You have no idea how much I needed to hear that." Over Trena's shoulder, she saw Steph and Eve stand. Eve stumbled into Steph as they began to walk toward the door. "Damn it."

Trena looked to them. "Is everything okay?"

"Look, I'm really sorry. I gotta go," Dusty said as she rose. "But thank you for telling me all that."

Trena stood and touched Dusty's cheek. "Thank you." She smiled and started back to her table and her waiting girlfriend.

"Hey, Trena, can I ask you something?" Dusty said as she pulled on her jacket.

"Sure."

"If you'd met your girlfriend first, would you have wanted to do all that for the first time with her?"

"Well, I wouldn't have met her without my night with you because I—"

"But just say you did. Would you have wanted her to be the first?"

Trena looked to her girlfriend with a loving expression then back to Dusty. "Yes, I think I would have."

"Yes," Dusty said, clenching her fist. She was right. "Thank you." She pressed her palms to Trena's face and kissed her full on the lips. She caught herself. She turned to the girlfriend and held out her hands. "Sorry," she called. Then to Trena, she said, "Thank you again."

She caught up with Eve and Steph in the parking lot. "Where you going, Eve?"

"We have a play date," Steph said, her arm possessively around Eve.

"Egzactly." Eve could barely stand on her own. "We hava play date."

"Do you even know what that means?" Dusty asked.

"It means Steph's goin' ta teach me what I wanna learn."

Dusty closed her eyes and released a sigh. She had to change strategies. If she couldn't talk some sense into Eve, she'd have to appeal to Steph. "C'mon, Steph, you know this is wrong. This goes against every tenet of safe and sane play. You're gonna get so much backlash from this when it gets out."

"I know," Steph said sweetly. "But sometimes it's worth it when you get offered something so tasty." She squeezed Eve's shoulders. "It's not often a *teaching* opportunity comes along."

"See? *She's* willing." Eve pointed a finger first at Steph then at Dusty. "She's a real friend."

Dusty rolled her eyes. "She's not a friend. She's a…" Dusty threw up her hands and turned in a circle. "Did she tell you what she's gonna do to you?" She shifted her gaze to Steph. "Isn't that one of the rules? Aren't you supposed to spell out up front what's gonna happen?"

"She's going to show me the ropes," Eve said with seemingly genuine innocence.

"Oh, please." Dusty glared at Steph.

Steph smiled. "You know, there might be another way, if you really want to rescue your little damsel here." Her eyes narrowed. "I might be willing to trade my scene with her for one with you." Her smile widened. "You know how much I've wanted to get you into my playroom."

Dusty stepped back. "No. Not going there."

"Okay, then." Steph began to walk, urging Eve along.

Dusty grimaced. Could she really let Eve go home with this woman, knowing what might lay ahead? She wasn't sure Steph would actually do a scene with someone who didn't know what she'd agreed to, but she was sure Eve would end up in *some* kind of situation she was unprepared for given that Eve really wasn't prepared for much of anything. How would Dusty live with herself? How would she face Eve tomorrow? Or Sammi? At least if Dusty took Eve's place, she would know what she was agreeing to, and who knew, maybe a good flogging would offset some of the emotional pain she was feeling.

"Okay, wait," Dusty said. "What would you want?"

Steph and Eve halted. "Hmm, this is getting interesting." Steph kept her hold on Eve. "Just some fun. We can work out the details later, before we start."

"Wait a minute." Eve held up a hand. "You're not taking her, are you? She already knows how to be with a woman." She turned on Dusty. "You're awful."

"Fine. Agreed." Dusty resigned herself. "When?"

"No time like the present, I always say," Steph said with an air of victory. She pushed Eve into Dusty's arms. "Take your damsel home—I don't think she should drive—and be at my place in two hours. The night is young."

"Your concern is touching."

Eve yelled at Dusty all the way to the car. "I hate you. You ruined everything. All I wanted was for you to help me."

Dusty opened the passenger door and plopped Eve sideways into the seat. "I'm about fed up with everyone blaming me for everything.

Just shut up." She took off her jacket and threw it in the back. She'd have to leave her bike and come back for it later. "I'll tell you something. As long as I'm around, I won't let you make dumb mistakes, especially when you're drinking. I won't let you do things that will hurt you, and I won't let anyone take advantage of you. *That's* being a friend, even if you're too stupid to know it. Now, get your feet in the car."

"I think I'm going to be sick," Eve said with an unfocused gaze. She leaned forward and threw up on Dusty's boots.

In the morning, Dusty let herself into the hotel room where she'd left Eve. The night before, she'd been halfway home with Eve passed out beside her, when she'd realized if Maggie had gotten up or Tess had come home, she'd have a lot of explaining to do. Besides, she couldn't bear the thought of facing that look of disappointment in Tess's eyes again. In fact, knowing Tess was seeing someone else, she couldn't bear the thought of facing her at all. She'd pulled off the freeway, gotten a room, and tucked Eve into bed. She'd taken her clothes just to ensure the stubborn little brat didn't go anywhere if she woke up, and left a note saying she'd be back to get her. She'd had nothing to worry about, though. Eve was still sound asleep.

She eased the door closed behind her and headed straight into the bathroom for a shower. She wanted to get cleaned up and hopefully a second wind before moving into a new day. Her body ached. A low burn simmered deep in her muscles from activities they weren't used to, and a few areas of reddened skin felt like they might end up with some light bruises, but she'd surprisingly enjoyed her scene with Steph. It'd helped clear her mind of visions of Tess with other women and her heart of the pain of wanting something she couldn't have. Steph had actually turned out to be an ethical and skilled Domme and had admitted to Dusty before they'd even started that she'd never intended to do anything with Eve. She'd just used the situation to lure Dusty into her playroom, then she'd given Dusty the opportunity to call it off if she really didn't want to go through with it. Dusty smiled to herself when she realized that all it would've meant if she'd let Eve go, was that Eve would've thrown up on Steph's boots instead of hers. At least it was all over now, and life went on.

She dried herself and slipped back into her jeans. She slipped into the T-shirt she'd bought at Wal-Mart that morning to hide the marks on her back and shoulders that her tank top wouldn't cover then combed her hair. It wasn't until she brushed her teeth that she began to feel almost alive. She filled a glass with water and took two aspirin from the new bottle, then fished out four more for Eve. When she stepped back into the room, Eve was moaning.

"Oh, my God." She held her head in her hands. "At first, I thought I'd died. Now, I wish I had." A thin strip of sunlight from the small opening between the thick curtains spilled across the bed and onto Eve's bare shoulders.

"Here, take these," Dusty said, handing her the pills.

For once, she did as she was told, then lay back down on the pillow. "Why are we in a hotel?"

Dusty set the glass on the nightstand. "I couldn't very well take you home the way you were last night," she said. "I'd never hear the end of it."

Eve continued to look confused. She lifted the blanket and peered beneath it. "We didn't…" She looked back to Dusty. "Did we?"

Dusty laughed. "I didn't spend all night *not* sleeping with you just to sleep with you while you were passed out."

Eve relaxed. "What time is it?" She glanced around the room.

Dusty checked her watch. "Quarter to six."

"Quarter to six? I have to get ready for work." Eve sat straight up then grabbed her head again. "Or at least call in sick." She groaned.

"I'm thinking the latter." Dusty winced as she sat in the chair by the window and bent to put on her new tennis shoes.

"Where are your boots?" Eve asked.

"In your car. You threw up on them."

"Oooooh." Eve stared at the ceiling. "I remember that vaguely. I'm so sorry."

Dusty eased back in her seat. She wondered how many other things to be sorry for Eve would remember. "It's okay. But you're gonna need new floor mats." She relaxed. "You'd better make your call."

When the aspirin had kicked in, Dusty dialed room service and ordered coffee, croissants, and two cheese omelets.

"I want a shower," Eve murmured.

"Why don't you take one before the food gets here?"

Eve hesitated. "Close your eyes. I don't have anything on."

"Are you kidding?" Dusty asked in disbelief. "Yesterday, you were ready to seduce me, and this morning you're afraid I'll see you naked?"

Eve blushed.

"Besides, who do you think undressed you and put you to bed?"

Eve's blush deepened. She stared at Dusty.

"All right." Dusty sighed. "Closing my eyes."

Eve emerged from the bathroom wearing the lounge pants and T-shirt Dusty had bought for her just as the bellman wheeled the dining cart into place.

"Thanks," Dusty said and signed for the meal.

"Thank you for the clothes," Eve said, looking down at herself. "I couldn't even imagine getting back into that dress this morning." She sat across from Dusty. "And thank you for breakfast. You really are sweet."

Dusty grunted and took the cover off her omelet.

"Are you mad at me?" Eve asked.

Dusty stopped short and looked at her. "Do you even know what could have happened to you last night?"

Eve lowered her gaze to her own food.

"You don't just walk into a bar and start telling people you want to learn how to have sex. You could have really gotten hurt."

Eve looked surprised. "How? I was just going to have sex. You do it all the time."

Dusty's temper sparked. "No, you were going home with a Domme."

"A what?"

"Steph—the woman you were leaving with? She's a dominatrix, a Mistress. You could have ended up in way over your head and your backside covered in welts. Not everybody has sex the same way." Suddenly, the real danger struck Dusty. "Eve, you left the bar completely drunk with a total stranger, without your car, with no idea where you were going…" She pointed her fork at her. "You could have ended up dead."

Eve paled. "I'm sorry," Eve said, her voice small. "I was mad at you. I wanted *you* to teach me."

Dusty sighed, her anger ebbing. "All right. C'mere." She got up gingerly and moved to the bed. "I wanna show you something."

With a questioning expression, Eve sat in front of her.

Dusty took Eve's face in her hands. She'd thought a lot about what Trena had said about wishing the first time had been with her girlfriend. Maybe if Eve could make a comparison like Trena had, she would understand. She prayed she was right. She leaned in and kissed Eve, gently at first, just touching her lips. Then she trailed the tip of her tongue between them and slipped inside.

Eve let out a small gasp.

Dusty shifted, then claimed her mouth.

Eve's hands came up to Dusty's shoulders, and she pulled her closer.

They finished the kiss in a heated rush.

Eve opened her eyes and stared into Dusty's. "That was great."

Dusty held her breath. God, please let this work, she said in silent prayer. "Did it feel the same as when you kiss Sammi?"

Eve blinked. "No," she said with a thoughtful expression. "With Sammi it's…more. It's the physical, which is good…" She looked at Dusty then eased back. "But it's also what I feel inside. I want to share myself with her, not just kiss her. And I want her to share herself with me. Does that make sense?"

"Yes." Dusty felt some of her tension ease. "It does. Does it make sense to *you*?"

"It does."

"Okay, then. Making love with her is gonna be the same way. It wouldn't matter who else you slept with before Sammi. Making love with Sammi will be different because you have feelings for her. You want to share yourself with *her*, not just have a physical thing with someone else."

"But I still don't know what she likes."

"You *can't* know until you sleep with her. You could go to bed with a hundred other women, but until you make love with *her*, you aren't gonna know what *she* likes. If I go to bed with you, I'll end up knowing what you like, and you could end up knowing what I like, but neither one of us'll know what Sammi likes." Dusty clamped her hands around Eve's head. "You have to be with Sammi," she said with exaggerated articulation.

Eve gave a sheepish grin, then looked worried again. "How do I know if she likes something? If I'm doing it right?"

"Aaarg. How did you know with Jeremy?"

Eve laughed. "He moaned."

"Good start," Dusty said. "And I'm guessing if he moaned louder, you knew he liked it a lot. Just pay attention, then follow through. That's all it takes to be good in bed." She went back to her chair. "I'm hungry, woman. I'm gonna eat. I'm tired of talking about your problems."

Eve watched her with a smile. "Thank you, Dusty."

Dusty picked up her fork and scooped up a bite of her omelet.

"Wait a minute," Eve said, tilting her head. "*You* took my place with Steph. You went with her instead of me, didn't you?"

"So?"

"Why wasn't it dangerous for you?"

Dusty looked at Eve. *Jeez. This kid sister stuff isn't for the weak.* She couldn't remember a time when she'd had to explain herself so much. But then, it was kind of nice, too. "I know Steph. I've known her for a long time. I know where she lives, and I took my own car—well, your car. *And* I wasn't drunk."

Curiosity sparked in Eve's eyes. "What about the other thing? What about her being a dominatrix?"

Dusty sighed. "I know about that, too. I've done it before." She glanced down. "It actually helped last night."

"But you said I could have ended up with welts all over my backside."

Dusty pursed her lips and gave Eve a knowing look. She waited for it to sink in.

Eve's eyes widened. She stilled. "Can I see?"

Dusty laughed. "No, you can't *see*. What are you, a little Mistress in the making?" Dusty thought of the Dommes she knew who couldn't seem to resist running their fingertips over reddened flesh, no matter who'd made the marks. "That's something else you can explore with Sammi, but I'd recommend you just make love first."

Eve smiled shyly as a slight blush touched her cheeks. "Okay. So, what about you?" She returned to the table. "You and Tess."

Dusty went back to her breakfast. "There's no me and Tess. That was just sex, and it's over." Dusty tried to taste her food, but the bitterness of her words tainted all flavor.

"What? I've seen you two together. It's not just sex. You're in love with each other."

"Don't be stupid." Dusty bit into her croissant and chewed. "She's not in love with me. Yeah, I was an idiot and probably fell in love with her, but I'll get over it." She took a drink of coffee.

Eve pursed her lips in obvious thought. She ate a forkful of eggs and cheese. "I think you're wrong. I've seen her. If she thinks no one's watching, she looks like she's in love, too."

"Uh-huh. So why is she dating someone else?"

"Why were you in a bar last night looking so hot you could turn sand to glass?"

Dusty raised an eyebrow.

"Oh, don't even." Eve threw a piece of bread at her. "I promise you, you will rue the day you said no to *me*."

Dusty ducked and chuckled. She winced at a twinge of pain that caught in her back. "Roo? Isn't that the little kangaroo in Winnie the Pooh?"

"I'm serious about Tess," Eve said.

Dusty sighed. "I think it's time to just let things be. You and Sammi just let it happen. Tess can just go on dating this woman she likes." She couldn't help her curiosity. "What is she? Another professor?"

Eve seemed reluctant to answer. She nodded.

"So, see there. Someone who has a lot more in common with her." Dusty felt an ache that wasn't from her night with Steph. "I'll move on and just have fun in life like I always do. Maggie and Addison will do whatever they do. And the world just keeps on spinning."

Chapter Twenty-one

Maggie woke, her head pounding, each pulse of pain a rebuke. *Tequila is not your friend. Tequila is not your friend. Tequila is not your friend.* She groaned and pressed her fingertips to her temples. She was too old for this. What had she been thinking?

She opened her eyes and felt the sting of the morning sunlight streaming through her bedroom window. She squinted and turned away. Her gaze fell on a tall glass of water and two aspirin on her nightstand.

She sighed. *Thanks be to all that is for the people who love me.* As she gingerly rose onto an elbow and reached for the glass, she thought of her friends. Tess had been so gentle, so loving with her, and Dusty had kept her from drinking any more than she already had. *Oh, God...Dusty. The things I said to her.* She cringed. She would have to apologize first thing this morning.

She gulped down the entire glass of water before settling back onto her pillow to wait for the rehydration to take effect. She'd save the aspirin.

She had to get a grip on herself. This wasn't who she was. She didn't drink herself into a stupor to escape emotional pain—or at least she hadn't in a very long time. Maybe that was because she hadn't been in this much emotional pain in a very long time. No, she was wiser, now. She knew who she was, understood more of what life was about. Didn't she?

Who am I? She closed her eyes. *I am all I need to be.* She knew that. She was everything she needed to be to handle this and was surrounded by love and support. She knew everything she needed to know to move through whatever happened with Addison. Okay, now what did she know?

It had been almost three weeks since the Halloween party, since she had discovered Addison's affair and told her to leave. During that time, she thought she had put up a good front, but that's all it had been—a front. Inwardly, she had been a mess. She had been feeling sorry for herself, feeling like a victim.

How could she be a victim, though? She had known deep down that something was going on with Addison, and in all honesty, she had known what it was. She had been dragging around the fear of this exact situation the entire time they had been together. *Our thoughts create our experience. It is done unto you as you believe. As a man*—or, in this case, woman—*thinketh, so it is done unto her. Blah. Blah. Blah.* Every teaching had a version of it, and as much as she hated it in this moment, she knew it was true.

So, now that she was being more honest, what did she really feel? Nothing came. She opened her eyes and stared at the very spot where Addison had been standing, where Victoria had been kneeling. She hadn't been able to do that before. In fact, she had slept in Tess's room for several nights following the incident—the first purely for the comfort of a close friend, the next two because she couldn't bear the image of Addison and Victoria against the armoire. Finally, on the fourth night, she had forced it from her mind and reclaimed her bedroom.

Now, she recalled it.

A sharp pain pierced her heart. She sat with it and let it be. Okay, there was that to deal with, particularly if she and Addison ended their partnership. She let it be.

Then came the anger, certainly from that night, but now there was something else—something beneath the anger. What was it? Relief? Was that possible? She surprised herself with the revelation. This was it, the very situation she had been so afraid of for so long, and now here it was before her. Uncomfortable, painful, staggering even, but it still wasn't as horrible as she had always imagined. It wasn't the end of the world—not even the end of *her* world. She didn't know if it meant their relationship was over, but she knew she would go on. Her life would go on, although differently, perhaps. Hadn't it already begun to change, though?

Suddenly, she was free of the fear she had lived with, the anxiety that Addison would need to be with other women, to experience more than just Maggie. It had happened, and she knew she would survive—more than survive. It might take a little while, it would take some grieving, but she would be okay. A weight lifted from her heart. She nodded. She would be okay. She eased the covers back and slipped out of bed.

Following a thorough brushing of her teeth, another tall glass of water, and a long, hot shower, she headed downstairs feeling much more human. Between the pounding in her head subsiding to a dull ache and her true realization—not just lip service—that she would be fine regardless of what happened, she felt capable of facing the day. She found Tess stretched out on the sofa grading papers and Baxter sunning himself in front of the windows. He came to her and nuzzled her hand.

"Good morning." Tess smiled. "You look much better."

"I *am* much better," Maggie said with her newfound resolution. "As embarrassed as I am about you and Dusty havin' to deal with me the way I was yesterday, wakin' this mornin' with a hangover did me some good. It made me think about a few things."

Tess laughed. "Whatever works." She drew her legs up and made room for Maggie to sit with her.

"Yes. I never thought I'd be grateful for havin' too much to drink." Maggie ran her hand over Tess's foot. "Thank you for bein' so sweet and helpin' Dusty get me to bed."

"You know you don't have to thank me."

Maggie gave her a tender look. "Is Dusty around this mornin'?" she asked. She felt her cheeks warm.

"I haven't seen her." Tess looked away before rising. "What can I make you for breakfast?"

"Oh, darlin', you don't need to be waitin' on me. I can—"

"I know you can," Tess said softly. "But you take care of everyone all the time. Let me take care of you this morning."

Maggie chuckled. "Okay then. Nothin' elaborate, though. My stomach's a bit touchy. Maybe just some tea and toast?"

"Coming right up. Then you can tell me what you've been thinking about."

"Thank you, luv." Maggie smiled up at her. "I really need to apologize to Dusty. Did you see her last night?"

Tess shook her head. "She and Baxter were gone when I came downstairs. And I didn't see her later when I got home." Tess smiled, but her eyes held a hint of sadness. "I know you want to say you're sorry, but don't worry, Maggie. She knows you love her."

Maggie nodded, her regret still lingering. She settled back onto the couch and tried to accept someone making her breakfast when she was perfectly capable of doing it herself.

The doorbell chimed its tune.

Maggie winced. She *had* to change that. She hurried to answer it before it rang again.

"Addison Rae-McInnis?" the man asked, staring at a clipboard.

"No," Maggie said. "She isn't home. May I help you?"

He looked up. "Uh, well, I don't know. She was going to meet me here this morning."

"I'm sorry," Maggie said, confused. "When did she tell you that?"

"Oh…" He ran a hand over his short beard. "It's been a couple of months. I've been finishing up some other jobs. I tried to call to confirm, but I must've written the number down wrong." He stared at Maggie.

"I'm Maggie Rae-McInnis. I'm her…" Her words caught in the space of a flinch. "Partner. Can I help you with whatever it is you're here for?"

The man looked away and scratched the back of his neck. "I don't know." He shifted his weight. "It was supposed to be a surprise. I think I blew it."

Maggie smiled. "It's not your fault. She obviously forgot, so why don't you tell me what it is."

He gave her a thoughtful look before his expression relaxed. "I'm Randy Silva." He pulled a business card from his shirt pocket and handed it to her. "I'm a landscape architect and contractor. Addison hired me to build a gazebo in your backyard."

A gazebo? That *was* a surprise. She couldn't have been more caught off guard if he had told her he was there to raise a barn. She had wanted a gazebo beside the koi pond for years, but it had always seemed like such an extravagance. Any time they had discussed it, her practicality had won out. But now *Addison* had made the decision? Randy had said it was a surprise. "I'm sorry. When did you say she contacted you?"

"Let's see." He shuffled through some papers on his clipboard. "My guy came on the fourth of October to take the measurements, and…Oh, here it is. I got her initial call on September twenty-ninth."

It was long before the Halloween party, so it wasn't out of guilt. On the other hand, Maggie didn't know exactly how long Addison's affair had been going on. But September twenty-ninth? When was it she had first mentioned Victoria Fontaine?

"Ma'am?"

"Oh, goodness, I'm sorry." Maggie flushed. "Things aren't really…the same…as when she ordered this," she said, not wanting to go into detail. "Perhaps we should just cancel the order, if it wouldn't be too much trouble."

Randy looked undeterred. "She's already paid for two-thirds of it, and I've bought all the materials." He hooked his thumb toward a truck at the curb.

Maggie weighed the options. Should she call Addison? No. She wouldn't do that. She had made some progress in the processing of her emotions that morning, but she wasn't ready to take the chance of hearing Victoria Fontaine in the background. Maybe it could be postponed. But what was the point of that? They were heading into the holidays when everything got more hectic in general. She didn't want construction going on as well. And what was the harm? So, she would get her gazebo—hopefully not in exchange for Addison, but it *was* something she had wanted. "Okay," she said finally. "Let's go ahead and do it."

When she returned to the living room, Tess had toast, tea, and marmalade on a tray on the coffee table. "Who was at the door?" she asked. As Maggie finished explaining the situation, Tess smiled. "That's very sweet."

"I just don't know what to make of it." Maggie took a bite of her toast.

"What do you mean?"

"Why now, with everything else goin' on?"

"It sounds as though she ordered it before she met Victoria," Tess said gently.

"Hmm. I can't quite figure out the timin'. If it was before, at least I won't have to work through any feelin's of resentment that she did it out of guilt every time I look out into the yard or want to enjoy my coffee sittin' in it. I've been tryin' to figure out when she first mentioned the woman." Maggie still had difficulty saying her name.

Tess looked thoughtful. "Wasn't it the weekend Eve moved in? That Saturday Addison came home with the Chinese food and the two of you fought? I think that's when you said she brought up meeting her and you talked about making your relationship a higher priority."

She remembered. "Yes, you're right." Being reminded of that just confused her more. "And Eve moved in on October first." So, Addison hadn't done this out of guilt, but then, Maggie had already known that on some level. When Addison felt guilty, she withdrew as she had done during the last couple of weeks before the party. "Oh, Tess, I don't know what to think of it all." She sighed.

Tess took her hand. "I think it shows that whatever has been going on with Addison, whatever she was feeling prior to the affair, she hasn't stopped loving you. She hasn't stopped wanting to make you happy."

Maggie shot her a sharp look, but she knew Tess was right. In her heart, regardless of anything else, she didn't doubt that Addison loved her—no matter how twisted up and distorted it all seemed right now. She watched Randy and his helper stack lumber on the patio. "Her reason for comin' by yesterday *was* to make sure I was okay with Pete's passin' and all."

Tess squeezed her fingers.

She knew Addison cared. She knew Addison still loved her. And she loved Addison. That was a starting point. She recalled her conversation with Rebecca the morning Maggie had phoned her a few days after the party. *There's no right or wrong.* Rebecca had been gentle, while still reminding Maggie that she had her work to do in this as well. She wasn't a helpless victim. *This is a time for both you and Addison to look at some things within yourselves. You don't want to waste it.*

Maggie hadn't been ready to hear it then, but now…

It was the forgiveness piece, she remembered. That was the part she really hadn't wanted to hear, the most important part. Rebecca had reminded Maggie of the guilt she still carried for cheating on and hurting Julia. *God, does the woman ever forget anything?* Maggie had shared that with her at a birthday party for Dusty several years earlier, for whatever reason. Maybe precisely so she would have that information now. Who knew?

Maggie wanted to be able to forgive Addison. She would have to, regardless of whether Addison decided she wanted to come home. She would certainly have to in order for them to remain in a life partnership, but even to be friends, she would need to be able to leave this behind them. And truthfully, she couldn't imagine her life without Addison in it in some way.

And as Rebecca *always* pointed out, *the only real forgiveness is self-forgiveness. It's only through forgiving ourselves that we can let anyone else off the hook.*

So there it was. Maggie knew what she needed to do. She would be seeing Addison in two days for Pete's service and the following week for Thanksgiving dinner. She wanted both those days to be celebrations, unmuddied by undertones and tension, and she wanted to clear out anything she was holding on to that would get in the way of wherever their paths led them.

She ran her thumb over Tess's hand and released it. "I think Baxter and I are goin' to the beach today."

Baxter lifted his head from the floor beside Maggie and pricked his ears.

"I have some things I need to let be washed away. To be free of, once and for all." She smiled, and for the first time in weeks, felt it in her heart.

CHAPTER TWENTY-TWO

Thanksgiving day, Addison stood in the shadows behind one thick tree trunk and watched Maggie at the foot of the waterfall.

Maggie's face glowed from the spray and the flush from her hike. Her dark auburn hair shone in the sunlight, and her soft curves beneath jeans and a green, *Rottweilers Rule* T-shirt reminded Addison how good it felt to hold her. Maggie held out her arms and tilted back her head.

Addison knew at that precise moment she was enjoying the feel of the droplets landing on her face, aware of each one individually and the full sheet of water coating her skin at once. She thought of how Maggie loved to swim nude, reveling in the liquid caress on her body. She remembered that same expression of awe shaping Maggie's features throughout so many moments of their life—while she watched a sunset, holding the hand of a child, the first time she'd seen Baxter as a puppy, gazing down from atop Addison as they made love.

Maggie was beautiful, not like Victoria in that hot, sexy way that turned every head in a room, but in that way that put everyone around her at peace, let everyone near feel loved. Addison missed her so much. She truly hoped her realization hadn't come too late.

Tess walked up beside Maggie, Baxter at her heels, and slipped an arm around her.

Maggie encircled her waist and rested her head on her shoulder.

Addison missed that, too, her friends, her family, her dog. Everyone had tried. Tess had called her a couple of times, but the one conversation they'd had had been so strained that Addison couldn't bear the thought of another one. After the first week of complete silence, Dusty had left messages incessantly, at least once a day, sometimes twice. Addison had met her for a beer one night, but she felt too guilty to do it again. For some reason, it seemed as though she'd let Dusty down almost as much as Maggie. She'd told herself that as time passed it would get easier, but it hadn't. In truth, everything had gotten more difficult. She'd finally realized she just wanted to go home. How could she, though, after what she'd done?

Baxter dashed off after something in the trees on the other side of the falls, and Maggie and Tess sat down beside the water. They talked, but Addison was too far away to hear anything.

Had she made different choices, she'd most likely be sitting there with them today, involved in their conversation, rubbing Maggie's back, smiling at Tess, or maybe tromping through the woods with Baxter. She glanced around her. She wouldn't be hiding in a bunch of trees, watching like a stalker. Then again, had she made different choices, she wondered if she'd have the same appreciation for what she was seeing. She thought back to how she'd felt right before she'd met Victoria. She'd been restless, discontented. She'd known she still loved Maggie, but she'd felt something was missing in her life, or maybe it was that she'd missed out on something. She hadn't been able to put it into words, into clear understanding. Now, she understood, but at what cost?

She remembered the evening Dusty had caught her at Vibes with Victoria—and, yes, she now realized she'd truly been *caught* that night. She now comprehended she was already cheating on Maggie at that time. She'd been in Victoria's room earlier. She'd seen her naked and watched her dress. She knew what she was feeling on the dance floor. At any of those moments, she should've gone home, but she hadn't. She'd stayed. She'd exchanged e-mails with Victoria, knowing where it was heading but denying it to herself. She'd even yelled at Dusty when Dusty had tried again to talk some sense into her.

How *could* she fix it? Or could she? Maggie had told her the previous week that the house was still her home, but did that mean their bed was still her bed? Did it mean Maggie was still hers, or did it just mean she could live there in one of the other rooms? They could set her up in the art studio, turning part of it into a bedroom, or maybe if things worked out well between Eve and Sammi, Addison could take Eve's room.

Maggie stretched and eased down onto her back, her arms above her head.

Arousal swelled within Addison. She pictured Maggie naked, the bare skin of her full breasts dappled with the sunlight shining through the trees. She imagined herself on top of her, kissing her, the cool air fanning across their heated flesh. Addison had learned a few things from Victoria, had opened her mind, her body, to some new ideas and even to some she'd said no to in the beginning of her and Maggie's relationship. Maggie had been the more adventurous, the one with more experience, but she'd deferred to Addison's comfort level and seemed to enjoy what they did share. Victoria hadn't given Addison a choice. She wanted what she wanted, when she wanted it, and she took it. Looking back, Addison almost wished Maggie had done the same, but then, she wouldn't be Maggie.

Addison remembered the times Maggie had wanted to make love outside—once even right here at this waterfall—and the afternoon she'd asked Addison to go with her to The Pleasure Chest to buy some toys, and the night she'd tried to coax Addison into tying her hands and blindfolding her while they made love. Now, Addison wished she'd done all those things and more, now that she knew she could. Maggie had always voiced the concern that because they'd gotten together when Addison was so young, she'd not had the opportunity to experience a variety of lovers and discover what she really liked. Perhaps she'd been right.

Now, however, that Addison had experienced about fifteen lovers in Victoria alone, she knew she liked trying new things, and she'd found out she actually liked a lot of those new things. She'd learned how excited she became using a strap-on—yet another one of Maggie's denied requests—and watching the arousal in the eyes of the woman beneath her build to orgasm then plunging in deep to eke every tremor of pleasure from her lover. She looked behind her into the thickening trees and found the perfect spot where she and Maggie could satiate each other with the breeze caressing their skin and vowed that if Maggie would take her back, it would be one of the first things they did.

Baxter bounded out of the water and dashed up to Maggie and Tess. He shook himself, spraying them with a blanket of droplets.

Both women shrieked.

"No, Baxter," Maggie yelled through laughter.

Baxter stopped and rolled on the ground.

Maggie and Tess stood, looking down at their wet clothing. They turned and started down the trail.

Addison heard Maggie in her mind. *And with that, I guess it's time for us to be gettin' home and bakin' some pies.* As Addison watched, Maggie turned and whistled for the dog. She grinned when Baxter flipped upright, leapt to his feet, and ran to her. Her smile filled Addison with longing for what she very well might have lost.

A light breeze stirred the treetops and wisped through Addison's hair. She froze as Baxter stopped, sniffed the air, and turned his head in her direction. He seemed to be looking right at her. How would she explain her presence after sitting here spying on Maggie for the past hour? By telling the truth—that she wanted to come home but was afraid to ask?

"Baxter. Here, laddie," Maggie called over her shoulder as she walked.

With only the slightest hesitation, he ran after her.

After they'd gone, Addison sat at the base of the tree for a while. She wanted to be certain she didn't follow them back to the parking lot too closely. She'd taken a lot of precautions to make sure Maggie didn't know she'd come up here today just to be close to her. She'd left at six in the morning to get here early and killed time for an hour and a half. She'd searched out the perfect spot from which to watch. She'd even rented a car so Maggie wouldn't recognize the Explorer.

Now, as she waited to head back down, she thought about what she needed to do. After her epiphany from watching Maggie all morning, she knew without a doubt she could never sleep with Victoria again, that it was truly over. With the realization that she wanted to go home, she could make, and keep, that promise Maggie had asked of her.

Victoria had been in the Bay Area the past few days and was due back that night. Addison knew she'd been with her family for Thanksgiving. Addison knew she *had* a family in spite of what Victoria had initially told her. The phone in Victoria's room had rung early one morning while she was in the shower, and Addison had taken the call, thinking it might be something important about one of the restaurants

"I'm sorry, she's in the shower," Addison had said. "May I tell her who's calling?"

"Oh? Are you a friend of hers?" the caller asked, sounding curious.

She supposed—a friend who's in her bed at six in the morning. "Yes. My name's Addison."

"Oh. Hello, Addison. This is Beverly Fontaine, Victoria's mother. Would you please tell her I called and would like her to call me back as soon as she gets a chance? Let her know it's about her sister's wedding."

Mother? Sister? Addison had hung up, astounded. What happened to the mother who'd died when Victoria was young, the father she hadn't seen since he'd beaten her for being gay? Then there were the two brothers she hadn't spoken to since she'd run away from home. She'd wondered what other lies Victoria had told.

Victoria had come back into the room wrapped in a towel. "You're awake." She sat on the edge of the bed.

Did it really matter that she'd lied, or why? The truth was, Addison had always known deep down that Victoria wasn't who or what she claimed to be. Very early, she'd done some research on Fontaine's in San Francisco for the Los Angeles ad campaign and found out it'd been in business for four years. How does a fifteen-year-old runaway from Utah make her way to northern California, finish high school, put herself through college, and have the money to open a restaurant by the age of twenty-two? "I am," Addison had said and pulled away the towel.

She never mentioned the call from Victoria's mom, nor did Victoria. If Beverly Fontaine ever asked about a woman named Addison who'd answered Victoria's phone, it was clear Victoria didn't want to talk about it.

As Addison started back to her car, she knew what she needed to do.

❖

Addison pushed the button on the panel, buzzing Victoria's room. She heard the door open and waited.

To her surprise, a tall woman with spiked, blond hair opened the gate. The fit of her black leather vest and faded jeans accentuated her muscular frame. She was the poster child for *butch*. "Hey there," the woman said. "I'm Roni."

"Hi." Addison waited, not sure what else to say.

"Victoria's inside." Roni eased back and gestured for Addison to go ahead of her.

"Hi, lover," Victoria said as Addison stepped into the sitting area.

Roni moved into the room behind her.

Victoria hung a blouse in the closet, then turned to face them. "Look at the two of you," she said in a sultry voice. "Mm, mm, mm."

Addison tried to smile, not comprehending. She glanced over her shoulder.

Roni just smiled back at her, *her* expression revealing some understanding.

Addison felt like there was a joke she wasn't getting. It didn't matter. She was here for only one reason, to have a conversation with Victoria. She cleared her throat. "Can we talk a second?"

"Sure, we can talk as long as you want," Victoria said.

Roni walked around Addison and sat on the edge of the bed.

"There's something I want to talk to you about, too," Victoria said. "Did Roni introduce herself?"

"Uh. Well, yes." Addison wanted to stay on point, but she was curious as to who this woman was and why she was here. "I mean, she told me her name."

Victoria frowned. "She's my…" She looked at Roni again and raised an eyebrow. "Partner? Maybe?"

Roni shrugged. "Sure," she said as though this were being decided right at that moment. Knowing Victoria, that could very well be.

Addison felt as though she'd gone down the rabbit hole. She remembered wondering earlier what else Victoria had lied about. Here was something. She'd said there was no one special in her life. Again though, it didn't matter. None of this mattered. "Okay," she said, shifting her glance between them. "So…what? Are you here to kill me?" she asked Roni. She laughed but felt a little uneasy. She wondered what Dusty would do in this moment. She was sure something like this must've happened to Dusty, at least once or twice.

"Of course she isn't," Victoria said. "In fact, just the opposite."

What's the opposite of being killed?

"It's simple, really. I fuck Roni." Victoria tilted her head in that way Addison liked so much. "And I fuck you." She stopped as though no further enlightenment were necessary.

Maybe not for someone else, but Addison was more lost than ever.

Victoria sidled up to her and slipped her arms around her. "Now, I want you both," she whispered.

Addison waited, still unclear. Then it hit her. "At the same time?"

Roni chuckled.

Addison looked at her.

"Yes, lover." Victoria pressed her fingertips to Addison's cheek, redirecting her attention. "At the same time." She kissed her. "I want you both in my bed. Together."

Addison stared at her.

"You are so cute." Victoria giggled. "You've liked everything else we've done. You'll like this, too. I promise."

Addison looked again at Roni. She was hardly her type. It would be like sleeping with Dusty—on steroids. She shook the thought. "Look," she said, turning back to Victoria. "I came by tonight to tell you something."

"No," Victoria said. "You came by tonight because I told you to. And I told you to so that I could feel both my lovers' mouths and hands on me at the same time, both their cocks fucking me."

In that moment, Addison realized that's how it'd been from the start—Victoria wanted something, and Addison did it for her. She assumed the same was true for Roni. And if one was going to be someone's plaything, Victoria was certainly an excellent choice. If she hadn't already decided to go home, she might've done this just for Victoria. She could understand—maybe—the desire to sleep with two people together who you enjoyed separately, and she'd liked making Victoria happy. *But not as much as I want to make Maggie happy.* "Victoria, I'm going home."

"No, you're not." Victoria kissed her again, this time more deeply. She rubbed her thigh between Addison's just the way Addison liked.

Addison wrapped her arms around Victoria and returned the kiss. She let herself sink into it, knowing it would be the last.

Victoria moaned and pressed against her. "That's it, lover. Come on." She eased away and took Addison's hand. She started to lead her toward the bed.

“That was good-bye, Victoria,” Addison said, her tone gentle. She liked Victoria. She’d had fun with her and had learned a lot about herself and her life through this experience, but this wasn’t what she wanted. Even if Maggie didn’t take her back, she knew she was done here. “Thank you for everything.”

Victoria stopped. “Thank you?” She echoed. Her hands went to her hips. “You can’t just say thank you and leave me. People don’t leave me.” Her voice rose on the last words.

“I can’t leave you,” Addison said. “I was never with you. We were just enjoying each other. Isn’t that what you said?”

Victoria studied her. “You’re going back to Maggie.” She almost spat the words. “After *me*, you’re going back to that…” She let out a laugh filled with disdain. “Fine, go ahead, but you’ll regret it. After a couple weeks of being back in that boredom, you’ll regret it.”

Addison smiled at the thought of the *boredom* of sharing morning coffee with Maggie, watching a movie cuddled up on the couch together, laughing at all their funny memories and creating new ones, trying all the things with Maggie that she’d said no to before. She now realized that *she’d* been the boring one. “No,” she said. “I won’t regret it. I need it. It’s where I belong. But I don’t regret this either. I needed this, too.”

“What do I care? I was about done with you anyway.” Victoria strode to the bed and sat on Roni’s lap. “*This* is where *I* belong. You were just an amusement.”

Roni slipped her arms around Victoria’s waist.

Addison smiled. She was glad Victoria had someone, whatever the two of them had. “Be happy. Both of you.”

Victoria glared at her.

“Thanks,” Roni said. Something about her expression suggested she understood more than she was going to voice.

Addison nodded and let herself out into the cool night air. As she started her engine, she couldn’t stop grinning. She was going home. Whether or not Maggie would take her back right away, no matter what she had to do to make that happen, she was going home.

Addison stepped up into the illuminated pool cast by the porch light and reached for the doorbell. She stopped herself. Maggie had said this was still her home. If there was ever a time to take her at her word, this was it. She adjusted the strap of her duffle bag on her shoulder and took a deep breath. She turned the knob and stepped inside.

The smell of pumpkin and pecan pies caressed her senses. It was the scent of every winter holiday since she'd met Maggie thirteen years earlier. It was a scent that encapsulated everything it meant to be a part of Maggie's life. It was a scent that strengthened Addison's resolve to make a place for herself there once more. She crossed the foyer into the living room doorway.

Baxter met her, carrying his ball. His whole back end wagged.

Maggie and Tess sat hunched over the pieces of a jigsaw puzzle spread out on the coffee table.

"Eve says you'd best have your side of the bathroom cleaned up before Sammi comes over tomorrow," Maggie said without looking up.

Addison smiled. *That bathroom.* She scratched Baxter's ear. "I'll get right on it," she said, her tone less confident than she'd have liked.

Maggie spun around in her chair. She stared at Addison. Her lips parted, but she made no sound. "I thought you were Dusty," she said.

Addison shifted her weight. "I hope so," she teased her. "I'm not really here for the housekeeping job."

A dozen questions drifted through Maggie's pale blue eyes like white, puffy clouds on water-colored sky. She dropped her gaze to the bag then brought it back to Addison. "Are you home?" Her voice held a slight tremor.

Addison's throat closed. Her chest tightened. This was it. "If you'll have me," she answered. She choked back unshed tears.

Maggie rose. "Are you sure, dawtie?"

The endearment stole her breath. She nodded.

Maggie took a step, then paused. The corners of her mouth lifted almost imperceptibly and the playful glint Addison loved so much flashed in her eyes. "What makes you think I haven't rented out your spot?"

Addison grinned. "My parking space was empty."

Maggie laughed and threw herself into Addison's arms. "I've missed you so much." Tears spilled down her cheeks.

Addison held her tightly, soaking in the wonder of such a perfect fit, of the familiarity, of the possibilities for the future, but mostly of the flawlessness of that specific moment. In that moment, she knew they'd always been together and would always be. She eased Maggie back and covered her mouth with her own. She kissed her long and slow and deep. She didn't even remember the last time they'd kissed that way. Feeling the moisture on Maggie's face, on her own, she didn't know whose tears they were, and she didn't care. "Thank you for loving me," she whispered.

Maggie cried harder and buried her face in Addison's neck. "Thank you for coming home."

They held each other for a long time.

Addison breathed in the fragrance of the cocoa butter cream Maggie used on her skin, the milk and honey shampoo she used in her hair, the rich, sweet scent of Maggie herself.

They parted at the sounds of movement and pans clattering in the kitchen. Their eyes met and held. They were both grinning like children on Christmas morning.

"Let me help Tess real quick," Maggie said.

"I'm not going anywhere." Addison ran a finger over Maggie's lips. "Ever again."

Tess looked up when they walked into the kitchen. She smiled. "Welcome home, Addison. I missed you."

Addison closed the distance between them in three strides and scooped Tess into a huge hug. "I missed you, too." She spun her around.

Laughing, Tess embraced her and kissed her on the cheek.

Addison set her on her feet again and turned back to Maggie. "Where's Dusty?"

"I don't know." She looked at Tess. "Do you?"

Tess shook her head.

"She hasn't been around much lately," Maggie said. "It seems she's gone back to a bit of her old ways. She should be here tomorrow for dinner, though."

"Okay," Addison said. "I'll see her then." Her gaze held Maggie's with the question Maggie had always been able to read.

Maggie smiled and arched an eyebrow. "I'll be up in a—"

"Oh, no. You two go." Tess grinned and turned her back. "I'll clean up down here."

"Thank you, darlin'," Maggie said, her eyes never leaving Addison.

In their room, Addison dropped her bag on the floor and pulled Maggie to the bed. "I want to show you something," she said, her desire igniting. "I saw you this morning." She tugged Maggie's T-shirt out from the denim waistband.

"This mornin'?" Maggie looked confused.

"At the waterfall." Addison coaxed Maggie's arms over her head and stripped off the shirt. "I just wanted to be close to you today, but I was afraid you'd say no if I asked to be with you." She unfastened Maggie's jeans and slid them down over her hips.

Maggie encircled Addison's neck. "Dawtie, I wouldn't have said no." Her breath came faster.

Addison quickly dispensed with her own clothes. "That doesn't matter now," she said, taking Maggie in her arms. She unhooked her bra, freeing her breasts, and stepped back. Her breath stopped at the sight. It seemed forever since she'd seen the woman she loved naked. "What matters is this." She eased Maggie onto the bed. "When you laid back on the ground with your arms over your head…" She grasped Maggie's wrists, pinning them to the mattress, duplicating the exact position from that morning. "All I could think of was *this*." She took Maggie's mouth in a fervent kiss. Her need flared as she lowered the full length of her body onto Maggie's.

Maggie gasped and arched against her. Her lips parted, and she met Addison's tongue with her own, but she let Addison take her.

And Addison did. She kissed Maggie hard and deep then gently bit her lower lip as she thrust her mound against her.

Maggie moaned. "Oh, dawtie."

Addison shifted. She teased one of Maggie's nipples with the tip of her tongue.

Maggie let out a low groan.

Addison circled the hardening flesh, enjoying the feel of it growing with pleasure when she grazed it with her teeth. Her own body responded as though she were on the receiving end.

Maggie shuddered and tried to press it into Addison's mouth.

Addison struggled to hold off, but she couldn't. There would be plenty of time for teasing later. She sucked the nipple in fully, massaging it with her lips.

Maggie gasped and moved her hips. She tried to pull her hands free, but Addison held them firmly.

As the images from the waterfall returned to Addison's mind—Maggie lying just like this, naked beneath her, Addison kissing her, sucking her, filling her—she nudged her knee between Maggie's legs and opened her. She sucked the other nipple.

Maggie's moans grew louder. She tried to squeeze her thighs together, but Addison held them apart with her leg.

As she kept a grip on Maggie's wrists with one hand, she trailed the other down Maggie's body until her fingers dipped into Maggie's wet folds.

Maggie cried out and lifted her hips, opening herself more.

Addison waited, savoring the moment. She was home with Maggie, in their bed, making love to the only woman she would ever want again. Tears filled her eyes as she released her own moan. She sucked harder on Maggie's nipple and eased two fingers deep into her center.

Maggie's whole body tightened and she clamped down around Addison. "Yes, dawtie, yes."

Addison pulled out and thrust in again. She caressed Maggie's clit with her thumb as she began an easy rhythm.

Maggie whimpered, her breathing fast and ragged. Occasionally, she tugged at her wrists but relaxed at the first resistance. She squirmed under Addison's mouth and fingers.

Addison feasted on Maggie's breasts. When Maggie's leg muscles begin to tighten, she quickened her pace.

Maggie's body went rigid, and she screamed her release.

Addison stroked softly as Maggie relaxed. She kissed each nipple fully. She released Maggie's wrists and looked up into her eyes.

Maggie was crying.

"Are you okay?" Addison whispered.

Maggie slid her arms around Addison and pulled her close. "I didn't know if I'd ever feel you again. If I'd ever hold you. If I'd ever taste you."

Addison winced with guilt. "I'm so sorry."

"I know," Maggie said, pressing her fingertip to Addison's lips. "And we're okay. Just let me hold you now. Let me taste you. I want to taste you."

Addison's body surged with desire. She'd missed Maggie's mouth, her touch, her knowledge. Without another word, she rolled onto her back and pulled Maggie on top of her.

Maggie began with Addison's lips, then made her way along every inch of her body—kissing, tasting, suckling—until Addison was on fire. As Maggie neared her burning center, Addison said a silent prayer of Thanksgiving—for love, for forgiveness, for Maggie. She threw her head back and moaned as Maggie's mouth found her need.

She was home.

CHAPTER TWENTY-THREE

Dusty left Emily's early and took the surface streets home to avoid the Black Friday traffic. She hoped to slip in, grab some clothes, and slip out before anyone was up and moving.

She'd spent a couple of days with Emily and Seth and joined Rebecca and Jessica for the Thanksgiving dinner they always gave for anyone with nowhere to go for the holiday. While that wasn't technically true for Dusty, she felt like that this year. Being at home made her nervous because she was never sure when she'd run into Tess, and ever since Eve told her about JoAnn, Dusty had found it more difficult to deal with her feelings. The icing on the Pop-Tart had been the conversation between Tess and Maggie that Eve overheard about JoAnn possibly coming to Thanksgiving dinner today. Dusty knew she couldn't get through that. Then the ideal solution had presented itself.

She turned the corner onto Skycrest Drive and caught a glimpse of dark green as she squinted against the early morning sun. Was it? She stared. It was. Addison's Explorer sat in its parking space in the driveway. Dusty pulled up beside it and let her Harley idle. What was Addison doing here at seven a.m.? The last time she'd come by was to help Maggie with Pete's death. Had something else happened? Had something happened to Maggie? Her gut clenched.

She punched the garage door opener and pulled her motorcycle into her spot. As she yanked off her helmet, she took the front steps two at a time and rushed into the house. It was quiet. "Maggie?" she called. "Addison?"

No answer.

She made a quick check of the downstairs, then headed to the second floor. She only scanned the hallway before racing up the flight of steps to the third. "Maggie," she called again, bursting into the master bedroom, her heart pounding at the possibilities of what could be wrong.

Maggie sat up in the king-sized bed, holding the sheet to her breasts. With sleepy eyes, she blinked at Dusty. "What's the matter, darlin'?"

Beside her, Addison raised up on one elbow.

They both stared at her.

Dusty felt her mouth drop open. Addison? In bed with Maggie? She stared back. "Wh—" What was the right question? She looked to Addison. "Are you?" She glanced down and saw a duffle bag beside the door. She looked up again and pointed at Addison then to Maggie. "Are you two…"

They both grinned and nodded.

"Yes." Dusty pounded her fist into the air. "Yes. Yes." She ran across the room and leapt into the bed.

Maggie and Addison laughed, each rolling to the side, letting Dusty land between them.

Dusty flipped onto her back and kicked the mattress. "Yes. Yes. Yes." She straddled Addison's thighs and sat up on her. She grabbed her shoulders and pulled her up into a hug. "I'm so glad you're home." She squeezed her tightly then, loosening her hold, began planting kisses all over her face.

Addison batted at her. "Knock it off." She choked with laughter.

Dusty's cheeks ached from her broad grin. She eased Addison back to arm's length and looked at her. "Buddy, I'm so glad you're home." It was the only thought in her mind.

Addison smiled. "Me, too."

Happiness surged through Dusty, taking control of her once more. She clamped her arms around Addison and began kissing her again.

Addison fought to get away. "Maggie, help. Get her off me."

Maggie laughed. "Oh, no. You're the one who left. You have to pay the consequences now."

Dusty flopped onto the bed between them and exhaled a deep sigh of satisfaction. "This is so great." She wrapped an arm around each of them and pulled them to her.

They rested their heads in the hollows of her shoulders and laced their fingers together across her stomach.

"I'll second that," Addison said, relaxing into the new position.

"I'm so glad you're home," Dusty said yet again.

Maggie chuckled. "I think we've made someone very happy," she said, obviously to Addison.

Addison released Maggie's hand and stroked her cheek. "I think we've made everyone very happy."

The three of them lay still for a long moment, Dusty feeling more contented than she had in a long time. Then she realized where she was. "I oughta probably get out of your bed now, huh?"

"Yeah," Addison said. "I'm thinking that'd be a good idea."

Dusty started to move, then remembered Maggie's comment about consequences. She turned to Addison. "Did she make you sing The Super Sorry Song?"

Addison grinned. "I sang a different kind of Super Sorry Song." She arched her eyebrow.

"All right!" Dusty held up her fist.

Addison bumped it with her own.

"*I* am *right* here," Maggie scolded them.

Dusty's cheeks heated. "Sorry, Maggie Mae." She scooted down to the end of the bed. She turned to face them once again. She smiled and backed toward the door. "Yes," she said, punching her fist into the air one last time. She turned to leave.

"In case you're thinkin' about goin' anywhere today, our Thanksgivin' dinner's at five," Maggie said. "But we'd love to have you with us for the whole day. If you can, that is."

Dusty halted, remembering her reason for coming home that morning in the first place. She looked over her shoulder.

Addison and Maggie had moved to the center of the bed and lay in each other's arms.

Dusty would've liked nothing more than to spend the day celebrating their reunion and joining in on bringing the household back together as it used to be. It would never truly be as it used to be, though—not for her—because it used to be that she and Tess shared something nice, something maybe a little special, even if it wasn't everything Dusty wanted it to be. It used to be that Tess wouldn't have a date today at dinner. It used to be that Dusty wouldn't have to sit and make conversation with some woman who was probably doing the things to Tess that Dusty loved to do, in addition to sharing things with her that Dusty never could. No, it would never be what it used to be, and Dusty wasn't ready to face that.

"Oh, sorry." She feigned nonchalance. "I'm not gonna be here today."

"At all?" Maggie asked, clearly surprised.

"Where you going to be?" Disappointment was evident in Addison's eyes.

A dull ache swelled in Dusty's chest. "You know, I met this girl." She averted her gaze as she lied. "And we're gonna hang out for a couple of days. I just came home to pick up some clothes." She felt Maggie and Addison watching her.

"Okay, luv," Maggie said, resignation in her voice. "You have a good time. But we'll be missin' you."

Dusty clenched her teeth. She'd miss them, too. She'd miss sharing everything about this day with them. Could she stand it, though, being there with Tess and her damned date? No, she knew she couldn't. "Hey, well, I'll be back. I'll see you then." She gave a wave and slipped out the door.

She packed some clean jeans and several T-shirts along with some bathroom things. She jerked the zipper of her bag closed, angry that she'd miss this special day with everyone, angry at Tess for wanting someone else, but mostly angry at herself for being so stupid. At the bottom of the stairs, she ran into Eve coming in the front door. "Hey," she said. "How was your family thing?"

"It was great. I had a good time cooking with my sister-in-law. And Enos actually stayed at the table when the shrimp cocktail was served."

Dusty raised an eyebrow in question.

"He's afraid of seafood," Eve said. She eyed Dusty's bag. "Where are you going?"

"Uh, I met this girl—"

Eve rolled her eyes. "You're such a liar. Where are you really going? You're just avoiding Tess."

Dusty clamped her hand over Eve's mouth. "Shh." She pushed her into the hallway behind the kitchen. "I'm not avoiding Tess," she whispered. "I just don't want to be here with her and that woman.

Rebecca's brother's out of town. He said I could stay at his place a few days." She released Eve. "It's at the beach," she added, as though that were the point.

Eve's features fell. "You mean you're not going to be here all day?"

"I can't." Dusty hated admitting it, but at least it was only to Eve. "I can't watch her with someone else. Not yet."

"Dusty." Eve pouted. "It's my first holiday with you, with Sammi, with my new family. It won't be complete without you."

"I'm sorry. I know it's important for you, and…hey. Did you know Addison's home?"

Eve's eyes widened. "She's home?" She squealed. "You mean she's actually home as in living here again?"

Dusty grinned and nodded. "She spent the night." She was grateful they were on a different subject.

"Oh, my God, that's fantastic," Eve said. "I saw her car outside, but I just thought she came over early to help or something."

"Nope, she's upstairs in bed with Maggie."

Eve eased back and looked at Dusty. "How do you know that?"

"Good morning," Tess said as she came down the stairs.

Dusty and Eve dropped into silence.

"Am I interrupting something?" Tess stepped into the foyer. She wore her red silk robe and carried a book in one hand. Her thick hair hung loose and flowing.

Dusty wanted to bury her face in it. "No," she said a little too quickly. "Good morning. Happy Thanksgiving." She remembered the times her fingers had loosened the tie of that robe and wondered what Tess would be reading with her morning brew of spiced butter rum. Then she realized she wasn't entitled to those thoughts. Someone else was. Someone named JoAnn.

"Happy Thanksgiving." Tess smiled. "How was your day with your boys yesterday?" she asked Eve.

"It was fine."

"Oh. Well, I'm glad." Tess's expression was questioning, but she apparently decided to let Eve's curt answer go without comment. She turned her gaze to Dusty.

Dusty almost melted under the warmth of those soft brown eyes. It was so much harder to be around Tess now that she'd admitted she'd fallen in love with her. She had to get over this.

"Do you have a minute?" Tess asked. "There's something I'd like to speak with you about." She pulled her lower lip between her teeth.

Dusty tensed. *A minute to hear about the woman you're seeing who's better than me? Who gets to be here today instead of me?* "No. I don't." Her tone held more of a bite than she'd intended, but the fragile skin of the moment between them had been broken. It was too late to take it back.

Tess hesitated. "Okay. Well, maybe when you get home."

"Sure," Dusty said, feeling guilty for the uncertainty and hurt in Tess's eyes. Hadn't she lain with Tess in her arms one night and made a silent vow to never let anything hurt her again? Now, here she was doing it herself. She looked away. "When I get home."

To keep from falling to her knees and begging Tess to choose her, Dusty turned and fled.

❖

Eve brushed past Tess and went up to her room. Annoyed, she tossed her purse onto the seat of her rocking chair and flopped onto her bed. She couldn't believe Dusty wouldn't be home today. She'd been so touched when Maggie had said they'd celebrate Thanksgiving on the day after just so Eve and Sammi could be a part of it, and now with Addison home, it would've been so perfect. Even Aunt Carolyn was planning to stop by this evening to introduce her new boyfriend. It could've been an occasion where all the people who'd been so wonderful to her during her confusion and journey of self-awakening were in the same room with her at the same time, on the very day dedicated to gratitude. She was so grateful to them all, but mostly to Dusty.

Dusty had been the one to take her to Seth's birthday party where she saw how unfounded her concerns were about being a mom *and* a lesbian and where she'd met Sammi. Dusty had put up with her the night of the Halloween party and talked her through her fears about how her first kiss would take place. Most importantly, Dusty had *not* taken her up on her idiotic request to teach her how to have sex and insisted she go to Sammi herself for that. Eve only hoped the whole incident with the dominatrix and throwing up on Dusty's boots would never be mentioned—miraculously, it hadn't been as yet—but she knew she owed Dusty for that as well. Now, Dusty wouldn't even be present at this first gathering of all the new people who'd become so important to Eve. She wouldn't be there because of Tess.

What was wrong with Tess? Dusty was in love with her. Dusty was sweet and funny and patient—as long as one didn't mind being made fun of a little bit—and she was cute and hot. Was Dusty right? Did Tess want someone smarter? Someone more educated? Dusty was smart. She'd known enough to save Eve from herself, to give her wisdom and sound guidance.

A light knock drew Eve's attention.

"Yes?" she said, still deep in thought.

The door opened, and Sammi poked her head around it. "Can I come in?"

Eve smiled. "Of course you can. You don't have to knock."

"I didn't know. I've never been in your bedroom before." She winked.

Eve rolled onto her back and raised one knee. Her ankle-length skirt still concealed what lay beneath, but she saw Sammi's eyes shift. "Get in here and close the door, and I'll give you a tour."

Sammi scooted inside and slipped onto the bed beside Eve. She took her in her arms and kissed her deeply. "I've missed you," she whispered against Eve's lips.

"Mmmm." Eve pressed against her. "I've missed you, too."

Their first time had been amazing—and so had their second, and third, and fourth, and however many times they'd made love over the past week. After giving herself one night of recovery from the ginormous hangover she'd had following her evening at Vibes, Eve had taken Dusty's advice. She'd gone to Sammi and simply let it happen. She'd walked in, kissed her, slid her hands beneath Sammi's sweater, and reveled in Sammi's moan.

"What about the tour?" Laughter danced in Sammi's eyes.

"You're on it." Eve pulled Sammi's face to hers. "Beneath you is the bed. In front of you is…me."

Sammi chuckled and captured Eve's mouth with hers.

Eve loved those lips, that tongue. She would always remember the thrill of their first touch to her sensitive flesh, the first time Sammi had feasted on her need. She'd never felt anything so exquisite, so soft yet demanding at the same time. Sammi's lovemaking with her mouth, her hands, her body, was all Eve had dreamed it would be. Eve's doubts of her own knowledge and talents had been baseless, as Dusty had predicted, and what Eve needed to know about Sammi in particular, Sammi had told her, if not with her body's innate responses, with words themselves.

It was Eve's body that responded now.

Sammy left Eve's lips and trailed the tip of her tongue along Eve's jaw in small circles down her neck, into the hollow of her throat. She slid her hand around the back of Eve's raised knee and coaxed her onto her side. She draped Eve's leg over her, then ran her fingers along her open thighs through the fabric of the skirt.

Eve gasped.

"Can I make love to you here?" Sammi breathed against Eve's skin. She continued her caress.

Eve's breath came faster. "How can I say no when you're doing that?"

"Is that a yes?" Sammi moved her mouth lower.

Eve moaned. It all felt so good. She wanted more. She also wanted to help Maggie, though. "Who answered the door?"

"What?" Sammi left the vee of Eve's legs and unbuttoned the top button of Eve's blouse. "Uh, Tess."

Eve twined her fingers into Sammi's thick hair and brought her mouth to the swell of her breasts. "Did you see Maggie?"

Sammi undid the next button. "Honey, we could be done in the time it takes to have this conversation." She dipped her tongue into Eve's cleavage as she slipped her hand between them to cup Eve's mound.

Eve groaned and thrust into her grasp. "Yes."

Sammi squeezed, drawing a deep moan from her, then finished with the buttons. She coaxed Eve onto her back again and ran her hand over the bare flesh of her sides and tummy. On her second pass, she gripped Eve's skirt and pulled it up to her waist.

Eve yanked the straps of her bra off her shoulders and pulled Sammi's mouth to a hard, aching nipple.

Sammi's lips closed around it, and she sucked it in as her fingers slid into Eve's panties and through the wetness of her arousal. They both groaned as she stroked Eve's folds.

Eve thrust her hips, meeting each caress. Sammi was right—this wasn't going to take long. It'd been two days since they'd seen each other, since they'd made love, and it might as well have been two months. With each of Sammi's strokes, Eve let out a cry. Within seconds, her climax racked her body.

As Sammi's hand stilled, Eve tried to catch her breath. "Now you."

"No argument." Sammi's voice was hoarse. She was just as ready as Eve had been, maybe more. She straddled Eve then pulled her T-shirt and sports bra off over her head.

This hadn't been what Eve had in mind, but the sight of Sammi on top of her like that, transfixed her. Seemingly of their own volition, her hands reached for Sammi's breasts. She cupped them and ran her thumbs over her stiff nipples.

Sammi let out a whimper and arched into Eve's caress. She pumped her hips.

Eve couldn't wait to feel her. She stopped long enough to unbutton Sammi's jeans and yank down the zipper, then she returned one hand to Sammi's breast and slipped the thumb of the other into Sammi's fly. She found her slick, hard need immediately.

Sammi released a loud groan.

Eve rubbed Sammi's clit as she rolled an erect nipple between her fingers.

Sammi stifled a cry, trembled, then collapsed on top of Eve. She didn't move for a long moment.

Eve held her and trailed her nails over Sammi's soft skin. She couldn't stop touching her.

"If you keep doing that, we're never going to get out of this room," Sammi murmured.

Eve sighed. "Okay, but I want more later." She stilled her hands. "And I want it slower." Eve felt Sammi's facial muscles shift on her flesh and knew she was smiling.

"You got it, hon."

After cleaning up, they went downstairs and found Tess at the kitchen sink peeling potatoes.

Eve frowned. "Where's Maggie?"

Tess glanced over her shoulder and smiled. "She and Addison ran to the store. Did you know Addison is home?"

"Yes, Dusty told me." She tried to think of something else to say. The only thing that came was, it's your fault *she's* not home. She needed to get over her grudge against Tess. Who Tess dated was none of her business.

"Really? That's fabulous," Sammi said. She turned to Eve. "Why didn't you tell me?"

Eve looked at her in disbelief and folded her arms.

Sammi grinned and backed away. "Need some help, Tess?"

"You can grab the other peeler from that drawer over there." Tess continued her task. "We have ten pounds of potatoes here. Maggie wants plenty of leftovers for potato pancakes in the morning."

"What can I do?" Eve asked.

"The dishwasher needs to be unloaded."

"Okay." Eve knew she'd asked, but it irritated her that Tess was telling her what to do. She'd wanted to help Maggie, but she supposed having an empty dishwasher would be of help to her later. She opened the door and pulled out the top tray.

"Did you two have a nice Thanksgiving?" Tess asked.

"Yeah, mine was good. Melissa and I went to my parents' house." Sammi's tone was congenial.

That annoyed Eve, too. "We weren't together." She felt the need to correct Tess's question. She heard the sharpness in her own tone. She put away some glasses.

"I'm sorry." Tess glanced at her. "I didn't mean anything."

"It's okay," Sammi said. She shot a questioning look at Eve. "We were each with our kids yesterday, and today we're together."

Eve felt Tess's eyes on her.

"Eve, are you upset with me about something?" she asked.

Eve stopped. She *was* upset with Tess. Why shouldn't she tell the truth? Dusty had held back with her, and it'd caused all kinds of problems. She wished she were fine with Dusty not being there, but she wasn't. She wished Dusty were fine with Tess dating JoAnn, but *she* wasn't. Dusty was gone and hurt and sad. The anger Eve had been trying to assuage flared. "Yes." Eve felt Sammi's hand on her arm but ignored it. "Yes, I *am* upset with you."

Tess rested her arms on the edge of the sink, potato and peeler in hand, and stared at her. "Why?"

"Because you're mean. You're mean and selfish and, really, not very intelligent for someone with your education."

"What?" Tess's eyes shone with genuine bewilderment.

Sammi reached for Eve. "What are you—"

"No, it's okay." Tess held up the potato peeler. "Let her speak."

"Dusty loves you, and you just threw her away." Eve was on a roll now. "You want someone smarter and more intelligent because you think you're better than her. But I'll tell you something. Dusty *is* smart. And she's kind. And she's sweet. And you're not going to find anyone who'll love you like she does. And it's your fault she isn't here today and hasn't been around very much. And I really want her here." As Eve took a breath, she became aware of Tess's stunned expression.

Tess looked at her, lips parted, eyes unblinking. "Dusty's in love with me?" she said finally.

"Yes." Another wave of anger broke in Eve. "But what do you care? You'd rather have some college professor."

Tess's gaze shifted and she gave a slight shake of her head as though she were trying to clear it. "I…Who?"

"That JoAnn you've been dating. Dusty's not coming today because *she's* going to be here."

Tess sighed. "JoAnn's not coming today." She set the potato and peeler in the sink and looked out the kitchen window.

"She isn't?" Eve's thoughts came to a crashing halt. Her whole premise had just crumbled. "I thought you…"

Tess shook her head. "No," she said absently. "I stopped seeing her because…"

She returned her attention to Eve. "All those things you said about me wanting someone smarter and thinking I'm better than Dusty. Is that what Dusty thinks?"

"Because why?" Eve asked.

"Is *that* what Dusty thinks?" Tess repeated, this time with more force.

"Except for the part about you thinking you're better. That's more mine." She felt a blush creep into her cheeks.

Tess pressed her hands to her face. "I need to talk to her."

"Because why?" Eve stepped closer.

"What?" Tess seemed to finally see her.

"Why did you stop seeing JoAnn?"

"Eve, I need to talk to Dusty. Where is she?"

"Are you in love with her?" Eve had to know before she let Tess go find her. The last thing Dusty needed was a conversation about anything other than Tess loving her. "Are you in love with Dusty?" Eve's voice rose.

"Yes," Tess yelled. "I'm in love with Dusty. Now where is she?"

"Oh, my God." Eve broke out in a wide grin. She hugged Tess. "She's at Rebecca's brother's house, but I don't know where that is."

"I'll call Rebecca." Tess hurried upstairs, and when she returned, she carried her purse and keys.

"Did you find out where she is?" Eve asked.

"Yes," Tess said. She hesitated. "Please don't call her and tell her I'm coming. I want some time to think, and I don't want her waiting for me to get there. Or worse, I don't want her to leave."

"Tess, she wouldn't leave. She loves you so much. But I won't call her." Eve took Tess's hand. "I'm sorry for the things I said."

Tess smiled. "No need for apologies in a family. Besides, if that's what it took for me to finally hear all this, then I'm glad it happened." She squeezed Eve's fingers. "Oh, and please don't say anything to Maggie or Addison about any of this, either. I should have been confiding in Maggie all along. I want her to hear about it from me now—however it turns out."

Eve nodded. "Good luck."

"Thank you. And thank you for telling me." She turned to leave. "I *will* be home for dinner, with or without Dusty."

"Wow," Sammi said as soon as the front door closed. "A lot happens around here in a day. I should get you out of here before you run off with someone."

Eve laughed and snuggled up to her. "In case you haven't noticed, I've already run off with someone."

Chapter Twenty-four

Tess checked the numbers on the houses as she drove along Pacific Coast Highway. She spotted Dusty's Harley up against a garage door. She blanched. Now that she had found her, was she ready to hear from Dusty's own lips what she had to say? Tess had ended things with JoAnn so she could take the time to fully get over Dusty. She hadn't expected to be confessing the very feelings she had been trying to deny for so long and facing the moment of truth regarding Dusty's. She turned into the driveway and sat motionless.

She had been so certain as she had left home, so elated to find out that Dusty felt the same as she did. Now, doubts engulfed her. What if Eve was wrong? What if Eve just *thought* Dusty had feelings for her because she had walked in when Dusty was massaging her feet that one day and seen them in the backyard after the party? What if because Eve was in love, she just made it up everywhere? That happened sometimes when people fell in love, and Eve could be a little flighty, after all. Maggie had said Dusty was spending a few days with some girl. What if that was true and that girl was here? How embarrassing would that be, not to mention difficult? She couldn't imagine seeing Dusty with another woman. Tess glanced around. The only other cars were parked at different residences, but who was to say Dusty's friend hadn't ridden here on the back of the motorcycle? Surely, Rebecca would have said something if Dusty was here with someone else. All Rebecca had said was, "Lord have mercy, it's about time," whatever that meant. Then she had given Tess the address.

She had to do this. She had to know. She steadied herself and climbed out of her car. At the front door, she rang the bell and waited.

No one answered.

She rang it again. Should she leave? What if Dusty was in bed with someone? Tess pushed the blurred outline of the image from her mind before it could sharpen into focus. She walked around the side of the house and down its length. Out the other end of the passageway, she saw the waves breaking on the sand beneath the clear, morning sky and sea gulls swooping and screaming over the water. A beautiful wooden deck stretched across the back of the house, decorated with lounge chairs, potted plants, and a blue and white umbrella that slanted down over a table. A barbeque stood beside the open sliding glass door. A curtain moved.

Tess held her breath until she realized only the breeze rippled the thin cloth. She sighed. Why was she so anxious? It wasn't as though her life would be different if Dusty didn't love her in return. Actually, though, she knew her internal life would be. She had spent almost a year knowing that Dusty was there for her when she needed her. She suspected now that what they had shared had never been just sex—not for her. From the very first kiss, Dusty had been giving her something, not merely a physical thing but the reassurance that she wasn't alone, that she once again had something worthwhile to offer a woman, that she was wanted and desired and honored. She had given her something—someone—she could count on, someone to hold her, to play and explore with, someone to fill Tess's thoughts and heart. Wasn't all of that what a love relationship offered? And now, this relationship could be over before Tess had even realized she was in it, and there would be a hole in her life, just like the one left by Alicia.

What had Tess given Dusty in return? Anything? She thought for a moment. She didn't know, but Dusty must have been getting something from her. She had been home more these past several months—and usually in the same room as Tess, now that she thought about it. So, Tess had given her *something* to come home for, to *be* home for, even if Tess didn't know what it was, and she always seemed happy any time they were together, not only when she was in Tess's bed. That was something, wasn't it?

A dog barked, and a child whooped.

Tess looked out to the beach.

A family strolled along the sand, carrying chairs, an ice chest, and towels. The wind picked up, and the umbrella twirled with it.

Tess started.

In the far corner of the deck, Dusty stood with her elbows on the railing, staring out to sea.

Tess let her gaze travel over her—the soft blond hair, windblown and messy, the straight, taut back Tess had run her hands up so many times, the toned legs beneath jeans rolled up to the knees. Her bare feet and ankles were covered with wet sand, evidence of a walk along the water's edge.

Anxiety, doubt, excitement, desire, and love all clamored for precedence. Tess hushed her emotions. She had made up her mind to find out the truth, and she intended to do so with clarity. She set her things on the table. Her keys rattled against the glass top.

Dusty turned. "Tess." Hope flashed in her eyes but vanished just as quickly. She stood, still and silent. "What are you doing here?" she asked finally.

Tess bit her lower lip. It wasn't the response she had wanted, but she wouldn't be deterred. She collected herself and walked to the railing. She looked out over the beach. "Eve told me something earlier, and I came to find out if it's true." She felt Dusty tense beside her.

"What'd she tell you?" Dusty asked, returning to her previous position.

Their shoulders lightly met.

Tess waited. She wanted to prolong the contact. "I was wondering why both she and you seemed irritated with me this morning," she said, "and I asked her if I had done something to upset her." She could feel Dusty's warmth where they touched.

Dusty looked down at her hands. "What'd she say?" She sounded resigned.

"She said yes. That I'm mean and selfish. And that I'm the reason you weren't going to come to Thanksgiving dinner."

"I'm sorry," Dusty said softly. She straightened and turned to face Tess. "She shouldn't have said that. It's not true. Look, I didn't mean to cause any problems. I was just getting out of there to give you some room with your new girlfriend."

Tess saddened at Dusty's meaning. She now knew the only girlfriend she wanted was Dusty, but Dusty didn't have girlfriends, that old voice in her head said. Eve had implied some things had changed, though. She glanced around the deck. "This actually looks like a nicer place to explore a new girlfriend." She tried to sound bold, flirtatious even. She turned her attention to Dusty. "That is, if you want one."

"What?"

Tess looked up at her. "Eve said you're in love with me."

Dusty reddened. She sighed then shifted her gaze above Tess. "Damn it, Eve," she murmured. "I am," she said, her voice coming back stronger. "But I'll get over it. It won't affect you at all."

Tess watched her. Her expression was so sincere, her tone so earnest. Tess wanted to ask why Dusty hadn't told her, but how could she when she had never shared her feelings with Dusty, either? She looked back to the ocean. "We're a couple of idiots."

Dusty laughed. "I know I am, but why are you?"

"For the same reason."

"What do you mean?"

It was way past time for all this to end one way or another. Resolved, Tess turned, cupped Dusty's face in her hands, and kissed her. "Dusty Gardner, I am so in love with you," she whispered. "Deeply, hopelessly, deliriously in love with you."

Dusty stiffened for the briefest of instants before her arms went around Tess and she crushed her to her. She trailed the tip of her tongue between Tess's lips, then parted them and sank into a deep kiss.

Tess moaned. She slid her hands into Dusty's hair and pulled her even closer. The kiss was long, tender, the possibility of fulfilled desires, future moments, and shared dreams. "Will you make love to me?" she asked. She pressed more firmly against Dusty, their mouths coming together once more. All the desire she had been restraining for the past several weeks flooded through her.

"Yes," Dusty whispered. "I mean, wait. What did you say?"

"Make love to me," Tess repeated. Her nipples hardened against Dusty's breasts. The silken caress of Dusty's hair between her fingers brought a moan from within her.

"No," Dusty said. "I mean, yes, I'll make love to you—always. But what did you say before that? The thing about if I want…one. Did you mean a girlfriend?"

Tess paused, her lips still lightly touching Dusty's. "I want to be yours. I want to be with you every day and every night." She began to tremble. What if Dusty only wanted what they had had? She didn't know if she could settle for that after realizing how much she wanted something more.

Dusty released a rush of air. "Yes. Oh, baby, yes." Her tone was desperate, as desperate as Tess felt. She claimed Tess's mouth in a passionate kiss and lifted her into her arms. She strode toward the open door.

Dusty had said yes. Relief surged through Tess. Dusty wanted to be with *her*, too.

In the master bedroom, Dusty lowered her onto the quilted comforter of the queen-sized bed and started to lie down beside her. She stopped. "Damn it."

Her arms still locked around Dusty's neck, Tess panted. "What?"

"I'm all sandy." Dusty groaned. She pulled from Tess's embrace. "I'll be right back. Don't go anywhere," she said, palms out to Tess. "Don't move. I'm gonna clean up, and I'll be *right* back." She was so frantic. What had happened to the cool, suave Dusty Gardner? After everything it had taken to get them here, did she really think Tess would leave?

Tess laughed softly. "I won't move," she lied. "I promise."

Dusty kissed her once more then dashed from the room.

As soon as Tess heard the water, she rose and undressed. In the bathroom, she watched for a moment through the clear shower walls.

Dusty stood, bent over, hurriedly rinsing her legs and feet.

Tess moved in behind her and ran her hand over the smooth, slick flesh of Dusty's backside.

Dusty moaned and straightened.

Without a word, Tess took the nozzle from her grasp and fitted it into its holder. She knew what she wanted—a slow, luxurious, hot, sensuous shower. She had dreamed it, fantasized about it, even considered trying to orchestrate it during the past few months. Her body raged with want, with the need for the release only Dusty had ever been able to give her, but she wanted this, too. She stepped beneath the stream of water and, lifted her hands to her hair and let herself be soaked.

She watched as Dusty's eyes raked over her naked body. She could feel them as tangibly as though they were fingers running over her, touching her, teasing her, taking her. Her desire heightened even more.

As Dusty's gaze grew hungrier with each passing moment, Tess lathered some shower gel between her palms and stepped close. She gasped at the touch of her erect nipples against Dusty's warm, supple flesh.

Dusty slipped her arms around Tess's waist as Tess slid her soapy hands up Dusty's back. She stroked, made circles, dipped low, traced Dusty's spine, until her entire backside was slick and sudsy. The sensations from their bodies working against one another teased Tess at least as much as she intended to tease Dusty. She squeezed her thighs together, trying to allay her craving for Dusty's touch. Then she moved her hands to Dusty's front.

Dusty stood straight. She dropped her arms to her sides, a curious, small smile on her lips. Her breathing was ragged, her eyes hooded.

Starting at her shoulders, Tess spread the gel down to Dusty's hands, sliding her fingers in and out between Dusty's. She caressed Dusty's stomach and made her way to her breasts, palming her stiff, engorged nipples, massaging them between slippery fingertips.

Dusty groaned. Her lips parted. She began a slight thrust of her hips.

Tess moved closer, pressing herself to Dusty's mound. She slid her hands lower, wanting to feel Dusty's arousal, but before she reached it, Dusty gripped her wrists.

With a jerk, she pulled Tess against her and claimed her mouth. As she sucked her bottom lip, she turned them both and pushed Tess against the hard tile.

Tess fell into sweet surrender.

Dusty's mouth stilled. She gazed at Tess. A teasing glint, one that said something like, *you wanted to play?* burned in her eyes. She held Tess's body against the wall with her own then raised Tess's arms above her head and pinned them.

Tess's desire flared hotter. She released a low groan.

Dusty began to move. She slid her breasts, her stomach, her mound, her thighs against Tess's, the lather creating a sensuous glide. She set an excruciatingly slow pace, circling up and down, from side to side, occasionally slipping a thigh between Tess's.

Tess's nipples grew larger, tauter, and the pulse between her legs more intense with each stroke of Dusty's flesh. She moaned under the pressure, whined each time Dusty brushed her throbbing need.

Dusty kissed her, hard and deep. Then, she leaned back and let the warm jets of water stream between them, rinsing away the lather, tantalizing Tess's aching nipples. She sucked one engorged nipple into her hot mouth.

Tess cried out and thrust against her.

"Oh, yeah." Dusty moaned. She grazed the tip with her teeth while she stroked the other nipple between skilled fingers. She took her time, suckling, circling, savoring, slowly driving Tess insane.

Tess hissed in a gasp. "Yes." She whimpered. Whatever Dusty was doing with her mouth, it was that thing she did that could almost give Tess an orgasm all by itself. She never knew what it was exactly. She just knew how much it made her ache. She tried to pump her hips, but Dusty pressed her too tightly. She wanted release, needed it, and yet, she didn't—not *quite* yet. She groaned. How did Dusty know that? How did she always know? Tess's knees grew weak, and her legs began to shake.

Dusty slid a thigh between Tess's and moved it against her. "Now?" she asked. She leaned in more firmly.

Tess's arousal rose in her throat. "Oooh, yes," she cried.

One hand still at Tess's breast, Dusty moved her mouth to Tess's ear as she caressed Tess's wet center. "Let me hear you." Her breath was hot. "I've always wanted to hear you." She thrust her hips, quickening her pace.

Tess met each with her own. She let out a cry with each stroke. Her orgasm built. As it peaked, she gripped Dusty's shoulders and pulled against her. She screamed with pleasure as spasm after spasm racked her body.

"Oh, Tess. Baby." Dusty nibbled her ear. She continued a deliberate yet gentle rhythm until the last of Tess's shudders subsided.

Dusty held Tess against the shower wall and breathed her in like a fine wine.

Head back, eyes closed, her breath feathering through parted lips, she was so beautiful.

Was Dusty dreaming? Had Tess really come to her and told her she loved her? Had they really just made love with no restraint, no restrictions? Had Tess *really* said she wanted to be hers? How had all that happened in just a few hours? Dusty's mind burned with questions as fiercely as her body flamed with need. She placed a gentle kiss on Tess's lips. "Baby?" she said.

"Hm?" Tess only slitted her eyes. She smiled. "I love you."

Dusty went weak. Her breath caught. "I love *you*," she managed.

Tess twined her arms around Dusty's neck and moved her lips over Dusty's in a languid kiss.

Dusty felt overwhelmed—too much emotion, too much desire. "Come to bed with me," she murmured.

"Yes."

They toweled each other dry, caressing one another between more kisses. In the bedroom, Tess backed Dusty onto the bed and crawled up over her.

If Dusty *was* dreaming, she had no intention of waking any time soon.

Tess lowered herself fully onto Dusty's length and buried her face in her neck. She lay motionless.

Dusty held her and drank in the moment. Her body ached with need, but so did her heart. Her heart needed this closeness. It needed a minute to savor Tess's earlier words. *I want to be yours.* Could this truly be happening?

Tess's mouth moved on Dusty's skin. "It's been so hard being away from you," she murmured. She sucked Dusty's earlobe and flicked the tip of her tongue over the sensitive spot behind it.

Desire throbbed between Dusty's thighs. Her memory of her grief over the past couple weeks mingled with the overwhelming feeling of completeness in what was happening now, bringing a hard lump into her throat. "I just thought you were done with me," she said. Her voice trembled. She knew Tess would hear the tears that threatened, but she didn't care.

Tess stilled again. "I doubt I will ever be done with you," she whispered. Her tears spilled onto Dusty's neck.

She tightened her grasp around Tess.

Tess gently bit Dusty's earlobe and tugged it. She caressed the other one between her fingertips.

Dusty closed her eyes and moaned. She slid her hands down Tess's sides. With all the months of exploring each other, Tess knew exactly how to excite Dusty, but today, it probably wouldn't have mattered what she did. Dusty was flying high.

"I want you."

"Yes, baby. I'm yours." Dusty gripped Tess's hips and lifted her own, pressing her mound against Tess's.

Tess drew in a sharp breath. She kissed Dusty's neck—once, twice, sucked it, nibbled it, until Dusty's thrusts reached a steady pace. Then she rose, straddling Dusty and shifting backward.

Dusty stared, unable to tear her attention from the view of Tess above her, naked, gazing down at her with—yes, there it was—love. The light of day bathed her skin—a sight Dusty had never seen before—and she was flushed with her own desire once again.

Her eyes never leaving Dusty's, Tess moved down and parted Dusty's thighs. Her warm breath on Dusty's swollen flesh drew a deep moan from her, and Dusty raised herself to meet Tess's luscious mouth.

Tess kissed her, a full, unrestrained kiss. She pressed her lips firmly against Dusty then slid her tongue inside her heat.

Dusty opened wider for her just as Tess licked her full length. She cried out and clenched her fists into the comforter. As Tess's mouth worked against her, she felt Tess's fingers tenderly coax hers open and intertwine with them.

Her tongue moved slowly at first, stopping occasionally to suck and kiss.

Dusty's breath came hard and fast. One of Tess's hands slipped from hers, and she felt gentle fingers slide inside her. She pressed back into the mattress. "Oh, yes, baby, yes," she cried.

Tess thrust in deeper at a steady pace while still sucking and licking Dusty's hard clit.

Dusty's orgasm ripped through her. She writhed on the bed, giving Tess every jolt, every pulse, every shudder of her release. Finally, with a groan, she relaxed, her fingers combing through Tess's hair.

In seconds, Tess was over her on her hands and knees. Need, not love, burned in her eyes. She lowered her torso, offering Dusty a stiff engorged nipple.

Dusty took it hungrily at the same instant she found the apex of Tess's open thighs. She entered her with a quick thrust.

Tess moaned and pushed against her fingers.

Dusty sucked hard on her nipple and waited for Tess's hips to begin to pump. She knew they would. She let Tess wriggle on her unmoving fingers for just long enough to feel her muscles clamp around her before she shoved deep inside and ground the heel of her hand against her clit. She took Tess completely, the way she knew Tess wanted it when she was like this. With her free hand, she softly pinched Tess's other nipple.

"Ooh. Oooh." Tess's voice was hoarse. "Oooh, Dusty." Tess keened and ground herself into Dusty's grasp.

Finally, they lay in each other's arms, listening to their breathing, their calming heartbeats, the breaking surf against the beach.

"Thank you," Tess said.

Eyes closed, with images and declarations of the past hour drifting through her mind, Dusty felt the words more than she heard them. "Mmm. If we're gonna be together, you're gonna have to stop thanking me every time we make love."

"Or maybe I should thank you more," Tess said, a smile in her voice.

Dusty considered the statement. She turned onto her side and faced Tess. "I'm confused," she said.

Tess brushed a lock of hair from Dusty's forehead. "About what?"

"Why…" How could she put it? "Why, all of a sudden, do you want to be with me?"

"It isn't all of a sudden. I've wanted it for a while. I just thought you wouldn't want a relationship with me. With anyone, really, but certainly not with me."

"You're the only one I've ever wanted a relationship with," Dusty said.

Tess studied her. "Why?"

"I…I dunno." How stupid could she sound? Wasn't this the moment she was supposed to have all those romantic, perfect things to say? "I've never fallen in love with anyone else. I think you're the one I'm supposed to be with." She touched Tess's swollen lips. "I'm a better person since I fell in love with you."

Tess kissed her fingertip. "I don't know about that." She smiled. "You've been pretty amazing with me from the start. You brought me back to life, Dusty. You and Maggie."

There. There was one of those perfect things. Embarrassed by the significance of the statement, Dusty blushed. "You mean your *friendship* with Maggie, right?" The joke lightened the moment. "Not you and Maggie like this." She wiggled her finger between them.

Tess laughed and stroked Dusty's cheek. "Yes. My friendship with Maggie. I haven't been with anyone but you in four years."

Dusty thought of JoAnn, the Halloween party, Tess's frequent absences for the past several weeks. She knew she didn't have the right to feel any particular way about JoAnn, but she couldn't stop herself. She averted her eyes. "What about…"

Tess cupped Dusty's chin and brought her gaze back to her own. "I haven't been with anyone but you in four years," she repeated. "And I haven't wanted to be."

Dusty felt ridiculously happy. She'd never been the jealous type, but the thought of Tess with JoAnn had tortured her. Or maybe it'd been the thought of not being with Tess ever again that'd tortured her. She shrugged it off. She was right here with Tess now, and JoAnn was nowhere in sight. "I haven't wanted to be with anyone else for a while, either. I mean, it hasn't been four years." She grinned and gave a small shrug. "It's been five months, except for the night I found out about JoAnn. But five months is kinda a long time for me."

Tess fell silent, tenderness in her eyes. "Yes, it is. I didn't know that."

"How would you?" With a start, Dusty realized they were talking, not just about Baxter or where Maggie was or what needed to be done around the house before a gathering. They were talking about themselves, about their feelings, about actually being together. They were having the conversation she'd been wanting. It was time to say everything. "Tess, I love you. And I don't want anyone else ever again."

"I love *you*, Dusty." Smiling, Tess closed her eyes. She looked like she was just taking in the words and their meaning. "This is the most remarkable day I've ever had. Who knew, even when we woke up this morning, we'd be lying in each other's arms talking about really being together?"

"I did." She rolled onto her back and slipped her arm around Tess. "All that being snippy with you and leaving and coming here was just a ploy to get you alone for once. I even paid Eve to help."

Tess cuddled against her and laughed. "Oh, really? Well, you were certainly clever about it. I didn't suspect a thing."

Dusty chuckled. "I'm very good, you know."

Tess sighed. "Yes, you are." She circled Dusty's bare nipple with a fingernail. "*Very* good."

Dusty slipped her hand over Tess's and squeezed it. "I do have one concern, though."

Tess stilled. "What is it?"

"I dunno how compatible we are. Really," Dusty said, drawing out the words.

Tess lifted her head from Dusty's shoulder and gazed up at her. "We are different, but a lot of couples are different."

"Yeah, but you voted for blue M&Ms. What's up with that?" Dusty shook her head. "Now purple, that's a solid, respectable, gay color. You know, there're lavender triangles and there's lavender jewelry."

Tess narrowed her eyes. "Blue's in the pride rainbow."

"Yeah, but really—"

"Do you want to know the real reason I voted for blue?" Tess snaked onto Dusty's body and kissed her lightly on the lips, her breasts cushioned against Dusty's.

Dusty sighed, desire stirring within her. "Sure."

Tess gazed at her. "It's the color of the eyes of the woman I love," she whispered.

Dusty stilled. She knew she'd never get tired of hearing those words, of being that woman, but she couldn't let this pass. She laughed. "I don't even think we were sleeping together, then."

Tess moved against her. "We were. And even though I might not have known I was in love with you—or would fall in love with you—I *had* looked into those beautiful eyes while you held me." She hugged Dusty's shoulders, rubbing her breasts against Dusty's. "When you moved closer to kiss me." She flicked her tongue across Dusty's lips. "While you were inside me." She slid her hand between Dusty's thighs.

Dusty groaned.

They made love again and then drifted off to sleep, entwined around one another.

When Dusty woke, she found Tess resting on an elbow, looking down at her. "Hi," she said. "Whatcha doing?"

"Staring at you. And thinking."

"'Bout what?"

"I have a dilemma." Tess trailed a fingertip along Dusty's collarbone. "I want to go home with you, to *our* home, and have

Thanksgiving dinner with *our* family. I want to tell them I'm in love with you and that I want to spend the rest of my life in your arms. I want to go to sleep tonight with you and wake up with you tomorrow and the next day and the day after."

Dusty kissed her. "Sounds like a great plan," Dusty whispered against her lips. "I don't hear the dilemma."

"I also want to stay here with you and have some time to ourselves."

"Mmm, equally great, as far as plans go," Dusty said. "How about this? We get up and go home for dinner and share our news with everyone. Then we come back here and make love and walk on the beach and eat takeout for the next two days. I have the place through the weekend."

"And I thought I loved you before."

"So, are you ready to get dressed and head home for dinner?" Dusty grazed Tess's cheek with her thumb.

Tess hesitated. "What time is it?"

Dusty glanced at the clock on the nightstand behind Tess. "Three-ish."

Tess lowered her eyelids. "One more time?"

Dusty groaned and eased Tess onto her back.

CHAPTER TWENTY-FIVE

Addison lifted the turkey from the oven and set it on the rack on the counter. It smelled and looked delicious, as did anything Maggie cooked. Eve and Sammi were putting the finishing touches on the table setting, and Maggie was busy pulling out serving dishes for all the trimmings and sides. The holiday dinner was ready, and Addison was so happy to be home, but she felt a hole in the celebration with Tess and Dusty absent.

Dusty, they'd already known that morning, wouldn't be there. She was just out doing what Dusty did—though Addison did feel, given it was her homecoming as well, Dusty could've changed her plans—but where was Tess? She'd told Eve she'd be back in time for dinner. It wasn't like her to just disappear without telling anyone where she was going.

"What are you thinkin' about, luv?" Maggie slipped her arm around Addison's waist and shifted her away from the cupboard that held the accessories to the good china. She opened the door and squatted in front of it.

"Just wondering where Tess is, and wishing Dusty was here." She took the gravy boat from Maggie and helped her to her feet. She pulled her into her arms. "But I'm glad you're here."

Maggie smiled. "And I'm oh so glad you're here. It's the best surprise you ever could've given me." Maggie snuggled into her and hugged her for a quiet moment. "I am a bit shocked, though," she said, returning to the dinner preparations.

"About Tess?" Addison opened a drawer and found the electric knife.

"About both of them, really," Maggie said. "Certainly Tess. For her to vanish for a whole day…I don't know whether to be worried or simply know she's somewhere doin' somethin' she enjoys. Even Dusty, though. She seemed to be changin' over the past several months, so I was a bit taken aback at her takin' off with some girl rather than bein' here with us. I didn't notice it at first, but she was startin' to be home quite a bit more and seemed much more aware of other people."

"What do you mean?" Addison asked.

"She helped Eve a lot with her fears and just seemed more—" The phone rang. "Maybe that's Tess." Maggie had said that every time the phone had rung.

"I'll get it," Addison said, reaching for the receiver. She'd enjoyed surprising people throughout the day. "Hello?"

"Hi, Addison, it's Tess."

"Hey, Tess. Where are you?"

At the sound of the name, Maggie, Eve, and Sammi all turned to listen.

"We're almost home," Tess answered, a smile in her voice. "We just stopped at the store to pick up something. We'll be there in about fifteen minutes."

"Great." Addison grinned. "I'll hold off carving the turkey till you get here. Are you going to tell us where you've been all day?"

"Oh, yes." Tess laughed. "You'll know all about it, soon."

"Okay then. See you in a few." Addison hung up the phone. "Tess stopped at the store. She said they'll be here in about fifteen minutes."

"They?" Maggie asked.

Eve let out an odd squeak, but when Addison looked at her, Sammi was kissing her.

"Is JoAnn with her?" Maggie asked.

"She didn't say." Addison retrieved a roll of foil and began to cover the bird.

"Hm. Maybe she changed her mind about havin' her over," Maggie muttered, clearly lost in thought.

While they waited, they all worked on the jigsaw puzzle laid out on the coffee table. It'd been a project the four of them had shared throughout the day in between some card games and a movie about a whale. Addison had enjoyed getting to know Sammi and watching her and Eve in the early stages of love. It reminded her that she and Maggie had the opportunity to start over, and of her plans to do just that. When the chimes on the door sounded, they all turned.

Tess walked across the entryway, Dusty close behind her.

Eve stood, squealed, and clapped her hands.

Dusty grinned and, after setting a bag she carried on the credenza, strode to her. She picked her up and planted a long kiss on her lips. Eve wrapped her arms around Dusty's neck and, kicking her feet, squealed again.

Finally, Dusty set her back to the floor. She stepped away and looked at Sammi. "Sorry. I had to thank her."

"I understand completely," Sammi said with a broad smile. She held out her hand and shook Dusty's. "Congratulations."

Tess moved to Eve and took her into a long embrace.

Addison looked at Maggie, who appeared just as confused as she was. "Do you get the feeling we don't know something everyone else does?"

"I definitely get that feelin'," Maggie said, staring wide-eyed at the scene unfolding. "Is someone goin' to explain it to us?" She caught Tess's eye.

Tess released Eve. "I'm so sorry, Maggie. I know I should have told you. You're my best friend."

"Don't be sorry, darlin', just tell me, now." Maggie stared. "Is it what it looks like?"

Tess took Dusty's hand in her own. "I hope so." She giggled like a teenager.

"You tell them, baby," Dusty urged her. "I want to hear it again."

Tess smiled. "Dusty and I are in love."

"What?" Maggie cried, laughter claiming any other response. She leapt to her feet and grabbed them both in a tight hug. She released them but held on to Tess's hand. "I've suspected *somethin'* between the two of you for a while now—a spark or somethin'—but *this*..." She embraced them again.

In love? The words reverberated in Addison's mind. She knew she'd been gone a while, but...in love? She grinned. "How did that happen?"

Dusty put her arm around Tess and pulled her close. "We'll tell you all about it, buddy. But first, we have champagne." She grabbed the bag from the credenza and held it up. "We'll celebrate all of us."

Dinner waited while Dusty and Tess shared their tale from the very first kiss. They clinked champagne flutes to Dusty's and Tess's story, to Maggie's and Addison's reunion, to Eve's and Sammi's new love. Addison watched and listened, knowing this was her true family and exactly where she belonged. Finally, they rose to put dinner on the table.

As Addison uncovered the bird and picked up the knife, Dusty stepped up beside her. "What do you think, buddy?" she asked. "Did I do okay?"

Addison paused and looked at her. "Man, I don't even know who you are. I leave for a few weeks and the tiger is tamed." Addison grinned. "And yeah, you did fantastic. You can't get much better than Tess. And Maggie, of course," she said quickly.

Dusty chuckled.

"I hear you helped Eve out, too."

Dusty glanced into the dining room where Eve and Sammi were putting mashed potatoes and gravy on the table. "Yeah, that worked out pretty good, too, didn't it?"

"It sure did. Sammi seems great." Addison turned back to her task. "I'll tell you something, though. If you're going to be all domesticated like the rest of us, you'd better pay attention to how to carve a bird. Watch and learn."

"Why?" Dusty draped an arm over Addison's shoulders. "Tess and I are gonna be spending all the holidays with you guys anyway."

The truth in the statement brought a smile to Addison's face. She realized in that moment how much she'd grown to love Dusty. "Hey, I'm sorry I was such an asshole about Victoria."

"Really?" Dusty turned and leaned against the counter. She picked a piece of crispy skin off the turkey and took a bite. "Sorry enough to sing the Super Sorry Song? And *not* the way you sang it for Maggie."

Addison laughed. "You're pushing it."

Dusty grinned.

She glanced around to make sure no one else was listening then bent toward Dusty and sang softly. "I know I blew it big time. I know I'm such a pig rind," she sang. "But don't you worry…cuuuuuuz, I'm super sooorrrrry." She finished with a flourish and a small bow.

Dusty laughed out loud. "I never get tired of that."

As they sat at the table, Addison looked into each face and knew that everyone's Thanksgiving offering would be the same—*I am thankful for love, friendship, and a beautiful life.*

She smiled and squeezed Maggie's hand. *I am thankful for home.*

About the Author

Jeannie grew up in Tehachapi, CA, a small town in the southern foothills of the Sierra Nevada mountains, the kind of town where everyone knew everyone and lived with unlocked doors. Summer days were long and filled with bike riding, fort building, tree climbing, and lots of freedom. Raised by an English teacher, Jeannie has always been surrounded by literature and novels and learned to love reading at an early age. She tried her hand at writing fiction for the first time under the loving encouragement of her eighth grade English teacher. She graduated from college with a bachelor's degree in English.

Jeannie's loves include her beautiful family, an amazing circle of friends, and her four-legged best friend. She enjoys many genres of novels, movies, and theater, is a cliché as a George R. R. Martin fan in her grumblings about the wait between Song of Ice and Fire books, and is deeply committed to her spiritual path.

In addition to being a novelist, Jeannie is a freelance ghostwriter and editor and is working on a new novel.

Books Available from Bold Strokes Books

Making a Comeback by Julie Blair. Music and love take center stage when jazz pianist Liz Randall tries to make a comeback with the help of her reclusive, blind neighbor, Jac Winters. (978-1-62639-357-8)

Soul Unique by Gun Brooke. Self-proclaimed cynic Greer Landon falls for Hayden Rowe's paintings and the young woman shortly after, but will Hayden, who lives with Asperger syndrome, trust her and reciprocate her feelings? (978-1-62639-358-5)

The Price of Honor by Radclyffe. Honor and duty are not always black and white—and when self-styled patriots take up arms against the government, the price of honor may be a life. (978-1-62639-359-2)

Mounting Evidence by Karis Walsh. Lieutenant Abigail Hargrove and her mounted police unit need to solve a murder and protect wetland biologist Kira Lovell during the Washington State Fair. (978-1-62639-343-1)

Threads of the Heart by Jeannie Levig. Maggie and Addison Rae-McInnis share a love and a life, but are the threads that bind them together strong enough to withstand Addison's restlessness and the seductive Victoria Fontaine? (978-1-62639-410-0)

Sheltered Love by MJ Williamz. Boone Fairway and Grey Dawson—two women touched by abuse—overcome their pasts to find happiness in each other. (978-1-62639-362-2)

Asher's Out by Elizabeth Wheeler. Asher Price's candid photographs capture the truth, but when his success requires exposing an enemy, Asher discovers his only shot at happiness involves revealing secrets of his own. (978-1-62639-411-7)

The Ground Beneath by Missouri Vaun. An improbable barter deal involving a hope chest and dinners for a month places lovely Jessica Walker distractingly in the way of Sam Casey's bachelor lifestyle. (978-1-62639-606-7)

Hardwired by C.P. Rowlands. Award-winning teacher Clary Stone, and Leefe Ellis, manager of the homeless shelter for small children, stand together in a part of Clary's hometown that she never knew existed. (978-1-62639-351-6)

No Good Reason by Cari Hunter. A violent kidnapping in a Peak District village pushes Detective Sanne Jensen and lifelong friend Dr. Meg Fielding closer, just as it threatens to tear everything apart. (978-1-62639-352-3)

Romance by the Book by Jo Victor. If Cam didn't keep disrupting her life, maybe Alex could uncover the secret of a century-old love story, and solve the greatest mystery of all—her own heart. (978-1-62639-353-0)

Death's Doorway by Crin Claxton. Helping the dead can be deadly: Tony may be listening to the dead, but she needs to learn to listen to the living. (978-1-62639-354-7)

Searching for Celia by Elizabeth Ridley. As American spy novelist Dayle Salvesen investigates the mysterious disappearance of her ex-lover, Celia, in London, she begins questioning how well she knew Celia—and how well she knows herself. (978-1-62639-356-1)

The 45th Parallel by Lisa Girolami. Burying her mother isn't the worst thing that can happen to Val Montague when she returns to the woodsy but peculiar town of Hemlock, Oregon. (978-1-62639-342-4)

A Royal Romance by Jenny Frame. In a country where class still divides, can love topple the last social taboo and allow Queen Georgina and Beatrice Elliot, a working class girl, their happy ever after? (978-1-62639-360-8)

Bouncing by Jaime Maddox. Basketball Coach Alex Dalton has been bouncing from woman to woman, because no one ever held her interest, until she meets her new assistant, Britain Dodge. (978-1-62639-344-8)

Same Time Next Week by Emily Smith. A chance encounter between Alex Harris and the beautiful Michelle Masters leads to a whirlwind friendship, and causes Alex to question everything she's ever known—including her own marriage. (978-1-62639-345-5)

All Things Rise by Missouri Vaun. Cole rescues a striking pilot who crash-lands near her family's farm, setting in motion a chain of events that will forever alter the course of her life. (978-1-62639-346-2)

Riding Passion by D. Jackson Leigh. Mount up for the ride through a sizzling anthology of chance encounters, buried desires, romantic surprises, and blazing passion. (978-1-62639-349-3)

Love's Bounty by Yolanda Wallace. Lobster boat captain Jake Myers stopped living the day she cheated death, but meeting greenhorn Shy Silva stirs her back to life. (978-1-62639-334-9)

Just Three Words by Melissa Brayden. Sometimes the one you want is the one you least suspect. Accountant Samantha Ennis has her ordered life disrupted when heartbreaker Hunter Blair moves into her trendy Soho loft. (978-1-62639-335-6)

Lay Down the Law by Carsen Taite. Attorney Peyton Davis returns to her Texas roots to take on big oil and the Mexican Mafia, but will her investigation thwart her chance at true love? (978-1-62639-336-3)

Playing in Shadow by Lesley Davis. Survivor's guilt threatens to keep Bryce trapped in her nightmare world unless Scarlet's love can pull her out of the darkness back into the light. (978-1-62639-337-0)

Soul Selecta by Gill McKnight. Soul mates are hell to work with. (978-1-62639-338-7)

The Revelation of Beatrice Darby by Jean Copeland. Adolescence is complicated, but Beatrice Darby is about to discover how impossible it can seem to a lesbian coming of age in conservative 1950s New England. (978-1-62639-339-4)

Twice Lucky by Mardi Alexander. For firefighter Mackenzie James and Dr. Sarah Macarthur, there's suddenly a whole lot more in life to understand, to consider, to risk…someone will need to fight for her life. (978-1-62639-325-7)

Shadow Hunt by L.L. Raand. With young to raise and her Pack under attack, Sylvan, Alpha of the wolf Weres, takes on her greatest challenge when she determines to uncover the faceless enemies known as the Shadow Lords. A Midnight Hunters novel. (978-1-62639-326-4)

Heart of the Game by Rachel Spangler. A baseball writer falls for a single mom, but can she ever love anything as much as she loves the game? (978-1-62639-327-1)

Getting Lost by Michelle Grubb. Twenty-eight days, thirteen European countries, a tour manager fighting attraction, and an accused murderer: Stella and Phoebe's journey of a lifetime begins here. (978-1-62639-328-8)

Prayer of the Handmaiden by Merry Shannon. Celibate priestess Kadrian must defend the kingdom of Ithyria from a dangerous enemy and ultimately choose between her duty to the Goddess and the love of her childhood sweetheart, Erinda. (978-1-62639-329-5)

The Witch of Stalingrad by Justine Saracen. A Soviet "night witch" pilot and American journalist meet on the Eastern Front in WW II and struggle through carnage, conflicting politics, and the deadly Russian winter. (978-1-62639-330-1)

Pedal to the Metal by Jesse J. Thoma. When unreformed thief Dubs Williams is released from prison to help Max Winters bust a car theft ring, Max learns that to catch a thief, get in bed with one. (978-1-62639-239-7)

Dragon Horse War by D. Jackson Leigh. A priestess of peace and a fiery warrior must defeat a vicious uprising that entwines their destinies and ultimately their hearts. (978-1-62639-240-3)

For the Love of Cake by Erin Dutton. When everything is on the line, and one taste can break a heart, will pastry chefs Maya and Shannon take a chance on reality? (978-1-62639-241-0)

Betting on Love by Alyssa Linn Palmer. A quiet country-girl-at-heart and a live-life-to-the-fullest biker take a risk at offering each other their hearts. (978-1-62639-242-7)

The Deadening by Yvonne Heidt. The lines between good and evil, right and wrong, have always been blurry for Shade. When Raven's actions force her to choose, which side will she come out on? (978-1-62639-243-4)

Ordinary Mayhem by Victoria A. Brownworth. Faye Blakemore has been taking photographs since she was ten, but those same photographs threaten to destroy everything she knows and everything she loves. (978-1-62639-315-8)

One Last Thing by Kim Baldwin & Xenia Alexiou. Blood is thicker than pride. The final book in the Elite Operative Series brings together foes, family, and friends to start a new order. (978-1-62639-230-4)

Songs Unfinished by Holly Stratimore. Two aspiring rock stars learn that falling in love while pursuing their dreams can be harmonious—if they can only keep their pasts from throwing them out of tune. (978-1-62639-231-1)

Beyond the Ridge by L.T. Marie. Will a contractor and a horse rancher overcome their family differences and find common ground to build a life together? (978-1-62639-232-8)

Swordfish by Andrea Bramhall. Four women battle the demons from their pasts. Will they learn to let go, or will happiness be forever beyond their grasp? (978-1-62639-233-5)

The Fiend Queen by Barbara Ann Wright. Princess Katya and her consort Starbride must turn evil against evil in order to banish Fiendish power from their kingdom, and only love will pull them back from the brink. (978-1-62639-234-2)

Up the Ante by PJ Trebelhorn. When Jordan Stryker and Ashley Noble meet again fifteen years after a short-lived affair, are either of them prepared to gamble on a chance at love? (978-1-62639-237-3)

Speakeasy by MJ Williamz. When mob leader Helen Byrne sets her sights on the girlfriend of Al Capone's right-hand man, passion and tempers flare on the streets of Chicago. (978-1-62639-238-0)

Venus in Love by Tina Michele. Morgan Blake can't afford any distractions and Ainsley Dencourt can't afford to lose control—but the beauty of life and art usually lies in the unpredictable strokes of the artist's brush. (978-1-62639-220-5)

Rules of Revenge by AJ Quinn. When a lethal operative on a collision course with her past agrees to help a CIA analyst on a critical assignment, the encounter proves explosive in ways neither woman anticipated. (978-1-62639-221-2)

The Romance Vote by Ali Vali. Chili Alexander is a sought-after campaign consultant who isn't prepared when her boss's daughter, Samantha Pellegrin, comes to work at the firm and shakes up Chili's life from the first day. (978-1-62639-222-9)

Advance: Exodus Book One by Gun Brooke. Admiral Dael Caydoc's mission to find a new homeworld for the Oconodian people is hazardous, but working with the infuriating Commander Aniwyn "Spinner" Seclan endangers her heart and soul. (978-1-62639-224-3)

UnCatholic Conduct by Stevie Mikayne. Jil Kidd goes undercover to investigate fraud at St. Marguerite's Catholic School, but life gets complicated when her student is killed—and she begins to fall for her prime target. (978-1-62639-304-2)

Season's Meetings by Amy Dunne. Catherine Birch reluctantly ventures on the festive road trip from hell with beautiful stranger Holly Daniels only to discover the road to true love has its own obstacles to maneuver. (978-1-62639-227-4)